A Blind Eye Crying

By
Christopher Britton

A BLIND EYE CRYING

Author: Christopher Britton

ISBN-13: 978-1981494095
ISBN-10: 198149409X

Although the author of this novel lived in North Carolina, attended Duke University, and became a lawyer. This novel may seem very real, however, the events and persons in *A Blind Eye Crying* are fictional. The events never happened, the people never lived. Any resemblance of any character to any person living or dead is purely coincidental.

For permission, please contact:
Christopher Britton
cqbritton@hotmail.com

Cover design by Richard Bayer
Cover photo by Kelly Jett

Book layout/design by David Larson

Other Books
by Christopher Britton

Paybacks

No More Forever

Bill,
Hang in there.
A multitude of friends
are cheering for you!
Chris

In Memory of Janeen Kerper

A great lawyer and a better friend

ACKNOWLEDGEMENTS

Many thanks to Dr. Joy Kennedy, Georgia Quinn, Candace Carroll, Susan Podolsky, Dr. David Braff, Dr. Carl Jepson, Parker Bell, Esq. Hon. Leo Papas, Bob Grimes, Russ Block, Phyllis Bush, Donna Roof, Wendy Patrick, Lindsey Burroughs, Rhonda Turner, Lynn Schwartz and the Tuesday Morning Writer's Workshop for all their assistance and encouragement, and most especially to my wife, Nancy, who has endured my long silences as I pondered my story and who has been the source of great editorial advice.

TRIAL

Like a soldier
In the war.
No sleep tonight,
Only dozing.
Thoughts, ideas,
Never ending,
Enemies of rest.
Strange how deadly
Words can be –
Sometimes weapons
Ripped across
The no-man's land
Before the bar,
Or muttered softly
To your fears,
No less lethal
To the spirit
So tired of being
In harm's way.
Longing in
The hours of waiting
For combat
To resolve the question,
What do things mean?
How will things be?
There is a drum
In this battle
Sometimes beating
Deep and slow;
At other times
A quick tattoo.

Sometimes only
Marking time;
Sometimes summoning
Red-rimmed eyes
To day long vigilance
And night long too.
"Beware, beware,"
The drummer warns,
"The things that kill you,
You will not see.
You can care too much;
You can care too little.
In war you must learn
To balance woe."
Morning comes
And the march resumes.
Tasteless food
And yellow paper.
Wild highs
Dissolving in hours
Of sweaty tension,
Obliterating memory.

Frank Marello

PART I
CHOICES

1

Monday, December 24, 1973

With no family and having outlived all of her friends, Claudia Wilmer hadn't wanted to give anyone a Christmas present for a long time. The thought of doing so once more filled her with happiness. Reaching for the curtain above the kitchen sink, she pushed it aside and looked into the parking lot. She had a little gift she wanted to give to her neighbor, Livia Marello.

Oh, good, she thought. Their car's still here. She pulled on her everyday sweater as she headed for her back door, picking up a small gift-wrapped package from the kitchen table. Claudia turned a hard right as she emerged from her apartment and stopped in her tracks. The backdoor of the Marello's apartment was wide open. What's that girl doing leaving the door open in this cold? Claudia glanced around to see if Livia was out at her car or coming from the laundry room, but she was nowhere in sight.

"Hello, Livia, Merry Christmas!" Claudia stepped into the entryway and stuck her head into the Marello's kitchen. "Livia, are you home?" Louder this time. Gift wrappings covered the kitchen table. Oh, she's wrapping presents. She took a step inside. "Livia …" Claudia looked down as she spoke. "Oh! Oh My God!" She recoiled, dropping her package.

Livia Marello lay on the floor, clad in her bathrobe and slippers, eyes open, unblinking, staring up at her, head lolling to the left. One foot pointed towards the ceiling, the other at a forty-five-degree angle pointing at the stove, where a mangled teakettle glowed over a high flame.

A retired nurse, Claudia Wilmer didn't startle easily. Regaining her composure, her heart slowing back down out of its red zone, she reached to turn off the burner as she knelt and picked up Livia's left wrist. No pulse. Straddling Livia, Claudia put her ear to the younger woman's chest and listened, then put both palms together where her ear had just been and pushed hard. Again and again and again. "C'mon, girl. Breathe. C'mon." Nothing. Standing and stepping over Livia's body, Claudia reached for the phone.

Frank Marello twisted and snaked his left arm into the back seat, retrieving a bag full of parcels in Christmas wrappings as Mark Josephson drove over the bump at the entrance to the parking lot."

"Look, Frank."

Frank glanced up. Two police cars were parked side by side in the small lot.

"All the students have gone home for the holidays," Frank said. "Maybe someone broke into an apartment."

"Frank, your back door's open."

"Hmmm. Good. Livia's probably in the laundry room. Maybe I can get these packages in before she gets back."

Frank Marello got out of the car, shopping bag in hand, and walked around to the driver's side. "Merry Christmas, Mark." He bent over so that he could see his friend. "Have a great holiday."

"You too, Frank," Mark said. "See you next year, I guess."

They shook hands.

As Frank entered the apartment, he almost bumped into a large man in a brown uniform and wearing a Smokey hat. At the sound of Frank's entry, the man turned towards him.

"Who are you?"

"Frank Marello. Who are you?"

"I'm Sheriff Hatcher. This is Deputy Julius. Do you live here?"

"Ye ... Yes, I do. Why are you here? What's going on?"

Sheriff Hatcher made a nodding motion over his shoulder, glancing down as he did so. On the floor a blanket covered a body. The slippers on the feet protruding from beneath were Livia's.

"Wha…" Frank recoiled, but could not help craning his neck to see, then thrust his arm out toward the kitchen table for support.

Sheriff Hatcher looked at him, silent for a moment. "I hate to tell you this, but we're investigating a homicide. Your neighbor discovered the body of this woman, whom I suspect was your wife, an hour ago. Appears to have been murdered."

"Livia … murdered … wha … what happened?" His hand came up to his face covering his mouth agape, but with no words coming out. He shook his head.

The Sheriff and deputy exchanged glances.

"Howard, keep inventoryin' these items." The Sheriff gestured around the kitchen.

"Mr. Marello, would you mind walkin' out to my car and talkin' to me for a few minutes? I need to ask you some questions."

Wednesday, April 10, 1974

The Bailiff, a uniformed deputy, rose and spoke in a loud voice: "The Accused and his counsel will rise."

The already quiet courtroom became even more silent.

Judge Charles Hunter was blind, but he stared down at Frank Marello. Frank, tall, skinny, bespectacled, stood up awkwardly, all arms and legs needing to be untangled.

"Franklin Allan Marello, having been convicted by a jury of your peers by unanimous verdict of the crime of murder in the first degree of Livia Elaine Marello, I hereby order that you be remanded to the custody of the Warden of the North Carolina State Penitentiary, there to be executed by hanging. May God have mercy on your soul."

A buzz raced around the packed gallery of the courtroom. Reporters with deadlines charged the door in a race for one of the two public phones. The lawyer standing beside Frank sank back into his chair as the Judge growled for "Order in the Court." Frank continued to stand, numb and unlistening, as the Judge thanked the jurors for their service, dismissed them, adjourned the court and left the bench.

"My God," Frank thought, "how can this be?"

Somewhere to his left Avery Carlton, the lawyer, was speaking now, something about a "miscarriage" and there still being "an appeal," but Frank Marello was thinking about being dead. First Livia, now me. He wished he had faith. If he believed in God and heaven, he could find comfort in the belief his execution would transport him to a place where it would be known he hadn't done this crime, where he could once again be with Livia, could tell her all the things he never got a chance to say.

Frank laughed to himself. In the endless hours of confinement since his arrest four months earlier, he'd read a lot of religion and philosophy. Without faith such thoughts were a distraction, not a comfort. He knew some Eastern ways of thinking believed all thought, all activity, was a distraction from existence, and that followers of such beliefs sought to distance themselves from distraction through meditation, seeking to retreat into the blankness of life's essence. He tried to meditate away the monumental distractions of his life, find some respite from the accusation he killed the one person in the world he loved, but without success. Religion was just another thing he wasn't good at, he decided.

"Frank ... Frank ... are you all right?"

Someone was touching his shoulder, shaking him out of his reverie. He looked around and there was his friend, Rhonda Enright, another of his lawyers, staring at him. Behind her stood his dad and brother.

Frank nodded and tried to smile. "Yes ... yes, I'm all right. I'm not having a heart attack or stroke or anything."

The idea of a fatal attack suddenly didn't seem so bad. At least it would save the State of North Carolina the trouble of killing him. Why don't more prisoners under sentence of death commit suicide?

Frank seldom heard of that happening. He supposed the authorities probably denied them the means.

"Frank," Rhonda was saying, "I'm not going to tell you not to let this get you down, but don't give up on this fight. It's a long road from where you're standing now to the carrying out of that sentence, and that jury's guilty verdict is by no means the last word on the issue. So don't give up. Will you promise me that?"

Frank nodded. What is there to give up? He would just go back to his cell, and the fight for his life would swirl on somewhere out beyond the place where he dwelled. If successful, fine. He had already done all he could do. He had taken the stand and told the jurors how much he loved Livia and that he hadn't killed her, and they hadn't believed him.

His dad and his brother, Jim, would continue to pay the attorneys to file their briefs and argue their appeals. If they won, great, but nothing that happened since that awful Christmas Eve gave him any cause for hope. Murder, arrest, trial, conviction, sentencing – looking back, he'd been swept away by an avalanche tearing a path of destruction through his life, nearing the bottom now, where its rampage would end with his execution. "I need to get ready to die," he thought. "How do I go about that?"

On the way back across the street to the jail, Frank walked more slowly than usual. It was a beautiful spring day, blue sky, dogwoods in bloom on the town square, an enormous pink azalea bush spreading across the front of the jail. His thoughts of impending death were swept away, and Frank found himself back in the present, a tall, still living organism moving through the sweet air, breathing, feeling his lungs fill, revitalizing him. For the first time since the announcement of his fate, Frank Marello felt like crying, not because he would soon be denied such visions – sooner or later everyone was denied – but in gratitude for one more glimpse of beauty and the ability to appreciate it.

"I feel like running," he said to Tubby Mayes, the deputy escorting him.

"Wh ... what..." Tubby reached toward his pistol.

"I don't mean escape. I just mean I feel like running. I've always worked through my troubles that way - the one sport this giraffe body of mine always could do. I'd like to take off and run forever."

"You bettah not try it, Boy. I'd have to put you down, an' I don' wanta have to do that."

Thursday, September 2, 1976

> It having been determined that references by the prosecution during final argument to the homosexuality of the accused were unsupported by presentation of any evidence during the evidentiary phase of the trial, and that the unsupported references to homosexuality may have unduly prejudiced juror decision-making regarding the issue of guilt or innocence, the conviction of Franklin Allan Marello, is hereby VACATED, and the matter is remanded to the Superior Court of Johnston County for appropriate action in accord with the findings and orders of this Court.
>
> September 1, 1976
>
> David M. Roberson, Justice Supreme Court of North Carolina

Rhonda Enright folded the paper from which she'd been reading aloud and looked up at Frank Marello, who sat across the partition from her.

"We did it, Frank. We won. This means the State has to start all over. A new trial - a fresh shot at acquittal. How do you feel?"

"I feel like I used to when I had to mow the lawn while growing up."

Rhonda stared. "What do you mean?"

"We had a power mower, the kind you push. In order to start it, you had to pull on a rope. I'd pull and pull, and it would never start. I'd get so mad and frustrated that sometimes I'd actually kick the darn thing. After pulling about a thousand times, eventually I'd go get my dad or Jim. They'd come out and usually it would start for them on the first try, which always made me even more mad and frustrated. Anyway, ever since Livia was killed, the justice system has seemed like that lawn mower to me. I just couldn't get it started working for me, no matter how hard I tried, but now I feel like we finally got it cranked."

Rhonda, no stranger to stubborn lawn mowers while growing up, laughed. "Well, we still have a big lawn to mow."

2

Friday, September 3, 1976 - Predawn

The ringing bludgeoned its way through the cocoon of sleep in which Mike Taggart had been floating. Groping for the phone, he bumped into Marcia, who had somehow wound up on his side of the bed.

"May I speak to Mike Taggart please?" A woman's voice, refined, but with a slight trace of a southern accent.

"Um … this is Mike."

"Mike, this is Rhonda Enright."

"Rhonda Enright … law school Rhonda?

"Yes, 'Law School Rhonda.' As a matter of fact, I'm back at Duke again, teaching this time. It's 'Professor Rhonda' now. Listen, I want to talk to you about the possibility of helping me on a case. It involves a friend of mine who's in a lot of trouble."

Marcia's face loomed in front of Mike in the dimness. She was mouthing the words, "Who is it?"

Mike shook his head to put her off and tried to collect his thoughts about Rhonda Enright. "Jesus, Rhonda, what time is it? How'd you get this number?"

"Oh, I know it's early out there. It's seven-thirty here. What's that make it, four-thirty California time? I wanted to be sure to catch you before you went off to court or something. I got your number from the Alumni Office. This can't wait."

Nothing's changed. When Rhonda Enright focused on a problem, any problem, everything else took a back seat. "What kind of trouble is your friend in?"

"Murder. He's accused of murder, but there's more to it than that. Lots more."

"Murder! How much more trouble can he be in than that?" Taggart was suddenly wide awake.

"Plenty. You see, he's already been convicted once and sentenced to death." Rhonda paused while that fact sank in. "The North Carolina Supreme Court just threw out the conviction on appeal. So now he's going to be retried."

"Why'd they throw it out, bad confession?" Taggart had been a deputy sheriff for three years while in law school, when the Supreme Court started throwing out confessions for failure to warn persons of their right to remain silent.

"No, no. No confession. He's innocent and has always said so."

"Rhonda, why do you need me? There are lots of lawyers in North Carolina with more experience. Why not handle it yourself?"

"Mike, I know the law. I handled the appeal. But you've tried capital cases. I haven't. Plus, the case is out in Marlborough. Having lived out there, you've probably drunk beer with half the prospective jurors in Johnston County."

Marlborough. A kaleidoscope of images spun in Taggart's head. Law school, the little cinderblock house where he and Cathy lived in the days when they'd been happy, Stick Hatcher, the Sheriff for whom he'd worked, the West End Tavern. Marlborough had been like a three-year visit to Mars sandwiched between the before and after slices of his life. Taggart wasn't sure drinking with the boys down at the West End was much of a credential, but a trial in Marlborough aroused his curiosity. "Tell me some more about this case."

"Well," Rhonda said, "that brings me to the rest of the trouble I mentioned ... You see, Frank, 'Frank Marello' is my friend's name, is a professor at UNC, or was, and he's homosexual. The first conviction was overturned because the prosecutor alluded to his homosexuality during final argument despite there being no evidence of it at trial. He won't have to mention it this time though, because there won't be a juror in all of Johnston County who doesn't already know about it."

"Who's Marello accused of killing?"

"His wife, his pregnant wife, on Christmas Eve 1973. The prosecution contends he strangled her in a domestic quarrel."

"Were they fighting?"

"One of the neighbors says she heard an argument the night before."

"What about ... the fact that Frank liked the boy next door better than her?"

There was a momentary silence on the other end of the line. "Taggart, that's not funny. If you're going to do this, you have to give Frank a chance in your own mind. He needs somebody who doesn't come into the case pre-judging him because of something having nothing to do with it."

Taggart grimaced at the telephone receiver. *Hard to believe Marello's homosexuality has nothing to do with the case.* "You're right, Professor. What were they arguing about?"

"Money, according to Frank. He says they didn't have any. Livia, that was his wife, wanted him to ask his parents for some, and he didn't want to. It was Christmas Eve, and there weren't any presents under the tree; there wasn't even a tree. She was upset."

"What happened to Marello's lead counsel? Did he get dumped when he lost, or did Marello run out of money?"

"It was mostly mutual. The family had lost confidence, but he was sick of the case. Money's not a problem. Frank's family's very well off. You'll get paid. Anyway, you'll be good for this case, if the homosexuality thing doesn't bother you. I think the last guy was more uncomfortable than maybe he was even aware."

"But you think I'd be 'comfortable' with it?"

"Well, I know you and I can work together unless one of us has changed more than most people ever do. I actually thought of you as being open-minded back in law school, although what I took for open-mindedness may simply have been you not giving a damn. Sometimes it's hard to tell with you."

Sounds like something Cathy would have said. Mention of Marlborough brought back thoughts of his ex-wife. When Taggart came back from Viet Nam, she had accused him of caring too much and too little all at the same time.

"Mike, I'm not kidding. I need to find someone I think can help Frank Marello. You've got to decide. Is this something you're willing to do? Because if it isn't, I have other calls to make.

"Taggart, are you still there?"

"I'm still here." Mike's reminiscence evaporated. "Listen, I can't decide this without talking to my partner, see if it's even possible to rearrange the workload. How soon do you need to know?"

"The Supreme Court announced its decision yesterday. The County Solicitor immediately announced plans for a hearing Monday to set the new date. Can you let me know today, maybe by two o'clock your time?"

Wow! Taggart stared at the phone he'd just hung up.

"Is it okay to come back in?" Marcia walked back in from the bathroom. "No more privileged communications?" She plopped down on top of the covers.

Mike shook his head and grinned. "No, no more 'privileged communications.'"

"Couldn't help overhearing that someone named 'Law School Rhonda' wants you to handle some case. What's it all about? Who's Law School Rhonda?"

"Rhonda Enright, probably the smartest person I've ever met ..." Taggart's memories of Rhonda overtook his reply. Half way through their first semester in law school, he'd been walking across campus in a drenching rain, when Rhonda stopped and offered him a ride. Glancing in the back seat, he saw her law books piled there still wrapped in their cellophane. She'd finished first in their class, was Editor In Chief of Law Journal, had been a Supreme Court law clerk. Big deals in the law business.

"I asked her once how she did so well," he went on. "She said she had a photographic memory. 'How does that help when you never read anything?' I asked. 'I don't know,' she replied. 'It just does.' We were assigned to be partners in the first year moot court competition."

"Before I got to know her, I assumed she must be from some big city in the East, Vassar, fox hunting, debutante balls, those sorts of things, but she's from Cody, Wyoming, a small town kid like me. We were friends the rest of the way through law school. Even Cathy thought she was great. But except for a letter or two while I was in Viet Nam, I hadn't heard from her."

"So, what's this case she wants you to handle?"

Mike summarized what Rhonda told him. "Retrying a case is always tough, especially a murder conviction and death sentence, especially in a place as resistant to change as Marlborough. Town's turned a blind eye towards a lot of injustice in its day. I'm not sure this emergent 'New South' I've been reading about has reached Marlborough."

"I thought the University of North Carolina was in Chapel Hill."

"It is. But Chapel Hill is in the same county as Marlborough, if not the same century, and somehow Marlborough wound up being the county seat. So that's where the courthouse is. Marlborough's about fifteen miles west of Durham. I think I told you about my being a deputy sheriff there."

"That's right. You were Barney Fife in an earlier life." Marcia laughed. "Well, are you going to do it?"

3

Friday, September 3, 1976 - Midmorning

Tom Horn, had been Taggart's law partner for four years, ever since Mike's return to San Diego from Chicago after everything with Cathy fell apart. They'd been best friends since Viet Nam in '69.

"So that's the deal." Mike came to the end of his account of Rhonda's proposal. "What do you think?"

Horn was leaning back, feet up on his desk. He took off his glasses, held them up to the light to see if they were dirty enough to clean and put them back on. "We could use the money. I guess North Carolina's money is as good as California's.

"As far as this guy being gay goes, I suppose homosexuality's still illegal somewhere. Who knows? You've represented a lot of people guilty of worse things. Anyway, that's not what he's charged with. Sounds like a good case if you're not too hung up about that. What difference does it make to you?

"What about Marcia? What does she think, or does that matter? You're going to be gone a long time, and you won't be flying back and forth much on our budget, even if you have the time."

"I don't think Marello being qu … gay makes any difference to me." Mike addressed the easier of Horn's questions. "But my first response was to make some sarcastic joke, and that makes me wonder a little. Never stopped to think about it before. Never had to."

"Now you do."

Shortly before noon, Taggart walked down to the waterfront and followed it all the way out to Harbor Island, his thinking place, a couple of miles from downtown. It was a typical San Diego day, cloudless, warm, but not hot, with a light breeze.. He sat on a bench staring at the water, watching occasional sailboats skim by, listening to the distant drone of aircraft engines from the air station across the Bay. Marcia Banning, not Marello, occupied his thoughts.

4

March – June 1975

Eighteen months earlier, the spring he and Horn decided to coach a youth baseball team, Taggart was leaning against the chain links of the backstop listening to Tom explain to a group of seven and eight-year olds how to hold their gloves during the first day of practice.

"Which one is yours?" A woman's voice.

"None of 'em." Mike turned around to see who was asking.

The speaker was about his own age, tall, at least 5'10", dark complected, wearing a plaid flannel shirt and jeans. He was struck by the blueness of her eyes, a striking contrast to her black hair.

"Which one is yours?" he asked.

"The little one over there on the far side of the group. Matt Banning. I don't want to point because it would embarrass him if he noticed. I'm Marcia, Matt's mom."

Mike saw the resemblance. Matt Banning was the spitting image of his mother, a little darker maybe, but with same coal black hair and blue eyes.

"Glad to meet you, Marcia. I'm Mike Taggart. That's Tom Horn out there trying to explain how to catch a baseball. If you have any questions about what we're doing or why, just ask, okay?"

"Okay. I probably will ask some really dumb questions as the season goes along. Matt's just getting started and it's just the two of us."

For several games Taggart had no opportunity to speak to Marcia Banning again beyond nodding "Hello" through the fence at each game, although he found himself always looking to see if she was there. She always was.

Matt was the smallest and youngest player on the Brave German Shepherds, the name the players chose for the team. If his birthday had been two days later, he would have been too young to play that year.

Jimmy Testa was the biggest and best player on the team. If his birthday had been two days earlier, he would have been playing in an older division. Big and fast, a twelve or thirteen year old in an eight year old's body, but sullen, mouthy and mean. So when Mike heard Jimmy say, "C'mon Banning, let's you and me warm up," at the beginning of a mid-season practice, he was suspicious of the mismatch.

Jimmy's first throw was a rocket that was on top of the unsuspecting Matt way before he was ready for its arrival, and he barely got his glove up in time to ward it off. Matt picked up the ball and tossed it back to Jimmy, who immediately fired back at him so hard that the ball blew past Matt's glove, brushing it aside and hitting him in the shoulder.

Mike had seen enough. He picked up his own glove. "Matt, why don't you go warm up with Jason and Andy." He indicated two nearby players. "I want to play catch with Jimmy." He held out his glove, and Matt underhanded him the ball. Mike could see Matt was fighting tears and struggling not to rub his shoulder. "You okay?" Mike asked.

Jaws clenched tight. Matt nodded and jogged over to the other group.

Without any apparent effort, Taggart whistled his first throw back at Jimmy chest-high. "Pop." It smacked into the glove Jimmy only just managed to get in front of the onrushing ball.

That's about right. Mike immediately raised his glove towards Jimmy in a signal for him to throw the ball back. After three more throws, on each of which Jimmy, grimacing, had turned sideways to make himself a smaller target, Mike walked up to him. "Now you know how Matt felt when you were throwing to him, but you already knew that, didn't you?"

"Knew what?"

"C'mon, Jimmy. You knew if you threw that hard at an inexperienced player like Matt, someone a lot younger and smaller than you, he'd be scared.

Jimmy shrugged and looked over Mike's shoulder towards the outfield, waiting for the conversation to be over.

"We're here to play baseball. If Coach Horn or I see you do anything like that again, you won't play any more this season. Is that clear?"

The next day, Jimmy quit the Brave German Shepherds, who didn't win another game all season, but had more fun.

Two days after the season ended, Mike's phone rang.

Shifting the half-empty pizza box off his lap, he tossed a piece of crust to his dog, Feodot, turned down the ballgame and answered.

"Is this Coach Mike?" A child's voice.

"Sure is."

"Coach, this is Matt. My mom and I want to invite you over for dinner."

Taggart smiled. *Great kid.*

"Sure, Matt. I'd love to come. When?"

"Here's my mom. She'll tell you."

"Hello, Mike, this is Marcia Banning. Like Matt just said, we want you to come for dinner this weekend. How about Saturday night?"

"Saturday night's great. Can I bring something?"

Five thirty-five Saturday afternoon found Mike standing at the front door of 2410 Martin Way, along with a plate full of brownies.

One nanosecond after he rang the bell, Matt opened the door. He was wearing his Brave German Shepherds shirt.

"Hi, Coach." Matt grinned. "C'mon in."

"Hi, Matt. How's it going?"

"Great. MOM, COACH IS HERE!"

Marcia appeared around the corner drying her hands with a dish towel.

"Hi, Marcia." Taggart held out the brownies. "Here's my contribution to the feast."

"Hey, I told you I had the food covered. You didn't have to do that. They look good though. Bake'em yourself?"

"Yep. Never hurts to have some depth in the dessert department. Isn't that right, Matt?"

"Well, come on into the kitchen," Marcia said. "It's the nerve center of this operation. Want something to drink?"

"Sure. What do you have?

"Beer, wine, lemonade, soft drinks – bar's full."

"Too many choices. What're you drinking, Matt?"

"Lemonade. Mom says I'm too young to drink beer."

"My mom used to say the same thing. I think I'll have what Matt's having."

Matt hustled over to the cupboard for the glasses. "What'd you do today, Coach?"

"Played baseball this morning. Just laid around and read a book this afternoon. What'd you do?"

"BASEBALL. You play baseball too? That's neat. Mom and I cleaned the house this morning 'cause you were coming over and went to the store. I went swimming this afternoon, 'cause it was so warm. We've got a pool. Wanna see it? Wanna see my room?"

Matt's room was upstairs in the opposite corner of the house, which was about three times as big as Taggart's two bedroom apartment. En route they passed through carpeted rooms, furnished in bright, attractive colors. Things went together. There was artwork that wasn't an old Janis Joplin poster. *Gee, it looks like a grown-up lives here.*

"Here's my room, Coach." Matt waved his arms at the space.

Against the far wall was a bed with a bedspread with pictures of jet planes on it. There was a bookshelf stuffed with books and games, a coat tree on which hung Matt's Brave German Shepherds hat, and a desk where the Brave German Shepherds' team picture and a photograph of a young man in a Marine flight suit wearing captain's bars and holding a flight helmet. He was standing on a carrier deck in front of an F-14 that bore a name in script, "Bad News Banning."

"That's my dad. He was a Marine, a fighter pilot ... He died in the war."

Taggart swallowed hard. "I'm very sorry that happened, Matt. Your dad looks like a great guy."

"Yeah, he was. Mom tells me all about him 'cause I wasn't born yet when he had to go to the war."

"Show me some of your books," Mike half-croaked, not knowing what more to say about Matt's father. "What's your favorite?"

Out beside the pool, a table was set for three.

"Nice place, Marcia ... and this ..." Taggart gestured at the pool deck and adjacent flowerbeds, "this is beautiful."

"Coach, what kind of a baseball team do you play on? Did you ever play for the Padres?" With those questions, Matt sparked a run of conversation that carried the three of them two hours past dinner and covered, in addition to Mike's emphatic disclaimers of any participation in professional baseball at any level, the Padres' season's prospects, Matt's plans for summer camp, his best friend, Charley, Charley's dog, Marcia's explanation why she wouldn't let Matt have a dog – something about her having been badly bitten as a child, Mike's dog, Feodot, and half a dozen other burning second grade subjects.

About nine-thirty Mike nodded in the direction of Matt sitting on the couch in the living room, where they had moved when it began to get cool out. He had fallen asleep. "Marcia, look."

"Oh, I know. I tell him he can stay up late on Friday and Saturday nights, and he never makes it much beyond nine. I'm surprised he lasted this long tonight, because he was so charged up all day about you coming over. Do you want to carry him into his room for me? I can still lift him, but just barely. He's getting so big."

Ever so gently Mike worked his hands beneath the sleeping boy and scooped him up, one arm under his bottom, the other supporting his back and neck. Matt's arms flopped around Mike's neck. Mike carried him into his room and slowly lowered him on his bed.

"I'll get his PJs on and be out in a minute," Marcia whispered.

As Taggart was tiptoeing out, he heard Matt murmur, "G'night, Coach."

By the time Marcia emerged from tucking Matt in, Mike had cleared the dinner table and was loading the dishwasher.

"I want to thank you for being such a good coach for Matt all season," Marcia said as she pitched in. "Especially for what you did with Jimmy Testa. Matt told me about that the day it happened."

Taggart straightened up from putting the last dish in the dishwasher. "I'd forgotten about that."

"Well, Matt and I want you to know we appreciate everything you did all season. Tom too, but that thing with Jimmy was special."

"You're welcome." Mike looked around. "Time for me to be heading home. Thanks for the wonderful dinner. That's more nutrition than I've had in three weeks. You have a lovely home, and Matt's a great kid."

As they walked to the door, Marcia said, "I suppose Matt showed you the picture of his dad when he showed you his room."

"Yeah, he did. Tough loss. I'm really sorry that happened to you."

Marcia gave a wan smile. "Tough loss. Yes, it was a 'tough loss.' Still is, but it's been more than seven years now. Tonight was Matt's night, but maybe you and I can get together some time and talk about something other than second grade. I'd like that."

"I'd like that too. Good-night, Marcia." Taggart stepped off the porch and walked to his car without turning back.

That was how it all started.

Two weeks later Mike and Marcia went out to dinner. It was a velvet evening - soft air and the sound of surf a quarter mile away, dim as twilight in the background. They sat on the outside patio at Guiseppi's, an Italian restaurant a couple of miles from Marcia's house. Once they had ordered, Marcia said, "So, Matt made me promise to ask whether you played baseball again this morning?"

"Yeah. Most Wednesday nights and Saturday mornings."

"It probably won't surprise you to learn Matt wants to come to one of your games."

"Sorry, can't ever let that happen."

"What ... why not?" Marcia missed Mike's grin.

"It would destroy me in Matt's eyes. Once he saw how poorly I play, I'd lose all credibility. I'm very much a 'do what I say', not 'do what I do' type of coach."

"Yeah, I'll bet. I think there's not much chance of that. If you're still playing baseball at what ... how old are you anyway?"

"Thirty-four."

"If you're still playing baseball at thirty-one and like the sport enough to coach a bunch of seven and eight year olds when you don't even have one of your own, I doubt you'd be risking much loss of credibility. Why did you do that anyway, coach the Brave German Shepherds, I mean?"

"A great guy named Al Weiss, who didn't have any kids, spent a lot of time coaching teams I played on as a kid. If I could do for just one kid what Al Weiss did for me, I'd feel like I really accomplished something."

"What did he do for you?"

"Made me believe in myself, that I could play and not let the inevitable mistakes wreck my confidence. So, I had a debt to the game, to Al. Horn felt pretty much the same way, so we decided to coach."

"How come no kids?"

"No wife. Probably ought to get one of those first, don't you think? Actually, that's a little deceiving, 'cause I had a wife once upon a time, but we didn't have any kids. We got a divorce a couple of years ago."

"Mind if I ask what happened?"

"I'm still asking myself that question. Cathy, that was my wife's name, and I had dated since high school. Got married the summer before law school. But when I returned from Viet Nam, things weren't the same. Probably my fault. There were days when I wasn't exactly all the way back from the war."

Marcia waited to hear what that meant, but Taggart, who had stopped to take a sip of wine, did not resume talking. The few guys Marcia had dated since Tim's death had all seemed eager to tell her more than she wanted to know about themselves. But now that she had found someone in whom she was interested, he was practically laconic. "How long after your return before you split up?" Marcia asked, hoping for more.

"For good? A couple of years. Long ones. How about you? Matt said his dad died before he was born. What's happened to Marcia Banning since then?"

Taggart's marital history well had evidently run dry, at least for now.

"Not much. I was working for a landscaper when Tim left for WesPac. I'm the manager of the place now. As for motherhood, I didn't even know I was pregnant when Tim left, but it had been a fond farewell. I was five months along when he died. Four months later I was a single mom, and that's what I've been ever since.

"It took a long time before I felt like dating. Eventually I started to go out occasionally. But there's never been anyone I cared about. I haven't gone out with anyone more than three or four times. They stop calling, at least all but one of them, and I'm not sorry when they stop. Probably they can sense I won't be sorry, and that's why they stop."

"All but one?"

"Yes, all but one. There's this guy, Bill Sullivan. I only went out with him twice. He's a Navy doctor. Seemed nice at first, but on the second date he turned into one of those guys who think the so-called 'sexual revolution' wrote them a blank check. When he found out there was no money in his account as far as I was concerned, he got nasty. He has a slight limp, some car accident a couple of years earlier. Said I was rejecting him because of that, even though the limp had nothing to do with it."

"Wonder how he got in the Navy with a limp," Taggart said.

"I think the accident happened after he was in," Marcia replied. "Anyway, since then it's as if persuading me to go out with him again is his special crusade. Calls at least once a month, sometimes more, acts as if we just went out the night before last. I always tell him to stop, but he doesn't. Lately, I've seen him drive by the house several times. He drives a red Corvette - hard to miss. That scares me a little, because he doesn't live around here. But he's never stopped or done anything weird."

Within a few minutes, the conversation lightened up – swapping stories about growing up mostly. By the time they had finished their coffee, it had become eleven o'clock.

"Gee, that went fast." Marcia glanced at her watch. "I'd better get home. My in-laws are baby-siting. They might start worrying."

Mike agreed with her about the time going fast.

"We certainly did what we said were going to do," Marcia said as they stood on her doorstep saying good-night.

"What do you mean?"

"We said next time we got together we'd talk about something other than second grade. I think we accomplished that."

"Yeah. Hope I didn't bore you with the saga of my youth."

"Not at all, Mike." Marcia touched his shoulder as she spoke. "Those are the kinds of things a girl needs to know. I had a wonderful time. Thanks."

"Glad you enjoyed it. I had a good time too. I better take off before your father-in-law starts flashing the porch light. Say 'Hi' to Matt for me."

As he turned to go, Marcia began to open the front door but then turned back towards the retreating Taggart. "Oh, Mike, one more thing."

Half way down the sidewalk Mike looked back in her direction.

"You're not one of those guys I want to stop calling." She disappeared inside her house.

As Mike opened his car door, a red Corvette drove by.

5

July – September 1975

Of course, Mike did not stop calling. Just the opposite. Following up on Matt's wish to see him play, Mike invited Matt and Marcia to his game the next Saturday morning. Marcia brought a picnic lunch and they'd spent the afternoon at the park. Feodot came too. When she and Matt saw each other, it was love at first sight.

The rest of the summer had been filled with weekend hikes, bicycling, swimming – Marcia was game for anything outdoors. She could make a Frisbee land wherever she wanted and had more moves jumping rope than a professional fighter. Matt and Mike played endless games of catch, batting practice and Big Time Two Man World Series of Baseball, a game Mike invented. Matt put a picture of the three of them along with Feodot on his desk between the Brave German Shepherds' team picture and the picture of his dad. Marcia began to receive calls from someone who hung up whenever she answered.

In September Mike accompanied Marcia to her friend Sharon Page's wedding. The ceremony was on the lawn of the Admiral Kidd Club, a Navy officer's club on the shore of San Diego Bay across the water from downtown. Mike had met Sharon and her fiancé, Bill Bagosian, a couple of times, as well as a number of the other guests, at parties he and Marcia had attended during the summer. He liked Marcia's friends.

"Congratulations, Bill," Mike offered the groom his hand as they stood next to each other at the bar early in the reception. "Beautiful spot." He gestured towards the water and the distant lights beginning to twinkle in the dusk.

"Hey, thanks, Mike." They shook hands. "When we gonna be doing this for you and Marcia?"

"You know something I don't know, Bill?" Mike smiled.

Bill smiled back. "Just idle speculation, my friend. Idle speculation." He turned to accept congratulations from another guest.

Back at their table, Mike handed Marcia her drink. "Want to engage in a little wager?"

"I don't know. What do you have in mind?"

"When Bill and Sharon feed each other their wedding cake, do you think one or both of them will shove it in the other's face?"

"Oh, Sharon wouldn't do that."

"What about Bill?"

"I don't think so. He'd better not."

"So you think it's unlikely?"

"Yes, I think it's unlikely."

"Then you should probably give me odds if I'm going to take the other side of this bet."

Marcia studied Taggart's deadpan expression. "What are we betting?"

"How about a shoeshine?"

"A shoeshine! What do you take me for? I don't have a single pair of shoes that take more than a minute to shine. Your size ... whatever they are, what? Twelve? They could take me an hour."

"That's where the odds come in. These are your friends. You know their personalities far better than I. Based on that, you think cake-in-the-face unlikely. Therefore, my risk of losing is higher if I take the other side of the bet, so I should get more if I win."

"I liked you better as a little league coach than as a lawyer," Marcia made a face at Mike. "But okay. A shoeshine it is."

Dinner progressed, toasts were drunk, darkness fell. At last the cake, a traditional multi-layered pile of sugar, came under the knife. Gently, Bill put his hand over Sharon's along the handle, and together they cut the first slice and laid it on a plate. Then they cut the slice in two. Carefully Bill picked up one half with his fingers and fed it to Sharon. Under the table, Marcia nudged Taggart with her foot. As she did so, Sharon lifted the other half to Bill's mouth and then, with a sudden twist of her hand smeared cake across his face.

Taggart was the first to applaud. After a moment the rest of the guests, with the notable exception of Marcia, followed suit, as Bill laughed and tried to lick frosting off the tip of his nose.

Mike glanced at Marcia out of the corner of his eye and found her staring at him, shaking her head. "You're so lucky. I would have bet a hundred dollars that Sharon would never do such a thing."

"Ah," Taggart smacked the heel of his hand against his forehead, "and to think I settled for a shoeshine."

As they were finishing their own pieces of cake, the moon began to rise, huge and orange, across the water behind the downtown buildings. By the time the band started to play and the traditional first couple of dances had been danced, it was high enough in the sky to be mirrored on the water.

Marcia eyed Mike, who was leaning back on the rear legs of his chair watching as guests poured onto the dance floor. Marcia loved to dance. She was afraid Taggart might be more watcher than dancer. Unexplored territory.

Suddenly, the band broke into *Johnny Be Good*. Mike grabbed her hand. "C'mon."

They didn't sit down for the rest of the evening except when the band took a break. Tall and graceful, Marcia seemed to float. Whether the song was fast or slow, it was as if her feet didn't touch the floor. "I had no idea you liked to dance," she told Mike during a break between songs. "You're pretty good."

"What I lack in grace, I make up for with enthusiasm."

Marcia laughed as the next song, a slow one, began to play and she stepped into Mike's arms. "I'm glad you do."

Toward midnight, the bandleader announced the next number would be the band's last. Only a few couples were still on the floor as the first few bars of *The First Time Ever I Saw Your Face* began to play. Marcia nestled her head on Mike's shoulder, her arms wrapped around his neck, his around her waist, their dance a slow-turning embrace.

"I wish this song would never end," she whispered in Mike's ear.

Afterwards, they walked to Mike's car hand in hand. Driving home, Mike said, "It's too bad you stepped on my toes so many times tonight. It's going to take a lot of work to get all those scuff marks out of my spit shine."

Marcia had forgotten about the bet. "Oh, right. I'm surprised you're not limping."

Walking up to her front door, Marcia said, "Matt's at his grandparents for the weekend. Do you want to come in?"

Taggart hesitated for a long moment before replying. When he finally spoke, his voice was husky, "I had a great time tonight, Marcia, a wonderful time. But it's late, and I think I'll just head home."

As he spoke, he gave her a hug and opened the door she'd just unlocked. Almost before she knew it, Marcia was standing inside and alone, trying to digest what had just happened or failed to happen. She walked to her front picture window, pushed the curtain back slightly and watched Mike drive away.

6

October 1975 - June 1976

"So, what's it like to be an old married lady?" Marcia asked. She and Sharon Bagosian sat drinking coffee in Sharon's kitchen a couple days after Sharon's return from her honeymoon.

"About the same as the last two years Bill and I lived together. A lot better than that first year." Sharon rolled her eyes. "That took some getting used to."

"But what about you. How are things going with Mike?"

"Tough question." Marcia held her cup out for a refill. "Matt loves him, and in many ways Mike's like I always imagined Tim would have been as a father. It's like we're on the same page wherever parenthood's concerned." She took a sip. "I love Mike. He makes me laugh and feel safe." Marcia smiled at the thought. "I miss him when we're not together. These last few months we've had any number of wonderful, gentle moments, moments that begged for next steps to be taken, but do you know what?" She paused. "He's never even kissed me."

"Snork." Sharon inhaled an ounce of steaming coffee, coughed, wiped her mouth and blew her nose with a napkin, shook her head and stared at Marcia.

"It's true. Each time we seem to be right on the brink of intimacy, he backs away. I haven't dated that much the last few years, but nothing I've read or heard makes me think boys have stopped kissing girls, especially ones who want to be kissed."

"Maybe he doesn't like girls," Sharon said. "He was married before, wasn't he?"

"Yes, to his high school sweetheart for almost seven years, although they weren't together the whole time. He also was involved with another woman who seems to have been important to him. I don't think he's uninterested in kissing girls, either in concept or me in particular. Something else is going on. I'm not sure what."

At the end of October, three weeks went by with no call from Mike. When Marcia called his house, he didn't answer. Finally, she called him at work.

"Mike, what's happened to you? Why haven't you called?"

"Too blue to call. Feodot died. It's like I lost my heart. "

Although half blind and enfeebled by arthritis, Feodot had been a big part of that summer's activities. No ball had ever been hit or thrown that she would not chase down and return, no sock she would not chew, no open car window out of which she would not thrust her head, outsized ears flowing backwards in the wind. Whenever possible she was to be found curled up on Matt's lap once they became acquainted.

"Oh, Mike, I'm so sorry. I wish you'd told me. Maybe we could have done something to make it easier. This is going to tear Matt up."

Mike didn't say anything.

"Mike, why not come over for dinner tonight?" Then, before he could answer, "On second thought, let's go out, just you and me, is that okay?"

Marcia picked Mike up for a change and drove to "Taco King," a tiny hole in the wall in a nearby strip mall, that she knew to be Taggart's favorite restaurant in the entire world. Mike said nothing during the five minutes it took to get there.

Once settled in their booth, Mike with a beer and a burrito the size of a catcher's mitt swimming in enchilada sauce, she with a fish taco, Marcia said, "Mike, I thought it would be better if just the two of us got together, because it seems to me we have some things to talk about that aren't second grade things."

Taggart met her gaze, but didn't say anything.

"I know you loved Feodot, but why make her loss a reason not to see me, not to see Matt?"

"I don't know. It just seemed like it was my problem. I didn't want to bother you with my stuff."

"But you know that Matt loved her too? Your stuff's become our stuff."

Taggart shook his head.

"For that matter, you know that Matt loves you, don't you?"

"I know." Mike shook his head again. "I love him too, both of you. I love both of you. That's the problem."

It did not surprise Marcia that Taggart loved Matt, loved her. It did surprise her that, although he had seldom even held her hand, he recognized his own feelings and was prepared to acknowledge them. "Why are those feelings such a problem?"

"Because I'm afraid I'll disappoint you. When it comes to love, I've disappointed some wonderful people. When Feodot died, my first thought was to call you. I wanted to call. I just wanted to put my head on your shoulder and weep. But that wanting made me see like never before just how far down the road I was where you and Matt are concerned. The more I give you of me, the more you will come to expect it, and rightly so. Then, if I stop, there'll be a lot of sorrow. Maybe that's a risk any two people take when they become involved, but the last thing in the world I want to do is break Matt's heart."

Marcia thought something like this was coming. "Is that why you've never kissed me?

"Yeah." Mike picked up his fork. "Sex changes things. I thought if I slowed way down, maybe everybody would be protected, but it doesn't work that way." He laughed. "Just means lots of cold showers."

"Mike, look at me." Taggart raised his head. "You're too late. You know you are. If you ever stop giving yourself to us, there are going to be broken hearts all over the place. Where romance is concerned, I had my dukes up for seven years, both for me and especially for Matt, because we're obviously a package deal, and, even more than you, I *really* don't want his heart broken. But I dropped my guard with you almost before I knew what was happening. I love you, and I know Matt does too. Nothing could be more clear. So, it's time for you to stop taking cold showers."

Thus had begun a mostly wonderful year. They did not live together nor did Mike spend the night at Marcia's until, after the passage of almost nine months, Matt went camping for a weekend with his best friend, Charley, and Charley's family. So, when Marcia called, "Matt, Charlie's here. Grab your things and c'mon," she and Mike were looking forward to Matt's weekend absence every bit as much as Matt. Matt charged down the stairs, dragging his duffel bag banging along behind him,. "'Bye, Mom. 'Bye, Coach." He gave Marcia a running kiss and disappeared into the waiting van. "Hey, Charlie."

"I know what we can do," Marcia said with a grin as the intrepid campers pulled away from the curb.

"Get him out of here!"

The sleep-shattering command burst over Mike and Marcia like a bomb.

"Get him out of here! Get him out of here!"

"What … " Marcia stammered, reaching for Mike. Moonlight illuminated the bed. Beyond it, standing in shadow, Taggart saw the silhouette of a tall man demanding, "Get him out of here!"

Holy shit. The words spewing out of the dark hollowed Taggart, shrinking, withering him with fear he hadn't felt since the war. He willed himself to calm down. Without having to be told, Mike knew he was about to meet the driver of the red Corvette.

"Get him out of here!"

"Okay. Okay. I'm going." Not wanting to further antagoinize their assailant, Taggart rolled out of bed. "Let me get dressed."

"Mike, don't!" Marcia sat up.

Reaching for his pants on a nearby chair, Taggart strained in the dimness to see whether the man was armed.

"Mike, what are you … "

"Get him out of here!!!" Their antagonist shouted, waving his arms as he repeated his demand. The instant he saw the man's hands were empty, Mike threw his pants in the man's face. "UUHHH!" Right behind the pants came two hundred pounds of angry, naked ex-Marine smashing into the intruder's midsection, driving him face first to the floor. Instantly, Mike was on top of him, pinning the man flat into the carpet with a forearm on the back of the his neck, his right leg bent back all the way to his butt and his left arm jerked behind him at an angle that threatened to tear it off his shoulder.

Recovering from the shock of being taken down, the man began to thrash.

"Lie still or I'll break your fucking neck." Mike thrust even more weight on the forearm pinned against the base of the man's skull. The thrashing stopped.

"Marcia," he sensed more than saw she was on her feet. Glancing up, he saw her standing, equally naked, brandishing a baseball bat. "Good. Get me something to tie him up and call the police."

It was after three by the time they were back in bed, intruder arrested, statements given, Marcia's post-traumatic tears finally flowing. She nestled in the crook of Mike's arm, snuffling, chest heaving.

"Marsh, take it easy," Taggart said, stroking her cheek. "It's over now … Look on the bright side."

"Bright side? What bright side?"

"Well, there's no longer any doubt what Sullivan's up to, and the authorites know about it."

"Oh, Mike, do you think it's really over? Won't there have to be a trial? Will we have to testify?"

"Probably."

Marcia shuddered, daubed her eyes with the edge of the sheet and snuggled closer to Mike. "That'd be awful."

7

January 1, 1976

"Mike, I know we haven't been at this very long," Marcia said, "but where do you think this thing is going?"

She and Mike stood at the sink in Mike's apartment doing dishes on New Year's morning after ringing in 1976 with the Bagosians, Horn and his maid of the moment. Taggart was washing. *Why didn't we clean up this mess last night?* He chiseled away at some dried guacamole. *I feel like a dirty dish.*

"'This thing?'"

"Us. You know what I mean. We've been together almost six months. I'm not looking for any final answers or anything, but as of this moment, what do you foresee for us?"

Holy shit. "I don't know. I'm not sure I 'foresee' anything. It seems like we're becoming closer. Whenever I think about what that means, all the old misgivings loom up."

Marcia turned to look at Mike, hands on hips. "So what you're saying is, you're no closer to resolving your 'misgivings' than you were right after Feodot died?"

He blinked as if that would help him clear his hung over head, so unready for such a conversation. "I don't know. Closer? Farther? I don't think like that."

Marcia looked at him for a long moment and then looked away. She set the champagne glass she was drying down on the counter.

"I sometimes wonder whether your hesitancy has to do with inflicting your 'bad self,' or whatever you want to call it, on Matt and me, or you're just plain afraid to commit."

"'Afraid to commit?' It's not like I'm off living it up in some different life six nights a week. You two are pretty much my whole life."

"Yes. But you could walk away tomorrow without breaking a single promise. That doesn't give me and Matt much to rely on."

"So could you. Seems to me that's a good way to keep either of us from taking the other for granted."

"Mike, I want you to take me for granted. I want to take you for granted. When I think of you, of us, I want to take for granted that ten years from now, twenty, there'll you'll be right beside me, me and Matt, because you've told us so. It's not going to change who I am, how I act. It's just the security of knowing what tomorrow's going to bring. Otherwise, I've no better foundation for planning a future than that girl Tom brought to the party last night."

What is there to say? Taggart didn't say anything.

Standing on her tiptoes, Marcia reached up to the top shelf of the cupboard and took down a champagne glass, set it beside the one she just finished drying, and reached for another.

"What ... what're you doing?"

"My champagne glasses on your shelf are me taking you for granted, Mike. If that's not something I should be doing, then I need to take them ..." The glass she was reaching for toppled off the shelf onto the counter, atomizing into an infinity of glass shards.

"Shit! Shit, Shit, Shit."

Ignoring the mess, she reached for another, her vision blurred by tears and her hand shaking. It, too, eluded her grasp and fell, but was caught by Mike, who kissed the glass and handed it to Marcia.

"Your glasses don't seem to want to leave."

Marcia looked at him across the tears welling up along the edge of her lower lids. From somewhere deep inside an impulse to laugh at herself, at Mike, at the situation came bubbling up. She flexed her face to fight it back, but the mirth refused to be suppressed.

"Phhh." Her laughter came spitting out. She put her forehead against Mike's chest to hide her face.

Taggart expelled a deep breath of his own. He smoothed her hair.

Marsh, please don't leave. I love you and Matt. I don't know what I would do without the two of you in my life. I know we have to move forward. But like you said, we haven't been at this very long. Give us some time. Things will work out." He reached for the broom.

8

September 4, 1976

As Taggart drove up to Marcia's house, almost a year without cold showers had passed, nine months since the cascade of champagne glasses on New Year's morning, one day since Rhonda's invitation to help her defend Frank Marello. Matt answered the door. "Are you having dinner with us tonight, Coach?"

"No. I think your mom and I are going out for dinner tonight."

"Can I come?"

"No." A voice from behind Mike. "Grandma's coming over, and the two of you are going to order pizza. If you went with us, you'd have to wear a necktie."

"Coach isn't wearing a necktie."

"It's in my pocket, Wise Guy." Taggart pulled a tie from his jacket.

"Will you be back before I have to go to bed?" Matt went on. "It's Saturday, so I can stay up late. Coach, I want to show you my new bunk beds. Mom got'em so I can have friends over."

"Better show'em to me now, Matt. I don't know what time we'll be home. We have time, don't we?" he asked, glancing at Marcia.

"I guess," Marcia said without even looking at her watch. She gave Taggart a funny look as she replied.

"Look at this." Matt was bending over the bottom bunk. "It makes into a couch during the day. Isn't that neat?"

"Yeah, it's terrific." Mike gazed around the room at walls covered with Padre's pennants, Chargers' team photos. His eyes halted momentarily at the desk beside the bed, where Matt's personal photo gallery was on prominent display. Taggart appeared in all but one.

The waiter poured their coffee and departed the table as Mike finished describing to Marcia his decision to take the Marello case. "So, it's a lot of money for our struggling little enterprise as well as a chance to handle a really tough case. A win might help bring other good cases in the door.

"Re-trial's expected to be in about two and a half months, but I need to get out there now and get started. I'm leaving Monday afternoon. Maybe you can come out for part of the trial, put some faces on all the names and places I'll be telling you about."

Marcia shook her head. She was crying.

"Mike, I can't go to North Carolina. I can't even see you any more."

"Can't see me ... why?"

"Same thing we've talked about. Someday I want to get married again, have another child. I'd hoped that would happen with you, but it doesn't seem to be."

"Marsh, I thought you were willing to give me some time to think about it. You had a good marriage; I had a lousy one for which I was largely to blame. I need to be sure that won't happen again."

Marcia was still shaking her head. "You can never be sure. If I thought you wouldn't be a good husband and father, we wouldn't have dated this long, but I can't wait. Matt loves you too much already."

"What do you mean, 'Matt loves me 'too much?'"

"Just what I said. Oh, Mike, can't you see it? Matt wants you to see his bunk bed; he wants you to go to his games. He wants to be with you twenty-four hours a day. Today, when we were setting up that bed and rearranging his furniture, all he could talk about was what you would think of it. He even asked me if he should put his dad's picture in the drawer. He said he thought it might make you sad that you weren't his dad."

Jesus. Mike could picture Matt saying it. The image sawed at his heart like a rusty knife. Marcia's words echoed, "Matt loves you too much ... "

"I'm not making any of this up, Mike. It about broke my heart, not because Tim's so obviously been completely eclipsed as Matt's hero, but because his replacement won't step up to the plate. I'm not going to let his affection for you become any deeper only to have you decide you don't have what it takes for marriage. If it was just me, I'd hang in a while longer, but Matt needs someone he can count on long term,"

Taggart sipped his coffee in silence. Nothing Marcia had just said was wrong. "This is a hard time to bring this up with me headed for North Carolina and a murder trial for the next three or four months."

"No, Mike, it's the perfect time. There's always going to be another trial. You're a lawyer, for heaven's sake. Trials are what lawyers do. I don't mind if you're distracted for weeks or months at a time. I'd help you through, so would Matt. You know we would." Marcia pushed her chair back, ready to leave. "Go try your case. There's nobody else in my life - not even close, not the way you've been. Nothing's going to happen in three months. If you come back and want to get married, fine. No, more than fine – Great! If not, don't come back, at least not to us. It will be the best possible transition for you out of Matt's life ... and mine."

PART II
REUNIONS

9

Monday, September 6, 1976.

Rhonda Enright watched Taggart drifting toward her down the river of humanity along the concourse. He was darker than she remembered, had lost his law school pallor. Otherwise, not much different; the windbreaker he was wearing might be the same one he wore in law school, boots too. "Some big time trial lawyer you are. Flying around the country in blue jeans and carrying a backpack. Do you have your suits wadded up in there?"

"Gosh, Rhonda, you look great … in a law professor sort of way," Mike gave her a one-armed hug.

"You could have gone a hundred years without adding that last part. Good to see you again."

Rhonda never looked particularly great. Neither short nor tall, fifteen pounds overweight, little or no make-up, law school pallor prominent, dark brown hair combed, but certainly not fussed over, she looked exactly as Mike remembered – reasonably attractive, but too busy to make herself more so.

Rhonda pulled out of the parking lot onto the rain-swept highway. "Court set the re-trial date this morning. Monday, November 15. We need to get busy."

"We kind of got hung up on the homosexuality thing on the phone the other morning," Mike said. "Where does Marello say he was when his wife was killed? If he didn't do it, who did, and why?"

"I can tell you all about it as we drive or you can wait and hear it from Frank. He's been transferred back to the Marlborough jail. We can go over there now if you want. There's one thing I need to tell you, though."

"What's that?"

"There's a witness, Tremaine Troutman He testified Frank asked him to kill his wife, twice offered him five hundred dollars, and, on the day of the murder, admitted to him, Troutman, that he had done it. I don't be--"

Taggart half turned in his seat. "You're kidding me."

Rhonda gave a small shrug and shook her head.

"Maybe you should have called a magician instead of me, ... or a priest. You might have mentioned this before I came all the way out here."

Rhonda looked back at Taggart. "If I'd told you, would you still have come?" She grinned.

Good question. "What else can you tell me about Troutman?"

"Black guy. About fifty. Got one bad eye. Works in the garage where Frank used to take his car. Also works as a handyman. He painted Frank and Livia's kitchen a couple of weeks before she was killed. He had a key for a while, and the Sheriff suspected him originally, but he has an alibi. His story doesn't make any sense though. Even if you assume Frank killed her, what possible reason could he have for confessing to Troutman?"

Taggart fell into a silence. It was the same old story. On a witness scale of one to ten, there were no tens. Troutman sounded like about an eight for the prosecution, but maybe a five for the defense. *Would Given Watson, the Solicitor, like those odds well enough to use Troutman again?*

"C'mon, Mike. You're a trial lawyer. What's the old saying, 'in litigation there is no truth, only versions?' I wouldn't have called if this was going to be easy. So, what will it be, hear the Marello version from me or from Frank?"

Deciding it would be better to get the facts straight from Marello instead of strained through Rhonda's legal perceptions, especially since Marello was apparently readily available, Mike decided to spend the evening reviewing the police report of the investigation. What made Stick Hatcher, the Johnston County Sheriff, think Frank Marello killed his wife?

Taggart sat back and tried to relax. The already overcast late afternoon sky had turned even darker, and rain spattered the windshield. In the shadow of the low clouds, the heavily forested hills looked black in the distance. The windshield wipers swung back and forth through their arc like a hypnotist's pendulum, mesmerizing Taggart. It seemed like a long time since he had replaced the autumn rains of North Carolina with the arid brownness of Southern California.

Mike blinked to jar himself back to the present. He glanced at Rhonda. She, too, seemed lost in thought. *Where have the years taken her?* Plenty of time for that later. Life stories were distractions at times like these.

10

Tuesday, September 7, 1976 – 69 days to trial.

Marlborough had been the capital of North Carolina during the Revolutionary War – sort of a substitute capital while the British occupied Wilmington, the real one, over on the coast. It seemed to Taggart that in some ways nothing in town had changed since. The County Administration Building sat in the center of the town square, with the jail across the street to the east, the Court House to the south. "A festival of red brick," Cathy used to say.

The jail had been built just after the Civil War, and Jack, the jailer, "Mr. Jack" to any prisoner who knew what was good for him, had, according to town legend, been there since it opened. Nobody could remember when he wasn't.

Mike walked into the receiving room the morning after his arrival and spotted the ancient innkeeper at the far end sitting with his chair tipped back on two legs in the morning sunlight streaming in the window. "Hello, Mr. Jack."

Mr. Jack looked up and squinted, and then, much to Taggart's surprise, recognized Mike across the room. "H'lo Depity." Jack stood up. He was scrawny, except for a little pot belly, and bandy-legged. His three days growth of bristly whiskers were approximately the same length as the few remaining hairs on his head. "I heard you was comin' back ta town." Jack spit a gob of tobacco juice in the direction of a spittoon beside the leg of his chair. "So you's a lawyer now?"

"That's right, Mr. Jack," They shook hands. "Just goes to show that anybody can get to be one these days."

"Seems to me as how jist about everybody already has." Mr. Jack shook his head. "You been over to say 'hello' to Stick yet?"

"I was over at the office, but Stick was out. I saw Johnnie and Miss Carrie, and Howard, and they said Bobby and Mack were out on patrol. Tubby's off today.

"I hear you have a famous guest these days, Mr. Jack. Any chance of us getting to see Professor Marello?"

"I reckon so, you his lawyer." Jack reached for a big ring of keys hanging on a peg. "Kinda disappointed you repa'sentin' that fudge-packer."

Taggart winced, pained, but unsurprised. Once Howard Watkins, the only black deputy, had asked Mr. Jack if he'd ever gone to school. "I went long enough to know the difference between a nigger and a white man," said Mr. Jack. *Why should gays be any different?*

"Mr. Jack, you already know Miss Enright here, don't you? She and I are working together on the Marello case.

"Umpf," Mr. Jack turned and started up a flight of stairs leading through the wall opposite the outside entrance. Mike and Rhonda exchanged glances. What passed for cordiality with Mr. Jack evidently only extended to former deputies.

At the top of the stairs was a narrow corridor with three tiny cells on the right, the jail's south wall on the left. Each cell was separated from the next by only a shared wall consisting of steel bars, no privacy. At the far end of the corridor Mr. Jack stopped and unlocked the cell door. Inside stood a tall, skinny man, young-looking despite a receding hairline of black, curly hair, wearing glasses with clear plastic frames.

From the back wall of the cell hung a wooden platform fastened to the wall by hinges enabling it to swing down to make a bed or bench supported by a chain at either end. There was a thin canvas mattress folded double and a couple of blankets, a pillow and a sheet also neatly folded at one end. Apart from a metal commode with no seat and a metal sink, the bed was the only furniture in the cell.

The absence of privacy didn't bother Mike. The place was just as he remembered it, and there were no other prisoners. *Professor Marello's mom taught him to make his bed.* "Thanks, Mr. Jack. We'll give you the signal when we want out."

After Mr. Jack left, Frank Marello said, "What's the signal? I may need to use it sometime."

"Mr. Jack or anybody giving you a hard time?" Mike asked. "He can be a little brusque. You have any complaints?"

Marello shook his head. "Beats death row." He had a soft voice, but masculine. "I've no complaint … under the circumstances."

Taggart, antennae out, tried to sense what kind of a witness Marello would be. *Not bad.* In his first three sentences Marello had displayed more of a sense of humor than Mike suspected he'd have had under similar circumstances. Marello didn't seem to be a whiner, and he had a decent speaking voice. *Things could be worse.*

"Why don't you and Frank sit on the bed, and I'll sit over here." Rhonda sat down on the commode. "It will be easier for you to take notes over there."

As Mike sat down, his eyes met Rhonda's as she sat on the low lidless toilet. Both started laughing. Rhonda folded her hands in her lap. "This is how I want you to always remember me."

"Mind if I smoke?" Frank took a pack of cigarettes from the breast pocket of the blue cotton shirt he was wearing. "Never smoked until all this happened." He patted his pockets in search of some matches.

Taggart reached in his pocket and tossed Marello a book of matches. Marello caught them with his left hand.

"You a lefty, Frank?

Marello nodded.

That fact come out at trial?"

Marello nodded again. "Of course." As he spoke, Marello studied Taggart. There was a vague resemblance to Jim, Frank's brother. Maybe Taggart was a little taller. Frank wasn't sure he could stand another Jim in his life.

"Tell me about yourself, Mr. Taggart. How many death penalty cases have you tried ... More importantly, how many have you won?"

"First thing, call me 'Mike.' I've tried four death penalty cases. As for how many I've won, that depends on how you define 'winning.' None of the four got the death sentence, although one was convicted of murder, but it was overturned on appeal. Another was convicted of manslaughter. Two were acquittals."

"Have you had a chance to read the investigation reports in this case?"

"Yes."

"What's your assessment?"

"Hard to say without having talked to any witnesses. The prosecution's alleged motive seems pretty thin. Twenty-five thousand in insurance money isn't much. The other side of that coin, however, is, if you didn't kill her, who did?"

Frank Marello nodded to indicate he understood. "Do you think you can win?"

Taggart looked Marello straight in the eye. "This case is winnable, Dr. Marello, but it's also losable. You've already found that out the hard way. I can't give you any guarantees. All I can say at this point is, if the evidence lines up again the way it did the first time around, I think you should win."

Mike paused and held up his hand. *Marello shouldn't take too much heart from "should win."* "Trouble is, this isn't the first time around. The mere fact you've already been convicted once may be of some influence on the jury. There's also your relationship with Mr. Josephson, which wasn't part of the first trial. It turned out to be your salvation on appeal, but it may be what condemns you this time. Depends on whether the prosecution decides to make a big deal of it."

Marello said nothing.

After a few seconds, Mike said, "One thing you can count on, I'll bust my tail for you. If we lose, it won't be because some stone was left unturned."

"Well, Rhonda says you're my best hope. That's good enough for me. I know there are no guarantees."

"Good. We've got two months. Let's make the most of them."

Taggart had been sitting on the hard wooden bench for more than three hours; dozens of pages of the spiral notebook on his lap had been filled with notes; he was on his second ballpoint pen. He had no sense of the passage of time. Frank Marello had taken him at his word, when Mike asked him to start at the beginning.

"I first met Livia, my wife, ... Livia Lindholm in September 1969. I was a graduate teaching assistant working on my Ph.D. at the University over in Chapel Hill. Livia was an undergrad in one of the discussion groups I led."

Mike remembered Chapel Hill, a University town, twenty miles south and two centuries in advance of Marlborough. It was where he and Cathy went to movies.

"At first, Livia was just another student, one more semi-bored face, in a group of fifteen or twenty. But as time went on I began to get the feeling she really liked me. I don't mean liked the course or liked my teaching, but *liked me* personally, even though we had no contact whatsoever apart from class. I don't remember ever talking to her outside of class.

"I wasn't a very good teacher back then. Students, undergraduates, especially in the low level classes I was teaching, can smell blood. If they care enough to ask a question, they're usually just trying to prove whatever I said was wrong. But Livia's questions weren't like that. They weren't particularly bright or incisive, no more than average, but they were kind. I came to think sometimes she was coming to my defense, asking questions to give me a chance to make my point in a different way.

"Throughout my life girls had never liked me ...not the way they liked Jim, I mean. Look at me, Ichabod Crane reincarnate. I was losing my hair in high school. When I talk, my Adam's apple makes me look like I've swallowed a hatchet head." Marello gave a little laugh as he spoke. "I've always looked like a scarecrow."

Taggart was struck by the sadness of someone so without friends that he interpreted the absence of open hostility as an affirmative act of friendship. "Who's Jim?"

"My older brother. You remind me of him. Jim's kind of the anti-Frank, handsome, athletic, popular. You'll meet him. He and my Dad came to the first trial every day. They'll be here again for the retrial."

Marello picked up the thread of his account. He and Livia bumped into each other on campus some months after the end of the course. Headed in the same direction, they walked together, talking about her interest in books and literature, and wound up having a cup of coffee. "Actually, Livia had tea, always tea." Marello's voice, already gentle, softened at the reminiscence.

"Books and literature were my passion too," Frank went on. "In those early days of our friendship, I think the strength of my feeling for the written word created a momentum that swept Livia up, heightening her feeling not only for the reading, but for me as well."

Taggart studied his new client. Marello made it sound like the girl loved the subject, not him.

"Livia was a lot of things I wasn't. She had lots of friends, a sorority girl, went to all the football and basketball games. I lived alone, spent most of my time in the library studying, working on my dissertation, getting ready for teaching. I sometimes think Livia had some vague idea there was an 'intelligentsia,' if you want to call it that, at the University, and was able to feel a part of it through her friendship with me, even though nothing else about her life fit that mold."

Rhonda had become uncomfortable and shifted to the floor. Frank interrupted himself long enough to toss her one of his blankets to sit on. She watched as Frank talked and Taggart listened. Listening, really listening, was so critical, and Frank's first lawyer hadn't been very good at it

Livia had given Frank a book she liked. He read it, and they met to discuss it. She had called him that first time, and eventually their relationship evolved into a two person book club. They would get together in the late afternoon once or twice a month to discuss what they were reading. "A couple of times she brought along a boyfriend, but I never saw the same boy twice. Usually it was just the two of us, a cup of coffee for me, tea for her, and a book."

At the end of her senior year Livia enrolled in summer school to complete the remaining credits she needed for graduation. One night she invited Frank to her apartment for dinner. Before that night they had never even held hands. That night they slept together. It was Frank Marello's first sexual experience with a woman. He was twenty-nine years old.

"I'd been saving myself for marriage." Marello laughed a small laugh.

Mike heard something besides humor in the laughter, but filed it away without comment, preferring instead to get Marello's whole account of his relationship with his wife out in one uninterrupted lump. Time for clarification would come later.

"Livia finished school and started teaching in a private school over in Durham, and after about a year, she asked me where I thought our relationship was going. I hadn't thought about it, but she obviously had. She said it was like we were just standing still, and we needed to either go forward and get married or stop seeing each other, and she wanted to get married."

Sounds familiar.

"I said 'Okay.' I was happy. I didn't stop to think what marriage meant or whether it would change anything. I kind of took the line of least resistance as a way of preserving what had become the status quo. It sounds stupid and callous on my part, and I don't mean it that way. I thought Livia was the best thing that ever happened to me in an otherwise pretty empty life, but it hadn't been a life I was particularly unhappy with."

Frank Marello and Livia Lindholm married in June, 1972. Things went on as before. He got his doctorate the following January, and received an appointment to the faculty in the English Department at the University as an Assistant Professor. His special area of interest was Nineteenth Century English literature, his special author, Thackery.

Ugh! Taggart, who had been force-fed *Vanity Fair* in a freshman lit class, grimaced at the mention of the author's name.

"Money was tight, but between our two salaries we were making it," Marello said. "We were waiting to start a family, so we didn't need much. But then Livia got pregnant, and we knew that was going to change things. We had just learned about the pregnancy a couple of weeks before she died."

"Tell me about the day before she died. What did the two of you do?"

Frank Marello took a deep breath. "Livia had gone over to Greensboro, Christmas shopping with her mom and sister on Friday, the twenty-first. She didn't get home until about three on Sunday. I didn't go; I had papers to grade. We were going to drive back to Greensboro to be with Livia's family on Christmas morning. After she got home, Livia read, played Christmas carols and did housework, wrapped gifts for her family. I remember she wasn't feeling well, because we both associated that with the pregnancy.

"We went to bed early, but she woke up in the middle of the night and got up for a while. When she came back to bed, she was upset, because we didn't have a Christmas tree or Christmas lights. She had been looking out at all the lights in the other windows. There was a Christmas tree still lighted in one of the other apartments. She said it was all so pretty and was unhappy we didn't have any."

"Why didn't you have any lights?"

"We'd agreed. We were facing lots of extra expenses related to the baby, and when Livia had to quit working it would cut our income. So we were trying to save where we could. She was regretting our decision, said she wanted to get a tree anyway the next day."

"What did you have to say about that?"

"I was probably short with her, annoyed she'd awakened me with something that could just as easily be discussed in the morning. I remember asking where she thought the money for the baby was going to come from, and she said her folks would probably help, and maybe mine could too.

"That was kind of a sore point with me. I didn't want to take money from our parents. I was thirty-two, a bit old to be asking Mom and Dad for help, except in a real unforeseen emergency. But that's not the way we left it. I said we could work something out in the morning, and that made her happy. She talked for a little bit about where she thought would be the best place to put the tree, not that there were all that many choices, and that's the last thing I remember before drifting back to sleep.

"I know Ms. Wilmer, our next door neighbor, testified that she heard us fighting in the middle of the night, but it wasn't a fight. We weren't angry. Neither of us raised our voices. It was just a mild disagreement that evaporated when we talked about it. The apartment walls were thin." Marello shook his head and stared at his hands as his voice trailed off.

"What happened the next morning?"

"Livia was asleep when I got up. That wasn't unusual. She liked to sleep late on days she didn't have to work. After having been up in the night, she needed the sleep, so I didn't wake her. There was no reason. I'd made plans to go Christmas shopping with a friend of mine ..."

"Christmas shopping? I thought the two of you had decided against that?" Mike was immediately mad at himself for interrupting. He wanted Marello to tell the story his way, but his compulsion to cross-examine had the better of him. Taggart bit his lip and told himself to shut up.

"We were always going to buy each other something, just not spend much. My friend, Mark ... Mark Josephson, and I went over to Durham that morning, to North Ridge Mall. We left a little after eight and spent most of the morning over there. I bought a sweater for Livia. Around noon we returned to Chapel Hill and picked up some odds and ends, you know, stocking stuffers, at a couple of places on Franklin Street.

"Mark dropped me off around one. I walked in, and Sheriff Hatcher and a deputy were standing in the kitchen. And there was Livia under a blanket on the floor. I was stupefied. It was like someone hit me over the head and killed me for a moment or two, I don't know how long. Sheriff Hatcher and I went out to his car and talked. I don't even remember what I said."

Taggart closed his notebook and stood up. He knew what the scene of the crime looked like and what happened after Frank arrived from the police report. "We've been at this a couple hours, and there are many more ahead of us, but enough for today. It's a lot to think about, and I want to spend some time with the transcript of the first trial this evening." He extended his hand. "I'm glad to finally meet you, Frank."

11

Tuesday, September 7, 1976 – 69 Days to Trial - Evening

After leaving the jail, Mike and Rhonda had supper at the General Johnston Café, a coffee shop out on the Marlborough exit off of I-85, right next door to the The Rebel Yell Motel. General Joseph Johnston had been the last Confederate general to lay down his sword, and the surrender had taken place nearby. Joe Johnston also had a local highway named after him. It always seemed strange to Taggart that the little café would be named after a general thought to be lacking in aggression and short on victories.

"What do you think of our client?" asked Rhonda.

"More questions than answers."

"What?"

"Well, first, in retrospect, I need to jettison some stereotypes. Stupid as it sounds, it wouldn't have surprised me if Frank had been wearing a skirt or something. That's an exaggeration, but you know what I mean. So, it was a good meeting from that standpoint. His bearing and manner are okay, unlikely to antagonize a jury.

"On the other hand, even though the story he tells suggests a mild affection for his wife, there's no passion. It's bland. On the spectrum of romance, he's no more than half a notch beyond indifference. He makes their relationship sound like a plate full of Kraft dinner."

"Maybe it has something to do with having already told the story five hundred times. Maybe he's just on automatic pilot."

Taggart pursed his lips considering. "After five hundred times you'd think he'd get it right."

They ate in silence for a time, thoughts of the case receding with the arrival of their food. *Hushpuppies. It's been a long time.*

Rhonda regarded Taggart as he sat there stuffing his face full of ribs. When Rhonda and Mike had parted at the end of law school, he and Cathy were married, apparently happily, and planning to live in Chicago where Mike was going to work for a large firm. Now he was divorced, living in California and practicing with one other guy.

"I never had you figured for a Californian, Mike. I thought Chicago was just where you ought to be, you and Cathy. What happened?"

Mike looked up from his ribs and slowly wiped the barbeque sauce off his fingers with a towel-sized napkin. "I totally fucked things up. You know, when we graduated from law school, we, or at least I, had a pretty strong belief that the world largely worked the way it should, at least the American part of it. It certainly always had for me. Pretty naïve, huh?

"Well, it didn't take long for the Republic of South Viet Nam to disabuse me of those notions. Everywhere I looked, something awful was happening, and the source of much of it, one way or another, was us."

Rhonda, who had been deeply involved in the anti-war movement, nodded.

"But at the same time, in my little corner of the war, every now and then I would witness an act of courage so unselfish, so without any expectation of reward, that it made me want to weep for the nobility of man.

"Poor Cathy. When I came home, she met me at the airport expecting the person she'd put on the plane a year earlier. Instead, she got this stranger with a gigantic chip on his shoulder for a lot of the things she valued and a love/hate relationship with the Marine Corps that made him crazy.

"Anyway, we split up, got back together, went to Chicago, which she loved and I hated. Eventually she came to believe I was always going to find something not to like about whatever I was doing, so she said she wanted a divorce."

"How'd that make you feel?"

"At the time I thought it was probably for the best, and probably it was, at least for Cath. But I still can't get the thought out of my system. I mean, I had been in love with Cathy since ninth grade. How could I screw up something that went so deep? I still have dreams about it. It's like the war. It's been three years since I went back to San Diego alone, and I still think about how things fell apart every day. Other people let go of that kind of stuff. Why can't I?"

"Haven't you met anyone else? That might help."

Taggart sighed. "I'm involved with someone right now, or at least I was up until a few days ago. Her husband was killed early in the war. She has an eight year old son."

"Does this woman have a name?"

"Marcia Banning. Son's name is Matt."

"What do you mean ' ... at least up until a few days ago?'"

"Well, we had the 'this relationship doesn't seem to be going anywhere' conversation just before I left, the upshot of which was either come back after this trial and get married, or don't come back."

"You love her?"

"Yeah, I do."

"Ready to be a dad?"

"I think so. Matt's a great kid. Couple of my best days ever were when he and I went backpacking overnight."

Rhonda made a face. "Walking up and down hills carrying a heavy pack's not my idea of fun. "

"Yeah," Mike said. "After the Marines, I swore I'd never sleep on the ground again, but I changed my mind. This was kind of magical."

"Magical how?"

"Well, it began the first night we made camp..." He and Matt had lain on a starlit hillside after dinner, picking out constellations using a star chart Mike's dad had given him when he was Matt's age.

"See those three stars all in a straight line and pretty close together?" Mike pointed.

"Yeah, yeah. I see'em."

"That's known as Orion's belt. Orion was a mythical hunter, and ancient people thought they could see him holding an animal he killed outlined by stars. Those three I pointed out are his belt. Can you see the rest of him?" Mike, who never could, asked.

"Oh yeah. Look," Matt pointed at the sky, "there's his head and there's his shoulders, and he's holding a spear. And look over there," Matt swung his extended arm half way across the sky. "There's a pig."

Taggart looked. "What else do you see?"

The conversation had continued thus, with Matt identifying several more hitherto undiscovered constellations, until after a few minutes, Mike heard Matt's gentle slumbering breath and nothing else on the silent mountainside. Carefully, he took off Matt's shoes and socks, scooped him up and laid him in his sleeping bag, stuffing Matt's jacket into a nylon sack for a pillow.

"Good night, Matty. Pleasant dreams."

Sitting beside the sleeping boy, Taggart resumed gazing at the stars, musing not about mythical hunters, but rather the tenderness filling his heart.

"So, yeah, I do like kids, but who knows? Husband ... father ... I keep thinking what if I lapse back into my 'fuck the world' attitude that torpedoed Cath and me. It comes and goes. Some days I just wake up really pissed off at everything."

"How often does that happen?"

"Not too much any more. But it still happens now and then. Marcia and Matt, they don't need that."

"You talk it over with Marcia?"

"Yeah, sorta. She knows I became kind of a hard guy to be married to last time around. I don't know if I gave her much in the way of specifics."

"Well, whatever you told her apparently wasn't enough to scare her off. You know, you told me one time that you knew guys, athletes, who were so scared of losing, they couldn't bring themselves to take the risks necessary to win. You thought there might be lawyers like that too. Are you sure you aren't one of those guys when it comes to marriage?"

"I don't know, maybe. Never thought of myself that way."

"Mike, if you really love these two people, don't screw it up by being your own worst enemy."

As they were walking out of the General Johnston, a fat woman wearing a mumu style dress was walking in. Mike held the door for her. She walked past them without thanking him and gave Mike a funny look.

"Do you know her?"

"Yeah, I arrested her once. She recognizes me, but she can't think from where."

"Arrested her?"

"Yeah, Myrna Lipscomb. She and her husband run the motel next door, The Rebel Yell. Back in '66 they were being picketed because of their 'Whites Only' sign. One of the protesters lay down across the office doorway so anyone walking in had to step over him. Myrna walked out, hiked up her dress, squatted over him and pissed on his face."

"Gaaakh!" Rhonda grimaced and wiped her face as if she'd been Myrna's target.

"Anyway, Tubby Mayes and I were monitoring the party, and I ran her in for assault. I think she got off with 'Urinating in Public.'"

Rhonda peered out at the motel sign at the edge of the highway. "At least the 'Whites Only's' gone."

"Yeah, but I bet Myrna's still not putting mints on any Black pillows. She was a hero to some folks in town. Probably still is."

They were standing beside Rhonda's car in the parking lot. Mike had rented a semi-furnished two-bedroom apartment at the north end of town, a short mile up from the General Johnston. "Rhonda, I think I'll walk back to the apartment. It's going to be tough to get much exercise. Besides, I need to re-acquaint myself with this place, visit some old ghosts."

As Taggart walked slowly up Church Street through the three-block business district, past the library and into the residential area just to the north, he contemplated the strange little town that had already once sentenced Frank Marello to die. Both sides of the street were lined with sycamores and sweet gums. Mike kicked at the leaves just beginning to fall as he walked past the post office, Grissom Ford and Arthur Lund's drug store and coffee shop. Lund's fat wife, Edna, had been a first-grade teacher with Cathy. To Edna, Cathy and the other wives who were teaching while their husbands finished graduate degrees at nearby Duke or UNC were always "you Yankee girls," and the two Black students in her "integrated" class of thirty-eight "mah dumb lil' nigras."

Arthur had been elected Mayor of Marlborough while Mike was in law school. His only campaign promise had been to put the "ugh" back in Marlboro. There had been an ughectomy in the Thirties. According to Arthur and his upper-crust, Colonial Baptist pals in the caste-conscious town, the additional syllable would be a return to Marlboro(ugh)'s colonial heritage. It had been an enhancement unappreciated by Buck Brown, the manager of the town baseball team, and the other guys who hung out at the West End Tavern across the street from the textile mill where most of them worked. "Cain't spell the name of my own damn town no more," Buck had grumbled. Stick Hatcher, the Sheriff, hadn't liked it either, because he had to have all the Sheriff's stationery re-printed. That hadn't been in the budget.

What were the attitudes of the Arthur Lunds and Buck Browns and all the citizens somewhere in between towards Marello now? If Mr. Jack's opinion was any indication, there was abundant cause for concern.

In the midst of such reflections Mike walked up the driveway of his apartment and climbed the steps to his front door. Inside the transcript of Marello's first trial, all twenty-seven hundred pages, and many long days and nights awaited him. He sat, eyeing the enormous pile of paper as if it was alive. He was glad the phone company hadn't gotten around to installing his phone. What he wanted to do most was call Marcia.

12

Friday, September 10, 1976 – 66 days to trial.

The sun had shone for the last three days. Taggart spent the time indoors poring over trial transcript. Now, when he needed to be outside, it was raining. He peered through the downpour trying to spot the address he was looking for as he drove slowly along a broken asphalt street on the west edge of downtown Chapel Hill beyond the campus. The houses looked like places students probably rented, needing paint, patchy grass in the yards, lots of cars parked in front and in the drives, many bicycles. Finally, he spotted 406½, a brick building. The lower floor looked as if it might once have been a small corner grocery store. It was empty now, but there was a light in a window on the second floor.

Mike parked the car and walked around the building, trying to avoid puddles, looking for the entrance. Naturally, the stairs were on the outside, unsheltered from the weather. Made of wood, they wobbled slightly under his weight. At the top he pressed the bell, heard no ring, and followed with a knock. After a few seconds, a tall middle-aged Black man with a cloudy right eye came to the door, opening it a few inches,

"Who you? Whatcha want?"

"My name's Michael Taggart. I'm looking for Tremain Troutman. Are you Mr. Troutman?"

"What you want him for?"

"I'm a lawyer. I represent Frank Marello—"

The door slammed. Mike stood on the landing, the wetness of the rain multiplied by the runoff from the gutterless roof. He knocked on the door again. "Go 'way." He squished his way back to the car.

"You going to try again?" Rhonda asked, when Taggart told her of Troutman's unwelcoming attitude. "Maybe we should hire an investigator. You lawyers make people too nervous."

"I thought about that. I wish we had the guy I use in San Diego, friend of mine named Eric Gonchar. Interesting guy. He can get anybody to talk to him. But it's not worth the money. We've got the signed statement Troutman gave Stick plus his trial testimony, both pretty far-fetched. I bet the prosecution's of two minds about him as a witness. Wonder what Stick really thinks about Troutman."

Monday, September 13, 1976 – 63 days to trial.

Mike had been looking forward to seeing Stick Hatcher again for more reasons than merely learning his opinion of Tremaine Troutman. Jackson "Stick" Hatcher had been Sheriff of Johnston County almost from the moment of his return from a couple of hard years in the South Pacific with the Marines during World War II. A big man in more ways than one, by the time Mike Taggart met him in 1965, Stick had become the unlikely combination of the most powerful and most well-liked man in the County. Because of Stick, Mike had been able to see a side of the law most lawyers never see. They'd met while Mike was playing baseball with Stick's son, Micah, on the town's team during Taggert's first summer in Marlborough. At season's end Stick offered Mike the opportunity to become a deputy.

"Mostly what ya'll be doin' is mannin' the department radio at night, so you can study. But ya'll be on call in case extra manpower's needed in the field," was how Stick had put it. It was the mid-Sixties. Between, Civil Rights unrest and moonshiners, more manpower had often been required.

"Your nose don't point up in the air like a lota Duke folks," Stick said when Mike thanked him for the offer. Stick was a diehard

Carolina man in the rivalry that was as much a part of the State's personality as tobacco.

Now Stick and Taggart were having coffee in Mayor Lund's drug store.

"That boy a yours is guilty as sin." Stick sipped his coffee and studied the south end of Betty Lou Combs, the waitress, as she bent over to get something from a low cabinet.

"You mean Marello?"

"Far as ah know, he's the only client you got."

That was closer to the truth than Taggart liked to admit.

Stick was as hard as a railroad spike, but he didn't jump to conclusions. He wasn't likely to think that just because Marello was gay, he was necessarily a murderer, although he probably regarded the two crimes as equally heinous. If there was some fact or circumstance beyond what was to be learned from the investigation report, Taggart wanted to know about it.

"What makes you so sure he's guilty?"

"Well," Stick took a long drag on his cigarette, "we know the victim wasn't raped and doesn't appear to have been robbed, so the motive must have been something else. We also know he and the Miszrus were havin' domestic difficulties. Despite that, your Professor had just bought a bunch of life insurance on her. She didn't strangle herself, and there were no fingerprints in the place 'cept the victim's and Marello's. The fella he went shoppin' with is what ya'll out in California call 'openly gay. That's the word, ain't it? Ah don't reckon the late Mizrus Marello was too happy about that, do you? Seems to me it was pretty much like he told Tremaine Troutman - when he couldn't talk Troutman into doin' it, he did it himself."

"Mizrus," the North Carolina version of 'Mrs." The word stopped Taggart in his tracks every time he heard it. He shook his head to clear it of the peculiarity. There was nothing new in what Stick was telling him. To the extent Mike had an answer to such incriminating circumstances, there was no use sharing his rebuttal with Stick.

Whatever arguments he might have, he would save for the jury. Stick drank more coffee with Given Watson, the County Solicitor, than he drank with Mike. There was nothing to be gained by tipping his hand. There was one thing though…

"So, you think Troutman's believable, Sheriff?"

"Can't see as how he had any reason to lie. Why would he say such things if they didn't happen?"

"Maybe to deflect suspicion from himself?"

"Suspicion of what? Robbery? Rape? If he had either of those in mind, he forgot to do 'em. 'Sides, he has an alibi."

Mike didn't think that was necessarily the end of the analysis when it came to Troutman's role in the case. He held his hand over his coffee mug as a signal to Betty Lou he didn't want a refill; Stick did the same.

"Well, Sheriff, I guess if you didn't have a pretty good case, you wouldn't have convicted him the first time. Makes me think I better get to work. Thanks for calling me back," Mike added as they slid off their stools. "Good to see you again.

"You're welcome. Thanks for the coffee. Say, how's your wife? Cathy's her name, isn't it? Sorry, I had it in mind to ask when we got together, but then I got distracted by somethin' else when we started talkin'."

"She's fine, Sheriff," Mike answered, "except she's not my wife anymore. We got a divorce about four years ago. Things didn't work out. She got remarried and lives in Chicago now and has a couple of kids."

"Sorry to hear that. The two of you have any kids?"

"No."

"Well, at least that's somethin'." Stick stuck out his huge hand and they shook.

13

Tuesday, September 14, 1976 – 62 days to trial.

On Taggart's second visit to Frank Marello, he went alone. Rhonda was busy teaching, and Mike thought it just as well. He needed to establish his own relationship with Marello.

"You and I need to get to know each other real well, Frank. You need to be able to trust my judgment, and in a case like this, a lawyer needs to know as much about his client as possible, not just facts relating to the actual charges. This is especially true in this case because of the part homosexuality may play."

Frank Marello was standing up, leaning against the cell wall. "Do you think the prosecution will bring that up? I mean, that's what caused the conviction to be thrown out. I thought they would stay completely away from that subject this time."

"Good question. I saw Given Watson, the Solicitor, try a lot of cases while I was in law school, even testified in a couple. He's not lazy and he's not dumb. My guess is he'll try to strengthen his case in the area of motive. What was his theory in the first trial - that you killed your wife for twenty-five thousand dollars worth of life insurance and because she wanted to ask your parents for some money to boost your finances? That's a little thin."

Taggart suspected Watson thought so too. In Mike's opinion, that was why Watson dropped the reference to Frank's homosexuality unsupported by any evidence into the final argument hoping only the jury would notice. It had been subtle, a simple, but oft repeated reference to Frank as " … the kind of man he is …"

It might have worked. There had been no objection at trial. Luckily Rhonda had been smart enough to make a big deal of it on appeal.

"If I was Watson, I'd try to figure out a way to make homosexuality relevant. Even with Chapel Hill and the University, this County is predominantly Baptist, very conservative, not particularly tolerant. Homosexuality is something a lot of people are uncomfortable with. The prosecution will try to use that discomfort and intolerance against you, so I need to understand as much as I can about what role it could possibly play and plan for it – to think through the issue before it's raised.

"We might be able to deflect at least some attention from the issue if there was someone else we could point to who had a motive and at least some opportunity to kill your wife, somebody besides this guy Troutman"

"I know ... I know ... if I didn't do it, then who did?" Frank began to pace back and forth, a huge bird, a flamingo or a heron, in an undersized cage. "Troutman is the only person I can think of. But if he hadn't come forward and said all those things about me, I'm sure I wouldn't even have thought of him. Not one word he said is true, not one word. Why would he have said such things, if he wasn't trying to deflect suspicion from himself?"

"Frank, let's put Troutman aside for a minute," Taggart said, forcing himself to change the subject. "It's hard to talk to anyone about their sexual preferences. Normally, it's none of my business, but in this case, it is. I'm sure I've made a lot of rude, insensitive references to homosexuality, told lots of jokes, without even thinking. Just human nature, I suppose, to dump on things that are different, but I want to understand ... need to understand. Just tell me. Are you homosexual? Where does everybody get that idea?" Even for someone in the business of asking hard questions, that one was tough. It had been all Mike could do not to stammer.

Frank stared at the man across the cell from him. You're right, Mr. Taggart, he thought. Nothing you've ever experienced can be a patch on what it's like.

"That's not an easy question, Mike. I have a feeling you were good at all the things I was bad at as a kid. Here's an example. There were these twins, Dean and Dewey Larue ..."

Frank Marello had a good voice and a love of words well used. As he talked, Taggart could see the flat, dusty school yard, patches of grass here and there, battered survivors of daily use by six hundred pairs of young feet, a ball diamond with base paths worn, not chalked, into the ground. Boys standing at a home plate of discarded paper, eleven years old, jeans grass-stained, already perspiring from having run through the Louisiana heat from the confinement of their classroom to this far corner of the playground.

"Who gets Marello?" a boy standing at the center of the group asks.

"We don't want him," replied Dean Larue. "Maybe he doesn't want to play."

"The rule's that we've got to let everybody play," the first boy said.

"Not if he doesn't want to," Larue answered. He turned to Frank. "You don't want to play, do you Four Eyes."

Before Frank can answer, Larue shoved him hard in the chest, pushing him backwards over Dewey, who had sneaked behind Frank and knelt on all fours. Frank fell hard on his tailbone and back. The impact knocked off his glasses. Several of the boys laughed. No one offered Frank a hand.

"My guess is Frank doesn't want to play," Dean said. "C'mon, or recess will be over before we get started.

Frank felt for his glasses, found them. One bow was bent. He tried to straighten it, but it came off his hand.

"Can't play without your glasses, can you Four Eyes?" Dewey said.

"I should have known better than go out there. I didn't even like playing, but I thought I ought to try." Frank said. "I wasn't like Jim, my brother. I wasn't rough. Jim was very rough and tough. He was older than me, and he'd created expectations in my parents, especially my father, about how boys are supposed to be, and I didn't meet any of those.

"Even though Jim was older, I was always bigger, or at least taller, but that didn't make any difference. Jim could always take me."

Frank's stories described things Taggart had seen happen to kids he had known growing up. Was it as bad for them as it obviously had been for Frank? Mike had been a part of some of it and wished now he hadn't.

"One time, when I was twelve, they sent me to this camp in Florida – the same one they'd sent Jim to, more boy stuff, riding horses, canoeing, baseball, riflery, all that sort of thing, and, of course, I wasn't particularly good at any of it. I mean, I could do it, but not well, and I didn't enjoy it. I'd rather read. I started faking that I was sick and staying in my cabin. There was another boy, his name was Terry, who, it turned out, felt the same way, and we'd play together all day by ourselves.

"They made everyone go on an overnight group campout, and Terry and I shared a two person tent that night. During the night there was this big thunderstorm. It had been hot, and our sleeping bags were unzipped. When the storm hit, we huddled together, and we started feeling each other and, well, you can guess what happened. That was how I first learned how the equipment worked."

Listening to this, Mike, who had never been much of one for recounting his sexual experiences, could not imagine how it must feel to be telling such a story.

"The important thing was, even though I was scared someone would find out, and maybe a little embarrassed, I wasn't ashamed. It just made me like Terry more, and I think he felt the same way. Anyway, for the rest of the time at camp, whenever we could slip away, we did. Once we even kissed each other.

"After I came home from camp, I wrote to Terry for a long time. He was from some place in Florida. My folks thought it was wonderful I'd made this great friend. After a while though, the letters stopped. I don't remember which of us stopped writing, but you know how kids are.

"Anyway, before I was much older I started to hear guys talk about sex a lot more, and it became painfully obvious what Terry and I did was something others would think was terrible even though I didn't feel that way. So for a long time I just decided to be nothing. Why does anybody have to 'be' anything? I just went my own way, denying my feelings, suppressing them, trying to lose myself in books and music, neutral things that I could love, even though the kinds I liked isolated me even more. They weren't the popular kind."

"A couple of twelve-year olds on a voyage of discovery at camp, no particular affinity for sports, that seems pretty shaky for the assumptions you're making about yourself," Mike said. "Didn't you ever date?"

"A few times, sure," Frank replied. "I liked girls. I got along with them easily, probably because I didn't want to, what's the expression, 'get in their pants.' I wanted to be like everybody else ... more than anything, that's what I wanted, but I felt impulses, secret things that scared me, things I couldn't explain."

"What things?"

"Hard to describe ... Stirrings at the sight of a guy with his shirt off or in the dressing room for P.E. Who do you talk to about something like that? Certainly not my brother! My dad? In its own way that would have been just as bad. I wouldn't even let myself consider the possibilities, at least not consciously. I liked to read; I liked music. I was in a rock band, but all we did was make noise in our parents' garages. We never got hired to play for anybody, and that was okay too. It wasn't the kind of music I really liked. It seemed as if everything I really liked made me feel different. I spent a lot of time in my room. My folks just thought I was a moody teenager … and I was.

"Nothing made any difference. You are what you are. Nobody makes you or unmakes you. Did you make yourself straight? Did anybody else? Denial … being nothing, just led to loneliness, terrible loneliness."

"What about Livia?" Mike said. "How does she fit in? The two of you slept together. She was pregnant at the time."

"Yes, but by the time I met Livia I was twenty-seven. All that time, nothing … I'd had one or two experiences with men, 'one-nighters' I suppose you'd call, once with a man I met on a plane going to college, once with a fellow I met on vacation after I started working. Otherwise, all those empty years I had never even kissed anyone, no men, and certainly no women except my mother. Never wanted to. Tried not to think about why. That's what I meant when I said earlier that I was hiding from myself.

"Livia, she just came and found me where I was hiding. When we first started to sleep together, to make love, it was very new and nice in a sweet sort of way. But it was not something that evoked strong emotion in me, not the sort of thing that makes other men compose great poetry or launch a thousand ships or take cold showers or any of that. That wasn't what made me love her. What made me love her was that she was smart and funny and pretty and she loved me. For whatever unfathomable reason, she loved me and wanted to be with me all the time, the first person I can remember unquestionably feeling that way about me. The force of that experience, of having a real, true, intimate friend for the first time outweighed and obscured any lack of feeling for the sexual part of the relationship. Maybe that's what it took, I thought. Maybe the strength of her feeling would create what had been lacking in me for so long."

Marello had been pacing, but now he stopped in front of the cell door and stared through the bars toward the window in the opposite wall and the hills beyond the town. "I really miss her friendship, her companionship, whatever you want to call it."

Loneliness. That was something Taggart could understand, but loneliness didn't equate to being gay. Neither did a couple of isolated homosexual experiences. Beyond the lukewarm sexual relationship, Marello sounded like he really loved his wife. "Frank, I don't know anything about it, but it seems to me lots of people, husbands and wives, must live together in friendships without passion, and that doesn't make them gay."

"No," Frank said, "you're right. It doesn't, but things happened, one thing really, that led me to the realization that for me it was more than just a matter of not feeling a high level of sexual desire with Livia. Looking back, I can see that having been introduced to warmth and intimacy by Livia, my hunger for 'friendship,' which was how I was still thinking of it, had been awakened, but not fulfilled. The first half of my life was a secret game of hide and seek, and Livia found where I was hiding, only she wasn't 'it.' With her, I finally began to see what I'd been doing, but at first I thought it was from relationships I was hiding. Since then I've come to see I was hiding from what I really felt deep down, from what would really make me happy."

"Did you ever talk this over with anybody ... with Mark Josephson or Livia or your folks, with a counselor of some kind, anybody?"

"The first person I talked it over with was Mark. We went out to dinner one night when Livia was at her sister's helping with the new baby. Mark and I had gone out to dinner several times before and always talked about perfectly neutral topics, books, music, politics, that sort of thing. Things we both liked. We had a bottle of wine that night and even smoked a joint right there in the restaurant, the first one I ever smoked. Anyway, I was feeling very smart and sophisticated. For one of the few times in my life I felt in command of myself, like I was someone I really wanted to be. I was pretty candid with Mark that night.

"Frank," Mark had said, "I don't want to give offense, but I want you to know that I find you very attractive." The statement was accompanied by a look that made clear Mark wasn't referring to Frank's thoughts about Victorian literature.

In less time than it had taken Mark to say it, Frank realized this was something he wanted to hear. "I feel the same way about you, Mark."

"You turn me on," Mark continued. "Do you want to go home with me?"

Frank nodded.

When Frank woke the next morning, Mark was still asleep. The sun was just coming up, and the sky seen through the bedroom window was pink and gold. Frank stretched, still suffused with the excitement and tenderness of the night. But as he lay there, the immediate past subsided into the immediate future. *Livia. God. There's no way she deserves this.* Frank rose and went into the bathroom. Glancing in the mirror, he saw a breaker of trust, and turned away with a shudder, cringing at his thoughts.

Three hours later he was standing in class. "William Wordsworth was born in …" The words struggled out, disembodied from his brain, while in his mind's eye the thought of Livia entering their apartment, walking across the room to him, bore him down. She smiled, hugged and kissed him. "I missed you. How was dinner with Mark?"

At that point Frank's imaginings blurred. He didn't know what he would say, only that whatever he said would be a lie.

Frank Marello stared at Taggart across the chasm of his imagination. "I could see an endless downward spiral of lies. I knew

I wanted to be with Mark again, but the thought of it was crushing me."

"When was this? When did this happen in relation to when Livia was killed?"

"In September … late September. About three months before."

"What'd you do?"

"Well, I dragged myself back home after teaching. I just sat and stared at the walls for a time. Mark called and asked if I was okay.

"No. I'm not. I'm miserable. I'm sitting here dreading Livia's return and everything that means."

Mark paused on his end of the line, then said, "I can understand how you might feel that way, but … "

Frank interruped his friend. "I think it would be wrong for us to see each other again, Mark, even as friends, at least until I get some things sorted out."

"Frank, if what we've done was a mistake, it was only a mistake of timing. It would have happened sooner or later given the way we feel about each other. But go ahead, work your way through this, figure out where you belong. Then go there and stay. You'll be miserable in a double life, and you owe Livia more than that."

"Livia came home later that night, and it was just like I imagined. She was radiant, filled with stories, happy to be home and asking me what I'd been doing, and how was Mark, because she knew we were going out to dinner. I just kept looking at her moving around, talking happily while she was unpacking, and I was thinking 'God, Livia, what did you ever do to deserve me?'"

"Did you tell her?"

"No, not at first. I didn't lie to her, at least not in so many words, but every second I didn't tell her seemed like a lie. I just moped around brooding, my stomach in a perpetual knot. I listened to a lot of music. I would come home at night and put on the earphones to my stereo and just sit there, not reading or anything, just trying to decide what to do, or maybe just to block out what I'd done."

Taggart could see it would be a difficult thing to admit, even to one's self, that you had just had the most satisfying sexual experience of your life … and it had been with a man. He tried to picture what it would be like sitting down with Marcia or his Mom and telling either of them he was homosexual and had decided to live openly as a gay person. Mike's mother was as tolerant and unbiased as any person of her generation, but he couldn't imagine it.

"Livia knew something was wrong," Frank continued. "For a while she didn't say anything, but she knew. Finally after about two weeks of this, she confronted me. One night she just came up to me and lifted the earphones off my head. I wasn't even conscious of her approach. She said she knew something was wrong and it wasn't like me not to let her in on whatever was troubling me.

"Naturally I said nothing was wrong, but she wouldn't accept that. She kept demanding to know why I'd been sitting there listening to music through earphones for two weeks saying almost nothing. I kept denying it, and she kept demanding to know, until about two a.m. we were kneeling in the middle of our bed face to face, shouting at each other, two people who had never shouted at each other in their lives. I'm surprised the neighbor didn't testify about that, because the whole building could probably hear every word.

"She wasn't going to let this alone until I told her. It was never going to stop. Suddenly I just collapsed into her on the bed and hugged her around the waist and told her what had happened and how it made me feel, and how I felt about Mark, everything."

"What did she say?"

"Mostly she listened. I was crying, and she cried too, and she was hugging me. I'll never forget that night as long as I live, how we lay there, side by side, in the dim light of this one meager lamp on the nightstand, embracing, talking the rest of the night. We even made love that night. It was one of the most intimate moments we ever had. That was the night she got pregnant."

"The strangeness of everything makes it difficult to appreciate the strangeness of anything," one of Taggart's favorite sayings, floated into his brain. What bizarre twists love could take. "What happened after that? What did you decide to do?"

"Livia told me she'd been going to this counselor, a psychiatrist named Suzanne Lefler. Apparently, Livia had suspected I was gay. She was so smart. Somehow she knew before I did. Anyway, we decided to go see this Dr. Lefler together."

Eight years of legal practice had made Taggart skeptical of psychiatrists. "What'd the shrink say?"

Frank was looking at the ceiling, envisioning. "I can see us sitting there, Livia and me, across a coffee table from Dr. Lefler, while she talked about how homosexuality wasn't deviant behavior.

"Dr. Lefler," Livia asked, "is there anything I've done or not done that plays a part in this? I mean, maybe I'm an unsatisfactory partner."

"No, Livia," Lefler was quick to interject, "it has nothing to do with you. When it comes to sexual preference, the die was cast long ago. Based on everything I see, I think Frank really loves you."

Marello looked down at Taggart sitting on the bench, notebook in his lap. "It's strange, but Dr. Lefler's affirmation of my feelings meant a lot to me. Still does. She wasn't ready to concede I was homosexual based on a couple of encounters, but, if I was, she said those desires certainly would recur ... as would my need to act on them. She didn't think a person could change. I could deny it, try to abstain from it, but I couldn't change it.

"Dr. Lefler asked us what we wanted to happen. Livia really wanted us to try to stay together. She hoped I did too. We made up our minds to try. It was pretty clear that it was up to me. All Livia asked was, if things reached the point where I didn't want to try anymore, would I tell her? She didn't want me to sneak around, not for either of our sakes,' was how she put it.

"So, we were trying to make it work when she died. We made love now and then, more than before. At first it was bad, awkward. I think we were both thinking about me having been with someone else, but little by little it became more than just going through the motions. I know Livia was encouraged because she said so once."

"Were you encouraged?"

"Truthfully, I cared about Livia in so many non-sexual ways that her happiness made me happy. The sex was pleasant, but it was nowhere near the passion I had experienced with Mark. It was becoming clear what had happened hadn't spoiled sex for us, hadn't made it impossible emotionally, and that was encouraging. And then, of course, we learned Livia was pregnant, and that was another big reason to make marriage succeed. But I can't say I ever stopped wishing Livia was my friend and Mark was my lover, instead of the other way around."

Taggart shuddered but said nothing. If Frank Marello ever uttered that last thought on the witness stand, Given Watson would put it together with the insurance policy and the motive for killing would be indelibly fixed in the jurors' minds.

"Until I met Livia my life was mostly a desert," Frank was saying, "and she made it a green field. Mark made it a flower garden. The second half of my life won't be like the first, Mike," Frank was looking directly at Taggart as he spoke, "It will be a flower garden, at least if there is a second half."

PART III
COMPLICATIONS

14

Monday, September 20, 1976 – 56 days to trial.

Mike's living room was crammed with two rented desks, a table, bulletin board, blackboard and easel with a large tablet of newsprint. File cartons containing the transcript and copies of the exhibits from the first trial were stacked on the orange vinyl couch against the wall opposite the door.

Rhonda was at her desk reviewing Mike's notes from his long meeting with Frank that day; Mike had gone to his car for something. The phone rang, and Rhonda, expecting a call from the law school, picked it up "Hello." There was a long pause. "Hello," Rhonda repeated.

Another silence, and then a woman's voice said, "Is this Mike Taggart's residence?"

"Yes. Mike just went out to the car to get something. He'll be right back if you want to hold on."

"Yes, I'll wait."

Rhonda was about to put the receiver down, but changed her mind. "Is this Marcia?

"Yes."

"Hi, Marcia, this is Rhonda Enright. I've heard a lot about you in the last couple of days. We're using Mike's apartment as our office. He's schlepping in a typewriter. I don't know what Taggart's office in San Diego looked like, but it appears the Marine Corps didn't teach him much in the way of organizational skills."

Marcia laughed. The dismay she'd experienced at the unexpected sound of a woman's voice answering Mike's phone faded. "I don't know about organization, but no dust rag ever touched Taggart's apartment here in San Diego. How's the case going?"

"I think it's going to be an uphill battle, but Mike's certainly dived in headfirst. Our client likes him and is beginning to trust him. That's important ... wait, here's Mike now. I'll let him fill you in. It was nice to talk to you."

Taggart set a big IBM Selectric typewriter down on the table. Rhonda handed him the phone and silently mouthed, "Marcia," stood up and walked into another room, closing the door behind her.

Mike took a deep breath. "Hi, Marsh. I'm glad to hear from you. Kind of surprised you called. I've missed you. How are you?"

"Oh, I'm in a real dither. Tom gave me your number. I need to talk to you."

"A dither?"

"Mike, I received a subpoena from the District Attorney to testify in the case against Bill Sullivan for breaking into my house. Someone from that office called and wants to talk to me before the trial. I also got a call from Sullivan's attorney wanting to meet. Mike, what do I need to do about all this?"

Mike took another deep breath. He was disappointed Marcia's dither didn't arise from missing him too much, but at least she'd called.

"The only thing you're required to respond to is the subpoena. Both sides naturally want to talk to you before trial, size you up as a witness. But it's up to you whether you want to meet with either one of them. When's the trial?"

"Two weeks from today. Tom said the D.A.'s trying to reach you too. Apparently, they called the office. What do you think I should do about talking to them beforehand?"

"I think you should cooperate with the D.A. as much as possible. Anything you can do to maximize the case against this guy and create barriers against him ever bothering you again, you should do. As for Sullivan's attorney, I wouldn't talk to him if I were you.

He'll bring your refusal up at trial as an indication you're biased against his client. But that kind of goes without saying, given the charge. Who represents him anyway?"

"A woman named Sandra Lewis. Do you know her?"

"Yeah, I know her. She's known as No Limits Lewis."

"What's that mean?"

"It means she's likely to try anything, no matter how far-fetched. She probably holds the world record for number of times one lawyer has been admonished for irrelevancy."

It was a nice touch for a guy accused of stalking to have a woman attorney, but Mike didn't say it. "I think the only reason to meet with her is to satisfy yourself that she's not some Clarence Darrow, some great lawyer, so you don't worry yourself to death about being cross-examined. If I were you, I wouldn't do anything to help Sullivan. But if you decide to do it, make sure you take someone with you. That way you have a witness regarding everything that gets said during the meeting, and don't sign anything. You've already given the police a statement. Lewis has that. The more written statements floating around, the greater the chance for an inconsistency, no matter how inadvertent. You have a copy of the statement you gave to the police, don't you?"

"Yes."

"Regardless of whether you decide to talk with either one of them, make sure you review that carefully."

"Mike, they're going to want you to testify too, aren't they?"

"Yeah, I'm sure they will."

"You'll come back for the trial, won't you?"

There was too much to do in the Marello case for Mike to go anywhere before it was over, but whatever it took to keep Red Corvette guy from ever bothering Marcia and Matt again, Mike would do, even if he wasn't to be part of their future.

"Yes. Definitely. Who's the D.A.? I'll call him in the morning"

"William Malinzak. He sounded like a good guy over the phone,"

"Whitey Malinzak! Small world. I was in the Marine Corps with him. Good guy."

"That makes me feel better." Marcia paused for a moment. "Mike, maybe we can get together for dinner while you're home. Not seeing or talking to you is very hard."

Taggart drew his third deep breath of the conversation. "Hard for me too, Marsh. I'd like that. I'll let you know when I'm coming."

15

Sunday, September 26, 1976 – 50 days to trial.

"I read the first draft of your change of venue motion." Mike sat sipping a beer and watching Rhonda stir a pot of spaghetti sauce in her kitchen, "It's wonderful. I wouldn't change a word. We have to get Frank's case out of Marlborough if we can."

He and Rhonda had divided up the trial preparation. It hadn't required an organization chart. Among other things, Rhonda was responsible for drafting pre-trial motions.

"Thanks. Still needs some polishing, but I think we're on the right track." She paused, and went on. "Mike, let's not talk about the case for a minute. I need to apologize for the other night."

"Apologize ... apologize for what?"

"Oh, for giving you all that advice about Marcia, telling you not to be your own worst enemy. I'm the last person on earth who should be giving other people advice about their love life."

"I thought it was probably pretty good advice, not that I'll take it."

"In that case," Rhonda wiped her hands on her apron, "whether it's Marcia or someone else, you need to meet that special woman. Anyone who'd coach little league when he doesn't even have any kids, is a family looking for a place to happen."

Mike laughed. "Okay, what about you?"

"I don't need a special woman, Mike."

"You know what I mean. Are you going to be Professor Enright forever?"

"Probably." Rhonda nodded. "Here or somewhere else. It's hard to meet people here. Sometimes I think about moving to a larger city, but that would be tough with Louie."

"Louie. Who's Louie?"

"Louie's my horse."

"You have a special horse? I once knew a farmer back in Iowa who had a special goat."

Rhonda gave Taggart a look. "Yes."

"It figures. Girl from Cody, Wyoming has horse. Louie, huh?"

"What's the matter? You don't like the name 'Louie?'"

"It's not exactly 'Man O' War' or 'Bold Ruler.'"

"Well, Louie's a six-year-old gelding. He no longer has aspirations of world conquest."

"Ever think of going back into practice?"

"No, not full time. Maybe something like the appeal of this case. Something I can do in my spare time. I like teaching too much to give it up completely."

"On any better terms with your folks?"

Rhonda sighed and shook her head. "Mom comes back to see me a couple times each year, but Daddy won't. I don't think he'll ever forgive me for all the civil rights stuff. I haven't heard a word from him since I left Stanford for Alcorn State. Plus, he was for the war and all the bombing, and you know where I stood on that."

"Why didn't you call somebody from Patton & Black to help you on this case instead of me?" Mike asked. "The megafirms are always loaning out their lawyers to handle tough cases with social issues."

For two years after her Supreme Court clerkship before deciding to teach, Rhonda had worked at Patton & Black, a large law firm in Washington, D.C.

"Nobody there ever tried a murder case. They loan out people to get experience. In two years, I was never inside a courtroom. Whoever they sent would be somebody just like me – no experience. Frank needs a grizzled old fart like you who's actually done what he needs done." Rhonda stuck a heaping plate of spaghetti in front of him as she spoke.

As Taggart walked into his apartment following dinner with Rhonda, the phone was ringing

"Hello."

"Oh, Mike," Marcia's voice, "I've been trying to reach you for three hours."

"What's going on?"

"Sullivan's subpoenaed Matt to testify."

"Jesus," Mike swore. *No Limits Lewis is on the loose.*

"Mike, we've got to stop this. Matt wasn't even there. Why make an eight-year-old child a witness? Have you talked to the D.A. yet, your friend, what's his name – Whitey?"

"Missed him twice," Mike replied. "I'll call again first thing in the morning. I'll try to reach Tom tonight. He knows Whitey, too. It'll help to have someone, another lawyer, in San Diego who Whitey can call if he can't reach me - someone who is also pushing to put a stop to this."

"Okay." Marcia sounded like she was exhaling. "That makes me feel a little better. Oh, Mike, this whole thing's even more awful than I thought it would be."

"Yeah, it is, Marsh, but we'll do everything we can to keep Matt out. I promise. Try to relax and get some sleep. Nothing more you can do tonight."

"You're right. But I don't think I'm getting much sleep 'til this is over. You'll keep me posted, won't you?"

"Yes, of course. Tom will too, I'm sure."

"Okay, well, good-night, Mike. I love you."

Taggart's heart swelled at the sound of the words. "I love you, too, Marsh, both you and Matt. Talk to you in the morning. Pleasant dreams."

16

Sunday, September 26, 1976 – 50 days to trial – Late Evening

Frank Marello's question about whether the prosecution would try the case the same way the second time around inevitably led to the question whether the defense would try the case the same way the second time around. It hadn't worked the first time. Trial was now seven weeks away. It was beginning to look like Taggart wouldn't even be in town for several of those days. How much of the remaining time should be devoted to revisiting facts that appeared to be established beyond doubt? Which facts were those? In the aftermath of Marcia's call it was hard to even concentrate. After calling Tom Horn and telling him what was going on, Mike was reviewing his Marello To Do list, attempting to re-prioritize, when the doorbell startled him. He wasn't expecting anybody; it was late, almost eleven.

At the door stood a tall, young Black man dressed in a white shirt unbuttoned at the collar, a loosened black tie and some kind of uniform pants. "Mr. Taggart, do you remember me?"

"I sure do. Cornelius Kempton!"

As recognition dawned on Taggart, both men began to laugh.

"Cornelius, come on in. How are you?" They shook hands. "Gosh, it's great to see you!"

"It's great to see you too, Mr. Taggart. Hope you don't mind my coming over so late. This morning just before I had to go to work, I heard you were in town." He gestured at his clothes. "I just got off and decided to at least drive by. The light was on, so I took a chance."

"I'm glad you did." Mike marveled at the speed at which the news had spread, not only that he was in town, but where he was staying. He was also filled with warmth at the knowledge Kempton thought enough to come see him immediately upon learning he was in town. "Do you want a beer, Cornelius?"

"Sure, if you're having one."

"Clear some of those boxes off the couch, so you'll have a place to sit. Wow, how long has it been?"

During Taggart's first year in law school, Marlborough High School, the white high school, decided to "voluntarily" bow to the pressure to integrate by admitting five students from Fredrick Douglas High, the Black school. Coincidentally, all the students selected happened to be superior athletes. Most superior of all was Cornelius.

"Spring of '66," Cornelius remembered. "Ten years."

Glenn Carmody, the school's baseball coach, asked for Taggart's help teaching Cornelius to catch. It had been a classic case of a great and hungry student devouring everything a mediocre instructor had to teach. Within a few days following the start of practice Taggart's role had become yelling "keep up the good work." In the span of two seasons, Mike went from coach to mentor of sorts. Football was Cornelius's best sport. Mike helped him sort through the dozens of scholarship offers. Eventually he chose Michigan, Mike's alma mater.

"How's Josie? You two have any kids yet?"

"Sure do. A boy four and a girl two. Daughter's name is 'Tanya' and son's name is 'Michael.' Josie's just fine. She's working in the office at the Liggett plant over in Durham. Our moms take turns carin' for the kids during the day."

Mike had not missed the significance of Cornelius's son's name, but didn't know what to say. "Where're you working, Cornelius?"

"Skycap for Delta Airlines at Raleigh-Durham Airport. Been there five years. Just made supervisor on the morning shift last month. Had to work swing shift this evening too; someone didn't show up."

Taggart took a swig of beer as he digested that fact. "What happened to college?"

Cornelius gave him a wan look.

"You and Josie promised me and Cathy at your wedding that you wouldn't start a family if it meant quitting school. You crossed your heart. If I remember right, Josie was promising even more fervently than you. What happened?"

"You remember right, Mr. Taggart. An' we didn't start no family while I was in college either. Everything was going fine, until spring practice sophomore year. I'd started the last four games the previous season, my grades were good, and then I broke my leg and had to drop out of school before the end of the semester."

"You go back? Did it heal okay?"

"Draft got me that summer. I had a real low number."

Taggart took another swig, a big one.

"April of '71 I got hit bad in the back and both legs outside Pleiku and was medivaced back to the States. I was in the hospital in San Diego for about six months and then got my discharge." Cornelius pulled up his right pant leg revealing scarring all along both sides of his calf. "I can move around okay, but not good enough for Michigan football. No football, no scholarship. No scholarship, no college. No college, hello suitcases. That's how it goes." He shook his head.

April of '71, Jesus! Ten thousand bad old feelings beat on Mike's heart. April of '71, the month Cathy'd left. The whole time Cornelius was in the hospital, he'd been in San Diego. *Shit!* "Do me a favor, will you?"

"Sure, Mr. Taggart, what is it?"

Don't call me 'Mr. Taggart' any more. Call me 'Mike,' just like your son, a fact that makes me feel honored."

"Sure, Mr. ... Mike. Mike it is." They shook hands all over again.

Despite staying up until two a.m., Taggart awakened at five-thirty the next morning, head fuzzy from the four beers he'd drunk. His first thought upon waking was of Marcia and the subpoena for Matt.

At nine o'clock, six a.m. Whitey's time, the phone rang.

"Taggart, this is Whitey. Horn called me at home last night and filled me in. I didn't know about the subpoena. Just like No Limits to serve it on a weekend. Anyway, I thought you'd like to hear from me."

"Good, you know the situation. Any chance of getting that subpoena quashed?"

They discussed Whitey's assessment of their chances and how he was preparing.

"Sounds good," Mike replied. "What do you think No Limits is up to? I thought maybe that dirtbag Sullivan had taken a deal and pled out."

"No, no deals," Whitey replied. "No Limits was demanding the charge be reduced to a misdemeanor – Trespass in exchange for a guilty plea. That's bullshit. Breaking into a person's bedroom at two in the morning and threatening people is a felony. Sullivan's lucky you didn't kill him."

That's right.

"My guess is No Limits thinks her client might lose his medical license if he cops to a felony," Whitey continued. "So, no deals. But I don't know what she's planning. I'll keep you and Horn posted. By the way, I like your girlfriend. She's smart and classy. Too good for you."

Another Whitey opinion Taggart agreed with. *If she still is my 'girlfriend.'*

17

Monday, September 27, 1976 – 49 days to trial.

As soon as Taggart hung up with Whitey, the phone rang again.

"Mike," it was Rhonda's voice, "can you get over to the County Solicitor's office right away? Prosecution's got some new evidence in Frank's case it wants to disclose."

Without even knowing what lay in wait for him at Given Watson's office, Mike could feel the foundation of the case beginning to shift as the prosecution maneuvered for an edge. What kind of ambush awaited him? His stomach lurched.

Taggart walked into Watson's outer office and introduced himself.

"Oh yes." The receptionist handed him a five by seven-inch package about an inch thick wrapped in plain brown paper and tape. "This is for you." Mike signed an acknowledgement of receipt. Inside were approximately one hundred loose sheets of unlined paper containing some rather elegant looking handwriting.

"Livia Marello's diary," said a voice.

Mike looked up and saw Given Watson standing in the doorway to an inner office.

"Hello, Mr. Watson. I don't know if you remember me; I'm Mike Taggart. I--"

"I remember you. You don't have to call me 'Mr.' if I don't have to call you 'Depity.' Call me 'Given.'" He extended his hand. "C'mon in for a minute. Want a cup of coffee?"

Taggart's eagerness to know the contents of the diary was so strong it was as if the pages were alive, vibrating in his hand, but he didn't want to miss the chance to begin opening a line of communication with Watson. Many prosecutors Mike dealt with, like most police, treated defense counsel as if they were themselves criminals. If Watson was willing to be friendly, Mike was certainly ready to reciprocate. Stifling his curiosity, he accepted Watson's offer.

"Mind telling me what it is about this diary that suddenly makes the State of North Carolina think it's evidence my client killed his wife?"

"The late Mizrus Marello expresses her alarm about her husband's homosexual tendencies in there."

"What does that have to do with whether he killed her? I thought he was supposed to have killed her for the insurance."

"Coulda had more than one reason. Could be the two reasons fit together."

"How are you going to get it in evidence?" Mike held the package up to his nose. "Smells like hearsay to me."

"Oh, I wouldn't count on my not getting it in, if I were you." Watson didn't say how he intended to do it. There were so many exceptions to the rule excluding hearsay evidence that Mike had little doubt Watson would get the diary admitted.

"Listen," Watson said, "I don't know how familiar you are with your case, but I can tell you it's pretty open and shut for the State. The first jury wouldn't have recommended the death sentence if the evidence had been anything less. I'm not sayin' this to play games, but if Marello wants to plead guilty, it would save the State a lot of money, maybe even the cost of an execution, which is an economy he might appreciate."

Taggart was immediately on red alert. *What's this all about?* Rhonda had said there'd been no suggestion of willingness to plea bargain before the first trial. Given Watson held a lot of cards. The town had already demonstrated its willingness to sentence Frank Marello to death. Would Watson be willing to give up all possibility of the death penalty in exchange for a plea of guilty? Will Frank

Marello be willing to admit a killing he has steadfastly denied for the last two years in exchange for a guarantee he won't hang?

Try to sound nonchalant. "What are you offering?"

"What are you asking for?"

Taggart wasn't asking for anything, not at this point. This wasn't a decision anyone but Frank Marello could make, and Frank didn't yet know he was being given the choice. Mike and Given talked of other things long enough to finish their coffee, and Taggart departed, breaking into a jog for the nearest phone as soon as the door to the outer office closed behind him.

Two piles of Xeroxed pages sat on the desk in front of Taggart, the everyday life of Livia Marello whispering off the pages - quotes, poems she liked, including one Frank had written for her, notes about the weather, her job, daily tidbits, a couple of recipes, the births of friends' children.

The front door opened. "I came as soon as I could." Rhonda was still slightly out of breath from running up the front steps of Taggart's apartment. Without looking up or saying anything, he pushed the pile he'd already read across the desktop towards Rhonda, who picked them up as she sat down. They read in a silence that seemed to bore its way deeper and deeper into the room with each turn of a page.

"Hah!" After several minutes Mike exhaled a long sigh and handed the page he'd just been reading to Rhonda. She read it quickly and then again slowly, as if studying scripture. Finishing, she looked up at Mike, who was looking back. "Now I understand the meaning of 'paradox.'"

He nodded. "A little something for everybody."

They resumed reading.

When he reached the entries for mid-August, Mike lifted a page from the pile he was reading. "Listen to this. 'Thursday, August 15, 1973 – Frank and I haven't made love in two months. How can he be so kind and caring, but not want to have sex? God knows no man ever had a more willing partner! That sounds funny when I read it back to myself, but it's not. I'm scared. He sees more and more of this man, Mark Josephson, all the time. I think he's 'gay' or whatever it's called these days. I just can't believe Frank would sneak around or lie to me, but something's wrong.'"

Mike let the page drop back onto the pile in front of him. "You know, even if there wasn't a word about Frank's homosexuality in here, if I was the prosecutor, I'd want this diary in evidence just because of the woman who emerges from these pages. If the jury likes her half as much as I do, we're in trouble."

Rhonda opened her eyes wide and nodded. "I know. Livia was a sharp cookie. This makes me want to burn my own diary."

"Because you wouldn't want anyone to read it the way we're reading this one?"

"No, because she writes so much better than me. She can make the weather sound interesting. It's not easy writing about your feelings."

Taggart, a little surprised Rhonda kept a diary, could not imagine Livia Marello wrote better than Rhonda. "I keep asking myself how this will play with a jury. Almost seems like peeking, eavesdropping, something. Maybe the jurors will blame the prosecution for making them feel that way."

Rhonda tilted her head to one side as she considered Taggart's thought. "I don't think so. Watson has a legitimate reason to peek."

"It's interesting." Rhonda held up a page she'd just been reading, "One of the things that makes Livia so likable is the way she responds to Frank's sexuality problems as she comes to understand more about them – she humanizes the problem and Frank, too. Even this October 8 entry, the one right after he told her about his night with Mark Josephson - it's not 'Frank the Cad' or 'Frank the Unfaithful.' She goes way deeper."

Taggart nodded. When preparing for trial, he tried to put himself in the shoes of the people in the story he was getting ready to tell. So far, Frank's shoes hadn't fit very well, and Olivia's were proving no more comfortable. "Anything else that strikes you, now that you've read it?" he asked.

"Well, for whatever it's worth, we know Livia had no use for Jim Marello."

"I'm not sure how that helps us."

"Probably doesn't. I think we need to interview the marriage counselor, Dr. Lefler, as soon as possible. I can do that while you're back in San Diego"

"Maybe you won't have to if Frank's willing to go for a plea bargain. We have to get that sorted out before I go."

Arrest. The word had always disturbed Mike. He looked it up once just to see the dictionary's version. "To seize (a person) by legal authority..." It was the last part that bothered Taggart, "... by legal authority." It was one thing to be seized, to be in the control of another person, quite another to know the law was on the side of your captors, that no law-abiding citizen would lift a finger to help you. You were at the mercy of others, probably people who believed you guilty of whatever caused them to seize you in the first place. You could be punished, perhaps even killed, and no one, not your friends, not your family, not the police, especially not the police, could prevent it. Arrest was the ultimate vulnerability. If the evidence against you could not be overcome, hope was gone. Something had to happen to stem the tide, reverse its course. Someone had to make it happen - a lawyer.

In Frank Marello's case the law had already ordered his death. A court of law had passed judgment - it was okay to execute Frank Marello. All barriers against Frank being legally killed at the age of thirty-two had been removed, all save one - the appellate court.

Rhonda Enright had used that barrier to prevent Marello's death once, but the State wasn't finished.

Mike Taggart couldn't imagine what it must be like for Marello to spend all his days and nights in that tiny cell alone on the second floor of that ancient jail wondering what would happen. He tried to visit every day, even if only for fifteen minutes. He brought Frank newspapers, books, crossword puzzles. Now he and Rhonda were headed back to the jail to discuss Given Watson's overture regarding a possible plea bargain.

Rhonda hated the conversation about to ensue, hated the need to raise the subject with Frank, inasmuch as Watson had made no specific offer. "For almost two years Frank has sworn he didn't kill Livia." She and Mike pulled into a parking spot across from the jail. "Now we're about to ask him if he wants to admit killing her in exchange for a reduction in punishment for a crime he didn't commit?"

Taggart shrugged. "He can always say 'no,"

Rhonda grimaced, as if she had a bad taste in her mouth, "Just raising the subject suggests we think he might be lying. Morale's important. If Frank thinks his own lawyers disbelieve him, why should he think he has any chance with a jury of strangers?"

"Rhonda, even if we had a choice, how would you feel if we didn't tell Frank this lifeline may exist, and then he's convicted and sentenced to die? Frank's a smart guy. He's going to understand this is something we have to do."

Mike opened the back door of the car and took out two identical parcels. "Here, will you carry one of these for me? I can't manage them both with my briefcase."

"What are these?"

"You'll see. Let's go."

"Mr. Jack, we brought you something." Mike crossed the office and handed one of the packages to Mr. Jack, who began to unwrap it.

"It's a cake." Taggart explained. "We've got one for your guest upstairs too."

Mr. Jack tore away the brown paper and opened the lid of the pink bakery box. Inside was a multi-layer chocolate cake with the end of a large file sticking out of it.

"Oh … I gave you the wrong one." Taggart gasped in mock dismay.

Rhonda choked back a laugh. Taggart could joke with Mr. Jack, but she couldn't.

"I oughta throw you in the damn jail," Mr. Jack grumbled, clearly pleased at the joke, as he led Taggart and Rhonda up the steps to Marello's cell.

"You're the one who ought to be in jail, Mr. Jack," Mike replied.

"What're ya'll talkin' about?" The old jailer eyed Taggart as he unlocked the door to Frank's cell.

"Well, what's Stick going to think when I tell him I saw you defile a cake?"

Mr. Jack didn't get it; Rhonda's mirth was silent; Frank hadn't heard the joke.

I'm casting my pearls among swine. Taggart handed Marello the other cake, now thoroughly ventilated with fork holes from Mr. Jack's inspection. They all sat down, Rhonda taking her customary seat on the toilet.

"Something's come up, Frank…" Taggart bit his lip, considering his words, "but before we get started, you have to understand that the reason we're raising the subject we're about to discuss is because it's our duty as attorneys. Professional ethics require it. It has nothing to do with how we both feel, which is that you're innocent."

Rhonda nodded. Marello remained silent, listening.

"I talked to Given Watson this morning. His office called to let us know the State had some new evidence to produce. Turns out, Livia's diary's been found. I'll get to that in a minute. When I went to pick it up, Watson suggested the State might be receptive to a deal, a plea bargain."

"What are they offering?"

"Nothing right now. He just indicated his willingness to consider something. He wants us to make the first move."

"What do they want from me?"

"Whatever you're willing to agree to," Rhonda said. "You can say, 'I'll plead guilty in exchange for a guarantee that my sentence won't be more than five years.'" Rhonda's hands unfolded from her lap as if she was about to give Frank something. "Of course, if the prosecutors think your offer is ridiculously low in relation to what they believe can be achieved at trial, they may just reject it without making a counteroffer." She let her hands drop back. "So, if you want to try to make a deal, it's important to make whatever sentence you're willing to accept long enough for the prosecution to conclude agreement is possible. That way, they'll at least continue to negotiate."

"Why would I ever consider such a thing if I'm not guilty?"

"You shouldn't," Rhonda said. "If you're not guilty, it would be improvident--"

"Frank, it's this way," Taggart broke in. "You look at the chances you'll be convicted, and you look at the likely sentence. Then, guilty or innocent, you decide whether you're willing to risk receiving such a sentence in order to have a chance to be acquitted and go free. If not, if the risk's too high, maybe you decide to try to cut your losses and make a deal that will at least get you a lesser sentence."

Frank opened his mouth to speak, but Taggart held up his hand. "One more thing to think about. In order to make a deal, the

Court will require you to admit, under oath, that you really did kill your wife. You have to be prepared to do that, or there's no use negotiating."

Frank Marello had stood up and started pacing as Mike and Rhonda talked. Now he sank to a sitting position on the floor against the wall. "I didn't kill--" he began.

"Frank, I believe you didn't kill her." Mike said. "In my heart of hearts, I want you to reject any plea bargaining. I think you should reject it, but you owe it to yourself to hold off on your decision until you at least hear the odds."

"Okay, Mike," Frank raised his head to look Taggart in the eye, "what are the odds?"

"You know the evidence against you as well as we do, except for this diary of Olivia's we just received. We've scanned it once, and it makes clear homosexuality had become a big issue in your marriage. I'm more sure than ever that's going to be one of the alleged motives this time, so-called 'deviant sex' and the insurance."

Mike went on to describe the paradoxical content of the diary and the equally enigmatic role of Troutman. "It boils down to you being an outsider in a small, extremely conservative southern town, who was having marital difficulties arising not just from an affair, but something abominable according to the Good Book. In effect, we're going to be asking a second group of citizens to go against the judgment of their friends and neighbors on the first jury, to stand up in public and say those earlier folks got it wrong. It seems to me the second jury will have to have a lot more guts to acquit you than the first one needed. Do you agree, Rhonda?"

Rhonda nodded.

"Given that state of affairs and the evidence against you," Mike continued, "I'd say the chances in favor of you being convicted are about 60-40 first degree, maybe 65-35. There's nothing scientific about this analysis, Frank. These estimates are pure instinct born of some, but not a lot, of experience."

"And the sentence?" Frank asked.

"If it's first degree, the same as before," Taggart said. "Unless I miss my guess, that's the deal Watson has in mind: he'll waive all possibility of the death penalty in exchange for your guilty plea and agreement to a life sentence. I could be wrong, but if I was him, that's as far as I'd go. With good behavior you might be out in what ..." Taggart looked at Rhonda.

"Twenty-three, twenty-four years," she said. "Frank, you don't have to make this decision today, but one of the reasons for the prosecution's willingness to negotiate is to save itself the cost of getting ready for trial. If Watson has to prepare for trial anyway, much of the value of a deal is lost as far as he's concerned, so you have to decide sooner rather than later."

Frank sat leaning against the wall, knees pulled up against his chest, arms wrapped around his shins, forehead resting on his knees, saying nothing. Mike and Rhonda glanced at each other and said no more. After a time that seemed longer than it probably was, Frank stood up. "Fuck! This makes me furious."

Mike and Rhonda exchanged another glance, jaws dropping simultaneously.

"What would the life I buy by lying and saying I killed Livia be like? I would rather die than have even one person, let alone the entire world, believe on the basis of an admission by me that I killed her. Do you know that ever since I saw Livia lying there dead on the floor of our kitchen, the idea of dying, of rejoining her has tantalized me? The only thing that prevents me from saving the State the price of a hanging is my inability to believe that if I did manage to kill myself, it would somehow enable me to rejoin Livia."

Frank paused and pinched the bridge of his nose between his left thumb and forefinger. "I'm not going to kill myself. Don't worry about that," he said. "But believe me, when I say the one thing I do know about death is that it will be preferable to even one day of life purchased at the cost of saying even one time that I killed Livia. I didn't kill Livia. I loved her. No deals."

18

Tuesday, September 28, 1976 – 48 days to trial.

"Mike, this is Whitey. Just got back from court. We moved to quash the subpoena on the little boy. No Limits went berserk. Same old bullshit – prosecution is railroading her client, good ol' boy network. I'd never have made such a request if you and I weren't Marine Corps pals. Sullivan's being denied the ability to defend himself. Just because the mother says the child wasn't there doesn't mean he wasn't, the mother would say anything, etc."

"What'd the Judge say?"

"When No Limits finally calmed down, he asked her what evidence she expected to develop through the kid's testimony and whether there was some other way of getting at it without having to call a child to testify."

"And ..."

"She said there was no other way, and she shouldn't be required to disclose what she expected to get from him, because doing so would force her to reveal the defense's strategy prematurely.

"So, the Judge said that without any justification for calling an eight-year-old boy to testify, he wasn't going to allow it. Then No Limits offered to tell the Judge confidentially in chambers what she expected the testimony to be, and they marched back into chambers while Marcia and I sat there in the courtroom.

"After a few minutes, they came back out, and the Judge announced he's reserving his ruling until trial. If it appears the testimony No Limits expects would contribute anything meaningful to the defense, the subpoena will be upheld. Otherwise, it'll quashed."

"'Defense's strategy' my ass," Taggart said. "Her only strategy is to make the whole experience so awful Marcia will change her story to protect Matt."

"You think there's any chance of her doing that?"

"I can't imagine she would. All that would do is put Sullivan back on the street where he'd continue to threaten her and Matt. If putting him away requires Matt to testify, I'm pretty sure she'll do it. How'd Marcia handle the Judge's ruling?

"She didn't say much, but her jaws were pretty tight. If I was No Limits, I wouldn't get on the same elevator with her when leaving the courthouse."

Taggart laughed. *Winners and losers should never ride the same elevator.*

"This trial's supposed to start next Monday. When are you coming back?" Whitey asked.

Marcia Banning didn't go back to work following the hearing. She went to the beach. The tide was way out, the breeze just enough to take the edge off the sun's early autumn heat. Here and there, widely spaced, walkers, some solitary, some in pairs, otherwise mid-week morning emptiness. Marcia took off her shoes and stuffed them in her jacket pockets. The sand felt good, rough, but not too much. She scrunched her toes in it as she walked, as if to polish her thoughts through the soles of her feet.

"Tim, my love, are you listening?" Marcia stared out at the ocean that had swallowed her husband all those short long years ago. "We haven't talked for a while. Are you still watching over us, Matt and me?"

She walked on, imagining, remembering, crying just a little. "How did I get us into this mess, Tim? What makes this asshole Sullivan think he can do this to us and get away with it?"

Marcia's feet flirted with the water's fringe, in and out, absorbing the coolness. About a mile from where she left her car she plopped down just above the wet sand line, folded her arms around her knees where she rested her chin. She squinted into the light over the water, contemplating a lone surfer, remembering Tim on his board, riding as if he'd been born on it.

"Why'd you ever go away, Tim?"

No reply. Just the sound of the surf and the wind, both on the rise. Time passed. The surfer came in. Not Tim. Not Taggart. She was alone.

Two hours later, Matt came in the door and threw his backpack on the kitchen table. "Hi, Mom. How was your day?" he said before she had a chance to ask him the same question.

Marcia shook her head. Matt had started asking her that after hearing Taggart ask her. "Well, Matt, my day was kind of interesting. Why don't we have a glass of lemonade and talk about it?"

She poured the lemonade and they sat at the kitchen table. Matt looked so little and sweet sitting there, feet not quite reaching the floor. Marcia took a deep breath.

"Matt, I don't think I mentioned it before, but Mike and I are going to be in a trial next week, and it might even happen that you would get to be in it too."

"Trial, you mean like Coach does at his job?"

"Yes, that kind of trial. Only this time he's not going to be one of the lawyers. He's going to be a witness, one of those people you see on television who have to answer the lawyer's questions. That's what I'm going to be too."

"Why are you guys going to be in a trial?"

"Do you remember back when you went camping with Charley and his family a few months ago?"

"Yeah." Matt nodded.

"Well, while you were gone, a man broke into our house, and now there's going to be a trial to see if he has to go to jail."

"Into our house? Wow! What happened? Did he steal anything?"

"No, he just came in and started yelling at Mike and me. He scared me." Marcia bit her lip. She immediately regretted saying she'd been scared. It might make Matt scared now.

"Was Coach scared too? What did he do?"

"Well, if he was scared, he didn't show it." Marcia smiled at the memory of Taggart jumping out of bed with no clothes on and knocking Sullivan down. "Mike knocked the man down and tied him up. Then the police came and took the man away."

"Wow! I wish I'd been there. Can I have another glass of lemonade?"

Marcia refilled his glass.

"Mom, why would I be in the trial? I wasn't even here."

"I don't know, Matt. But the Judge says that you might have to be a witness too."

Marcia didn't want Matt to know the man who broke in was the one insisting he testify. It was too weird. Matt was silent for a few moments. Then he said, "Mom, can I wear a suit and tie and black shoes at the trial like Coach does?"

A lump the approximate size of Mount Everest immediately rose in Marcia's throat, and tears trickled down her cheek. "Sure, Matt, sure. We'll go shopping this weekend."

Friday, October 1, 1976 – 45 days to trial.

On Friday morning Rhonda drove Taggart to the airport. It was still dark, and Taggart seemed not only silent, but far away. Assuming he was thinking about the delicate interactions of the next few days with anxious-to-be-married Marcia, Rhonda chose not to interrupt his reverie.

"Rhonda, if you were representing a guy who was accused of breaking into the home of a woman he had dated briefly a couple of years earlier and confronting her and her boyfriend in bed at two a.m., screaming for the boyfriend to get out of the house, how would you defend a case like that?"

"I'd hope the guy had a good alibi."

"No alibi. I throttled the guy and the police came to Marcia's house and arrested him."

"And he's fighting it. No chance of a deal?"

"No deal. The guy's a doctor. If he's convicted, he has license problems. So how do you get him out of this mess if you're representing him? I should tell you that his lawyer has the guts to try anything. Her nickname's 'No Limits.' Nothing's too outrageous."

"Hmmm, no question he was in the house at two in the morning, eh? So, no alibi. Maybe I suggest to the good doctor that he was there all evening and you were the one who showed up uninvited in the wee hours and see if that's the way he suddenly remembers it."

Taggart glanced over at Rhonda. "Well, No Limits has nothing on you in the absence of ethics department. But that's a tough sell when both Marcia and I are saying it was the other way around."

"I'm just playing her role," Rhonda said. "It's still a swearing contest. Your version versus his. If what's her name ... No Limits, can think of a motive why Marcia might be willing to support you even though you were the actual intruder, she might be able to sell it. What about jealousy? That's often a plausible motivation for outrageous behavior."

"Jealousy? How do you mean?"

Rhonda explained the scenario she imagined.

Taggart was turned half-way around in the passenger seat staring at Rhonda. For about the thousandth time, Rhonda had come up with an answer in a few seconds to a problem that had been gnawing at Taggart for almost a week. "You're right. That's exactly the kind of thing No Limits might pull."

19

Monday. October 4, 1976 – 42 days to trial. 8:30 a.m.

Superior Court for the State of California, County of San Diego. Case No. K46325. *State of California v. Sullivan, William* - Breaking and Entering; Stalking, Assault; Vandalism.

Mike, Marcia and Matt arrived together. Ever since Marcia and Matt had picked Mike up at the airport Friday night, the embargo Marcia had placed on their relationship before he left for North Carolina seemed to have disappeared. For his part, just the sight of the two of them standing waiting for him, a sight he could no longer take for granted, made Taggart happier than he'd been in a long time.

Now the three M's, as Matt had christened them, were sitting together on a scarred bench outside Courtroom 2 watching the courthouse world on parade – prospective jurors, name badges prominently displayed, searching for assigned courtrooms, young lawyers with new briefcases, some eager, some frightened, headed for their destiny. Old lawyers with battered briefcases containing the entirety of their practice went by, others in pinstriped suits whose briefcases were carried by associates. Witnesses nervously awaiting their moment in the sun. Clerks, bailiffs, court reporters – carrying out, submitting to, praising, cursing the administration of justice, which by the end of the day would lead to the ruin of some, the vindication of others, the mere conclusion of another day on Earth for most. Not knowing what the day would bring made it interesting.

Whitey's case was simple. Marcia would go first, give the back story followed by her account of Sullivan's invasion of her home. Next Taggart, to back up Marcia's account; finally, the arresting officer describing what he found when he got there. The tricky part of Whitey's case would be his rebuttal following No Limits' defense. Mike had told Whitey of Rhonda's speculation.

Whitey's only response had been, "Well, if you're gonna lie, lie big."

"Coach, that guy's got a gun!" Matt's eyes were wide as he pointed to a uniformed bailiff walking by, pistol holstered on his hip.

"He's a marshal," Matt. They protect the courtrooms."

"Why do the courtrooms need protecting?"

"Oh, sometimes people get mad and start fights. Not very often, but some …"

"Okay, Marcia, you're up." Whitey stood in the door to the courtroom. "By the way, No Limits just finished her opening statement. Your friend in North Carolina must have a crystal ball."

Marcia, who had been holding Mike's hand, gave it a squeeze.

"Go get 'em, Mom," Matt stood, saluted Marcia in his best Marine imitation; Marcia saluted back and walked across the hall and through the courtroom door.

"That's what I always say to the guys on my team when they go up to bat."

"You call your teammates 'Mom?'"

Matt gave Mike a funny look. "What? No … you know what I mean." He was laughing. Of the three Ms, Matt was the least nervous.

Inside the courtroom, Whitey held the swinging gate open for Marcia. She glanced at the table where Sullivan and No Limits were sitting, then proceeded past the jury box filled with thirteen people and on to the witness stand, where the clerk swore her in, and she sat down.

"Counsel may examine," said the Judge.

Whitey wasted no time in getting into the story she had to tell. In response to his questions, Marcia described her first meeting with Sullivan, their two brief dates when she resumed dating almost four years after Tim's death, Sullivan's continued invitations despite her consistent refusals, the troubling drive-bys. She even presented a calendar on which she had noted the times she'd seen him drive by during one three month period – seventeen times in three months, the anonymous phone calls once she started dating Mike.

Then came Sullivan's appearance in her bedroom in the wee hours of November 9, 1975, Mike's first overnight at her place. She described her fright at being awakened by Sullivan's demand to "Get him out of here," Mike's apparently passive initial reaction followed by his tackling Sullivan and throwing him to the floor.

"No further questions. Thank you, Ms. Banning," Whitey said as Marcia finished her account of helping Mike tie Sullivan up, calling the police and, finally, the fear and anxiety she continued to feel, especially when she and Matt were alone in the house at night. It had all taken a little less than an hour.

"Ms. Lewis," said the Judge, indicating it was No Limits' turn.

No Limits stood up with a yellow legal pad in her hand and walked behind the prosecution table to the far end of the jury box. Of medium height, bespectacled, with sandy blonde hair, very slender, almost gaunt, she didn't look like the epitome of evil she had become in Marcia's mind.

No Limits put her pad down on the low wall separating the jury box from the rest of the courtroom, studied her notes for a few moments and began.

"Ms. Banning, you mentioned that Dr. Sullivan lived in Point Loma. You know that because you were at his house when you were dating, weren't you?"

A: We drove by and he pointed out where he lived. I never went inside.

Q: Now, with respect to these alleged "drive-bys," you mentioned Dr. Sullivan's Corvette?

A: Yes, a red one.

Q: A small car, built low to the ground?

A: Yes.

Q: How tall are you Ms. Banning?

A: Almost five ten.

Q: When you would see this red Corvette go by, would you usually be standing outside your house?

A: Usually standing or walking in the neighborhood; playing catch with Matt once or twice. A couple times I saw him out my front window.

Q: So, given your height, relative to the low-slung red Corvette, it would have been impossible for you to see who was inside the car?

A: Sometimes yes, sometimes no. I actually saw Dr. Sullivan in the car on some occasions when he drove past.

Q. Dr. Sullivan's car isn't the only red Corvette you've ever seen, is it?

A. Probably not, although I don't specifically remember any others.

Q: So what you were really seeing on most, if not all of these occasions was just a red Corvette driving by your house, not necessarily Dr. Sullivan?

A: No, it was Bill ... Dr. Sullivan. I know, because even if I didn't see him, I saw that Wyoming license plate he has.

Q: Anyway, on no occasion during any of these alleged "drive-byes" did Dr. Sullivan ever stop?

A: That's right.

Q: He never said anything to you?

A: No, he didn't.

Q: He was just driving down your street.

A: Yes.

Q: Never bothered you enough to do anything about it.

A: Like I said earlier, I considered doing something, but never did.

Q: So your answer is, "No it never bothered me that much."

A: I suppose it is.

Q: When you and Dr. Sullivan were dating, did you ever discuss physical fitness?

A: I don't recall one way or the other.

Q: Dr. Sullivan was very physically fit throughout the time you were dating, wasn't he?

A: If you mean during those ten days three years ago, the answer is, I don't have any idea of his fitness level. He looked reasonably fit.

Q: Now, just a few days before last November 8 you saw Dr. Sullivan at the Von's grocery store, didn't you?

Marcia paused and looked down at her lap, thinking back. She knew the answer was "yes." So far, No Limits had asked her no questions Mike hadn't already asked in their hours of drills except for the thing about Sullivan's physical fitness. Marcia took a deep breath and looked up.

A: Yes, I think so. I did see him at the grocery store one time, and it was probably not too long before that weekend, because I think on that occasion I was there to buy Matt something he wanted to take to eat on his camping trip. I didn't speak to him, I mean Dr. Sullivan, but I did see him.

At the prosecution table, Whitey groaned in silence. Marcia was volunteering, instead of just answering the question and waiting for him to fill in the blanks on redirect - the temptation of every witness,

Q: You're sure you didn't talk to him?

A: Positive.

Q: Ms. Banning, think very hard. You not only spoke to Dr. Sullivan, you invited him to dinner the following Saturday evening, didn't you?

A: I certainly did not.

Q: Maybe this will help you remember. When did you and this fellow Taggart first start to date?

A: June, 1974.

Q: So by November of the following year, the two of you had been dating for about sixteen months?

A: Approximately.

Q: By the time November 1975 rolled around, how long had the two of you been sleeping together?

"Objection." Whitey was on his feet. "Relevance."

"What's the relevance, Counsel?" Judge Kagara asked No Limits

"Your Honor," No Limits began, "the defense maintains…"

"Your Honor," Whitey interrupted, "If Ms. Lewis is going to give a speech, can it at least be at side bar?"

"Very well, Mr. Malinzak. Counsel will approach the bench."

Marcia sat there while the lawyers conferred with the Judge. She was so happy Law School Rhonda had foreseen No Limits' strategy, thereby enabling Marcia to have a weekend of practice with Mike to steel herself against the emotional impact of such questions.

After a few moments the lawyers headed back to their respective tables.

"The prosecution's objection has been overruled. The reporter will re-read the question," the Judge announced.

The reporter read the question.

A: I think the first time we slept together was sometime in October, 1974.

Q: So, by November, 1975, you and this Taggart were pretty deeply involved?

A: Yes.

Q: You were very much in love with him.

A: Yes.

Q: And he with you?

A: I certainly think so.

Q. You had introduced him to your son?

A. Yes, he had been Matt's first Little League coach. That's how we met.

Q: Your son loved him?

A. Absolutely.

Q. You wanted to get married.

A: Yes, I did.

Q: But this Taggart didn't want to?

A: I'm not sure I agree with that.

Q: Well, you discussed your wish to get married with him, didn't you?

A: Yes.

Q: Several times?

A: Yes.

Q: And he was unwilling to marry you.

A: That's not quite right. I'll be happy to explain if you wish.

Q: The bottom line is that you said, in substance, "Taggart, let's get married," and he did not agree?

A: That's true.

Q: He didn't respond by proposing?

A: No.

Q: And he still hasn't?

A: No.

Q: So, after getting nowhere discussing the subject of marriage with Mr. Taggart, when you saw Dr. Sullivan in the grocery store, you decided to change tactics and make Taggart jealous by inviting Dr. Sullivan for dinner on the coming Saturday evening - November 8?

A: No. Absolutely not.

Q: You and Dr. Sullivan were sitting in your front room having coffee on that Saturday night, when Mr.Taggart showed up?

A: No.

Q: Taggart became angry?

A. No.

Q: Instead of proposing to you, this Taggart attacked Dr. Sullivan and beat him up?

A: No.

Q: He broke Dr. Sullivan's nose?

Whitey was on his feet again. "Your Honor, the issue here is who broke in to this woman's house, not the extent of Dr. Sullivan's injuries, if any. This is irrelevant."

"Overruled."

A: Bill's nose bled some, but I don't know that it was broken.

Q: Taggart separated Dr. Sullivan's shoulder?

A: I wouldn't know.

Q: Once Dr. Sullivan was lying there bleeding on your floor, you saw that your plan had backfired?

A: I had no plan.

Q: You feared Dr. Sullivan would call the police on your boyfriend?

A: No.

Q: You knew that wouldn't increase the chances of him marrying you?

A: No such thought ever entered my mind.

Q: You and your boyfriend decided to call the police yourselves and say Dr. Sullivan was the intruder?

A: We never made any such decision until Bill Sullivan broke into my house and started screaming at us as we slept, but yes, we called the police when that happened, because Bill Sullivan was the intruder.

Q: You tried to start a conversation as he lay there on your floor tied up and bleeding, didn't you?

A: I never said a word to him.

Q: You tried to apologize to Dr. Sullivan, didn't you?

A: No.

Q: Don't you think you should apologize to him now?

"Objection," Whitey said, throwing down his pencil.

"I'll withdraw the question," No Limits said before the Judge had a chance to rule. "I have no further questions."

"Mr. Malinzak, redirect?"

"Yes, Your Honor.

Q: Ms. Banning, in response to a question by Ms. Lewis, you offered to explain to her what Mr. Taggart responded when you told him you wanted to get married, but she didn't take you up on your offer. Will you tell the jury Mr. Taggart's response?

A: Mr. Taggart essentially said he loved me and Matt, and he wanted to get married, but that when he came back from Viet Nam, he'd been moody and brooding, and not a very good husband to his first wife, and that he wanted to make sure he'd overcome those feelings before getting married and becoming a father to Matt.

Q: How did you feel about that?

A: I believed he truly did love us and wanted to get married and become a dad to Matt, and that his determination to go slow was an act of unselfishness towards me and Matt, not towards himself. I told him to take his time.

"No further ... oh, one further question," Whitey said. Ms. Banning, did you ever introduce Dr. Sullivan to your son, Mathew?

A: No. Insofar as I am aware, Dr. Sullivan never even saw Matt unless it was during one of his drive-bys.

"No further questions, your Honor."

As Marcia walked out of the courtroom through the door Whitey was holding open, she heard him say, "Good job," under his breath. She shot Taggart a glance as he walked past her, and he smiled in return on his way through and on to the witness stand.

Mike echoed Marcia's account of being startled into sudden wakefulness by the tall man silhouetted in the dark, more a shadow than a physical presence looming at the foot of the bed. He described how he didn't want to antagonize Sullivan until he could see whether he was carrying a weapon, attacking as soon as he saw

Sullivan was unarmed. "Are you some kind of martial arts guy?" Whitey asked.

A: No, I'm not. I wouldn't know a judo chop from a pork chop.

Taggart told of the firmness of Marcia's reaction at the outset, brandishing her ball bat, ready for action and of her tremors and tears when it was over, once the police had taken Sullivan away.

Then it was No Limits' turn. She resumed her place at end of the jury box, as close to the jury as she could get.

A: Mr. Taggart, you'd been dating Ms. Banning about sixteen months as of November 8, 1975, correct?"

A: Yes.

Q: The two of you dated steadily – neither seeing anybody else romantically?

A: That's right.

Q: The two of you were sleeping together?

A: Now and then.

Q: "Now and then?" C'mon Mr. Taggart, two healthy young people seeing only each other for sixteen months, you were spending the night together more than just "now and then," weren't you?

Whitey stood halfway up to object, caught a "Sit Down and Shut Up" glance from Taggart and resumed his seat without saying anything.

A: Well, Ms. Lewis, I didn't keep track, but it wasn't often. Ms. Banning has an eight-year-old son, and we both agreed he wasn't going to wake up and find me at the breakfast table unless and until his mom and I were married.

Q: Speaking of marriage, Ms. Banning had told you that she wanted the two of you to get married on at least one occasion before November 8?

A: Yes, we had had that conversation.

Q: She'd also told you her son wanted you to be his dad?

A: Yes.

Q: She said she loved you?

A: Yes.

Q: And that Matt loved you?

A: Yes.

Q: But you refused to get married?

A: At that time, yes.

Q: "At that time?" The two of you still aren't married, are you?

A: No, we're not.

Q: Not engaged?

A: No, not engaged.

Q: You haven't proposed?

A: No.

Q: Now, I'm going to ask you a series of questions about the night in question, and before answering, I want to remind you that you're under oath. You understand that, don't you?

A: Yes.

Q: You understand what being under oath means?

A: Yes, I believe I do.

Q: It means that you have sworn to tell the truth. Is that your understanding?

A: Yes, that's my understanding.

Q: Good, now, keeping that in mind, on the night of Saturday, November 8, you went over to Ms. Banning's home about eleven p.m.?

A: No, I had been there since around nine that morning when I came over to help Matt get ready to go camping.

Q: When you arrived at the Banning house, you saw Dr. Sullivan's car parked outside?

A: No.

Q: You knew what Dr. Sullivan's car looked like, didn't you?

A: Yes.

Q: When you saw Dr. Sullivan's car, you decided to let yourself in instead of ringing the bell, didn't you?

A: Nothing like that happened.

Q: You had a key to Ms. Banning's house, didn't you?

A: Yes.

Q: When you entered the house, you found Ms. Banning and Dr. Sullivan sitting on the couch in the living room drinking coffee"

A: Nothing like that happened.

Q: You felt betrayed?

A: No.

Q: When you and Ms. Banning had discussed marriage, she had told you to take your time?

A: Yes.

Q: Yet here she was with this guy that she'd formerly dated, some doctor.

A: Is that a question?

Q: Did that make you angry, finding the two of them like that after having been told you should not feel as if you needed to hurry up and decide whether to get married?

A: Nothing like that ever happened.

No Limits was just using these questions to get Sullivan's version in front of the jury one more time, notwithstanding the denials, an old tactic of hers. Whitey could object, but he and Taggart had discussed what to do in case she tried it and decided to let Mike handle it with simple, straightforward denials. Better that than to keep objecting and appear to the jurors as if they were trying to keep some damaging piece of evidence from them.

Q: In a rage, you hit Dr. Sullivan in the face and knocked him down?

A: No.

Q: Do you deny breaking Dr. Sullivan's nose?

A: I don't know whether his nose broke when he hit the floor. He landed kind of face first when I took him down. Like I said earlier, his nose bled some, but not too much. I never touched his face.

Q: You also separated Dr. Sullivan's shoulder, didn't you?

A: I have no idea.

Q: You had his left arm wrenched behind his back in what is called a "hammerlock," didn't you?

A: Yes.

Q: As you were holding him down, you threatened to break Dr. Sullivan's "fucking neck?"

A: He was thrashing around trying to get away, and I told him if he didn't stop I'd break his neck.

Q: "I'll break your fucking neck" were the words you actually used, weren't they?

A: Could be. Like I said, I was angry.

"Yes," No Limits replied, "We both agree on that."

Q: If Dr. Sullivan escaped before you called the police, you were afraid he would report you to the police for beating him up?

A: That thought never entered my mind.

Q: You knew if you were convicted of assault and battery, you might lose your license to practice law?

A: The possibility of me being charged with anything never entered my mind.

Q: If you lost your license, that would have a serious affect on your career prospects, wouldn't it?

A: Sure.

Q: You might have to go back to being a southern sheriff?

Taggart laughed. "Ms. Lewis, I think my days in law enforcement are long over."

Q: You told Mr. Malinzak that you didn't know "a judo chop from a pork chop," did I get that right?

A: Yes, I think those were my words.

Q: But you aren't quite the neophyte at hand to hand combat that remark suggests, are you? You were a wrestler in college?

A: No.

Q: Are you telling me that you weren't a competitive wrestler?

A: It was high school, not college. I wrestled in high school.

Q: You had hand-to-hand combat training in the Marine Corps?

A: Yes, some.

Q: You fought in Viet Nam.

A: Yes, although never hand to hand. *Thank heaven*

Q: You were a southern sheriff back in the sixties during the civil rights era?

A: I was a deputy sheriff in North Carolina while I was in law school. My primary duty was to operate the short wave radio in the office during the night.

Q: You received self-defense training when you became a sheriff?

A: Some.

Q: You received training how to subdue suspects?

A: Some.

Q: You went out on patrol from time to time?

A: From time to time.

Q: You broke up demonstrations?

A: I helped break up some fights that occurred during demonstrations, but never the demonstrations themselves.

Q: You were one of those guys in big hats we saw on television beating up civil rights demonstrators?

"OBJECTION. NO FOUNDATION. ARGUMENTATIVE."

"Sustained," Judge Kitigawa immediately ruled. "Ms. Lewis, approach the bench."

"Ms. Lewis," the Judge hissed in a whisper loud enough for the last juror in the back row of the jury box to hear, "I've let you go on with these unfounded questions because you claim you will be able to support them later, and because they don't appear to be upsetting opposing counsel. But that last question and any like it have no place in this trial, and if I hear another, you will be found in contempt. Do I make myself clear?"

"Yes, Your Honor."

Mike could hear the entire exchange. No Limits didn't sound particularly chagrined.

"Do you have any further questions of this witness?"

"No, Your Honor."

"Very well. Mr. Malinzak, redirect?"

"Yessir. Mr. Taggart, you have stated that the fear of being reported by Dr. Sullivan to the police played no part in your determination not to let Dr. Sullivan escape. Why were you so determined not to let him escape?"

Mike turned to the jury. "This guy had been hovering on the edge of Matt and Marcia's lives and mine too, indirectly, for a long time, years, a threatening shadow. Now, at last, he had finally overplayed his hand. However, if he got away, he could still contend nothing ever happened, and it would only be our word against his. But there he was on the floor of Marcia's bedroom at two a.m. Let him explain that if he could. So we needed to keep him there until the police arrived."

"No further questions."

"Ms. Lewis, any cross?" the Judge inquired.

"No, your Honor."

"Very well. The witness is excused. Call your next witness, Mr. Malinzak."

Whitey called Detective Barnes, one of the arresting officers, who described the scene at Marcia's house when he arrived, including the time of arrival, Sullivan tied up on the bedroom floor, the rumpled covers on the bed, the fresh bloodstains on the floor of the bedroom in the vicinity of where Sullivan was lying, the broken garage window, the glass on the floor of the garage indicating it had been broken from the outside, and how Sullivan had complained of pain in his nose and shoulder, which caused the officers to take him to the emergency room for examination en route to the station.

On cross, No Limits began by establishing that Barnes and Mike Taggart had been stationed at the same base in Viet Nam at the same time. She then pointed out that Barnes had not seen how Sullivan came to be in the bedroom, had not seen who broke the window, had no first hand knowledge of what time Sullivan arrived at the Banning house or how he came to be in the bedroom, having only Marcia's and Mike's word for whatthem happened. She also established that although Barnes had observed no blood stains as he walked through the living room and hall, he hadn't specifically checked for blood stains anywhere except the bedroom.

With a flourish, No Limited crossed out the entire page of notes on the yellow pad she carried, as if Detective Barnes had just made her case for her. "No Further questions."

The prosecution rested.

20

Monday, October 4, 1976 - Afternoon

"For its first witness," No Limits said in a voice vibrant with energy, as if she couldn't wait to begin telling Sullivan's side of the story, "the Defense calls Dr. William Sullivan."

Having been excused as witnesses, Mike and Marcia could both be in the courtroom for Sullivan's testimony, but No Limits had refused to release Matt from his subpoena. Whitey decided Marcia was more likely to spot some detail of Sullivan's testimony that was vulnerable to impeachment than Mike because of her greater involvement with him, so Mike and Matt continued to wait in the corridor when court reconvened.

Now Marcia, sitting beside Whitey at counsel table, watched as Sullivan stood to take the oath - tall, at least 6'4", dressed in the dark blue uniform of a naval officer, his Lieutenant Commander's rank prominent on his sleeve and collar, a single row of ribbons over his right breast pocket. Black hair slicked back, pale complexion slightly scarred by acne, watery blue eyes, he made Marcia think of a snake.

"Please state your name and address," No Limits began.

A: William Shakespeare Sullivan, 467 Catalina Court, San Diego, California 92106.

Q: What is your occupation?

A: I am a doctor, a physician.

Q: Do you have a specialty?

A: General surgeon.

Q: Where do you practice?

A: Balboa Navy Hospital. I am a lieutenant commander in the Navy.

Q: When did you enlist in the Navy?

A: I enlisted in Naval ROTC while I was an undergraduate at the University of Wyoming and was commissioned upon graduation in 1964. However, I had been accepted to medical school, so I went on what is known as "extended leave" during my medical training. I did not go on active duty until April, 1974.

Q: Where did you do your training, Dr. Sullivan?

A: I went to undergraduate school at the University of Wyoming in Laramie, medical school at Washington University in St. Louis, Missouri. I performed my general residency at University of Colorado Hospital in Aurora, Colorado, a suburb of Denver, and my surgical residency at Scripps Hospital in La Jolla.

Q: Are you married?

A: No, … never.

Q: Dr. Sullivan, before we go one step further in this trial, let me ask, did you break into Marcia Banning's home on November 9, 1975?

A: No, I did not.

Q: Did you ever break into Marcia Banning's home?

A: No, I did not.

Q: Fine. Now that we have that firmly established, how did you and Marcia Banning meet?

Whitey glanced over at Marcia and shook his head. The gratuitous "firmly established" remark was classic No Limits, objectionable, but, unless it became more frequent and abusive, unworthy of objecting.

A: We met at a dinner party given by mutual friends, Len and Candy Marston.

Q: When was that party?

A: Approximately April, 1973.

Q: Was there a particular occasion for the party?

A: I had just arrived in San Diego. It was kind of a "Welcome Aboard" party for me.

Q: When did you and Ms. Banning first begin to date?

A: I guess you could say it began at that party. We were seated next to each other and began to talk, and Marcia offered to show me around town.

Sullivan hadn't been on the stand five minutes and already Marcia was fuming. "Keep a poker face, no matter what he says," Mike had commanded. "The jurors tend not to like much emotion on the sidelines. They resent the distraction."

Easier said than done. She hadn't "offered" to show Sullivan around town; he had asked her to do it. She supposed it was a meaningless detail, but suspected it was only a small sample of what was to come.

Q: How long after this dinner party before the two of you first went out together?

A: Oh, we went out the next day. It was a Sunday. Marcia gave me the grand tour from Torrey Pines Park to the Hotel Del. We had a wonderful time. We had dinner at a restaurant on the Bay. Being from Wyoming, I'm kind of a landlubber despite being in the Navy, so being near the water was a great new experience.

Q: How often did you date after that?

A: We dated pretty steadily for about a year, or at least as steadily as a surgical residency will allow. I was committed a lot of nights, weekends and holidays, and, of course, Marcia was working during the week and she had a young son. So, our opportunities were somewhat limited.

Q: Did you ever go out with other couples?

A: Once or twice, but not often because of my schedule. Usually it was just the two of us. Sometimes we did things with Matt, Marcia's son.

Whitey, who was listening intently, felt a nudge. Glancing in Marcia's direction, he saw the note she had pushed in front of him.

"He NEVER met Matt!!"

Q: With what other couples did you and Marcia go out?

A: I remember introducing her to my parents when they came to visit. We all went out to dinner.

Q: Where do your folks live?

A: They lived in Wyoming, in Lander, but they've both passed away now.

Whitey groaned. Of course, the one couple who can't be called to impeach him.

Q: What sorts of things did you and Marcia do with her son?

A: Well, once we went to a Padre game. Another time the three of us just went to the park across the street from her house for a picnic.

Q: Did you and Ms. Banning ever travel together?

A: No.

Q: You say you dated for about a year starting in May of 1973. What happened at the end of that year?

A: Marcia and I went out to dinner one night in June, 1974, and she told me she had met someone else and no longer wanted to go out with me. She was very nice about it – said she hoped we would always be friends.

Q: So, she dumped you?

A: I guess you could say that. I didn't think of it that way. I just thought it was one of those things that happens to people in the single world.

Q: In favor of whom?

A: She told me his name was Mike. I assume it was Michael Taggart, the fellow who testified this morning – the man who beat me up.

Q: Did you ever meet him?

A: Not before that evening in November last year, when he beat me up.

Q: How would you describe your relationship with Ms. Banning just before she broke up with you? Were you romantically involved?

A: I thought I was in love with her.

Q: Can you be more specific regarding the nature of your relationship – to what extent had you become physically involved?

A: There were lots of kisses, not just hello or good-bye, but long loving ones, but we never went further than that. I knew dating was hard for her after her husband was killed and that I was about the first guy she had gone out with. I didn't want to go any faster than she wanted to go.

A second note from Marcia. "UGH!!"

Q: After you and Ms. Banning broke up, how often did you drive past her house?

A: Maybe once or twice. Certainly, no more than that.

Q: Why did you drive by on those one or two occasions?

A: Well, I admit I was disappointed when she broke up with me. So, a couple of times on my way to the Y to work out, I did a little detour down her street just to see if she was outside.

Q: Did you ever see Ms. Banning?

A. On one occasion, but she was working in her flowerbed on her hands and knees with her back to me. I'm sure she didn't see me.

Q: Did you ever call her for dates after the two of you broke up?

A: I did call her a few times, like once when someone gave me tickets to a play at the Old Globe Theater. I knew she really liked live theater; she had showed the Globe to me on our tour of the City, so I took a chance. But she turned me down.

Q: How many times is "a few?"

A: I don't know the exact number. Maybe ten.

Q: Ever call and hang up when she answered?

A: Never.

Q: Did Ms. Banning ever call you?

A: Now and then she would call me just to talk. Once she called me at home in the middle of the night when Matt was sick and she couldn't reach her regular pediatrician. I called in a prescription for her. Another time she called and talked about how she wanted to get married, but how this guy Mike didn't want to.

Note to Whitey: "I NEVER CALLED HIM!!"

Q: How many times did she call you between the time the two of you broke up and the night of November 8, 1975?

A: I didn't keep track, but maybe a dozen. Sometimes the calls were pretty brief, just a few minutes. Sometimes they lasted an hour or more – you know, just catching up.

Q: Did you ever get the impression she was stringing you along?

A: Not back then, but in retrospect it kind of seems like that … Oh, can I add something to an earlier answer? I also called Marcia to tell her that my mom had died. Marcia had met her, and they really seemed to have hit it off on that occasion. They always asked about each other when they talked to me.

Q: So that's all you called her after the break up, approximately ten times?

A: Yes, best estimate.

No Limits paused and turned a couple pages of the legal pad on the table in front of her, lining out whatever she had written on them as she did so.

Q: Okay, Dr. Sullivan, let's turn to the evening of November 8, 1975. Where were you that night?

A: I was at Marcia's house. She had invited me for dinner. I arrived a little after seven.

Q: When did she invite you?

A: A couple of days before, when we bumped into each other at the Von's grocery store in downtown La Jolla. We talked briefly, and then she asked me to come over for dinner. She said Matt would be away that weekend, and we would have plenty of time to chat. I think those were her exact words.

Q: What did she say about her boyfriend?

A: She didn't say anything.

Q: Did you ask?

A: No. I was just happy to be able to see her again, whatever the circumstances.

Q: Describe your evening together.

A: Well, it was all very innocent. The table was already set when I arrived. Before we sat down to the meal, we had a cocktail. I think we drank it in the kitchen, because she was still putting the finishing touches on the meal.

Q: What did you have to eat?

A: She fixed leg of lamb. She remembered that was my favorite. We had some green beans and mashed potatoes and gravy and dessert, I think it was some kind of lemon tart.

Another note. "UNBELIEVABLE!!"

Q: What did you do after dinner?

A: I helped her clear the table. I offered to help with the dishes, but she said she'd take care of them later. We had lingered quite a while at the table, and I said something about it being about time for me to leave, but Marcia insisted I stay for a cup of coffee. So we went back in the living room to drink our coffee.

Q: What happened next?

A: Right in the midst of our coffee, Mr. Taggart barged in. I heard the front door opening and when I looked up, there he was.

Q: What did he do?

A: He came walking up to me clenching and unclenching his fists. I had stood up and was standing between him and Marcia. He looked at her over my shoulder and shouted, "Get him out of here!"

Q: Then what happened?

A: I started to tell him to calm down, but before I could get the words out of my mouth, he hit me right in the nose. I stumbled backwards and bumped into the coffee table and lost my balance. Before I could regain it, he tackled me and drove me face first down onto the floor with him on top of me. He had my left arm jerked up behind my back and one of his forearms bearing down on the back of my neck just at the base of my skull. He said he was going to "break my fucking neck."

Q: What did you do?

A: There wasn't much I could do. I asked him to let me up, but he didn't respond to that. Marcia said something like, "Mike, what are you doing?" But all he said was for her to get something to tie me up while they decided what to do with me.

Q: What did Ms. Banning say to that?

A: She hesitated, but he said he'd explain in a minute. Then she left the room and came back with a shoestring, and he tied me up.

Q: How did he tie you up?

A: First he tied my thumbs together. Then he took off my shoes and socks and tied my big toes together and then jerked my legs up and tied my toes to my thumbs. Once he was satisfied that I was tied good and tight and wouldn't get away, he said to Marcia to come with him in the other room for a minute. I tried to free myself, but it was no use. When they came back in, he dragged me into Marcia's bedroom to the foot of the bed. Marcia held the door for him. I think she was crying.

Q: What happened after they took you in the bedroom?

A: Not much. One of them, I don't remember which one, but I think it was Marcia, tried to stop my nose from bleeding, but it was too painful to even touch. Once Mr. Taggart asked Marcia where he could find a bucket and then went out of the room for a few minutes. I think he was trying to wash the blood out of the carpet in the living room and maybe the hall. While he was gone, I begged Marcia to untie me, but she said she couldn't. I asked her why, and she said she was sorry, that she had never intended for anything like this to happen."

When Mr. Taggart came back, I tried to ask him to untie me, but he just told me to "shut up" or he'd put a gag in my mouth. Mostly, we all three sat there saying nothing. I asked for water, and Marcia got me a glass with a straw so I could drink while lying on my stomach.

Q: How long were you in the bedroom?

A: A long time. I think it was after two o'clock when they called the police, and Mr. Taggart had arrived sometime around ten.

Q: Did you hear the call to the police?

A: Yes. Marcia used the phone on her nightstand.

Q: What did she tell the police?

A: That someone had broken into her house, but they had caught him, obviously meaning me, and would the police come. Apparently, the police said they would be there within ten minutes, because that's what she told Taggart after she hung up.

Q: What happened when the police arrived?

A: The first thing that happened was one of the officers, the one who testified right before lunch, said "Hi, Mike," to Mr. Taggart.

Q: Did you hear any other small talk between of them?

A: No, but they left the room together for a few minutes at one point. I don't know what they said to each other during that time.

Q: Did you hear what Mr. Taggart and Ms. Banning told the police about the reason for their call?

A: They ... I mean Marcia and Taggart told the police pretty much the same story you heard them tell this morning on the stand. The police untied me and put on the handcuffs and read me my rights and took me away.

Q: Did you say anything to the police?

A: I told them I didn't need a lawyer and that they were arresting the wrong guy.

Q: What was their response?

A: They didn't say anything, just put the cuffs on me.

Q: Did you say anything else to them?

A: Just told them my nose was broken and I thought my shoulder was separated.

Q: So you were injured when Mr. Taggart attacked you?

A: Yes. The police took me to the emergency room at Scripps, and it turned out I was right. I had a broken nose and a separated shoulder, just as I suspected.

Q: How long were you in jail?

A: About five hours once we got back from the hospital. I called my commanding officer, Captain Frank, and she arranged for my release.

Q: Have you had any contact with either Ms. Banning or Mr. Taggart since this incident?

A: No. After thinking about it for a long time I decided I wanted to talk to Marcia and let her know I forgive her for what she's done, but you told me not to.

Whitey was on his feet. "Objection, relevance."

"Sustained. The jury will disregard the witnesses' last answer."

"I have no further questions, Your Honor." No Limits sat down.

The ball was now in Whitey's court, and he wasn't at all sure what to do with it. He knew the methods of cross-examination as well as he knew his own face in a mirror, but the cardinal rule of questioning was to ask no question to which you did not already know the answer, whether from another source or by exercise of logic. By asking Sullivan to supply details of his fantasy account, Whitey might only be providing Sullivan the opportunity to cement his version in the jurors' minds by demonstration of his so-called "facts." Sullivan could say anything, and Whitey had no independent sources with which to impeach him – only Mike and

Marcia's denials. As Rhonda had said, it was a swearing contest plain and simple.

Betraying no hint of his misgivings, Whitey stood up without the least hesitation when No Limits sat down. He would wade slowly into the water and hope to find a place to dive.

"Your witness, Mr. Malinzak," said the Judge.

"Thank you, Your Honor. Dr. Sullivan, what is your home telephone number?

A: It's unlisted.

Q: Dr. Sullivan, what is your home telephone number?

Sullivan hesitated, staring at Whitey.

"The witness will answer the question," ruled Judge Kagara without Whitey having to request his assistance.

Q: Do you understand the question, Dr. Sullivan?

A: Yes, of course, I understand the question. My number is 619 225 3131.

Q: You knew Mathew Banning, Ms. Banning's son for approximately one year?

A.: Yes.

Q: You say you went on several outings with him?

A: Yes.

Q: How old was Mathew at the time of these outings?

A: Eight or nine. I don't specifically remember.

Q: What color hair did he have?

A: Brown.

Q: What was the name of Ms. Banning's late husband?

A: I don't remember.

Q: You say Ms. Banning called you for help when her son was sick?

A: Yes.

Q: She just called you on one occasion regarding Mathew's illness?

A: I only recall one time. She may have called again to let me know he was getting better. I'm a little foggy about that.

Q: What was wrong with Mathew on the occasion of her call? What did she say his symptoms were?

A: I'm not sure. I think it was an earache.

Q: Did he have a fever?

A: I believe he did.

Q: What did you prescribe?

A: Probably some antibiotic. I'm not sure which one.

Q: You wrote this prescription without actually examining Mathew?

A: Yes.

Q: Isn't that a violation of medical ethics?

A: I did it out of friendship for Marcia.

Q: You allowed your interest in Ms. Banning override your ethical obligations?

A: Yes, I suppose I did.

Q: You have a record of this prescription, don't you?

A: Probably not.

Q: You're aware that California law requires a record to be kept of all prescriptions you write?

A: Yes.

Q: This call you say Ms. Banning made regarding her son's illness, it was in the middle of the night?

A: Yes.

Q: After midnight?

A: Yes?

Q: After two a.m.

A: Around that time.

Q: You called the prescription into a drug store for her?

A: I beg your pardon?

Q: Ms. Banning didn't come over to your house and pick up the prescription, did she? You called it in to her drug store?

A: Oh, I see what you mean. Yes, I did. I called it in.

Q: To what drug store did you call it in?

Sullivan paused. "I … I don't remember."

Q: Well, it must have been an all-night drug store if you called it in in the middle of the night, correct?

A: Of course.

Q: Does that help you remember? There aren't many pharmacies open all night.

Two could play the gratuitous remark game. Whitey sneaked a sideways glance at No Limits, who made no reaction.

A: No, it doesn't help me remember.

"May I have a moment, your Honor?" Whitey asked, leafing through his notes. Was he missing anything? He didn't think he had scored many points and he didn't have much left.

"Take your time, Mr. Malinzak," replied Judge Kagara, that rare breed of judge who remembered what it was like to be a trial lawyer.

Whitey crossed out the areas of examination he had already covered. There was nothing else remaining on the page.

"No further questions."

"Any further questions, Ms. Lewis?"

"Yes, Your Honor."

Q: Dr. Sullivan, why didn't you keep a record of the prescription you wrote for Matthew Banning?

A: You know, it didn't even occur to me. As a surgeon, I'm rarely write prescriptions for patients. Other doctors usually take care of that. This call came out of the blue in the middle of the night.

Q: You weren't trying to hide anything?

A: No. If I was, would I have mentioned it here today?

Q: Why didn't you say more when the police ignored your protest that they had the wrong guy?

A: I could see they were on this guy Taggart's side. Both officers appeared to know him. They told me I needed a lawyer. When they ignored me, I decided they were right. So I shut up.

"No further questions.

No Limits' next called a character witness, Captain Margaret Frank, Sullivan's commanding officer. According to Captain Frank, Sullivan had what it took to be the next Surgeon General of the United States. Not only was he a terrific surgeon, but someone who made life and death decisions daily. Sullivan's judgment was such that, if Captain Frank needed surgery, she would go to him. She observed him on an almost daily basis and, in her opinion, the man was gentle and non-confrontational.

On cross-examination, Whitey established that Frank's opinion of Sullivan as a surgeon was based on hearsay. She was not a surgeon herself, nor had she ever observed Sullivan perform surgery. With the exception of semi-annual meetings when she gave him his fitness reports, Frank's opportunities to observe him consisted almost entirely of saying "Hello" as they passed in corridors. Upon being told Sullivan had just admitted writing a prescription for a patient he'd never examined and then failed to record it, Captain Frank conceded that she wondered what other lapses of judgment he'd committed.

Q: In a manner of speaking, Captain, the failure to make a record of a prescription is a way to cover up having written it. Do you agree?

A: Yes.

Q: A falsehood by omission?

A: Yes, assuming the failure to record wasn't just an oversight.

Q: Alternatively, the failure to record a prescription might suggest no such prescription was ever written?

A: What do you mean?

Q: I mean, if Dr. Sullivan was lying about ever having written the prescription in the first place, that would explain his failure to make any record of it, isn't that right?

A: I can't imagine Dr. Sullivan would ever do that.

Q: Because if he did, that would be perjury? Whitey came down hard on the last word of his question, attempting to drive the thought into the minds of the jurors.

"Objection. Argum—"

"Sustained."

"No further questions," Whitey's exasperated tone suggested Captain Frank's entire testimony had been a waste of everyone's time. Captain Frank stood and walked off the witness stand, seeming to look away from Sullivan as she passed.

Judge Kagara said., "Call your next witness, Ms. Lewis."

"Your Honor, the defense calls Mathew Banning."

"Your Honor," Whitey was on his feet, "may we approach the bench to confer regarding the next witness?"

"Is this the witness who was the subject of your pretrial motion, Mr. Malinzak?"

"Yes Sir, it is."

"Very well, counsel may approach."

Once assembled on the side of the Judge's bench, away from the jury box with the court reporter hovering with her stenograph Judge Kagara spoke. "All right, Ms. Lewis, what can this witness add that has not already been fully addressed by other witnesses?"

"Motive, Your Honor. Ms. Banning has admitted she wanted to marry Mr. Taggart, and he was dragging his feet, but I have reason to believe her son will testify that she had promised him she and Taggart would get married. This would give her added incentive beyond her own romantic feelings to do something to get Taggart to pop the question. It reinforces the inference that she invited Dr. Sullivan to dinner to make Taggart jealous. How could she make such a promise to a child without a plan?"

"Mr. Malinzak," the Judge turned his head in Whitey's direction, "what do you have to say?"

"What's the basis for her belief such a promise was ever made? It's one thing to say this is what I think a witness will say and another to explain the basis for such belief. Unless Ms. Lewis can provide a source for her belief, what she's talking about is merely her speculation – certainly no basis to require an eight-year-old child to testify."

"Ms. Lewis?"

"Your Honor, this is not speculation. My investigator has spoken to two sources. Both told him Mathew Banning told them his mom promised she and Taggart were going to get married."

Judge Kagara sighed, and with that sigh Whitey knew he had lost. As the accused, Sullivan was entitled to the benefit of every reasonable doubt. Judge Kagara would never be reversed for allowing Matt to be called, but he might be reversed on appeal for preventing Matt from testifying.

"The government's objection is overruled. Call your witness, Ms. Lewis."

Matt and Mike were sitting on a bench directly across from the door to the courtroom when the bailiff opened the door and said, "Mathew Banning." They both stood up. Taggart gave Matt a sharp salute that Matt returned with equal precision. "Go get 'em, Matty."

Matt grinned at the echo of his advice to his mom, turned and disappeared into the courtroom. Mike collected the three comic books and the cards from their half-finished game of slap-jack and entered the courtroom. Matt, already seated, peered over the low rail in front of his chair, the knot in his tie barely visible. His back was straight and his hands were folded in his lap. Every eye in the courtroom was fixed on him.

"Matt," No Limits began, "my name is Sandra Lewis. I'm one of the lawyers in this case. I just want to ask you a few questions. Will you please tell us your full name?"

A: Mathew Timothy Banning.

Q: Do you know your address?

A: 2410 Martin Way.

Q: You live there with your mom, Marcia Banning?

A: Yes.

Q: Do you know a man named "Michael Taggart?"

A: No … wait a minute. You mean Coach?

Q: Your mom's friend?

A: Yeah.

Q: Do you know Coach's real name?

Matt hesitated, looking perplexed. "Mom calls him 'Mike'."

Whitey stood up. "Your Honor, the government will stipulate that the man Mathew calls "Coach" is Michael Taggart."

"Thank you, counsel. Proceed, Ms. Lewis."

Q: Did your mom ever tell you she loved Coach?

A: Yeah. We both do.

Q: She told you she and Coach were going to get married, didn't she?

A: I told her to marry him.

Q: What did she say about that?

A: She said that would be very nice.

No Limits had hoped she could coax the boy into saying his mom had said she and Taggart were going to get married. Any such statement by a mother to her son would be the equivalent of a promise, but so far the questioning wasn't quite going according to the script running through her mind. Any trial lawyer, no matter how inexperienced, could see this boy was a very likable witness, and No Limits was not inexperienced. Aware she was playing with fire, she decided to give it another try.

Q: You thought your mom and Coach were going to get married, didn't you?

A: Yes.

Q: You told other people they were going to get married, didn't you?

Matt looked at his mom sitting directly in front of him beside Whitey and then over her shoulder at Mike. His eyes widened and he grinned. "Yeah, I did."

Q: Because that was what your mom said was going to happen, wasn't it?

A: Not exactly.

Q: Not exactly?

No Limits bit her lower lip. She had committed a cardinal sin for a trial lawyer. She had let herself be carried away by the witnesses' story. Her question allowed Matt to give her an answer she did not want to hear. She wanted her last two words back, but not enough to withdraw the question, because she knew if she withdrew, Whitey would certainly fill in the blank. Better not to underscore the blunder in the minds of the jurors.

A: I told people that, because that's what I wanted to happen. I thought if I wished hard enough, I could make it happen.

Could this get any worse? No Limits didn't know how. Nevertheless, she plunged ahead, "Do you know the man seated over at that far table, the one with the red necktie?" No Limits pointed at Sullivan.

A: I don't know his name, but I've seen him before.

Q: At your house with your mom?

A: No. Over by the Y. He offered me a ride home one day.

Sitting behind Marcia, Taggart could see her stiffen.

No Limits had trained herself never to show surprise at an unexpected answer, but after that one, she paused for a moment and looked over at her client.

"Do you have any more questions of this witness, Ms. Lewis?" the Judge inquired?

"May I have just a minute, Your Honor?" She bent over her notes to hide her dismay. "I have lost my place."

"Matt," No Limits resumed in her gentlest tone, "even though you may not remember this man's name, you recognized him when he offered you a ride, didn't you?"

A: Yes.

Q: You had seen him lots of other times around your house?

A: Yes.

No Limits began to breathe easier.

Q: So he gave you a ride home?

A: No. I ran away.

Q: Ran away?

A: Mom told me to run away if someone I don't know offers me a ride.

The judge, clerk, bailiff, twelve jurors and an alternate, three casual spectators, Marcia and Mike, anything but casual, Whitey, Sullivan and No Limits were in the courtroom – twenty-four people, apart from Matt. In the wake of his last answer, not one of them made a sound. Finally, No Limits asked, "But you said you had seen him lots of other times around your house?"

A: Just in his car, the red one with the cowboy on the bucking bronco on the license plate. He used to drive by our house a lot.

Q: You must have told your mom about being offered this ride, didn't you?

A: No. She worries a lot. Nothing happened. I didn't want her to worry.

Why hadn't she stopped when he balked at saying his mother had promised she and Taggart would get married? Stupid lawyer's pride – the vanity of believing she could tease out the testimony she wanted from any witness, let alone an eight-year old.

Q: Matt, did you talk to your mom about this trial at all?

A: Yes.

Q: How about Mr. Taggart ... Coach, did you and Coach talk about the trial?

A: Yes.

Q: What did your mom tell you about the trial?

A: She said you would ask me a bunch of questions, and I should tell you the truth.

Q: Anything else?

A: No.

Q: What did Coach tell you?

A: He said we could stop for ice cream on the way home.

Amid the laughter of jurors and court personnel alike, including the Judge, No Limits sat down, but not for long. Whitey didn't ask a single question. If it ain't broke, don't fix it.

After conferring with her client briefly, No Limits announced, "The defense re-calls Dr. Sullivan to the stand."

Sullivan took the stand, and the Judge reminded him he was still under oath.

Q: Dr. Sullivan, how old was Mathew Banning when you and his mother were dating?

A: No more than five.

Q: Didn't you say earlier that you thought he was eight or nine at the time?

A: Yes, I was mistaken. I did the math in my head as I was sitting here listening to Matt testify, and obviously he couldn't have been that old when Marcia and I were dating.

Q: How many outings did you have with Matt when you and his mother were dating?

A: Two or three at the most.

Q: Did you see him on other occasions?

A: Never, or at least almost never. Not with Marcia. I do not recall seeing him with her other than on those two or three occasions.

Q: You just heard Mathew Banning's testimony about you having offered him a ride home from the Y?

A: Yes.

Q: How did you happen to offer him a ride?

A: Not long after Marcia and I stopped dating, I began to see Matt over at the Y all the time. It was just a few blocks away from his house. One day I pulled out of the parking lot and, there he was, lugging a backpack that looked like it weighed more than he did. I thought he would remember me, so I offered him a ride. I didn't even think about it.

Q: What was his response to your offer?

A: Just as I finished speaking, another boy called to him, and he ran off without saying anything.

Q: Did you ever see him walking in the vicinity on any other occasion?

A: Now and then I would see him at the Y or just outside.

Q: Did you ever offer him a ride home on any occasion other than the one you've described?

A: No.

"No further questions."

"Mr. Malinzak..."

"No questions, Your Honor."

"Call your next witness, Ms. Lewis."

"Your Honor, the defense rests."

"Any rebuttal witnesses, Mr. Malinzak?" the Judge inquired.

In rebuttal Whitey called Elaine Williamson, Pacific Telephone's document custodian, who produced copies of phone bills for the home numbers of Marcia and Sullivan for the twenty-month period from April, 1973, when Sullivan and Marcia met through November, 1975, the month Sullivan was accused of breaking into Marcia's house. Ms. Williamson testified her review of the records revealed no calls from Marcia's number to Sullivan's, zero. However, they did show sixty-one calls from Sullivan's number to Marcia's. Of those sixty-one calls, thirty-seven had occurred after June, 1974, the date Sullivan admitted he and Marcia were no longer seeing each other.

On cross, No Limits asked only whether Ms. Williamson had also been asked to bring the phone bills from Sullivan's and Marcia's offices, to which the witness replied, "No."

Following Ms. Williamson's testimony, the Prosecution rested and Judge Kagara ordered the afternoon recess.

21

Monday, October 4, 1976 – Mid-afternoon

At one minute after three, court having re-convened, Whitey stood up and began his final argument. "Your Honor," Whitey gave Judge Kigara a courtesy nod and turned to face the jury. "Ladies and gentlemen, could the opposing versions you have just heard be more completely at odds? Clearly, someone is lying to you, and it's your job to sort it out. How should you go about doing that?

"Here's my suggestion: first, look for a motive. Second, look for a predisposition to act on that motive." Whitey paused. "The evidence clearly shows Dr. Sullivan had both. As for motive, he admits he carries a torch for Marcia Banning. As for a willingness to act on that motive, the undisputed testimony is that he continued to call her and drive past her house in the mere hope of seeing her. Sounds like an obsession. Normal thirty-one-year old doctors don't moon around over unrequited loves. They get on with their lives. If Dr. Sullivan was so derailed by his love for Marcia Banning that he placed sixty-one calls to her and repeatedly drove past her house, it's no stretch to believe obsession motivated him to break into the Marcia's home that night.

"Nor is it a coincidence that he chose that particular night to break in. He'd driven past the Banning house so many times that Matt recognized his car. Sullivan certainly knew Marcia had become involved with Mike Taggart. He admits it. Marcia and Mike had been dating for several months, but this evening, November 8, was the first time Mike spent the night at her place, because Matt was away. When Sullivan drove past, sometime after midnight, and saw Taggart's car there, the thought of Mike Taggart being with Marcia, the place Sullivan so obsessively longed to be, was too much for him to bear. So, in he went.

"Of course, the accused denies it. He has no choice. Doctors who break into the homes in the middle of the night and accost people in their bed lose their license to practice medicine. Naval officers who behave like that are thrown out of the Navy. Dr. Sullivan has every motive in the world to lie to you.

"Lest there be any doubt of his untruthfulness, consider the objective evidence. Dr. Sullivan testified that after he and Marcia Banning stopped seeing each other, he called her perhaps ten times, and she called him approximately a dozen times. But what do the phone records say? They say the accused called Marcia Banning sixty-one times, and she didn't call him a single time, not even once. This discrepancy between Dr. Sullivan's version and the hard evidence of what really happened is the best signpost you have when trying to decide whom to believe.

"Then we come to the accused's claim to have written a prescription for Matt in response to Marcia's telephone plea in the wee hours one morning. A prescription he says he wrote, but failed to record. Even if you believe that happened, despite the telephone records telling you it did not, isn't it interesting that Sullivan admits his willingness to break the rules of his profession where Marcia Banning is concerned? An obsession with Marcia strong enough to cause him to violate his medical ethics, standards he has taken a solemn oath to uphold, is certainly strong enough to drive him to break that garage window and climb through, to prowl through the darkened house."

As Whitey began to describe Sullivan in the act, he crouched slightly, rose to his tiptoes and took a couple of tentative steps, looking to his right and left as he moved, slowing his speech and lowering his voice. "... to reach for the knob of the bedroom door and slowly open it, to step to the foot of the bed, to stand in the dark above the sleeping couple, ...'Get him out of here! Get him out of here!' Whitey paused and took a drink of water while letting the jurors imagine how it would feel to be awakened in the middle of the night by a screaming intruder.

After a moment he continued. "What does the accused offer you to buttress his version? First, we have Captain Frank, his commanding officer, who testified the accused is a good surgeon. Of course, on cross-examination we learned not only that Captain Frank is not a surgeon herself, but she has never even seen Dr. Sullivan perform surgery. Be that as it may, the important thing to remember is, the accused isn't on trial for being a bad surgeon, but for stalking, something his surgical skills have nothing whatsoever to do with. They are irrelevant. The fact that the accused is a doctor means only that he has license to practice medicine. Where is it written that doctors are somehow immune from human failings? Indeed, by the time Captain Frank finished testifying, she admitted she'd begun to doubt Sullivan's judgment.

"Captain Frank, weak as her testimony was, is what is known in the law as a 'character witness.' When you think about it, Marcia Banning and Mike Taggart also have such a witness. Ordinarily, witnesses for the prosecution, such as Ms. Banning and Mr. Taggart, don't have character witnesses on their behalf, but in this case, it has happened inadvertently.

"I'm speaking, of course, of Mathew Banning, who, while he said nothing directly regarding their characters, supported their strength of character most eloquently by what he did say and the way he said it.

"Mathew Banning, an eight-year-old boy, marched up to that witness stand, took the oath and told it like it is. He described Mike Taggart, a man who volunteered to coach a bunch of seven and eight year old little leaguers despite having no child of his own, someone who earned for himself a place in Mathew's life such that Matt could look a room full of adults, strangers, in the eye and tell them that, not only does his mom love Mike Taggart, but so does he. Ladies and gentlemen, the accused points to Mike Taggart's experience as a high school wrestler, a deputy sheriff, as a United States Marine, as if it makes him a monster. But the man Matt Banning loves is no monster. You don't earn the love of a guy like Matt Banning if you don't have the character to deserve it.

"Same goes for Marcia Banning – naturally Matt loves his mom, but consider the boy who sat there and testified so straightforwardly, so without self-consciousness - an honorable man in a child's body. Ladies and gentlemen, Marcia Banning has been the only parent Matt has ever known, and you don't mold a man such as he has already become with words alone. You do so by example, by the demonstration in yourself day in and day out of the kind of character you expect your child to become. It's no accident Matt Banning has become the person he most obviously is – he is a reflection of his mother.

"Marcia Banning and Mike Taggart don't have the kind of relationship that requires tricks to create commitment. They are unquestionably in love. They have discussed marriage like reasonable adults. Mike has explained his concern about his ability to be the kind of husband Marcia wants and father Matt needs because of "misgivings," for want of a better term, he brought back from Viet Nam. Marcia understands. She has her own legacy from the war.

"These two intelligent, unselfish people want the best for each other and Matt. They talk to each other about their thoughts and feelings. They understand each other. Contrary to what the accused would have you believe, they have no need to *trick* each other into commitment.

"Ladies and Gentlemen," Whitey held his arms out from his sides, "the scales of justice are more than a metaphor. They are a decision-making tool. On the one side of the scale you have the testimony of three fine people, Marcia, Matt and Mike, the presence of the accused trussed up on the blood-stained carpet of Marcia's bedroom at two a.m., a cascade of unwanted phone calls and drive-bys and a broken garage window. On the other side you have a license to practice medicine, a permission by the government to make a living as a doctor, nothing more, and a denial impeached by telephone records and the absence of blood anywhere but the bedroom. Upon consideration of all the evidence, I am sure you will agree with me, the author Robert Louis Stevenson got it right – Dr. Jekyll by day, Mr. Hyde, a monster, by night. Thank you for your attention."

No Limits stood and walked around the defense table to a position directly in front of the jury box. "Ladies and Gentlemen, it's getting late, and I won't take much of your time, not because there isn't a lot to be said on Dr. Sullivan's behalf, but because all that's necessary for you to find Dr. Sullivan 'not guilty' is for you to have a *reasonable doubt* regarding the truth of the charges against him. Now that you've had a day long opportunity to observe Dr. Sullivan and hear him tell you in his own words what happened, there isn't a lot else that needs to be said to raise the doubt that requires you to acquit him.

"Dr. Sullivan very candidly told you he was in love with Marcia Banning when she dumped him, and that he carried something of a torch for her, hoping she would reconsider, at least to the extent he asked her out a few more times after the break up and drove past her house a couple of times hoping to see her. Those are the kind of admissions the male ego of someone who has just been dumped does not easily make. It certainly would have been better for Dr. Sullivan's case if he told you he'd just shrugged his shoulders when she dumped him without giving it a second thought. But that's not the way it was, and he opened up to you and admitted he still cared for her.

"But what I will call the 'Prosecution's version' is certainly not the way he behaved after she jilted him.

"Marcia Banning is clever. Certainly, clever enough to know Bill Sullivan still loved her, that she had him on a string, in reserve, in case she ever needed a substitute. So, when she bumped into him in the Von's that day early last November, she knew Dr. Sullivan was available to assist her, however unwittingly, in solving the problem of her boyfriend's foot-dragging when it came to marriage. Jealousy is a powerful motivating factor. Throughout history it has provoked far more drastic actions than a mere proposal of marriage. If she could just ignite a spark of jealousy in this guy Taggart, she might harness and drive it to the proposal she and her son longed for. What could it hurt?

"So, she invited the unsuspecting Bill Sullivan over for dinner, an invitation he admits he eagerly accepted. I doubt Ms. Banning foresaw that this guy Taggart would react by attacking Dr. Sullivan, but she knew he was coming over. He had a key and knew Matt wasn't home that night, an opportunity, as Taggart put it, for them to be together without Matt seeing Taggart at breakfast. When Dr. Sullivan said he needed to leave after lingering late at dinner, Ms. Banning urged him to stay longer, have another cup of coffee, because she wanted Taggart to discover that suddenly there was another man in the picture.

"Well, she got her wish in a way she probably never anticipated. Jealousy spoke, as it so often does, with violence rather than love. Taggart let himself in with the key she had given him, saw Bill Sullivan as he entered the living room, walked straight up to him and attacked him just as Bill was asking him to calm down. BOOM!"

No Limits paused and shook her head.

"What's the old saying, 'Oh, what a tangled web we weave, when first we practice to deceive.' Marcia Banning was about to learn how profoundly true that is. Because once that blow was struck, she really had no choice but to join in the lie required for Taggart to escape the consequences of what he had just done. The genie was out of the bottle. Otherwise, this icon, this saint that Taggart had apparently become for her son would be revealed to have feet of clay. He would go to jail. Mathew Banning had already lost one father. Marcia Banning was not going to let him lose another - not this way, she wasn't.

"So, she and Taggart dragged Dr. Sullivan, with his broken nose and separated shoulder into the bedroom. Then, after Taggart went out to wash the carpet while Marcia remained in the bedroom apologizing to Dr. Sullivan, they waited to unfold their story until a more believable hour. Finally, two a.m. arrived, and so did the police. Dr. Sullivan began to protest, but was *ignored* by the police, who, just coincidentally, were Mike Taggart's Marine Corps pals. You know what they say: 'No such thing as an ex-Marine.'

"If you believe the prosecution, this guy Taggart is everything but an Eagle Scout ... yeah right! Cowboy is more like it. An Eagle Scout who admits threatening to break Bill Sullivan's 'fucking neck.' He'd already broken his nose and separated his shoulder, so I guess his neck was the next logical candidate."

No Limits paused to let her words sink in, looking from juror to juror as she did so, making eye contact, commanding them to believe her.

After a few seconds, she went on, "The prosecution points to the telephone records as so-called 'objective evidence,' BAH! Subjective evidence, I say. Incomplete and self-serving. If the prosecution really wanted objectivity, why didn't Mr. Malinzak subpoena any records of Ms. Banning's office phone? At home she had an eight-year old to take care of, a million and one chores to handle, meals to prepare, all the burdens of a working single parent.

At work, she was the manager, with a nice private office, where in quiet moments she could just close the door and not be interrupted while she talked to her friend Bill Sullivan about the pressures and travails of her life. Reaching Bill during weekdays wasn't tough. As a surgical intern, nights and weekends were his working hours. It didn't happen often, maybe a dozen times over a fifteen-month period, but it was nice to have a sympathetic ear when she needed one. By so doing, she lulled Bill into believing in the possibility of resurrecting their relationship when she invited him over for dinner.

"If you want objective evidence, evidence from which you can reliably infer what really happened, how about 'admissions?' Marcia Banning admits she was in love with Taggart, that she wanted to marry him. Mathew thought the sun rose and set on Taggart. She had told her son how nice it would be for Taggart and her to be married but Taggart wasn't going along with the program.

"When you think about it, it's easy to see from Marcia's own testimony how she had painted herself into a corner with her son. Putting her own romantic feelings completely to one side, who could blame her if she dreaded to disappoint her son by failing to realize his dream of having 'Coach' for a dad? One cannot quarrel with her goal, only with her means of achieving it. 'Admissions,' Ladies and Gentlemen, those are the true objective pieces of evidence in this case.

"It's not my intention, nor certainly Dr. Sullivan's, to in any way scoff at or otherwise denigrate Mr. Taggart's Marine Corps service, but the hard fact remains that the Marine Corps is a famously rough bunch, an organization whose business is violence and war, whose business is confrontation, an organization known for its willingness to shoot first and ask questions later. Who among us hasn't heard the old Marine Corps' slogan, 'First to fight?'

"Contrast that with Dr. Sullivan's background. Mr. Malinzak says a license to practice medicine is nothing more than a governmental permission slip. Maybe that's all a license is, but the only persons who can get them are people who spend years learning to heal the sick and injured, more years I venture to guess than Taggart spent in the Marine Corps.

"People willing to make that kind of lifetime investment, people like Dr. Sullivan, do not break into people's homes, do not shout at them in their beds, do not act in any way to cause others to fear for their well-being. It's true that Bill Sullivan was still a little bit in love with Marcia Banning on the night of November 8, but it was a love big enough and unselfish enough to let her live her life the way she wanted to live it, with or without him, without doing anything to make her unhappy.

"Well, it's time for me to sit down and for you to put on your thinking caps. As you do, I leave you with the thought I began with – before you begin your deliberations, Judge Kagara will instruct you that, if you have ANY REASONABLE DOUBT that things happened the way the Prosecution would have you believe, it is your DUTY to find Dr. Sullivan 'not guilty.' Thank you."

"Mr. Malinzak, any rebuttal," the Judge asked.

By No Limits' standards, her misstatements of evidence were pretty mild. The later it gets, the less argument the jurors want to hear. Still...

"Just briefly, Your Honor," Whitey said, standing up.

"Ladies and gentlemen, Ms. Lewis asks why the prosecution didn't subpoena Marcia Banning's office telephone records. Let me ask her the same question. Dr. Sullivan asserts she made calls from her office. If that's his honest belief, not just some lawyer's desperate argument, why didn't he and his lawyer subpoena those records? Let me answer my own question. It's because both *know* they would show no such calls.

"Consider Dr. Sullivan's testimony that Marcia called him in the middle of the night about Matt's earache. There's no way such a call, had it ever occurred, would have been made from her office. The phone records from the Banning home number confirm *no such call was ever made*. It never happened, just like the ballgame and picnic with Matt never happened. This is all part of Dr. Sullivan's elaborate lie to escape responsibility for his after-midnight invasion of Marcia Banning's home.

"Ms. Lewis attempts to play the character card, making much of the accused's occupation as a physician. But, what of Marcia Banning? What of her character? The wife of a Marine pilot, widowed during her pregnancy, a single mother, who worked her way from a spot on a landscaping crew to manager of the business, all while raising Matthew, a terrific kid. There is no hint, no shadow anywhere on the character of Marcia Banning to suggest she would lie to you, whereas, doctor or not, you have irrefutable evidence of the accused's lies.

"I will say no more. The evidence speaks for itself. Thank you for your time and attention."

Whitey sat down.

After admonishing the jurors not to discuss the case with anyone, Judge Kigara recessed the proceedings until the next morning.

22

Monday, October 4, 1976 - Dusk

Marcia had taken Matt home as soon as he finished testifying. Mike went back to his office and called Rhonda in North Carolina to tell her he'd be returning tomorrow and give her his flight information in case she could pick him up.

"Do I dare ask how it went?"

"Too long a story to tell over the phone. You really nailed the defense's version, right down to the theory of why Sullivan was legitimately in the house. I think it's going to be close."

Horn was leaning against the doorway of Mike's office waiting to give him a ride home when Mike rang off with Rhonda.

"Close, huh?" Horn asked as they rode the elevator down to the garage.

"Closer than it ought to be. Sullivan was a good witness."

"Going to be hard on Marcia if Sullivan gets off."

"Yeah, especially with me not being here."

Preoccupied with thoughts of Sullivan, Marello's defense, dinner tonight with Marcia, Mike trudged up his front steps, steps that seemed steeper than usual. For years he'd come home from hard days to be greeted by Feodot, either at the door or, if taken by surprise, charging around the corner at the sound of his unexpected arrival, toenails clicking on the hardwood floor, ears flying, tongue adrift. Now, no more Feodot.

But it was beyond the loss of a friend, however great. For months, life had been getting richer, The Three M's, the melding of three lives. Yet here he was walking through the door of an apartment every bit as empty in any meaningful way as the one in Marlborough. Was he just trying one case so he could turn around and try another? What was it the old song asked, "Is that all there is to a fire?" All weekend long Marcia had been deep in the moment, never losing her sense of humor during the long hours of trial preparations, despite how much Mike knew she hated the whole process. Whatever distance had opened between them the night before his departure for North Carolina had closed, at least for the moment. He thought about how empty he'd felt while he was away. He thought about the nudge she gave him while he was telling Whitey about his confrontation with Sullivan, pulling her hands up to her chest as if covering herself with a sheet, so as to remind Taggart of his own nakedness. He thought he'd lost the intimacy her gesture bespoke. But now the trial was over. Would tonight be their last supper?

Mike needed to get cleaned up before heading over to Marcia's, but he flopped onto the couch without bothering to turn on a light, staring at walls that were just walls. How did he want his life to be? Mike's sense of time passing was both heightened and diminished. He contemplated the constancy of change. Minutes passed. Eventually, heaving a sigh, he stood, turned on a light and headed for the shower.

When Taggart finally arrived at Marcia's, Matt, already in his pajamas, was sitting on the couch waiting for him, yellow legal pad on his lap, sound asleep.

"I told him he could wait up for you," Marcia said, "but he couldn't make it. He's written some questions he wants to ask you about the trial on that legal pad you gave him this morning."

Mike picked up the pad and read:

1. Why did the lady lawyer stand over by the jury instead of at her own table?

2. What was the lady who sat in front of the judge with the macheen doing?

3. Why does the judge sit up so high?

Taggart smiled, wrote out his answers, corrected Matt's spelling and handed Marcia the pad. "Want me to carry him into bed?"

When Mike came back, Marcia was in the kitchen. "Did he wake up?"

"Nope, dead to the world."

"Matt just had hot dogs. By the time we got home there wasn't time for much else before he had to get ready for bed. Are hot dogs okay with you? I have some chili left over from a couple of nights ago."

"Sure." Taggart had never met a chili dog he didn't like.

"Marsh, ... "

Marcia was standing at the stove with her back to him. Something about the way he said her name told her Taggart was no longer talking about chili dogs. She turned around.

"I'd hoped to have this conversation when we were already celebrating Sullivan's conviction, but I have to go back tomorrow, and this can't wait. Let's get married. No more half-stepping by me. I should have asked you six months ago. I love you and I love Matt. I don't have a ring yet; that'll have to wait until Marello's over, but I don't want to go back to North Carolina unengaged."

Marcia's aspect, sunny and smiling most of time, became radiant as he spoke. In two long strides she crossed the kitchen to where Mike was sitting on a high stool.

"Coach," she said as she flew into his arms, "you've just made me the happiest little league mom in Southern California."

At least a dozen kisses and three chili dogs later they were still sitting at the kitchen table.

"How do you think it went today?"

"Hard to say, because I didn't see either you or Sullivan testify." Mike was hesitant to give her the slightly discouraging assessment he'd given Rhonda and Horn.

"Whitey did a good job, but 'reasonable doubt's' not a very high bar for Sullivan to get his chin over. One thing I do know - Matt deserves a ten-pound ice cream cone for his testimony. He was great."

Marcia sat back in her chair, left arm folded across her chest, chin in her right hand, reflecting. "What are we going to do if they find him innocent?"

For a moment Taggart considered explaining the difference between the concept of "innocence" and a finding of "not guilty," but decided it was a lawyer's distinction that made no difference to the point of her question. He knew what Marcia was asking.

"Nothing. We keep our eyes open. Hope a close call like this scares Sullivan enough to change his ways. We get married and live happily ever after."

Marcia shook her head. "All that for nothing. We'd have been smarter to throw him off the Ocean Beach pier while we had him tied up."

Taggart rolled his eyes. "Verdict's not in yet. Maybe you won't have to drown anybody."

Marcia stood up and reached for Mike's hand.

"No, it's not over yet." She brightened. "C'mon, husband-to-be, you must have time for a roll in the hay before you have to go home and pack."

23

Tuesday, October 5, 1976 – 41 days to trial.

"You look worn out," Rhonda said as Taggart climbed into her car at the curb in front of the terminal.

"Not much sleep last night. Early flight. Had to pack. Got engaged."

"Congratulations. Now put all thought of romance out of your head, because we're having dinner with Jim and Anthony Marello tonight. How's that for a 'Welcome Back?'"

Later, at dinner, after introductions were made and orders taken, before Mike even had time to finish what little he planned to say about his background and experience, Jim interrupted him. "Rhonda tells us you know the Sheriff."

Taggart nodded. "Worked for him for three years."

"You know the prosecutor too."

It wasn't clear to Mike whether it was a question or a statement of fact, but he agreed that he did know Given Watson. "Yes. He was already the Solicitor back when I was working for the Sheriff."

"Too bad you don't know the judge. You don't know him, do you?"

"We've been introduced. I testified once in a trial in which he presided, but there's no reason to think he'd remember me."

Jim shook his head but said no more for the moment.

"I suppose Rhonda's already told you about the discovery of Livia's diary," Mike said. "I expect Watson's going to use it to argue that Frank wanted out of the marriage because he'd come to the conclusion he was gay, but--"

"We need to fight this homosexuality claim from the git-go," Jim said.

After an acquaintance of less than fifteen minutes, Mike was struck by how different Jim was from his brother, and both were from their father, Anthony, a rotund giant. Jim stood no more than six feet tall with broad shoulders; Frank, at least six-four with shoulders narrower than Rhonda's. Jim's hair, full and light brown, was worn long and combed to one side; Frank's hair, that which remained, was dark, curly and looked uncombable. How could Frank, a professor of English Lit, have a brother who probably read nothing but car magazines? Jim's style was as direct and confrontational as Frank's was self-effacing and deferential. Jim's voice sounded like two pieces of fresh Velcro being pulled apart. Frank's was so soft, he seemed to be whispering even when he wasn't.

"You know, Jim, I agree we need to educate the jury that 'homosexual' and 'homicidal' aren't synonymous terms, but this defense can't be about what Frank isn't, especially when the facts don't support us. It has to be positive. It has to be about what Frank is, a smart, interesting, gentle man who, despite homosexuality, despite insurance, despite everything else, loved his wife heart and soul and under no imaginable circumstances would ever harm her."

"If this town thinks Frank's a que… homosexual, he's got no chance, none," Jim sliced his hand across the table palm down, a horizontal judo chop.

Taggart said nothing. *Jimmy wants me to defend him against the charge of having a queer brother.*

"What about this plea bargain you talked to Frank about?"

"What about it? It's standard pre-trial maneuvering. The prosecution wants to save money by getting the accused to plead guilty in exchange for some concessions by the government. Goes on all the time. Frank's not interested. That's the end of the matter as far as I'm concerned."

"Seems to me just listening to the invitation is a sign of weakness." Jim made a face like he had a bad taste in his mouth.

"Do you think Frank agrees with you?"

"What does Frank think? What does Frank know? Frank doesn't even mind he's in jail. Why should he? It doesn't interfere with his reading." Jim snorted at his own joke.

So it went for almost an hour. Finally, Mike pushed his chair back from the table where they were sitting because Anthony Marello was too big to fit into a booth.

"Gentlemen, I'm glad to finally meet you. It's been a long day, and I'm going to have to excuse myself. I'm sure we'll be talking a lot throughout the weeks to come." Rhonda was reaching for her purse when Jim said, "Rhonda, stick around for another cup of coffee. Dad and I want to talk a bit more with you."

Taggart was under no illusions about how poorly his first meeting with Frank's family had gone. It was hard to get much of a read on Anthony. *Jimmy dislikes me at least as much as I'm beginning to dislike him.*

The phone was ringing as he entered the apartment. "Hi, Coach. It's me, Matt."

At the sound of Matt's voice, all thought of Jim Marello melted from Mike's mind.

"Hi, Matt. How's it—"

"Mom says you're getting married an' you're gonna live with us from now on."

"That's right. Sorry I couldn't be there when she told you."

"Know what I think?"

"No, Matt. What do you think?"

"Well, when you and Mom get married, it's like you and me are getting married too."

Taggart bit his lip to keep from laughing out loud.

"You're right, Matt. The three of us are going to be a family."

"I think we already are, Coach."

This time Taggart bit his lip to keep from crying. "Me too, Matt. Me too."

"Hi," Marcia's voice replaced Matt's. "What do you think of Matt's take on the whole thing?"

"Smart kid. What's his mom's take on it now that she's had time to get used to the idea?"

"She hates these long engagements. She wants to get on with it. You must be worn out. I'll let you go, but just wanted to tell you that Whitey called. The jury's still out. Sounds like there are some dissenters from our cause."

It sounded that way to Mike too. The longer the jury deliberated, the more entrenched he imagined Sullivan's supporters must be. "No use worrying about what we can't control," he said.

"Ghost, you know anybody in New Orleans?" Taggart was on the phone with his friend, Eric Gonchar, 'Ghost' to all who knew him. Mike wondered whether Eric's mother called her son 'Ghost.' A former Navy SEAL, he was the private investigator Mike and Tom Horn used from time to time when preparing cases.

"New Orleans? Yeah. What's up?"

"I need to know everything you can find out about a guy named James Marello and his father, Anthony, but especially Jim."

"What do you already know?"

Taggart filled him in. "I don't know. Maybe the guy's just an asshole, but there's something about him, his hostility towards everything makes me think I need to know more. Anyway, see what you can find out."

"How soon you need this?"

"Week, ten days, if possible?"

"Shouldn't be a problem."

24

Wednesday, October 6, 1976 – 40 days to trial.

Wednesday afternoon about two o'clock Whitey called. "Tags, the Sullivan jury's back. "Not Guilty."

"Ah, shit. You talk to any of the jurors?"

"Yeah. One guy said it was a 'jump ball' in his mind, because it was so hard for him to believe a doctor would behave like Sullivan was accused of behaving. He said that was the equivalent of 'reasonable doubt' in his mind. Several others standing around agreed with that line of thinking."

Re-immersed as Mike was in the Marello trial testimony, the Sullivan problem seemed like something happening on Mars. *Next call with Marsh's going to be tough.*

* * *

At the sound of Jim's voice when Mr. Jack opened the door at the foot of the stairs - one jailer to another, the cell became suddenly smaller. Brothers, fraternity brothers, band of brothers, blood brothers. How on Earth did the word "brothers" ever come to symbolize camaraderie, loyalty, understanding, Frank wondered.

"Frank, we need to talk about this guy Taggart," Jim Marello said after Mr. Jack retreated back down the stairs. He stood while Anthony took up the bunk. "Dad and I don't like him. He's not the right man for the job."

"Why not?"

"He doesn't know what he's doing. We had a meeting with him and Rhonda the day before yesterday. Seemed like he hadn't even thought about how to deal with the homosexuality thing.

"Plus, what's he doing talking to the prosecutor about a possible deal? He's too friendly with everybody in this town. When push comes to shove, he isn't going to be willing to do anything that might antagonize his friends, no matter how much it might need to be done."

Frank Marello said nothing for several seconds and then asked, "Have you talked about your concerns with Taggart?"

"He knows we're unhappy. Rhonda knows we want to fire him."

"What did she say?"

"She said you were the only one who could decide. What else could she say? Taggart's her choice in the first place."

"Where are they this morning? This seems like a discussion they should be part of--"

"We don't need the lawyers to decide this. This is a family matter."

Frank Marello sniffed. "What did Mike say about homosexuality that you disapprove of?"

"I told him you were convicted because of those remarks about you being a homo during final argument in the first trial, so now the whole town knows about it. I explained that by proving you're not ... you know, homosexual, that will knock out the prosecution's theory of why you must be the one who killed Livia."

"What did Mike say?"

"He didn't think that should be the main theory of the case; that the main theory should be about how much you loved Livia despite all else. I got the impression he hadn't thought much about it."

"You know, Jim, Mike and I talked about this for hours a few days ago," Frank said. "You and he may not be on the same page when it comes to the defense theory, but he's thought about it."

"Okay, so he's thought about it. What's he going to do about it? That's what Dad and I want to know."

"Jim," Frank Marello looked his brother in the eye, "there's no way Mike and Rhonda can prove I'm not homosexual ... because it's true. Do you understand that? Clarence Darrow, Abraham Lincoln, couldn't convince a jury I'm straight."

Jim returned Frank's stare, blinking as if to clear his head of unwelcome information. Anthony stared at his shoes.

"I think what Jimmy's trying to say," Anthony spoke for the first time, "is that it's one thing for such a thing to be known inside the family, but outside ... that's different, especially when people are ready to condemn you for it."

Frank took a deep breath and sighed. "I'm sorry, Daddy, but it's too late to prevent that."

"You've been listening to this guy, Taggart, too much," Jim said. "You're giving up too soon. What's Livia's diary say, anyway? Mostly it's just what ... Livia's suspicions. Rhonda says they're going to try to keep it out of the case anyway. As for this guy, Josephson, maybe he won't be so crazy about admitting something like that. He's still got to sell insurance in this county, doesn't he? He's still got to make a living? Maybe he won't testify at all. Who knows? Lots of things can happen."

Frank had turned away as Jim spoke and stood slumped, glasses off, head bowed. But he straightened now, turning to speak, his eyes unused to the absence of his glasses, narrowed. "It's not about Taggart, is it Jim? It's the idea of admitting there's a queer in the family. That's it, isn't it? That's what's bothering both of you. You'd rather have a murderer than a queer, wouldn't you?

"That's bullshit, Frank, and you know it. How can you say something like that to either one of us, especially to Daddy? Haven't you brought enough shame on this family? Even if you don't care about us, this Taggart's realism is going to get you hung. You understand that, don't you?"

"Jim, I just don't want to discuss this any more. You picked the first lawyer. I never liked him, didn't feel like I could talk to him or that he even liked me, and we lost. I'm picking this one, and I pick Mike Taggart."

Frank turned to his father, who was sitting on the bunk listening to his sons, his arms on his knees, staring at the floor. "Daddy, I appreciate everything you've done for me. Without you, I wouldn't have a lawyer. I didn't kill Livia, but just saying so isn't enough. I don't know what's right, but I know this. Mike Taggart is in this for more than the money. He cares what happens to me. I don't care what Jim says. I trust him."

Anthony Marello raised his head. The old man was crying. "Frankie," he said, "I think Jimmy's right, but you gotta decide, not Jimmy, not me. If Taggart's the one you want, that's the way it'll be. You won't hear any more about it from us ... will he, Jimmy?"

"Bah."

"Don't worry," Anthony answered for him. "You won't hear any more about it from either of us."

The cell had become larger for Frank Marello. Jim muttered something about being afraid Taggart was going to give away the store, but Frank paid no attention. There were lots of different kinds of prisons. Frank felt as if he'd just escaped from one.

Through the window on the wall opposite his cell Frank watched Jim and his father walk across the town square towards their car. Had he done the right thing? Had he let Jim's dislike of Taggart make him say things he didn't really know? Turning away from the window, he dismissed such thoughts. It probably wouldn't make a difference.

25

Saturday, October 9, 1976 – 37 days to trial.

Seven witnesses testified for the prosecution in the first Marello trial, over fifty prospective jurors had been questioned. The verbatim transcript of what each had said sat on Taggart's orange vinyl couch awaiting dissection and analysis - a preview of what lay in store for Taggart in trial number two. Biases, opportunities to observe, foundational facts, investigative techniques – all waiting to be extracted from an almost three thousand-page pile of paper like a dentist pulling teeth. As he read and took notes, Mike tried to visualize how the testimony of each witness would unfold. He had been at it constantly, twelve hours per day for four days. So much for the glamour of trial practice. Despite his dislike of the telephone, he welcomed its ring Saturday evening.

"When ya'all comin' down ta the West End?" Taggart recognized the unmistakable voice. Johnny Cash was a soprano compared to Buck Brown.

Buck. Taggart mentally kicked himself for not finding Buck during the almost five weeks since he arrived. Buck didn't have a phone, and Mike wanted to see him when they would have plenty of time to talk. With everything needing to be done, he'd kept putting it off. Murder trial or not, Buck deserved better from Mike.

Buck had managed the Marlborough town baseball team and occasionally pitched for it, even though he'd been in his mid-forties during the three years Mike played. Buck had saved Mike's life once when an angry opponent had tried to end Taggart's career with a bat. Mike could still close his eyes and see that bat coming down towards his head like an axe, only to be checked by an unseen force - Buck flying off the mound to join the fight and smashing the assailant to the ground.

On another occasion, Buck had coldcocked a Baptist preacher who had connived to keep Mike from playing for Buck's church, the Church of God, in the town's softball tournament. "Well," Buck drawled in response to a post-game comment that it was bad policy to chance killing a Baptist preacher in Marlborough, "one thing's sure."

"What's that?"

"There's plenty more where he came from."

Anyone who would risk doing in a Baptist preacher in Marlborough for a Yankee like Taggart was a friend to be cherished.

"I've been real busy." Mike knew the words sounded lame as he said them.

"I know. You're here to represent that queer perfessor who killed his wife."

"Something like that. How the hell are you anyway?"

"Why don' ya'll come on down ta the West End an' see for yerself? Ya still drink beer, don't ya? It's Saturday night. Yer ol' lady's still lettin' ya out, ain't she?"

"That's not a problem. I'll be there in half an hour."

"Fifteen minutes'd be better. The boys are all down here, so haul ass."

West End Tavern, built with unpainted cinder block walls, a corrugated metal roof and a concrete floor with a drain for hosing out during infrequent cleanings, reminded Taggart of the boathouse where he'd worked in college, except not as nice. The wooden bar came up to the bottom of Taggart's rib cage. A cooler with a block of ice kept the beer cold, cans only, nothing on tap. Three pool tables and a television that hadn't worked the whole time Mike was in law school and still didn't, completed the furnishings. Stacks of cardboard beer cases leaned against the wall behind the bar. Light bulbs with green shades hung by bare cords from the ceiling over the pool tables. The only decoration, a red and black neon "Black Label" beer sign, flashed every few seconds.

A white paper "Notice," taped to the wall by the door, warned patrons about the dangers of drinking illegally distilled alcohol. Johnston County was dry, which meant no hard liquor could be sold. Taggart had watched a proposal to legalize liquor by the drink go down to defeat while in law school. The bootleggers and Baptist ministers had seen to that. West End Tavern sold only beer. Its customers were not much given to wine drinking unless the beer ran out, a situation that, despite the herculean efforts of its patrons, had never occurred.

The West End stood directly across the street from the textile mill, where most of its regulars, including Buck, worked, and around the corner from the Church of God, where a few worshiped and for which most played softball. Friday was payday at the mill. After the bar closed on Saturday night, some forlorn souls would spend the last few cents of yesterday's check at the 7-Eleven on the cheapest aftershave for purposes other than grooming. Taggart had carried the wreckage down to Mr. Jack at the jail on more than one occasion.

Mike stopped as he approached the open door of the tavern, which framed a familiar tableau. They were lined up at the bar inside, Buck, Bobby Mack, Big Roy, Alvin Wade, rough ol' boys with whom he had spent three years. He could see Jackie Brown, Buck's brother, back at the pool tables.

The one place in the world where nothing changes. There had been days Taggart wished he never left, but not any more. He walked inside.

"Hey, Boy, carry yerself on over here," Buck called, making a space for Mike at the bar. Taggart slid into his assigned spot, shook hands all around, picked up the Black Label Lester, the bartender, handed him and began to ask and answer questions.

"Ya'll look like you could still be playin' ball." Buck slapped Mike on the back.

"Still play some. Catching's wrecking my knees. I'm trying to become a third baseman. How about you?"

"Jist sof'ball for the church." Buck made a face. Softball was universally regarded as a lesser sport than baseball by the West Enders, but whether they played hardball or not, most played softball for Church of God, because that was how Reverend Bramlett waged war on the Baptists.

"Still managing the town team though." Buck got back to baseball. "Could use a catcher. Ain't had a good one since you left. Got plenty a third basemen."

"I'll be gone long before the season starts," Mike said. Then he nodded towards a large man, leaning against the end of the bar. His red and blue plaid flannel shirt had seen hard use, and he stared down at his beer as he silently fingered some coins on the counter in front of him. "What's the matter with Big Roy? He seems pretty quiet."

Big Roy Halderson used to be the most friendly, boisterous member of the team, always filled with jokes, stories, wisecracks.

"Big Roy's been quiet for the last five years." Buck shook his head. "His boy, Lonnie, got killed in Viet Nam in '71. He's never got over it."

Taggart felt a chill. *Guess the West End changes after all.*

Many beers later, the subject of Frank Marello came up.

"Ya'll gonna git this Marello fella off?"

"I don't know. What do you think?"

"How should I know? Ya'll the lawyer."

"Yeah, but you were here during the first trial, Buck. What do you think about the case? Did you follow it? Did you think he was guilty the first time?"

"I don' know. Lester here thinks he done it." Buck gestured towards the bartender, who was leaning against the other side of the bar, listening.

"Well, the jury convicted him, didn't it?" Lester said.

"Yeah," Buck said even slower than usual, "but that might could be on accounta what ol' Given Watson said about Marello bein' a queer there at the end of the trial."

"So what? That don' make him any less guilty."

"It don' make him any more guilty neither. Jus' 'cause a man's one thing, don' mean he's another."

"That's right." Bobby Mack was standing behind Buck. "Ever since I stole them tools ten years ago, whenever something's missin' around here, Stick comes askin' me where I was when the stuff disappeared, even though I've never took anything since I got back off the road."

Having actually been in prison, Bobby Mack was the Cool Hand Luke of the West End Tavern.

Mike listened, silently amazed. He had thought these guys would be ready to convict the world. Maybe he'd had more beers than he thought. Midnight came and Lester threw them all out. Can't sell beer on the Sabbath in North Carolina. The conversation continued as they walked out. Alvin Wade had some white liquor in the trunk of his car, but the guest of honor declined. Taggart needed to get home while he still could.

26

Sunday, October 10, 1976 – 36 days to trial.

Sunrise. Except there was no sun. No matter what the weather, no direct sunlight ever reached Frank Marello. The barred jail windows on the wall across from the door to his cell faced south and west, but the hills west of town blocked the afternoon sun.

"I'm like a bat," Frank muttered to himself as he lay on his thin mattress, his khaki colored blankets pulled up around his chin. He watched the black sky become a leaden, rainy gray. "I ought to start hanging upside down in here."

He had been awake a long time. Apart from running, Frank had never liked strenuous physical activity, but without even the exercise of walking around the small apartment or walking to class, he couldn't sleep more than four or five hours a night. The jail, quiet most nights except Saturday, was now soundless.

Prison had not been so silent. Metal doors clanged. Guards called to one another without regard to the hour. As a death row prisoner, Frank had his own cell, but his neighbors' occasional screams as they grappled with their private demons punctuated the night. One of them, a huge Black man named "Big Otis" once told him, "a death sentence makes you restless," and Frank found that was true. Even the slightest, most drowsy wee-hour awakening became a wide-eyed stare at the dim surroundings, illuminated always by the ever-burning lights in the corridor outside the cells.

What would happen? How would it feel? What's on the other side? Why is this happening to me? Who could have done such a thing? Why did I waste so much time? If I could once again be free, what's the first thing I would do? What would I change? What do I miss most? Endless questions and elusive, changing answers, danced in Frank's head during the earliest hours from which sleep had fled.

He had brought his death row sleeplessness back to Marlborough with him, and in some ways the quiet made it worse – fewer distractions from the torment of his thoughts. He shook his head at his own joke about being a bat. Was humor a sign of sanity? He hoped so. He had been feeling guilty about wanting to live when Livia was no longer alive. "That's stupid," he told himself, but his brain remained stubbornly unconvinced. The rain outside only deepened his melancholy. What had Livia already learned by dying that he might be about to find out?

In the midst of his musing he heard someone coming up the stairs. Mr. Jack bringing breakfast. Frank sat up and swung his long legs out of bed. The concrete floor felt cold on his bare feet. He was tired and unhungry. Jail's grim joke: wouldn't let you sleep, but neither would it let you completely awaken.

Balancing the tray with one hand, Mr. Jack fumbled for the keys and inserted one in the lock. Suddenly he gasped and the tray clanged on the floor, scrambled eggs flying in all directions. Frank had been rubbing his face to clear the cobwebs, and he looked up at the sound. He saw Mr. Jack grab his chest and open his mouth as if to say something, but no sound came out, and he collapsed on the floor amid the eggs.

"Mr. Jack? Mr. Jack! What's wrong?"

Wide awake now.

Mr. Jack neither moved nor made a sound.

"Hello ... Hello ... Is anybody downstairs? Hello ... Is anybody there?"

Frank stopped and listened. No sound came from down below. Apart from persons there to visit him, Frank seldom saw anyone except Mr. Jack in the jail, especially not at this hour on a Sunday morning. The drunk tank was downstairs, but he hadn't heard anyone being brought in last night. Frank never saw any of its occupants anyway. Mr. Jack lived on the first floor and never seemed to take a day off.

As Frank listened to the silence, he noticed for the first time the key hanging in the lock. He reached through the bars and opened the door, stepping outside the cell for the first time since the hearing two weeks ago. Kneeling beside Mr. Jack, he felt for a pulse.

He could feel one, but it seemed weak to Frank's untrained touch. He didn't know what was normal for a person of Mr. Jack's age. What about first aid? First aid for what? What should he do first?

Get help. Frank started for the stairs. Just the sensation of moving more than three steps in one direction without having to turn around and go the other way, of moving without handcuffs, caused other options to dawn on him. Seven-thirty Sunday morning. Through the window at the bottom of the stairs, the town square looked deserted. A civilian car in the lot between the jail and the Court House stood beneath a sign that said "Mr. Jack." The key to that car might be around somewhere, maybe on the ring of keys still hanging in his cell door, maybe in Mr. Jack's pocket. On the wall a shotgun hung chained to its rack. The key to that lock would be somewhere near by. Ammunition too. A vision of freedom blossomed, withered and died.

The thought of the shotgun brought him to his senses. Frank hated guns. Guns were Jim's thing, not his. Besides, where would he go? What would he do? Without having to think, instinct told him, if staying alive and free meant spending the rest of his life running, looking over his shoulder, constantly afraid he might unknowingly make the one mistake that would catch him up, then staying alive wasn't what he wanted to do.

"It's all up to you, Mike Taggart," he said aloud as he picked up the phone and called the hospital from the list of emergency numbers taped to the wall. Then, before running back upstairs, he called the Sheriff's office across the square. "It really is all up to you."

***

"What a pretty picture!"

From somewhere in the fog of sleep, Taggart heard Rhonda's voice. He attempted to raise his head and open his eyes, but was driven back into the pillow by a terrible blow from an invisible force.

"Get up, you sorry sack of ... stuff!" Rhonda's voice again. Maybe if he opened his eyes without trying to raise his head, they would work. He tried it and was met with a red flash more brilliant than a thousand suns.

"Get up or I'm going to throw a pitcher of water on you."

Thus motivated and shielding his eyes, Taggart opened them, wincing as he did so.

"What did you do last night anyway?"

"Um ... jury research. Surveyed some local attitudes down at the West End."

"How did you get home?"

"Drove, why?"

"Well, you kind of overshot the parking lot."

Taggart forced himself to his feet and lurched stiff-kneed towards the front window. There was the car Rhonda had loaned him parked in the middle of the lawn, with the door on the driver's side standing open.

He turned back towards Rhonda. "Sorry about that."

"You're going to need a lawyer if you keep that up. Shave and get dressed while I make some coffee. You remember we're supposed to meet Mark Josephson today?"

Josephson. Mark Josephson, Frank Marello's alibi witness; the prosecution's motive witness; the yin and yang of the case. Even without last night's thousand beers, the thought of Mark Josephson and what he might do to or for the defense of Frank Marello made Mike's head hurt.

"Prosecution called Josephson in the first trial," Taggart said to Rhonda, who was driving, while he inhaled coffee fumes, "to testify about the insurance. Why didn't Watson bring out anything about the homosexuality then? Didn't he know?"

They were driving through Marlborough, headed for Chapel Hill twelve miles to the south, where Josephson lived. As they passed the town square, Mike noticed an ambulance parked in the lot beside the jail, but thought nothing of it.

"I don't know what prompted Watson to allude to homosexuality during final argument." Rhonda shrugged. "He didn't really say much, just three or four seemingly off-hand references to Frank being '... one of those kind of men.' He didn't single out Josephson, just made insinuations. Maybe he heard a rumor during trial when it was too late to investigate; maybe he guessed. I just know, if Watson hadn't mentioned it, we wouldn't be here, and Frank would still be on death row. He might even be dead by now."

Mike was amazed Rhonda had been able to convince the State Supreme Court such an oblique reference was sufficiently prejudicial to compel the overturn of Frank's conviction. *Maybe some of the justices had been to Marlborough.*

"Mike, how much of a problem do you think homosexuality's really going to be? I mean, it's pretty clear from the diaries that Frank could have left any time he wanted to. He didn't have to kill her to leave. There's pain in those entries, but no anger. Livia obviously thought Frank still loved her."

Everything Rhonda said was true. But the Marlborough Mike knew still made him leery. Frank's own father and brother, southerners born and bred, were so uncomfortable with Frank's sexual preference, they could think of almost nothing else. If Frank's own family couldn't get past the issue, Taggart had little faith in

Marlborough's ability to see beyond and look at the rest of the evidence.

"Ladies and gentlemen of the jury," Mike role played as he stared out the car window at the thick timber through which the highway wound on its way to Chapel Hill, "stated as succinctly as possible, the uncontroverted evidence is that less than three months before Livia Marello's death, the Accused, her husband, came to her and told her that he was a homosexual and was having a homosexual affair with another man for whom he was experiencing very strong feelings. A few weeks later, the Accused went out and bought a $25,000 insurance policy on the life of his wife, whom he now loved 'just as a friend.' From whom did he buy this insurance? Why, from his homosexual lover, that's who! Two weeks later Livia Marello was murdered. Where does the accused say he was at the time of the murder? Why, with that selfsame homosexual lover. How convenient."

Taggart paused and turned his head a quarter turn to look at Rhonda. "That's just the first paragraph of the prosecution's opening statement. When it comes to closing argument, Watson will be pushing every fundamentalist, good Baptist, homophobic, family values button he can find. In a town that voted eight to one against liquor by the drink just a couple of years ago, how do you think our potential jurors will regard behavior the Good Book says is an 'abomination?'

"Do you remember when we were in law school? How all us down here from north of the Mason-Dixon line for the first time scoffed when we saw Jesse Helms spewing his nightly fifteen minutes of televised venom against 'nigras, homos and communists?' We thought he was nuts, but the citizens of this Commonwealth elected him to the United States Senate. Welcome to the Nineteenth Century.

"Look at that sign," Taggart gestured towards a billboard they were approaching. "People who erect billboards commanding 'Get

Right With God!' aren't going to have any trouble assuming the worst of someone whose lifestyle centers around a sexual preference so repugnant to their religion, it's referred to as 'that which cannot be named.'"

"Well, do you think we can overcome this?" Rhonda said. "Maybe Jim's right. What if we can't get the trial moved to some place that hasn't convicted Frank once already?"

"Let me tell you a story, one that gives me some hope. Do you remember my dog, that cocker spaniel named 'Feodot?' One summer day just before school started in 1965, Feodot and I went out for a walk along a dirt road north of town. It was maybe two months after Cathy and I got here ..."

As Taggart talked, Rhonda pictured Mike as she had known him eleven years earlier, wandering down a dusty road with the little black and white dog, imagining the events as Mike described them.

A car carrying five men approached as Mike and Feodot walked along. It slowed as it drew even with them, and Mike could see the driver studying him, trying to read the words on Mike's "Michigan Athletic Department" tee shirt. When the car was no more than five feet past, it accelerated sharply, spraying Mike and Feodot with a cloud of dust and gravel.

There's trouble looking for a place to happen. The sound of the car's engine died away and was replaced once more by the soft whir of insect life in the grass along the road's edge. Mike walked on another quarter mile with Feodot darting from one side of the road to another, investigating every scent, panting happily. Through the heat, almost like a mirage at first, and then far more real than Mike wished, the car reappeared, coming towards them once again real slow.

This time it stopped.

"Morning," Mike said with a friendliness he didn't feel.

The driver, a narrow-faced man about Mike's age with a cigarette in his mouth, pointed a shotgun straight at Mike, resting its barrels on the frame of the open car window. "Git in." Someone in the rear seat swung open the back door.

Taggart immediately put his hands in the air even though he hadn't been told to. "Sure, I'll get in ... but what's this all about? What have I done?"

"Let's jist say we don' want no freedom riders around here."

"Boy, have you made a mistake." Mike's hands still in the air. "I'm no freedom rider. I live here. My name's Mike Taggart. I'm a deputy sheriff. I work for Stick Hatcher."

"Stick! Boy say he works for Stick!" The driver turned to look at his companions. "What we gonna do now?"

Somebody muttered something from the backseat that Mike, who was edging sideways out of the shotgun's direct line of fire, didn't hear. Suddenly the car roared away spraying Mike and Feodot with a torrent of gravel that made their earlier dustbath seem a gentle shower.

An hour later Mike and Stick were standing in the outer office of the Sheriff's Department. Stick pulled down a large map of the county from a spindle hanging on the wall. "Show me where you were."

Taggart pointed to where he'd been waylaid. "Here's their license number." Mike handed Stick a scrap of paper. "Old green Pontiac four-door, about a '59."

"Probably not gonna need to run no license number. Bobby," Stick turned to Bobby Meachum, one of the other deputies, who was standing across the room at an open file drawer. Bobby had lived in and around Marlborough all his life.

"Bobby, Mike here says he was stopped by a bunch of boys out on the Duncan Store Road ... pointed a shotgun at him and wanted him to go for a ride. Thought he was a 'freedom rider.' Who you reckon that'd be?"

Bobby shoved his round-brimmed ranger style hat back and scratched his head.

"Out there by Duncan's you know Jimmy Lee Evanston's gonna be part of anything that goes on."

"Yeah," Stick said, "and Orv Murray."

"If those two's up to somethin'," Bobby said, "then Willkie Ferguson and Bevo Jones and Calvin Nickerson ain' gonna be too far away. They all drink white liquor together, and none of 'em works a lick."

Stick nodded. "Bobby, you and Tubby go round up those boys and carry 'em on in here. Mike, why don' you go on home. I'll give you a call when the guests arrive."

Two hours later Mike was back at the office.

"Mike," Stick stepped halfway out the doorway to his office, "c'mon in. I've got some fellas in here I'd like you to meet."

Over Stick's shoulder, through the open door, Mike saw five men standing side by side in front of the wall to the left of Stick's desk. Mike walked past Stick into the office, and Stick followed, closing the door behind them.

"Recognize any of these boys?" Stick asked.

Taggart looked from face to face. He'd only seen the driver's face, but he thought he'd seen most, if not all, of the men before, probably in the crowd at baseball games.

"These the ones, Mike?"

"That one on the far end was the driver, Sheriff. I couldn't see the faces of the others."

"Mike, this here's Orv Murray," Stick said, walking down the line until he stood facing the man. "Orv owns a green Pontiac, don't you, Orv?"

As Stick spoke, he hit Murray with a short, straight punch just above the belt, his big fist moving sharply forward in a powerful piston-like stroke. It was hard enough to knock Orv six inches back against the wall, but not hard enough to crumple him.

"Yessir, Sheriff," Murray wheezed and coughed.

"Now, Bobby tells me he found all five a you together leanin' on Orv's car out at Duncan's store and that there was a shotgun in the car. That wasn't no coincidence now, was it, Jimmy Lee?" Another short hard jab sent Jimmy Lee back against the wall.

"No Sir," the man gasped as he rebounded back into more or less upright position.

"You saw Orv point that shotgun at mah deputy, didn't ya, Willkie?" Stick moved further down the line, the question accompanied by another sharp blow to a midsection.

"Yes … yessir." The man gasped for air, "bu … but that shotgun wasn't loaded.'

"Shut up, boy. That ain' no excuse.

"And you, Bevo, you saw it too?" Whack!

"Yessir."

"And you, Calvin.?"

"UUUHHH!" Calvin grunted, and then rasped out a "Yessir."

Up and down the line Stick paced, explaining how pointing shotguns at people just "didn't git it" in his county, no matter who or what the person was, asking each man in turn whether he understood, punctuating his message now and then with another blow, playing no favorites, each man receiving his fair share of attention.

"And we don't take nobody for rides they don' want to go on in this County neither! Ya'll understand that?"

A chorus of "Yessirs."

"Now, Mike," Stick turned towards Taggart, who was hardly believing what he was seeing and wondering how he ought to be behaving, "it's clear to me that each of these boys is repentant of the mistake they made this mornin', and it's mah suggestion we let it go at that. That okay with you?"

"Yes, Sir." Mike was half afraid Stick might get carried away with his more emphatic means of communication.

"Well, then, why don' ya'll shake hands and be friends, and then you boys can go on home and don' be causin' no more trouble, ya hear?" Stick opened the door.

Mike shook hands with each of the five men, looking in their eyes for some craving for vengeance, but seeing none.

"It was like they knew they screwed up," Mike said to Rhonda, "and they were relieved nothing worse had happened. After that I saw those guys all the time, especially in the summer at games, sometimes down at the West End. Ran a couple of 'em in for being drunk in public once. Whenever I'd see them, they'd all laugh about what happened and the look on my face when I saw that shotgun, and what their faces must have looked like when they heard I worked for Stick, and we were all friends after that."

"What's your point?"

"The point is that despite all its prejudices and moralizing, even the reddest necks in town have a rough sense of justice. Not all those boys I was drinking with last night agreed that Frank was guilty of killing Livia even though they all think he's a 'queer' as they put it. I just hope the ones who have already made up their minds will tell us, and we can find twelve who haven't."

Rhonda looked across the front seat at Taggart over the top of her glasses. "That's fine if you can have Stick Hatcher beating the jurors into agreement for us. Otherwise, I still want to try this case somewhere other than Marlborough."

Just outside the city limits of Chapel Hill, in an area that had been pine woods when Taggart was in law school, they pulled into the parking lot of a large new–looking apartment complex.

"Look out for that lawn," Mike warned. "Sometimes these North Carolina lawns can jump right under your wheels when you're trying to park."

"I haven't done enough 'jury research' today for that to happen,"

The man of medium height who answered the door introduced himself as Mark Josephson. He wore a brown sport shirt, tan slacks and brown loafers with tassles. Color coordinated. The part in his hair was so straight, Taggart wondered if he'd used a ruler. Josephson offered coffee, and they sat down in a small neat living room. A bouquet of flowers sat on the coffee table.

Taggart struggled unsuccessfully to keep from reading something into everything he saw. Were dress or décor advertisements of sexual preference? Mike didn't want to think so, but found himself noticing nevertheless. What about his own apartment, where Marcia said she couldn't even detect signs of humanity?

"Mark," Mike began, "I've read the transcript of the trial. You testified about selling Frank and Livia some life insurance; also, that you and Frank spent time together on the morning his wife was killed."

Josephson nodded.

"Well, this trial's going to be different. The prosecution now knows that you and Frank had a homosexual relationship not long before Livia was murdered. They're going to make that part of the motive for the murder."

The news didn't appear to affect Josephson. He looked directly at Taggart. "It was hardly a 'relationship,' only an episode, nothing more. We were friends who became briefly involved one night, that's all."

Mike looked back at Josephson. "That's a distinction a Marlborough jury may find hard to appreciate, Mark. Do you understand what I mean?"

"Having lived in Johnston County all my life, I do understand. But I want to help. What can I do?"

Bit by bit, Taggart reviewed Josephson's activities with Frank, relieved that what he was hearing confirmed Frank's account of events. "So, when Frank suggested the two of you not see each other for a while—"

"I agreed with him. We just got carried away. Besides, I didn't want to be romantically involved with a married man."

Listening to Josephson, Taggart couldn't help envisioning him on the witness stand. The thought made him wince. Josephson's determination not to become "romantically involved with a married man," a statement that, coming from a woman would sound virtuous, was jarring and discordant to Taggart coming from a man. It made his skin crawl. *If that's my reaction, what will the jury's be?*

"In view of your agreement not to see each other, why did you?"

To Taggart's ear, Josephson's explanation provided more grist for the prosecution's mill than for Marello's.

"Besides," Josephson finished his account, "Livia had apparently changed her mind."

"What do you mean?" Taggart couldn't keep the surprise out of his voice.

"Not long after Livia learned about what happened between Frank and me, she called and said she wanted to talk. I was surprised. I'd only met her briefly, just enough to shake her hand and say hello.

"We met at a café in Chapel Hill one day. She came right to the point. She said she wanted me to stay away from Frank. He'd told her about us, and she wasn't blaming anyone, but Frank was determined not to let it happen again. She thought in order for their marriage to have every chance to work, it would be better if he and I were no longer friends."

"What was your response?" Mike asked.

"Do you mean how did it make me feel or what did I say?"

"I imagine it hurt very much to have someone say that to you, but we're looking at it more from the standpoint of what actually was said and done."

Josephson regarded Mike for a moment without speaking. Taggart's remark displayed a little more sensitivity than Mark Josephson was used to hearing. "Anyway, I told her Frank had already told me the same thing. I tried to explain to Livia that I wasn't some kind of gay evangelist. But, if Frank was really gay, simply suppressing those feelings would wind up leaving everyone unhappy."

Josephson paused and sighed. "But of course, I agreed to try to honor her wishes."

"But what about Livia 'changing her mind?" Rhonda prompted.

"Well, when Frank suggested we go shopping together, I asked something like 'what about Livia?' Frank said she was okay with it. Then, later, when I called to confirm times, and Livia answered the phone. She said she'd give Frank the message without any comment."

The interview drifted to other aspects of Mark Josephson's relationship with Frank, particularly what exactly Josephson observed on the day of the murder. Taggart only half-listened. He was partially distracted by the recurring thought that everything he learned about Livia Marello made her sound extraordinarily likable. One of the best defenses in a murder trial was the old "he got what he had coming" defense. It wasn't really a defense, but if the victim could be made sufficiently hateful, jurors tended to be more sympathetic toward the accused. A big part of any murder trial was damage control, keeping the death penalty at bay. Having a wholesomely sexy Mary Poppins for a victim wasn't going to help if the jury thought Frank killed her.

Half an hour later as Mike and Rhonda were leaving, Josephson remarked, "You know, in light of what happened, I've never visited

Frank. Not because I don't want to, but other people might try to make something out of it. Will you tell him that, and that I wish him the very best and want to help any way I can?"

"I'll tell him, Mark," Rhonda shook his hand.

27

Monday, October 11, 1976 – 35 days to trial.

Mike Taggart often wondered whether lawyers in other specialties became involved with as many dislikable people as he did in his criminal practice. Ironically, most of the people he disliked were not the accused. Criminal defendants were usually pretty clear about why they did whatever they were doing. Almost invariably they were acting in whatever way they thought best calculated to get out of the scrape they found themselves in or at least minimize the consequences. With others it was seldom quite so clear what game was being played.

"Why do you have to interview my Dad and me separately?" Jim Marello asked. "Seems like a waste of time."

"Tell me about growing up with Frank."

"I'll tell you one thing, Frank doesn't have the balls to kill anybody. The first time Daddy took us kids hunting, Frank started crying the first squirrel we shot.

"Not everybody's cup of tea, I guess."

"Nothing was Frank's cup of tea. Didn't like to wrestle or box. Wouldn't fight no matter what I did to him. One time we're playing basketball in the driveway, just the two of us, one on one. Every time he'd go up for a shot, I'd hit him in the nuts, not real hard, only a flick of the fingers to see what he'd do. Wouldn't fight. Just wouldn't play basketball anymore."

Jim paused. Taggart didn't say anything.

"When I heard Livia had been murdered, first thing I told Frank, don't make any statement to the police. It was obvious he'd be a suspect, and the law says he doesn't have to cooperate. There was no reason for him to make the cops' job easier. But he screwed that up too. He didn't even ask for a lawyer when they arrested him."

"When did you first hear about Livia's death?"

"Afternoon, around one-thirty New Orleans' time. Would have been two–thirty in North Carolina. Frank called me at the dealership. Said he'd been trying to reach Daddy at home, but couldn't find him, and he didn't want to tell Mama over the phone, but he had to tell somebody."

"Where was your dad?"

"Hunting. He got back later that afternoon. When Daddy stopped by work on his way home that day, I told him. I predicted Frank would screw it up somehow, and he did. If it wasn't for Daddy and me, Frank probably would have represented himself."

"So you thought Frank would be a suspect?"

"Husband's always a suspect when a wife gets killed, unless he's got an iron clad alibi. Everybody knows that. I knew Frank wouldn't have any alibi. And ... as it turns out, his attempt at an alibi is worse than no alibi at all, because he says he was off with this fairy, Josephson."

"You think your brother's a fairy?"

"Absolutely not." Jim almost shouted. "He's dumb, so dumb that he thinks he is, and he's a chickenshit, but he's not a queer. That's what that prosecutor is going to try to prove - that Frank wanted out of the marriage because he's a fairy, and he killed her because she was pregnant and wanted him to be a man and be a husband and father like he said he'd be. You prove Frank's not a queer, and you'll win this case."

"What about the fact he says he is?"

"What about the fact he had a wife who was pregnant with his child? When did he decide he was queer anyway? While he was in prison, right? No women around. Hell, he doesn't know what he is. Look at the evidence. How many queers are out there with a wife and kid?"

Taggart shrugged his shoulders and turned to other subjects. He hadn't counted how many queers were out there with wives and children, probably more than most people suspected. *No point in talking much further with Jim about Frank's childhood.* Taggart was glad it hadn't been his.

Anthony Marello was so big, any room he was in seemed crowded. He used up all the available air. Almost two inches taller than Taggart's six-two, Anthony didn't seem so, because he was what Taggart thought of as "beer keg fat" – fat, but with no softness. A great column of a man, easily over three hundred pounds, as thick as any two people anywhere you looked. Mike had a strong grip, but shaking Anthony Marello's hand was like shaking a brick with fingers, even though the top two joints of the little and ring fingers were missing.

Anthony Marello, with his enormous size, his red goatee and fringe of red hair surrounding an otherwise bald, but freckled size nine head and his incongruent little rimless spectacles, looked like a giant red devil. Mephistopheles in the flesh.

"You're a big boy, Mr. Marello," Taggart blurted out in an astonishment undiminished by having already met Anthony a few days earlier. He mentally slapped himself. *Not the most politic way to greet his client's father, the guy who was writing the checks.* "Frank tells me you're a car dealer"

Marello chuckled. "Call me Anthony." He reached into his shirt pocket, pulled out a card and handed it to Mike. It read, "THE KING OF CARS IN THE CRESCENT CITY" and bore a likeness of Mr. Marello's face wearing an outsize crown on his head.

Such an immodest slogan would ordinarily have negatively predisposed Taggart towards its bearer, but during their first meeting Anthony had surprised Mike with his quiet demeanor and apparent willingness to listen before starting to talk. Although abrupt and dismissive in a ponderous sort of way, when he did speak, it was with a voice both soft and hard at the same time – a blackjack wrapped in a soft southern drawl.

"Can't really see how I can tell you anything helpful, but I'll do anything I can. Rhonda must of told you money's not a problem." Anthony paused and gave Taggart a look that seemed to be assessing Mike's reaction to the confirmation of ready cash. "Anyway, I was hunting the day it happened. Stopped at the dealership on my way home, and Jim told me about it. Terrible thing. Turned this family upside down."

"Anthony, I appreciate the financial support," Mike said, "and I know Frank does too. I'm most interested in Frank's childhood, and what you thought about his marriage to Livia."

"Frankie never casused any trouble. Not like Jimmy. Jimmy, always raisied hell, but Frankie kept quiet. I tried to get him to come into the business with me when he graduated from college, like Jimmy did. You know, keep it all in the family, but Frankie wasn't interested. He just wanted to spend his time with his books, wanted to be a professor, so I said, 'Okay, be a good one.' I never had much education myself, and I told both boys I'd pay for their school as long as their grades stayed good, and Frankie's always were. Jim too, maybe even with less effort. Both smart boys."

So, Jim was a good student. One more thing for Frank to resent. "What did you think of Livia? Ever see the two of them fight?"

"Livia was a nice girl. Still can't get over what happened. She really wanted to have a baby, at least that's what she told my wife. Then she gets pregnant and this … You always think such things are going to happen to someone else's family, never your own.

"Never did see 'em fight, not her with Frankie, I mean. They'd been down to New Orleans for a visit the summer before all this happened and stayed with us. Seemed to get along fine. Ask my wife. She'll tell you the same thing. That's why I can't believe this stuff about Frankie bein' a … homo, not the way he always treated her.

"They'd been married a couple of years, and he was still holdin' her chair for her when she sat down and standin' up when she came into a room, things like I made 'em do for their mama. I know Frankie says that he is ... you know ... but I just think the prison's made him crazy. A lot of that stuff goes on in prison, you know. If he can beat this, I think he'll be all right."

"Jimmy was a handful. Every time I'd see Jimmy doin' something to Frankie, I'd wallop him, but you know, you never see everything that goes on with your kids. After a while they grew out of it."

Bullshit. Jimmy hasn't grown out of anything. Mike wanted to tell Marello how wrong he was, but what good would it do? As a father, Anthony'd done his best. Telling him he'd failed wasn't going to change anything. Might antagonize him. *Having one Marello dislike me is enough.*

28

Wednesday, October 13, 1976 – 33 days to trial.

"Sheriff, I'm wondering if you might do me a favor." Through the steam rising from his coffee Taggart stared at the glass counter case where slices of cream pie had begun to yield their freshness to time and gravity.

"I can only think of one thing for which you might be askin' me a favor," Stick Hatcher cooled his coffee by pouring it back and forth between his saucer and cup. "An' it seems unlikely I'd be so inclined. There." He put his cup back on his damp saucer. "Didn't spill a drop. What kind a favor you talkin' about?"

"Well, I've read the investigation report, and I understand one of Troutman's, the handyman's, fingerprints was found on the back door glass of Marello's apartment."

"Yeah, on the outside. Turned out he painted the door frame jus' a coupla weeks before the murder. Besides, Troutman had an alibi. Said he was with his mama all day, an' she backed him up."

Taggart knew all that from the report. Knowing his own mother would provide him an alibi even if he'd been committing genocide, Mike didn't necessarily accept the eighty year old Mrs. Troutman's verification of her son's whereabouts.

"Any other persons of interest you investigated, Sheriff?"

"If their names weren' in the report, I can't help you." Stick, still not looking at Mike, studied his coffee as he stirred.

"Yeah, but let's say you made inquiries about some folks that never panned out, never developed enough information to even justify a suspicion, so they didn't make the report. Anybody like that?"

"Taggart, I'm not havin' you going around botherin' law abidin' citizens of this County who've already been checked out. You just goin' to upset folks and waste your time both."

"What about Jim Marello? He doesn't live in the County. You checked him out pretty thoroughly, didn't you?"

Stick drained the last swallow from his cup and motioned to Betty Lou for a refill.

"You probably checked out the whole Marello family, didn't you?" Stick was softening. Otherwise he would have left after his first cup. "What'd you tell me one time, 'never accept the obvious without considering the obscure?' Don't you think Frank Marello's too obvious a suspect to just decide it was him without sniffing around a little further?"

Stick turned his head and looked at Mike for the first time since they sat down, but said nothing.

"I hear Mr. Jack wouldn't have made it without Marello's help," Mike went on. "You hear anything like that?"

More silence.

"You ever hear of a murder suspect who was already sentenced to die turning his back on a chance to escape in order to save his jailer?"

"Marello ain' sentenced to death no more, and ya'll know it," Stick said. "That's twistin' things around a good deal--"

"It's not twisting them around any more than it is to say he's not sentenced to die," Taggart said. "He's close enough. Most men would have run if they found themselves in Marello's shoes. You know that's true, don't you, Sheriff?"

"Listen," a pained expression clouded Stick's face, "there's nothin' to tell. Sure, Ah checked out the rest of the Marello family and your client's boyfriend, Josephson. A few others. Nothin' turned up."

"What did you learn about the Marellos?"

"Lotta money… New Orleans … ol' man's self-made … big Ford dealer, you must know all that. He was huntin' on the day of the murder. Jim, the other boy, he was at work. The mother, she was at home."

"What else did you learn about Jim?"

"Weak son of a strong father." Stick laughed. "Got a mean streak. Knows some rough people, likes playin' cards for money, but always pays his losses, or his daddy does, one. No reason to kill his sister-in-law."

"Anything else?"

Stick shook his head. "Nope."

"Did you ever check out the motorcycle? The one parked out front the morning of the murder, the one mentioned in the report?"

"Tried to. Not much to go on. Nobody saw who was ridin' it, 'n no one got the license number. It was just one of them big ol' easy rider-type a motorcycles, black, I think, with a long front fork. Between Johnston and Durham Counties, there's probably a hundred of 'em. Ain' no record a who owns 'em."

"What did you do by way of investigating the motorcycle?"

"Bobby went around to all the motorcycle shops in the County askin' if anybody knew someone with a bike like that. Deputy over in Durham County did the same. Got a few names, but everyone we talked to could account for their whereabouts that day. Folks tend to remember where they were on Christmas Eve.

"Why you askin' about that motorcycle?" Stick looked at Mike. "You got somethin?' 'Cause if you do, tell me. I will look into it."

"Wish I did, Sheriff. Just grasping at straws."

Taggart walked south out of Lund's drugstore half a block down Church Street and turned west on Duke Street heading for his car. He noticed the vacant building just across the sidewalk from where he'd parked. Walking down that same sidewalk one morning in June, 1965, Mike had been checking out the town while Cathy attended orientation for the Headstart program where she'd teach that summer. Nine o'clock, already ninety degrees. Mike was thirsty. He walked into the little coffee shop then nestled in the now vacant space, sat down at the counter and ordered.

While waiting for his drink, he began to look at the pictures covering the knotty pine walls. The first photo he saw showed people dressed up in white robes and pointed hats with masks standing around a large burning cross. Taggart did a double take. Glancing around the place, he saw that every of the dozens of photographs was of some Klan activity. Klansmen marching four abreast with lighted torches; Klansmen wearing fancy colored robes with crosses embroidered across the front; little kids in tiny sheets and hoods, a hideous misuse of bed linen.

Mike's stomach turned over. Growing up, he'd seen the pictures of the murdered Emmett Till; just last year there'd been the murders of the three civil rights workers fished out of a river in Mississippi; three months earlier the shooting of Viola Liozzo in Selma. The hair on the back of Taggart's neck stood up. He put some money on the counter and stood up just as his drink arrived.

"Hey, what about yer soda?" the clerk, a middle aged white man wearing blue jeans, a blue work shirt and glasses, asked.

"Not thirsty anymore." Mike walked out the door and took a deep breath of fresh air.

"I thought the Klan was some kind of secret organization, but there it is plastered all over the walls," he'd told Stick a few weeks after he'd been hired at the Sheriff's department.

"It is secret. That's why they wear masks. But the fact the Klan exists ain' no secret. They don't want it to be. Can't be scared of somethin' you don' know exists. Used to be you had to belong if you wanted to get elected to anything in this County."

Mike looked at Stick, afraid to ask the question, afraid of what the answer might be.

"No," Stick read the look, "I ain' in no Klan. Never have been. But I'm the first sheriff in this County since the Civil War that hasn't."

29

Friday, October 15,1976 – 31 Days to Trial

Taggart sat on the sunny bank of the Boxelder River less than a mile from where he and Cathy had lived during law school. He was thinking about how someone who liked the outdoors as much as he did could have wound up in such an indoor profession. Ten feet away Cornelius Kempton was fishing. A pole lay at Taggart's feet unused.

"Why ain't you fishin'?"

"Too lazy."

"Too lazy to fish. That's big time lazy. You thinkin' about your trial?"

"More like reminiscing about what it felt like to play hooky when I was in junior high school. I feel more guilty now than I did then. Do you suppose that's a sign of maturity?"

"Maybe so. They say a big part of growin' up is bein' able to foresee the consequences of one's actions."

They were both quiet for a few minutes.

"You ever think of comin' back to North Carolina to live? This town needs a good lawyer."

"I knew you had something like this on your mind, Cornelius, when you asked me to go fishing. Last time you wanted me to go fishing, you wondered whether I thought you ought to get married. Time before, it was to find out what college I thought you should choose. When you don't need advice, you ask me to go shoot baskets."

"You so old and out of shape, if I tried to talk to you while we're shooting baskets, you'd be too out of breath to answer. Anyway, you ever think of comin' back to Marlborough?"

"Why are you asking me that, Cornelius?"

"Let me tell you what happened to my Mama las' year. You know she worked for Reverend Claiborne and his family for fifty years. She raised him up from when he was a little boy. His daddy was the preacher at Colonial Baptist Church before the Reverend was."

Taggart nodded. Colonial Baptist sat atop the Protestant pecking order in Marlborough. Reverend Bobby Claiborne was the preacher who prevented Mike from playing for Church of God in the Marlborough Church League Championships, the guy Buck Brown slugged.

A year earlier, after she'd cleaned up the kitchen and was about to leave for the night, Jessie Kempton, Cornelius's mother, stepped into the Claiborne's living room where the Reverend and his wife, Mary, were watching television. "Reverend Claiborne, ma'm, I wants to tell you somethin'. Next month gonna be my seventieth birthday, an' I've decided to retire."

"Come sit down, Jessie." Reverend Claiborne got up and turned off the TV. "Mary, will you get us a pitcher of iced tea?"

At this, Jessie stood back up and took a step towards the kitchen.

"You stay put, Jessie." Mary Claiborne rose. "If you're serious about this retirement business, I need to get used to the idea of getting my own drinks." She disappeared into the kitchen.

Once they were all three settled with their tea, Jessie hastened to promise she would help them find her replacement. "Thank you, Jessie," Reverend Claiborne said. "We will appreciate that. You've certainly earned this retirement, but are you sure you have enough money to get along if you stop working?"

"Yes, Sir. Long as I been workin', I been savin'. Ten percent for the Lord; ten percent for the savin's account. I'm sure I'll be able to get by."

"Well …" the Reverend took a deep breath, "we will miss you every day you're gone from here, Jessie Kempton. You've been a wonderful blessing in our lives. I would love to do something for you to celebrate your retirement. Is there anything you especially need?"

Jessie's eyes moistened. "Yes, Sir, one thing. In all the years I worked for this family, I ain' never heard you preach, nor you daddy before you neither for that matter. Ah'd really like to hear you preach some Sunday."

"And so you shall! And so you shall, Jessie. It will be our honor. You will be our guest and sit with the family in our pew. May we pick you up around eight-thirty next Sunday?"

"So, it was all set," Cornelius and Mike sat leaning against a tree on the riverbank. "Mama was so excited. She'd been a world-class Baptist all her life. She wen' out and bought a new dress, new shoes, new hat. Wouldn't be surprised if'n she bought new underwear, though she'd never a said so."

Sunday came, the Claibornes waited out in front of Jessie's small house north of town at eight-thirty sharp. Everyone but the Reverend, who was already at church getting ready. Mary Claiborne was driving, the kids in the back seat. They drove to the church, parking in the spot in back reserved for the Reverend. They walked in through the side door near the front.

Mary lifted the red velvet rope across the entrance to the frontmost pew and stood aside as Jessie stepped past her and sat down, followed by Mary and the kids. Beautiful arrangements of white lilies stood on either side of the altar. An organ was playing. Otherwise, everything was quiet.

Jessie, almost transfixed with happiness, sat with her head bowed thinking about her love of the Lord. The Claibornes were her family almost as much as her own kin. They had never been anything but kind to her, and this church was the most beautiful place she had ever been. To think this baby she had mostly raised could have a church like this.

At nine o'clock Reverend Claiborne emerged from an unseen entrance and stepped into the pulpit. "Please stand and join me in prayer."

Jessie stood and bowed her head as did the entire Claiborne family standing to her right.

"Father," the Reverend's voice quavered, "we are gathered here this Sunday morning to give thanks for our many blessings. Among the foremost of our blessings is the friendship of others, of people who have shown us kindness and love and loyalty throughout our lifetimes, people who have lived good and faithful lives themselves, people who are friends, not just to us, but to you, God, and to the entire community. Friends, Christians, Citizens. Thank you, Father, for the ability both to be such people and have such people in our lives.

"It is also our prayer that you will forgive those among us who are blind, who cannot see the value of such friendship from whatever source it comes. Forgive them for their lack of Christian charity and fellowship. Forgive them for their pinched hypocrisy and mean-spirited lives despite the example set by your Son, whose teachings they all know so well. We ask this in the name of the Lord, Jesus Christ, Amen."

"AMEN," Jessie echoed, but no one else did. Oops. Maybe they didn't answer back in this church.

"Please remain standing and turn to Hymn number 53."

As Jessie withdrew the hymnal from the wooden pocket in the low wall in front of her and turned to number 53, the music of "Rock of Ages," which the Reverend knew to be her favorite, floated through the air.

As she started to sing, Jessie immediately knew something was terribly wrong. For one thing, it dawned on her no choir stood in the choir stalls. For another, no more than ten voices rose in song.

Jessie turned and looked back. In the pew immediately behind her stood Sheriff Hatcher, his wife and son, Micah, and his wife, and Susan Hunter, the Judge's wife. Otherwise, the sanctuary was empty. Jesse began to sob. She knew why no one was there. Mary Claiborne put her arm around Jesse.

"It's all right, Jessie. This is the most important sermon the Reverend will ever preach."

"He preached it too," Cornelius said, "prayed all the prayers, sang all the songs, even took up a collection as if there wasn't an empty seat in the house. God bless him. But somehow word had got around that Mama was comin' to Colonial Baptist on Sunday. I'm sure she didn't ever think to hide the fact and neither did the Claibornes, but when all the good folks of Marlborough heard that an old Black woman who had showed nothing but good-will for this town for almost seventy years was comin' to their church, they chose to stay away. I don't think Mama's been the same since. She just sad all the time."

The cruelty stunned Mike. The insult to Reverend Claiborne was one thing, but the sheer nastiness towards Jessie Kempton, who never hurt a fly, was another. It took Mike's breath away. Reverend Claiborne might be powerful enough to keep Mike out of a softball tournament. He might be powerful enough to prevent the adoption of liquor by the drink in Johnston County. But he didn't have the stature to impose the presence of one kindly Black woman on a congregation, most of whom had known her all their lives, for one hour of worship on a single Sunday morning.

"That's the most monstrous story I've ever heard in my life, Cornelius. You've wrecked my whole day, but I'm glad you told me. I'm really sorry Jessie had to go through that. Makes me ashamed to be White."

Mike rolled away from the tree trunk he'd been leaning against as he listened and lay silently staring at the cloudless sky.

"Just goes to show there's lots of prejudice still around. This town could use a good lawyer, one who would stand up for the rights of all the people the way you're standing up for the rights of this professor, no matter he's a homosexual."

"Plenty of civil rights lawyers are fighting that fight already," Mike replied. "Maybe not in Marlborough, but over in Durham and in Chapel Hill. I'll bet either law school, Duke or UNC--"

"Big issues, big cases." For the first time in his life, Cornelius interrupted Mike, "that's all they want to deal with. What I'm talkin' about is the day to day discrimination Black people in this town experience every single day of their lives, not just what happened to my Mama one Sunday morning. I'll give you an example. You know that town team you used to play on?"

Taggart knew where this was going.

"They play their games at a ballfield owned by the town, don't they?" Cornelius didn't wait for Mike to answer. "The uniforms they wear are paid for out of the town recreation fund, aren't they? In other words, it really is a 'town team,' isn't it?"

Mike nodded.

"How many Black players played on that team when you were playin'? How many Black players you think played on it last summer? How many Black players played on it any time in between? They won't even let Blacks try out. Why not? We're part of this town too."

Buck Brown's words from the other night rang sharp and clear in Mike's brain. "Could use a catcher," Buck had said, "Ain' had a good one since you left." The man sitting beside Mike was a better catcher than Taggart ever dreamed of being, and Buck wouldn't even look at him.

"Cornelius, you're right. But I don't know the first thing about such cases, and even if I did, now isn't a time when I could do anything about it. This Marello trial is only three weeks away. I'll talk to Buck though, and see what I can do."

Cornelius sat and stared down at the river flowing past. Taggart could tell he was disappointed, but he didn't say anything right away. "Mike, there's never gonna be a good time for cases like the ones I'm talkin' about. You can talk to Buck Brown, you can talk to Mayor Lund, you can talk to God, but you ain' goin' to change their minds. They're all together on this one. The only way Black people are ever going to get equality around there is to force it down the throats of the folks who have the upper hand. I wish you'd think about comin' back. This is a place where you could really do some good."

***

Friday night. Marcia and Matt had dinner with Tim's folks, Ed and Elizabeth Banning. As usual, Matt had fallen asleep on his grandparents' couch at nine o'clock while watching TV. They'd talked a long time. The Bannings had met Mike, of course, but knew little about him and had been hesitant to ask. For her part, Marcia'd made no secret of her involvement with Taggart, but seldom brought him up around her in-laws. Even after all this time, it might be a painful reminder of their loss.

Now, however, there was lots to talk about. Elizabeth wanted to know all about Taggart's proposal, wedding arrangements, Matt's feelings about Mike. Ed, asked about what happened at the Sullivan trial and what Mike was doing in North Carolina. After midnight, Marcia turned south onto Martin Way two blocks north of her house with Matt snoring softly beside her. As she completed her turn and her headlights played straight down the street ahead of her, a car parked near the end of the next block pulled away from the curb and drove away, its tail lights disappearing around the next corner.

Marcia didn't notice.

30

Wednesday, October 20, 1976 – 26 days to trial.

"Do you remember where the law library is?" Rhonda, the scholar, asked when Taggart announced he was on his way to do some research on North Carolina's law of evidence. "Did you ever know?"

"Are you kidding? Oliver Wendell Holmes is my hero. I sleep with a volume of *The Supreme Court Reports* under my pillow. What kind of a thing is that to say to the Intramural Chairman of the Class of '68?"

All kidding aside, Mike felt his 'library calm,' a sense of unhurried serenity coupled with unlimited possibility, settling on him as he walked into the Duke law library two hours later. One didn't go to law school to learn the law. One went to learn the "legal method," the system of analytical thinking. Those who possessed it could discover the law long after leaving law school. Learning the legal method, some said, was like having brain surgery. Once you began to "think like a lawyer," as Taggart's favorite law professor used to roar at faltering students, you never again thought as you had before.

Soon he was wrestling with questions such as when did the potential prejudice of a piece of evidence outweigh its probative value? Heady stuff. Books open to cases of particular interest rose in front of him like sandbags in the wall of a bunker, as he sometimes read, sometimes wrote, and sometimes sat thinking. Lost in his work, he didn't notice a well-dressed woman in her fifties walk by. A minute or so later, the same woman walked back in the other direction. This time she slid a sheet from a yellow legal pad under

Taggart's nose. The note read, "All work and no play make Mike a dull boy!"

Mike looked up and saw Susan Hunter, pretty as ever, standing above him. Before he could whisper a greeting, she nodded towards the door and started walking. Taggart followed her all the way out of the building onto the low steps in front of the school. Tall and slender, dark hair flecked with gray, she looked as good from the back as she did from the front. A couple of male students entering the building thought so too and turned to watch as she walked past on her way out.

"I was wondering whether you were ever going to phone," Susan said once they were outside. "I guess bumping into you like this saves me the disappointment of not receiving a call."

Taggart sighed. "Kind of awkward to be calling the wife of the judge in a murder case I'm about to try."

"Pah. Hizzoner would never know ... or care, for that matter. He never answers the phone. Besides, what's the harm of two old friends getting together after, what's it been, eight years?"

Once, years ago, Mike had asked Susan what she'd called her husband before he became a judge and she started calling him "Hizzoner."

"Asshole," she had replied, "on his good days."

Blinded by flack while bombing Germany, Charles Hunter returned from the war and went to law school. Wife Susan shepherded him through, reading his assignments aloud, taking notes in class while he listened, drilling him in study sessions, reading him the exam questions and waiting while he typed the answers. Through twelve years of private practice and fifteen years on the bench, Susan had been Charles Hunter's eyes without ever so much as a "please" or "thank you" from her husband. She never complained. She didn't have to. Everybody else knew how he treated her, because he treated them the same way.

They'd spent many long quiet nights talking at the Sheriff's office while Mike worked as the radio dispatcher and Susan waited to drive Hizzoner home when he finished working in his nearby chambers "Why don't you leave him?" Mike had once asked.

"I made up my mind that if he could go off and get blinded fighting for his country, the least I could do was support him in whatever way I could, in whatever way he'd let me, once he got back".

"You still the power behind Hizzoner's throne?"

"Still do a lot of his research for him," Susan replied in answer to Mike's question. "Write it up on a Braille typewriter; read briefs to him. But he listens; he's the one who decides things, not me." She smiled.

Based on what you tell him.

"What's happened to you since you left, Mike?"

Mike gave her the three-minute version, Marines, the war, Chicago, the divorce and return to California, his recent engagement. "What about you?"

"Marlborough." She laughed. "Marlborough's what's happened to me. Law library during the week, Colonial Baptist Church on Sunday." Susan paused. "I remember when you were about to graduate. Your future probably sounded more exciting to me than to you. But for you being married, I believe I'd have gone with you if you'd asked."

"That's one of the nicer things anyone's ever said to me, Susan. But for me being married, I might have asked."

"No, you wouldn't." Susan shook her head. "I'm old enough to be your mother. But thank you for saying so. Does me good to hear it." She kept smiling. "What do you think of your case? Now that you've had time to get into it."

For a moment Mike considered asking if his answer would stay between the two of them. Almost instantly he decided not to. He had every confidence everything they had ever said to each other was just between the two of them.

"I think I can win, if Marlborough will keep an open mind."

"In that case, watch out. Don't assume that's going to happen." She gave him a long look to see whether he was listening. Politics and religion in the various parts of Johnston County, relationships among County families - Susan talked; Mike listened. At the end of two hours, Taggart was wishing Susan could pick his jury.

They'd stepped outside in daylight. When they finished talking and went back in, it was dark.

31

Thursday, October 21, 1976 – 25 days to trial.

"Check your bags? Where you gentlemen flyin' this evening?"

Taggart squirmed. Cornelius Kempton came towards them as they lugged their bags up the curb in front of the terminal. It pained Mike to have his friend offering to check his suitcase.

While Mike tried to think what to say, Jim Marello said "New Orleans," and handed Cornelius his ticket. Taggart merely nodded to Cornelius, lined up behind Jim and Anthony and waited. "Hello, Cornelius."

"Hello, Mike. How's it goin' today? Flyin' to New Orleans, eh?"

"Yeah, I'm doing fine, Cornelius. How about you?"

"I'm okay. Say, did you ever have that conversation with Buck Brown we talked about?"

'Fraid you were going to ask that. "No, I haven't had a chance to see him. Can't call, because he doesn't have a phone. Besides, better to have that conversation face to face. But I haven't forgotten. It's a long time until next baseball season."

Immediately sorry he'd thrown in that last crack about it being a long time until next season, Mike winced. *This thing involves way more than baseball.* However, the remark didn't seem to bother Cornelius, and Mike resolved to go see Buck as soon as he returned from visiting Mary Sulah Marello, Frank's mother.

Cornelius stapled Mike's claim check to his ticket envelope and handed it back to Taggart. Reflexively, Mike reached in his pocket for a tip, just as he always did, just as Jim and Anthony had done immediately before him.

"Keep your money in your pocket, Mike. I don't work for friends."

"I'll talk to Buck as soon as I get back." Taggart withdrew his hand and waved to Cornelius as he walked towards the terminal door.

"You know that nigger?" Jim Marello said.

Taggart ached to smack Jim right in his nasty, arrogant mouth, but knew it wouldn't change a thing apart from making him feel better. He stared at Jim in silence, then walked towards the gate.

"How do ya'll like New Orleans?" Mrs. Marello stood from where she'd been kneeling, pulling weeds. The woman wasn't an inch over five feet tall and spare, no more than a hundred pounds, as little as Anthony was big. She was wearing a wide-brimmed bonnet, a full peasant skirt and long sleeved white shirt.

"Haven't seen much, but it seems nice," Mike lied. He'd been to the City twice before and thought it a hot, dirty, indoor place.

"Jimmy, you run on now." Mrs. Marello's drawl slow, cool, a steel dove cooing. "Mr. Taggart and I have some gettin' acquainted to do."

Jim opened his mouth as if to protest, but his mother gave him a hard look and then shifted her gaze back towards the house, silently ordering him to depart without any backtalk.

Mike watched Jim retreat across the lawn. "I don't think your son likes me very much,"

"Of course, he doesn't like you. He knows Frank likes you a lot. What's that sayin'? 'For every action there's an equal and opposite reaction?' Well, the same can be said for those two boys."

"Mrs. Marell—"

"C'mon now, Mike … it is 'Mike,' isn't it? We need to be on a first name basis. You bettah start callin' me 'Mary Sulah,' that's what everyone calls me. Let's go get out of the sun and have some sweet tea. I have a pitcher over on the table under the umbrella."

Although late October, it was a warm, muggy morning. Taggart continued to sweat even after he'd been sitting in the shade for half an hour drinking iced tea. Mary Sulah was talking again about the rivalry between her sons. "In a way, the deck was stacked against Frank from the time he was born."

Taggart surveyed the huge lawn, the pool and the gigantic house as he listened and wondered how growing up in such surroundings stacked the deck against anyone.

Mary Sulah didn't miss the question in his gaze. "Wealth can't buy you a father. What do they say, 'location is everythin''?' By bein' born first, Jimmy occupied the prime location in Anthony's heart, almost the only location when it came to children. Maybe if Frank'd been a little more like Jimmy, able to stand up for himself a little better, Anthony might have responded to him differently." She shook her head at the memory."

Mary Sulah paused while she refilled Taggart's glass and then her own. "It put me in a terrible spot, I'll tell you, tryin' to keep all three of them happy. I used to talk about it with Anthony, but he couldn't see what I was sayin'. He'd just say he was doin' for Frank the same as he was doin' for Jimmy, and he couldn't understand there was more to bein' a father than jus' doin'.

"When it come to showin' love, to bein' enthusiastic about what your kids are doin', Anthony only had room for Jimmy. I'll give you an example. Anthony never missed one of Jimmy's sports games when he was in school, but I don't think he ever went to but one or two of Frank's before Frank quit playin'. I'd tell Anthony he ought to be goin' to Frank's games too, but he'd just say that Frank never played, he just sat on the bench, so why should he go?"

Mary Sullah's example stabbed Mike's heart. Bill Taggart, his dad, had let a lot of hay get wet making sure he saw Mike play ball.

"I'm a little surprised Anthony's spendin' so much time worryin' about these charges against Frank. Oh, I don't mean I'm surprised he's payin' for the defense. Anthony always paid to get Jimmy out of his problems; he wasn't goin' to do any less for Frank.

Maybe it's because I can't go and be up there on account of this puny ol' heart of mine actin' up that he's doin' it, bein' up there in North Carolina all the time and what not. But maybe there's more to it than that. Maybe there's a side of ol' Tony Marello I haven't seen even after forty-five years of livin' with him."

"Mind my asking what kind of problems Jim got into? I'm just trying to put Frank's growing up in some kind of context."

"Oh, nothin' real big. Certainly nothin' like Frank's facin'. Jimmy went up to LSU and was in a fraternity an' all. He tore some things up, beat up a couple of boys, the way boys will, I guess. Made a girl pregnant in high school. Anthony always paid for the damage, paid for that girl to go to California, smoothed things over ... much against my wishes most of the time."

"Against your wishes?"

"Against my wishes, yes. In my view, if he was ever goin' to really grow up, Jimmy needed to face the consequences of his behavior. But my view didn't count for much with Anthony when it came to raisin' Jimmy. Maybe he was right. Jimmy seems to be stayin' out of trouble now that he's married and workin' and got kids of his own, although Livia didn't seem to think so."

"Livia ... Livia, Frank's Livia? What'd she have to do with Jim?" Mike tried to make his question sound casual.

"As little as possible, I think. The summer before she died, Livia and Frank came down here for a visit. Livia and I, we became real friends those two weeks. She and Frank stayed with us, but Jimmy and his family were over on weekends and to go swimmin' and what not, the way families will when one of them is in from out of town.

"Livia didn't like Jimmy though. She probably didn' like him to begin with because she knew what a hard time he'd always given Frank. Then, after bein' around him for a couple of days, she asked me if I didn't think Jimmy was a little too hard on his own boys and maybe Lauren, Jimmy's wife, too."

"Hard on them ... Taggart wanted to say just enough to keep Mary Sulah talking.

"Livia thought Jimmy might be abusin' his family. I told her I didn't think it came to that, although Jimmy's certainly not one to spare the rod. But Livia, she thought his whole family seemed scared. Lauren told me Livia had things out with him. Told him in front of Lauren and the boys she wasn't about to let him do to them the way he'd done to Frank, and if she ever found out he was hurtin' anybody, they could come stay with her and Frank, and she'd report him to the police."

***

Marcia Banning rarely fell asleep on her couch, but she and Matt had watched the final game of the World Series together. Reds 7, Yankees 2. Not a thriller. After Matt went to bed, she poured a glass of wine and began leafing through wedding magazines. No call from Mike, who said he was going to New Orleans to interview his client's mother. There was so much to think about. The next thing she knew, it was almost one a.m. and Johnny Carson was signing off.

She tossed the magazine lying open on her lap onto the coffee table, turned off the television and trudged upstairs to check on Matt before heading back down to bed. Lights out, doors locked, Marcia turned into her darkened bedroom. *Oops, forgot to close the drapes.* As she reached for the cord, a man's head and shoulders loomed, erupted up from her flower garden, no more than a foot away through the glass. There, and then not, the face disappeared in a blink, its outline etched in Marcia's brain as if by a diamond cutting glass.

Marcia melted and froze at the same time, her insides dissolving within the crust of her fear. She stifled her scream so as not to awaken Matt, and clawed for the light switch. One light, not enough. She grabbed the bat from beneath her bed, and turned on every light in the room. Armed and illuminated, heart racing, she dialed 911, shaking, it took three tries.

"San Diego Police Department Emergency Response. To whom am I speaking?"

"Mar … Marcia Banning," she managed to get out. "Marcia Banning. There's a man ... Oh, please send someone, please!" She felt herself beginning to cry and flexed her entire face hard in an attempt to keep back the tears.

"Where are you Ms. Banning?" The dispatcher's voice was calm. "Your address."

"2410 Martin Way in La Jolla, the Shores neighborhood. Please hurry."

"I'm sending someone immediately," the dispatcher replied. "Stay on the line. Where are you in the house?"

"On the floor beside my bed."

"That's good. Stay put and remain on the line. I'll stay with you until the officers arrive. It will only be a couple of minutes."

"I can't stay on the line. I have to check on my son."

"Ms. Banning, wait," the dispatcher began, but stopped when she heard the clunk of the receiver hitting a hard surface.

Head on a swivel, bat raised, fighting the urge to scream, Marcia plunged upstairs and along the hall toward Matt's room. The door was slightly ajar just as she had left it minutes earlier. A gentle nudge with her left hand, bat high in her right, she peered through, scarcely breathing. There Matt slept beneath his jet plane bedspread, safe and sound. Just then she heard the sirens.

Three forty-five a.m., New Orleans time. Pounding on Taggart's door.

Anthony wore a robe vast as a circus tent. "Ya'll have a phone call Mike. Someone named Marcia. C'mon, I'll show you where's the phone." Taggart padded down the hall in Anthony's wake, dreading what he knew could only be bad news.

"Mike, Sullivan's back."

"What happened? Are you and Matt okay?"

"We're both okay now." Marcia described what had happened. "The police went to Sullivan's house, but by the time they got there, he was home. Oh, Mike, who else could it be? Even in the dark I know it was Sullivan – just the way he stood there."

"I know it too. Listen, is there anybody there with you now, besides Matt, I mean? By the way, how's he handling all the excitement?"

"He's upstairs, still asleep. Slept through the sirens and all. Probably the only one in the neighborhood who did. The police are still here. They're outside checking for any sign of the guy, footprints, something like that, I guess.

"Mike, what am I going to do? I'm afraid to stay here alone. I'm afraid to let Matt go out to play, even just in the front yard. I'm afraid to let him walk to school by himself."

"Marsh, is there anyone you can call to come over for the rest of the night – your in-laws? Sharon and Bill? We'll think of something more long term in the morning. I'm going to call Tom. He may have some ideas. One thing you need to remember though."

"What's that?"

"We will get through this thing with Sullivan. He's not going to cast a shadow over our lives much longer. You have lots of friends who can help. More than you even know. Oh yeah, and one other thing – I love you."

"I love you too, Mike." Marcia, despite her fear, relaxed a millimeter. "I will call someone to come over. I know we'll be all right. It's just so frightening right now."

Taggart hung up the phone and dialed Tom Horn's number.

"Tom, this is Mike. Sorry to call at this hour, but Sullivan was back prowling around Marcia's tonight. She saw him looking in her bedroom window."

There was a pause. "She's sure it was Sullivan?"

"What do you think?"

"I think maybe it's time for a blanket party."

At his end of the line, Mike smiled. Blanket parties were the unauthorized last resort Marines sometimes used to communicate to one of their own that his behavior was unacceptable and had to change. Usually the recipient was asleep in his rack when a blanket was thrown over his head and he was beaten by unknown assailants. Sometimes the beating was accompanied by a spoken warning; sometimes the guest of honor was left to figure it out for himself.

"Maybe so, but I'm not quite ready for that. Maybe we should call Ghost. If it comes to a blanket party, Ghost will know how to set it up. My guess is he'll have some ideas about other things we should do first. I'm going to be on a plane tomorrow morning. Can you call him and explain the situation?"

"Good idea. I'll call Marcia too. See if she'd like to rent me a room for a while, at least until you get back."

32

Friday, October 22, 1976 – 25 days to trial

Just the thought of turning Ghost Gonchar loose on Sullivan calmed Mike down. He'd known Ghost since his flight to Viet Nam in 1969. Boarding the plane at Norton Air Base, Taggart had taken the first available aisle seat. There by the window, so slight he made the airline seat look oversized, sat a Navy lieutenant reading a giant book. As he sat down, Mike happened to glance at the Lieutenant's ear, if you could call it that. It was nothing more than an ugly red knob of twisted cartilage giving no hint of ever having been something to hear with apart from its location on the side of the Lieutenant's head.

"Hi," Mike extended his hand as he sat down. "Mike Taggart. Where'd you wrestle?"

"Eric Gonchar. Cornell University, Ithaca, New York. Everybody calls me 'Ghost.'"

"What weight?"

"123 the first two years. 130 my senior year. Growth spurt."

Gonchar wore a red and yellow Viet Nam Service Ribbon with four stars, among other ribbons, beneath the eagle and trident insignia of a Navy SEAL. This was not Eric's first trip to the war zone. Fourteen hours and eight thousand miles later Taggart and Ghost landed in Da Nang, fast friends.

Tom Horn walked into the Mandarin House restaurant in Pacific Beach and saw Ghost sitting in a booth at the very rear of the dining room with two beers in front of him. Ghost pushed one of the beers across the table towards Tom but said nothing.

"I don't know whether you've heard, but someone's stalking Marcia Banning, Taggart's fiancé. You've met Marcia haven't you?"

Ghost nodded. "I heard the guy got off."

"Yeah, he did. But the near miss apparently didn't cool his jets any, because he showed up again last night."

Ghost raised his eyebrows, but again said nothing.

"Last night about one o'clock. Marcia walked into her bedroom and there he was, looking in her window."

"Blanket party," said Ghost.

"Maybe, but first we want to make sure it's this guy Sullivan who's back in business and not some neighbor kid whacking off. It was dark, and Marcia didn't actually see the guy's face, but she's sure it's him. Me too, for that matter."

Tom stopped while the waiter took their order.

"Can you can keep an eye on him for a few nights, get some idea of his routine, confirm he's spending time around her place? Mike's out of town for a few weeks, so I'm staying at Marcia's, riding shotgun in case Sullivan decides to come indoors. So, if you need help on that end, I'll be there during the night, watching. You can reach me any time of night."

"Glad to." Ghost nodded.

"Here's the dope on Sullivan - name, physical description, where he works, car he drives, license number, home address. Let me know if you need anything else."

Ghost studied the paper Tom handed him. "Looks good."

Both men took a swig of beer. Ghost leaned back in the booth and sighed. "You think Mike will actually marry this woman, Marcia?"

"Yeah, I do."

"I liked Cathy," Ghost said.

"Yeah, we all did, but things change, you know?" Tom took another swallow.

"Even though he bailed on her, I sometimes think Taggart's still half in love with her."

Their food arrived, and both were quiet for a couple of minutes while they shoveled in their first few bites. Ghost put down his chopsticks. "Whatever happened to that television reporter he was seeing after he and Cathy split the first time?"

"Don't know for sure. Probably too soon after Cathy. Mike blames himself for a lotta shit."

"What do you think of this Marcia? I met her, but just once to shake hands," Ghost said.

"Good person. Viet Nam widow. Husband was a Marine pilot shot down over the North in '68. She's pretty level-headed, not going to get hysterical. Taggart said when Sullivan broke into her house last year, he looked up, and there was Marcia with a ball bat ready to brain the guy if he got away from Mike."

"Too bad she didn't."

"She's got a son about eight years old, great kid. I coached him in Little League last year. Tell him how to do something just once, and you can immediately see him trying to do what you said."

"Smarter 'n me," Ghost said.

They resumed eating, saying nothing more until the check arrived.

"Keep track of your time," Tom said as they walked out. "Tags'll pay whatever it takes to get this guy off their backs."

"I'll be in touch." Ghost walked off.

When Taggart arrived back in Marlborough, Rhonda was at the apartment working on the list of documents and other items they intended to use as exhibits in the trial.

"Your partner, Horn, called. Said to tell you he talked to Ghost and the situation's being taken care of, and for you not to worry."

Taggart nodded at the message but didn't say anything.

"Is 'the situation' what I think it is? Or do I want to know?"

"Probably the less either one of us knows, the better."

"Can you at least tell me who 'Ghost' is?"

"Real name's Eric Gonchar. He's the private investigator I mentioned when we were discussing what to do about Troutman. We've been friends since the service. Ex-Navy SEAL. Interesting guy. Doesn't say much, but once in a while when he's out beyond ten beers, he'll start hollering, 'I'm a ghost. I come and go unseen, appear as if from nowhere, infiltrate like fog, evaporate like mist. I see without being seen, hear without being heard and kill leaving no mark.' Hence the nickname."

Rhonda rolled her eyes. "Pretty dramatic."

"Only when he's drunk. He's half Chinese and otherwise pretty stoic. But he was a Theater Arts major. Likes disguises."

"Funny, I never meet anybody like that at faculty teas."

Leaving Ghost, they turned to Rhonda's meeting with Dr. Lefler, the psychiatrist Frank and Livia'd been seeing. Taggart was skeptical of psychiatric testimony. "You think she'll have anything useful to say at trial?"

"Maybe on the issue of what homosexuality is and is not. Whether she'll be prepared to offer any opinions beyond that remains to be seen. I gave her a copy of the diary."

33

Tuesday, October 26, 1976 – 20 days to trial.

Ghost Gonchar's heritage from his Buddhist Chinese mother suited him well for surveillance. The waiting often lasted hours, sometimes days. Ghost was very patient.

At the moment, he sat almost trancelike in his truck with the local cable company's name and logo painted on its side, his only movement his breathing, an empty peanut butter jar beside him in case he had to take a leak. Three hours earlier he'd climbed inside his own head and begun waiting for his target, which is how he thought of Dr. William S. Sullivan.

Twelve-fifteen a.m., an automatic garage door three houses down opened and a red Corvette emerged, turned away from where Ghost was parked and drove off. Once the car disappeared, Ghost walked to the convenience store at the end of the block and called Horn without ever losing sight of the residence.

"Tom, it's Ghost. Sullivan just drove away. Keep your eyes open. I'll call you again when he comes back.

Ninety minutes later, the red car returned and entered the garage. Ghost placed his call. "Sullivan's back. Any sign of him out there?"

"Twenty minutes after you called, he drove by real slow, went down to the end of the block, turned around and drove past again. About five minutes later, he showed up again and parked across the street in front of the house, but he didn't get out of his car," Tom replied. "He stayed there about thirty minutes, then drove away."

"If he shows up again tomorrow night, you want to call the police?"

"To report what? Someone parked across the street after midnight? Probably not a crime."

"Something else then."

On each of the next two nights, Sullivan repeated the routine, and Tom and Ghost repeated the same phone conversations except for the part about calling the police. On the third night, Sullivan got out of his car, walked around the perimeter of the small park directly across from Marcia's and sat on a picnic table smoking a cigarette and staring at her house.

The following day, Tom and Ghost had another Chinese lunch.

"I think he's trying to work up his courage to try something," Tom said.

"Probably no point in me sitting out in front of his house any longer," Ghost replied. "I think I should wait for him in the side yard in case he decides to visit."

"Me too," Tom said. "What are you going to do?"

Ghost looked at Tom.

Whatever Ghost did to Sullivan would be enough. Tom didn't care.

***

As much as Taggart loved sports, under ordinary circumstances when Rhonda offered him a pair of prime faculty tickets to the Duke v. UNC game just two weeks before trial he would have declined. But seeing Cornelius at the airport a week earlier had been a guilty reminder he owed his friend a conversation with Buck Brown, and Buck loved football.

Saturday dawned dark and threatening. When Buck picked Mike up at noon, rain seemed inevitable. By the time they parked in the law school parking lot it was pouring. Taggart had a windbreaker, and Buck an old army field jacket, but neither was going to be of much use withstanding this deluge. "What do you think?" Mike eyed the sky. He'd given up all hope Buck would make the unsolicited suggestion that they skip the game and just go have a beer somewhere.

"Hell, a little rain won' hurt us none." Buck reached into the back seat for his jacket. "I'd a thought the U.S. Marine Corps would have taught you to love weather like this."

Actually, it taught me just the opposite. Taggart got out of the car and they began the short walk to the stadium.

As they trudged through the parking lot, Mike noticed Rhonda's car parked in the faculty section. "Buck, I see a car that belongs to a friend of mine who works in this building. Let's stop and see if she has an umbrella she'll loan us."

Rhonda answered their knock and Mike introduced Buck.

"We've met before, at graduation in '68," Rhonda shook Buck's hand.

Mike had forgotten. Buck and some of the others from the West End, Big Roy, Bobby Mack, Alvin Wade, Lester and a couple of others had come to see Taggart get his sheepskin. The unexpected sight of Mike's pals among the proud and well-to-do parents there to see his classmates graduate, created a lump in Mike's throat almost bigger than he could swallow. The recollection as he stood dripping in the doorway to Rhonda's office made going to a football game in the rain with Buck seem like the least he could do. It did not lessen his dread of the conversation he planned. Rhonda gave them her umbrella, white with pink polkadots and a ruffle around its edge, saying she'd be in her office until at least five, so they could drop it off after the game.

Wallace Wade Stadium was a giant concrete bowl spectators entered from the top. It held in excess of forty thousand people. When Mike and Buck entered after walking through endless puddles topping Mike's shoes, it was five minutes before kickoff. Apart from teams, coaches and officials, no more than fifty people sat anywhere outside the press box. Even the cheerleaders were nowhere in sight. "Gonna have our choice of seats," Buck said.

They made their way to a section on the fifty-yard line half way up from the field, and sat down with a squish, huddled beneath Rhonda's umbrella. Buck reached inside his coat and took out two pint-sized Mason jars containing what looked like muddy water. "Got some white liquor to keep us warm an' our spirits high."

It was the stuff the poster on the wall at the West End warned could make a person blind. The few times Taggart drank it in the past, he thought he was going blind. He took a swig from the jar Buck handed him.

By the end of the first two series of downs, the players' jerseys were so mud-caked, it was impossible to tell the two teams apart, let alone which player was which. The program Buck had purchased turned into a sodden mass of runny ink and disintegrating paper. Taggart's teeth chattered as if he had malaria.

He took a deep breath as he was about to launch into his plea for Cornelius. *At least I won't be wrecking an otherwise good time.*

"Buck, you remember the other night out at the West End when you said the team could use a catcher and you hadn't had a good one since I left?"

"Yeah, I remember ..."

"Well, I know a catcher in town who's twice as good as I ever dreamed of being, and he'd like to play."

Buck half turned towards Mike. He thought he knew every man in town who ever played baseball. There couldn't be anybody he hadn't already thought of unless it was someone like Mike who'd moved there from somewhere else.

"Who would that be?"

"Cornelius Kempton."

"Cornelius Kempton." Buck knew exactly who Taggart was talking about. "You mean that boy who played football for the high school and got shot up in Viet Nam?"

"That's him. Not a boy anymore. He's a hell of a catcher. I coached him a couple of years. I talked to him, and he wants to play."

"What do ya mean 'ya talked to him?' Ya'll didn't tell that boy he could play, did ya?" Buck took a big drink. "Ah!"

"No, I just told him I'd talk to you. How about it? Is that something you're willing to consider?"

"Ya'll los' your fuckin' mind, Taggart?"

Mike immediately saw it had been a mistake to bring up the subject when Buck was drinking, no matter what his mood otherwise.

"Look at it this way, Buck. It's a town team playing on a field owned by the town. The town buys the uniforms and equipment. Cornelius is a citizen of the town. He's got as much right to play as anybody else if he's good enough, and, believe me, he's good enough. He'd help you."

Buck just stared at Taggart for a full fifteen seconds; he took another long drink from the jar, which was becoming dangerously low. "Look at it this way ... Yankee ..."

What name was Buck thinking of before he settled on "Yankee?" Not that "Yankee" connoted great affection in the lexicon of the West End.

"I let one nigger play, I'm goin' to have twenty more hollerin' to play. Pretty soon it'll be the 'Marlborough Nigger Kings' or somethin' like. There's no such thing as lettin' one nigger play."

Taggart wasn't angry, just sad. He might as well be talking to a wall, but he decided to try one more time. "Buck, you think of yourself as a fair man, don't you? You want to win, don't you?"

Buck just stared at him. Mike knew Buck thought of himself as fair and few people Mike had ever known wanted to win more than Buck Brown. "If Black players try out and do a better job than Whites, why shouldn't they play? What could be more fair? Isn't that the way you'll have the best chance of winning?"

Buck drained the last of his jar and stood up.

"Let'em try out for their own damn team, Nigger Lover." He tossed the jar down and it shattered. "Fuck this game," he turned and walked away.

Sitting in the downpour amid a thousand shards of glass beneath a ruffled polkadot umbrella, Taggart watched Buck climb slowly up the steps and leave the stadium. He didn't follow.

"You look pretty in pink." Rhonda strained to keep from laughing as she faced Taggart across her kitchen table. Her sweatpants fit him like knickers and the sweatshirt left at least three inches of his torso bare, the elastic sleeve and leg bands stretched to their limits.

"It's okay," Taggart said. "The blood flow to my brain has been insufficient all day. No reason to increase the oxygen supply now."

"I'm sorry about Buck." Rhonda reached out and touched Mike's arm.

"Thanks. I don't know which friend to feel worse about. Stupid of me bringing up the subject once Buck started drinking. I feel like I let Cornelius down."

"Wouldn't have made any difference," Rhonda said. "Maybe the conversation wouldn't have ended on such a harsh note, but you weren't going to persuade your friend to integrate. It's taken the Union Army, the Supreme Court, JFK, LBJ and MLK to get this far."

"I guess I hoped news of Jackie Robinson had made it to Marlborough," Mike said. "Thing is, I knew Buck would never go for it. Now it's as if I tossed our friendship away for a gesture."

"Yeah, but it was a gesture you had to make if you were going to be able to look yourself in the mirror, Mike. You know that." Rhonda patted Mike's hand. "Sometimes you have to let people go. Maybe Buck's one of those. I know … I let go of my own father, or he let go of me. He won't say a word to me, despite all my efforts to patch things up. If he answers the phone when I call, he hands it to my mom without a word when he hears my voice. I just don't think about it any more."

Obviously she does.

They were both quiet for a few minutes, just watching the rain in the darkening late afternoon sky. Somewhere in another room Taggart could hear his clothes clanking around in the dryer. The sound made everything else seem quieter. Finally, Rhonda said, "Mike, can I ask you something?"

"Sure, El Mysterioso stands ready to offer advice on all subjects." He drew his hand and forearm in front of his face, a wizard about to mutter an incantation.

"No, this is serious. Do you ever get scared? I mean, for instance, does this Marello case scare you like it scares me? I don't know why I'm doing this – the trial I mean. Sometimes when I think about it, I feel like throwing up."

The idea of Rhonda being frightened by anything having to do with the law took Mike a couple seconds to process. "Sure I'm scared," he finally said. "Being a little bit scared is a way of life, especially if you're competing, and that's most of life, isn't it? There's a little sip of fear associated with every 'what if' in life. How you handle that beverage makes all the difference."

"How do you handle it?" Rhonda said. "How do you handle the feeling you get when you think to yourself, 'My God, what if we lose this trial? What if Frank is sentenced to die again?'"

Mike thought for a moment. "Hmm, … well, I just try to be like a surgeon and make my best cut every time out, whether I'm defending a speeding ticket or a murder case like this one. Also, keep in mind there's someone on the other side trying just as hard to achieve the opposite result, someone just as afraid of their own 'what ifs' as you are of yours. You may still lose, but you shouldn't feel guilty." As he spoke, Taggart was remembering how scared he'd been at the beginning of his first trial, a fender bender for which he'd prepared as if it was the Rosenberg treason case. "The other thing to remember is how seldom you've lost at anything you really prepared for, that you have every reason to be confident. Sometimes that helps; sometimes you're going to feel like shit anyway."

"But why do we do the very things that make us scared?"

"Rhonda, wouldn't life would be pretty dull if you knew the outcome of every thing you attempted before you even gave it a try?"

"Oh, I suppose so," Rhonda said. "I mean, I know so. But more and more I feel scared and I don't even know what's worrying me. There's just this vague sense of apprehension. There's so much to do, and everything seems so daunting."

"I know what you mean," Taggart replied. "When I first came here, the prospect seemed overwhelming. Getting off the dime where Marcia and Matt were concerned helped. Getting to know Frank's helped too. His 'what ifs' are a whole lot bigger than mine. I only hope I handle mine half as well."

Wearing black clothing, gloves and a dark ski mask, Ghost checked his gear one last time. He lay down behind a small bush on the side away from the street in grass already wet with dew, deep in shadow in Marcia Banning's side yard. Then he waited.

At twelve-forty, regular as the mailman, Sullivan showed up, did his usual drive-by once, twice, and parked across the street five minutes later on his third pass. He sat inside the car for another five minutes, then got out, started to cross the street, stopped in the middle, paused, then turned around and went to the picnic table in the park where Horn had seen him the night before. Twenty minutes later, after smoking a cigarette, he stood up, returned to his car and drove away. Ghost waited thirty minutes to insure Sullivan was not returning, then went home.

34

Sunday, October 31, 1976 – 15 days to trial.

"Happy Halloween, Coach."

"Good morning, Matt. Happy Halloween to you. You going trick or treating tonight?"

"I'm going with Charley and staying over at his house. There's no school tomorrow. Hooray!"

"You have a costume?"

"Yeah. I'm wearing my suit and tie and being a lawyer and, guess what?"

"What?"

"I'm going to carry your old briefcase for my candy."

"Pretty smart."

"Yeah. That part was Mom's idea. She got me some glasses to wear too, black ones that don't have any glass in them. She wants to talk to you."

"Okay, put her on. Have fun tonight, okay? Don't eat too much candy. Make it last."

"Okay, Coach. Bye."

"So, how's it going in the Tarheel state?"

"Well, on a scale of one to ten, yesterday was somewhere deep in negative numbers." Mike described his afternoon with Buck. "How's it going out there? Any developments on the Sullivan front?"

"Don't worry about that. Your Marine Corps Protective Association has the situation well in hand. Matt can't believe Coach Tom is actually living at our house."

"I hope he's picking up after himself. He's kind of a mama's boy."

"Right, and I'm the Queen of England. What are you doing today? Trick or treating?"

"Going over to see Frank Marello this morning. Part social, part business."

"Social?"

"Just to keep him company. He's a good guy. Marlborough jail doesn't offer many creature comforts ... unless you're a rat. Time drags."

"Frank, there's something I've been meaning to ask you," Mike said, as the two of them sat playing checkers. "When we talked earlier and you said you'd racked your brain about who might have had a motive to kill Livia, why didn't you mention your brother, Jim?"

"Jim?"

From what I hear, there was no love lost between the two. Surely you knew that."

"Livia didn't like Jim. But did Jim dislike her? I don't ..."

"Your mom says when you and Livia were in New Orleans the last time, Livia confronted Jim about the way he treated his family. Accused him of being a bully, just like he'd been with you. Weren't you aware -- "

"No. I wasn't."

"According to Livia's diary, she and Jim had another confrontation over the phone in October," Taggart added.

"Even if true, and, if Mama says so, I suppose it is, what's the relevance for this case? You don't think Jim killed Livia, do you? He was in New Orleans. We talked about an hour after I learned of her death."

"I think he might have. Can't ignore the possibility. The fact he was in New Orleans doesn't mean anything. He could have hired someone. Professional job. That would explain no fingerprints."

Frank Marello stood up and began to pace. "You know, I dislike my brother, maybe even hate him for all the awful things he's done to me, but I don't think he hates me. He just doesn't respect me. What he feels for me is contempt, not hatred."

A meaningless distinction. "Yes, but Frank, I'm not suggesting Jim had her killed because of what he thinks of you, but because of what Livia thought of him and her threat to do something about it."

Frank rubbed his forehead. "I don't think so. Jim's a bully. He likes to hurt people, but he likes to do it himself. He's not much of a planner. No joy in hiring someone else."

Taggart didn't think Frank was giving Jim all the credit he deserved in the bad behavior department. "I guess it doesn't make much difference. One diary entry isn't going to give us much basis for pointing the finger."

Halloween. Matt had been at Charley's house since mid-afternoon. Marcia stayed home to welcome the early trick or treaters, the little ones, and then met Sharon and Bill Bagosian for a late movie. When Ghost arrived after the last of the neighborhood witches and goblins had straggled home with their candy, he approached the house through the back yard. Horn was waiting there for him, standing by the gate staring over the fence across the front yard into the park.

"Boo!" Ghost came up behind Horn, making Tom jump.

"Jesus, how do you do that?"

"Trade secret. Any sign of our boy?"

"Yeah. He's early. Did his usual drive-bys about half an hour ago, but must have parked his car around the corner. I saw him walk into the park, but he's not sitting at the table and no sign of a cigarette. Probably in the tree line at the back of the park. I watched him go in, but haven't seen him come out."

"Kind of poetic if we nab him on Halloween, huh? Remember, keep the window to the side yard open a crack, so you can hear what's going on, in case I need a bit of help, but don't do anything unless you hear me call." Keeping in shadow, Ghost walked through the gate. Crossing the flower garden next to the fence dividing Marcia's yard from the property next door, he lay down on the grass behind the usual bush.

Just before midnight Marcia came home. Lights came on and went out in the house. Half an hour after the last light vanished, a tall figure dressed in dark clothing walked out of the park and across the street into the side yard where Ghost lay watching. Once in the yard the figure stopped every few steps, looked around, then resumed walking until he reached Marcia's bedroom window. There he turned slightly towards the house and stood looking through the blinds Marcia had lowered, but left unclosed, just the way Horn had instructed her.

Tom and Marcia lay listening in the bedroom, Marcia fully clothed and quaking, bat in hand under the covers, Tom on the floor on the side of the bed away from the window.

An iron forearm closed across the prowler's windpipe, a sweet-smelling rag clamped over his nose and mouth. A whisper. "Take a deep breath, muthafucka, or die right here."

Taggart had a bowl of Halloween candy sitting beside his door, but not a single trick or treater rang his bell. He had eaten enough of it himself to become half sick. As he brushed his teeth while getting ready for bed, they felt like they'd turned to sugar. The phone rang. *Damn.*

"Mike, Susan Hunter."

"Happy Halloween."

"I have to see you right away."

"Tonight?"

"Yes, tonight. I know what time it is, but this involves your case."

"Marello … what about it?"

"Not over the phone. I'm serious. Not over the phone. I'll pick you up in front of your place in –"

"Whoa. Why don't I just meet you somewhere over by Durham, this town has eyes, Susan."

"Okay. Meet me at Honey's Restaurant on I-85 north of Durham as soon as you can."

Taggart called Rhonda and told her to meet him in front of the restaurant in half an hour, pulled on his socks and shoes and was out the door.

When he arrived, Rhonda was waiting. "Are we staying here or going somewhere else?"

"Staying here." He led Rhonda to the booth where Susan sat drinking a cup of coffee. "We're meeting someone."

"Susan, my co-counsel, Rhonda Enright; Rhonda, Susan Hunter."

Nodding, "Please sit," Susan patted the seat next to her.

"Why are we here?" Mike asked.

Susan reached into her purse, withdrew a white envelope and tossed it on the table in front of Mike. "Read this."

The envelope typewritten to "Mrs. Charles Hunter," was postmarked "Marlborough" two days earlier. No return address.

"Arrived yesterday, but I didn't notice until today."

Mike withdrew a single sheet of unlined white paper.
The neatly typed two sentence message read:

> Mrs. Hunter:
>
> Any favorable rulings for Frank Marello will be deeply appreciated. If you and your husband want to discuss the nature of this appreciation further, mention it to Michael Taggart.

The note was unsigned.

Rhonda, reading over Mike's shoulder, gasped.

Taggart thought he might throw up, and it had nothing to do with how much candy he'd eaten. *What's the target? An actual bribe or me?* But for his friendship with Susan, this letter might have put him in jail beside Frank. "Anyone else seen this?"

"No. The sender must know I do Charles' reading for him."

It was one of the few times Mike had ever heard her call her husband by his name.

"I know you don't have anything to do with this, but Charles wouldn't. He would make a whole lot of trouble."

Taggart sat staring at the letter, saying nothing.

Rhonda sat staring at Taggart and Susan, wondering, who wrote the letter? How does Taggart know the Judge's wife? How does she know he has nothing to do with it? What shall we do?

"Susan, I'll never be able to thank you enough for believing I have nothing to do with this letter."

"You're welcome," Susan said. "Now, what do we do?"

"Well, I think I know the author. Maybe we can turn things around on him," Mike said. "May I keep the letter, and will you let me know if you receive any more offers of appreciation?"

"Sure. I don't want anything to do with it. Let me know what you learn ... if you can."

Susan checked her watch. "I have to run. Here's for my coffee –

Mike held up his hand, stopping her. "Are you kidding?"

PART IV
DENOUEMENT

35

Monday, November 1, 1976 – 2:00 a.m.

Bill Sullivan awoke spread-eagled on what felt like a hard pad or mat. His head ached, and even beneath the blindfold the room was spinning. His arms and legs were stretched to their limits. They hurt. But what bothered him most was the absence of sound, no street noise, no birds, no planes, no TV, nothing. "Is anybody there?" His words floated in space.

No response.

Sullivan turned his head to one side, then the other, then began to push against his restraints. He screamed until he was out of breath. When he finally stopped, the only sound he heard was blood pounding in his brain. Minutes passed. A door opened and closed, but no footfalls. "Who's there? What are you doing?"

A scraping sound, somehow familiar, began and continued more than a minute, ending at last with a soft click. Whatever was making the sound must have been laid aside. He felt pressure against his abdomen, but not much, belt being unbuckled, pants unbuttoned. Fingers curled around the waistbands of his trousers and skivvies. A yank and they were jerked over his buttocks as far south as they would go down his splayed legs. The snipping of scissors cutting, his pants falling away, leaving him naked from the waist down. Cold.

Fingers explored his groin. Another flinch. The fingers lifted his scrotum. The scraping sound – stropping, a blade being sharpened in preparation for cutting, the recognition triggering the realization of things to come.

"Who are you? Who are you? Why are you doing this?"

Silence.

Sullivan erupted, arching his back with all his might, thrashing, thrusting his hips from side to side against his restraints, but no more than an inch no matter his exertion.

A blow drove his teeth deep into his lower lip. The salt taste of blood oozed onto his tongue and dripped into his throat forcing him to swallow. "Please don't do this. Please don't do this. I never hurt anybody. I never touched anybody." His voice a mumble from between lips already beginning to swell.

In the midst of his anguish he felt a speck of moisture fall on his now uncovered abdomen, and his surgeon's brain saw a syringe pointed upward, being cleared of any air, a tiny droplet escaping. As he felt the cool of alcohol being swabbed, the sting of the needle entering his scrotum, he began to sob, not softly or quietly, but with all the convulsion his bonds would allow.

The door opened and closed, surrounding Sullivan with a sensation of emptiness. Minutes passed, or were they hours being given him to contemplate his plight? What could he do? What could he say? After an unknown amount of time, the door opened and closed again.

"Listen, whoever you are, please don't do this. I'll never bother her again. She'll never see me. She'll never hear from me." Speech accelerated by desperation, he talked fast. "I will no longer exist in Marcia's world."

A faint squeaking sound interrupted his plea, a sound so soft as to be undetectable to all but ears hyper-sensitive to the progress of fate. A sound Sullivan himself had initiated hundreds of times, the protest of latex being stretched over fingers about to invade another human being.

Sullivan felt something brush against his side – the hip of his captor as he leaned over his patient? Pressure between his legs reappeared, but no pain, only the feel of being touched, lifted, turned, manipulated, and then of the vicinity being patted by something, maybe a cloth, followed by more manipulation, then more patting. Sullivan forced himself to be still, to submit, to do nothing that would trigger the slip of a knife, a razor, a scalpel, whatever device his assailant was using to propel him into a future impossible to contemplate. Sullivan discovered he was holding his breath, as if by halting this most fundamental of life forces, the alteration of his body and of his forever could be arrested. With an effort, he compelled himself to breathe. Time passed, punctuated only for a moment by a "Hmmm," during a pause in the midst of his handling.

The prick and pause rhythm of sutures being applied, only three. He lay there soaked in sweat, and, he was sure, blood. A door opened and closed and later opened and closed again, otherwise the void. As the anesthetic began to wear off, his groin began to throb. Eventually, he was untied, but immediately retied as he had been once before long ago. He was then rolled off wherever he'd been lying onto some kind of a cloth, a tarp perhaps, that felt rough against his skin, and dragged through the re-opened door and down a single step. After a few more paces, he was lifted by the waist and heaved over the edge of some vertical surface, into what he recognized as the trunk of a car at the sound of the lid closing above him.

36

Monday, November 1, 1976 – 14 days to trial.

"Dad used to say, 'if you can't chase the bull into the barn, let him chase you,'" Taggart said when Rhonda asked what he intended to do about the note.

"That's it?" That's your strategy? You think Jim Marello's trying to bribe the Judge and make it look like you did it, and your plan is something out of Barn Dance?"

"Be like water, Lady Lawyer," Taggart put his hands together in front of his chest and bowed slightly from the waist. "Do not clash with enemies; flow all around, absorb; use enemy's power, watch silently as opponent dissolves, erodes."

Rhonda laughed in spite of herself. Iowa Zen.

"Just follow my lead and don't say anything about having met Susan." They walked into the General Johnston to meet Jim.

"What's this all about?" Jim said. "Daddy and I were supposed to go home today. Why couldn't this be handled over the phone."

"Where is your dad?" Rhonda asked.

"He flew home anyway. Somebody's got to work to pay for all this."

"I'll get right to the point, Jim," Taggart said, "I received a call from a woman last night who said she wanted to know how grateful the Marellos were prepared to be if Frank's acquitted."

The look of annoyance on Jim Marello's face faded. "Who was this woman?"

"She didn't say. Probably wanted to make sure we were willing to listen before revealing anything."

"Makes sense. What'd you tell her?"

"Mostly I played dumb…" Mike didn't miss the look flicker across Jim's face that said he thought playing dumb was Mike's specialty. "which wasn't hard since I didn't know what she was talking about, only that she wanted to know how grateful was 'very grateful?'"

"What'd you tell her?"

"I said I didn't have any idea what she was talking about. Then she hung up."

"What? It sounds pretty clear to me she was interested in a bribe of some kind."

"I thought so too. But I didn't know what it was about. I thought maybe some reporter, or even the prosecution was trying to set me up. With no idea who was talking, I had to make clear I knew nothing about it."

Jim sighed. "That was really stupid. After that evaluation you gave my brother the other day, maybe you should have listened to what she had to say. Frank needs all the help he can get."

"Maybe you're right." Mike struggled to conceal the anger he felt. "Now that person will probably think she was being set up. I guess we lost our chance."

"Not necessarily."

Taggart stared at Jim with what Mike hoped was a look of non-comprehension.

"It has to be the Judge call—"

"No. This was a woman's voice."

"Of course, it was a woman's voice. You don't think the Judge was going to call himself, do you? It was his wife calling. She's the one who does everything for him."

"Oh, I don't think so." Taggart shook his head. "I've known Mrs. Hunter a long time. She'd never do anything like that. She's the most honest person in the whole town."

"Maybe you don't know her as well as you think," Jim said. "Call her up and feel her out on this, since you apparently know her so well. I think this is the break we need to really do something for Frank."

"Jim, I can't do that. What if you're wrong? If I call her and you're wrong, there goes everything. Frank's case is screwed and so am I, big-time."

"I'm not wrong."

"But what if you are. If you're wro— "

"Damn it, I'm ... I'm not wrong." Face flushed, Jim looked around to see whether anyone appeared to notice his outburst. "It wasn't a coincidence Mrs. Hunter called you. I contacted her anonymously and let her know the family would appreciate it if the Judge helped Frank. You don't have to worry when you call her back."

"What ... what'd you do?" Taggart's eyes were wide. "I have to know before I take a chance like that."

Jim Marello winced. Taggart was even stupider than he thought. "I sent her a note saying that if the Judge wanted to know what our gratitude for favorable rulings was worth to get in touch with you."

Bingo. Rhonda marveled at the whole exchange.

"Marello, you dumb shit. I don't know what you think you're doing..." There was no hesitation or confusion in Taggart's voice now.

"Doing? I'll tell you what I'm doing. I'm trying to keep you from getting my brother hung. That's what I'm doing." Jim pointed his finger in Mike's face. "I don't like you, Taggart. Hiring you was a mistake. We need a defense counsel, not a psychologist junketing off to New Orleans on our money, asking my mother all sorts of questions about me, getting her upset."

Jim stood up as he finished speaking, but leaned over so he was nose to nose with Mike. "It's not too late for us to get a new lawyer,

Taggart. So, if you want to keep those pay checks coming, I suggest you make that call."

"Sit down, Jimmy." Mike's voice was low, but it sounded to Rhonda as if he had shouted. Jim sat down.

"I don't care what you think about me, but you've meddled in your brother's defense for the last time. From now on you're going to do as I say, and if you don't, Mrs. Hunter and I are going to the Judge with this note and an explanation of where it came from. Then there'll be a second Marello in need of a lawyer. Do you understand what I'm saying?" Mike held up an envelope as he spoke. Jim grabbed it and tore it up.

Mike laughed. "Piece it together, Jim. You won't find any note, not in that one."

"How're you going to prove anything? What if I go to the Judge first and tell him you sent the note?"

Rhonda glanced at Mike as Marello asked the question.

"Smile, Jim," Mike said. "You're on Candid Camera ... sort of." With that, Taggart reached in his jacket and removed a small, pocket-sized recorder, being careful to keep it out of Jim's reach. Unclipping a small microphone that had been fastened to the inside of his cuff, he reeled the cord to which it was attached back through his coat sleeve. "I'm through trying to figure out why you're such an asshole, Marello. But, if you interfere with our defense of your brother in any way, you're going to have to answer for this note and the explanation on this tape. Is that clear enough for you?"

This time Mike and Rhonda stood up first. Marello continued to sit at the table staring at no place in particular, ignoring their departure.

When they were in the car, Rhonda finally spoke. "That was great, Mike, except for one thing. It's against the law in North Carolina to record a private conversation without the permission of the person being recorded. The legislature just passed the law last year after Watergate."

"I know it. There's no tape in the recorder."

***

Shortly after 3:30 p.m. the phone rang at the Taggart & Horn law office, Whitey Malinzak calling for Horn.

"Just thought you'd like to know, Dr. Sullivan was picked up at a turnout on Sunrise Highway tied up, wrapped in a tarp."

"Dead?"

"No, but he was babbling about having been castrated."

"What ... no shit?"

"Except, he wasn't castrated. His nuts were all bandaged up, and he was wearing an adult diaper when they found him. According to the detectives, Sullivan said a big guy jumped him from behind when he was getting into his car out at Fashion Valley shopping center. The guy knocked him out and took him somewhere. When he awakened, he was tied up and blindfolded. Then someone cut off his nuts without ever saying a word. Police found his wallet without any cash in it beside his car in the parking lot by Robinson's department store. Detective says when they untied Sullivan and took off the bandage and his balls were still there, he passed out."

"Too bad the guy didn't cut'em off."

"I didn't think you'd be overcome with compassion at news of Bill's travails. One interesting thing though. When they found him, his big toes and thumbs were tied together, just the way they showed us in the Corps – the way Tags tied up Sullivan when he broke into Marcia's house. Probably a coincidence, but you and Tags might get a call from the detectives in light of Tags' recent involvement with Sullivan, just to ask where you all were last night. Thought I'd let you know. Pass the word to Tags, will you?"

37

Tuesday, November 2, 1976 – 13 days to trial.

Talking to Buck about letting Cornelius play on the team had been hard. Mike knew telling Cornelius the outcome would be just as tough, even though Cornelius wouldn't be surprised. They were shooting baskets outside the high school. Cornelius watched Taggart take two dribbles, stop, shoot a jump shot from the top of the circle and miss. "Man, you shoot like … like I don't know what," Cornelius laughed as he grabbed the rebound and dribbled out to take a shot of his own.

Refusing to fill in the blank, Taggart said, "You basketball players think you're such hot stuff just putting a ball in a basket. Hell, you get penalized just for bumping someone on the other team. Basketball would be better without any rules except the team with the most baskets wins."

"Yeah, if it's so easy, how come you miss most of your shots even when nobody's guarding you?"

"I'm used to shooting against resistance."

Cornelius cocked his head as if trying to understand a difficult concept. "That why you scored one basket last game instead of none?" In the midst of this day's banter, Cornelius stopped. "Who were those two guys I saw you going to New Orleans with a few days ago?"

"Marello's family. His dad and brother."

"So that's who they are." Cornelius rebounded another of Taggart's errant shots.

"Yeah, why? You seen them before?"

"Sure. I've seen 'em going in and out of the airport all the time the last couple years. That daddy, he's a big 'un. He looks like a devil. I just didn't know who they were."

Cornelius was silent for a moment. "Say, you ever talk to Buck Brown?"

"Yeah, I did. He said 'no.'"

"Is that all he said? Just, 'no?'"

Mike shook his head, "He said some other things, but you don't want to hear what they were. They didn't weaken his refusal any."

Cornelius took a shot and made it. Taggart caught the ball as it swished through the net and threw it out to Cornelius for another shot. He made that one too. As the ball rolled away, Cornelius chased it down, then looked up at Mike without taking another shot.

"Mike, what can we do? Baseball, hell, that's just a freckle on an elephant in this town. There's much bigger issues. How long ago'd they march in Selma and Montgomery? Almost twenty years since Little Rock. What about the Civil Rights Act?" Cornelius dribbled the ball hard one time as if for emphasis. "Things were supposed to change. They took down the "Whites Only" sign outside the restrooms and Robert E. Lee's picture at the Courthouse. But do you see much difference? Six hundred students at Marlborough High School, eleven Blacks. Three hundred-fifty at Douglas High School, none white. You call that integration?" Another hard bounce.

Obviously not. Taggart shook his head.

"Black people look up to me, Mike. They know I had some college. They think because I was a leader in sports, I can make a difference somehow. I want to, but can't, not without help. If you'd help me, we could do it." Cornelius Kemption, an already big man, grew before Taggart's eyes while at the same time Mike was shrinking. "One lawyer in this town willing to stand up and demand Blacks be given the things we shouldn't have to be askin' for … someone who'll file the papers that'll get the courts going on ordering Blacks be given equal rights would make a big difference." Cornelius threw a hard bounce pass to Mike.

Not missing the gesture, Taggart caught the ball. "I told you before, I'm not that kind of lawyer, Cornelius."

"What kind of a lawyer are you anyway, Mike? C'mon," Cornelius took a swipe at the ball Mike was holding, knocking it loose. He retrieved it and dribbled off towards the car without waiting for an answer. "Let's go. I'm tired of playin'."

***

After dinner, Mark Josephson leaves the Man In The Moon Café. He has been sitting at a table by the window watching the trees just outside begin to stir in the gathering dusk. First, the leaves rustled ever so slightly, then with greater agitation, branches bent before the unseen force of the wind. The weather is turning.

Two motorcycles cruise slowly past and vanish into the night. Their sound, follows their disappearance, making the street seem even more quiet and empty than before. Mark pays the check and departs, thinking about Frank Marello and the approaching trial. The prospect of testifying makes him feel as empty and dark as the deserted street. The crucifixion of Frank front and center, Mark hanging on a cross off to one side. Collateral damage.

When the two of them discussed Mark's testimony and his dread of being on the stand, Frank's lawyer said the ordeal wouldn't last forever. Maybe for the lawyer it wouldn't last – he'll go back to California. What about those who stay behind?

A moment after Mark turns in the direction of his car, footsteps sound behind him. At first, he gives the sound little thought, assuming from the rate of the steps that they will soon overtake and pass him. But no. As they draw near the footsteps slow. Two persons walk behind him. Mark picks up his pace. His followers walk faster … or is it his imagina--"

"Hey, Mister, you walk like a girl."

Ignore, ignore, ignore. The advice of every mother to every child who ever complained of being teased. Don't let them know they're bothering you.

"Hey, Miss," Another voice. "Do you suck cocks?"

Chuckling.

Don't turn around. Keep walking. Half a block to the car. Unlock the door, get in, drive away. Mark Josephson bites his lower lip. Afraid, he walks faster.

Footsteps behind him walk faster. Keeping pace.

"Hey Mister," the voices right behind him now, the feet almost stepping on his heels, "are you a queer?"

More laughter.

A rough tap on the shoulder.

"Hey queer, don't you know it's bad manners not to answer when you're asked a question?"

Josephson turns and is confronted by two young white men, both big. One holds what looks like a bottle in a brown paper bag. "Look, fellas, just leave me--"

"What's the matter, queer, aren't we your type?" The man without the bottle gives Mark's left soulder a hard shove, and Mark takes an involuntary step backwards.

"Please, don't hurt--"

"Goddamned right we're not his type," the other man says. As he speaks, Mark turns his head slightly in his direction.

"Don't turn away from me when I'm talking to you, you fucking fairy," the first man says. He punches Josephson on the right cheek with his fist, knocking him off balance so he stumbles into his second assailant. "I'll teach you some manners!"

"Don't touch me, you fucking faggot!" The man against whom Mark has fallen strikes him in the stomach. "Are you trying to make a pass at me?" He giggles at his own humor. "Do you love me?"

Mark Josephson has never felt such terrible hurt as the pain that stabs his stomach. The blow went clear through him, he can't breathe.

"Pl ..." He tries begging them not to hit him, but has no air and merely gasps.

Another blow, this time to Mark's nose, knocks him down, making his eyes water. A kick.

"Fucking queer."

"Kick him in the nuts. He don't need 'em."

The voices become indistinguishable. So do the kicks. Many kicks. Mark vomits. A red flash of pain - something sharp, glass, strikes him just behind the right ear. On and on, blows and kicks. No more talking, only grunts of destruction.

Lots of blood, his own. Mark opens his eyes, but can't see. Where did they go? They were here, kicking, gone now. The blood tasted salty. Mark's teeth hurt, ribs too, groin. He can't get up. No balance. Rest a minute. Maybe someone will come. The pavement is cool, rough against his skin. Mark's call for help, only a whisper, no air. Mark sighs on the sidewalk; the wind sighs in the trees nearby.

Friday, November 5, 1976 – 10 days to trial.

"Hospitals give me the creeps. I hate hospitals."

How many times had Taggart heard those words? Now Rhonda was saying them as they walked together down a long corridor, silent except for short bursts of sound from televisions escaping from each room they passed. The call from Stick had come three days ago, and Mike had been checking whether Mark Josephson could have visitors ever since.

"420." Rhonda paused at the threshold of the first room past the nurse's station. "This is it."

There was no television playing. Mark Josephson's room was dark. Taggart entered first to make sure all occupants were fully clothed. A heavily bandaged person, presumably Mark, lay in the bed farthest from the door. The bed nearest the door was empty. Mike beckoned to Rhonda. Thinking Mark was asleep, neither spoke.

"Who's there?" the human shaped bandage mumbled, turning its one uncovered eye in the direction of the sound of their footsteps.

"It's Rhonda Enright and Michael Taggart," Rhonda replied. "We came to see you. We were told you were beaten up."

"Do you feel like visitors, Mark?" Taggart said.

"I … I think so. I wasn't asleep. I hurt all over. May I have a drink of water?"

Rhonda poured water into a paper cup and held it up to Mark, where his lips could reach the straw.

"Can't do anything without hurting, even breathe … the ribs, I guess, or spleen. I just lie here and wait for the pain to go away."

"What do the doctors say?" Rhonda bit her lower lip in an attempt to keep from crying at the sight of the mangling. "How long will you have to be in here?"

"Another week maybe. They don't know yet."

Now that his eyes had adjusted to the dimness, Taggart could see Josephson was speaking through lips swollen three times their normal size and laced with stitches.

"My spleen's gone, maybe my left eye, I'm supposed to lie perfectly still, because something might tear."

"How …" Rhonda's voice was husky. Mike turned to look at her and saw she was crying. "Do you feel like telling us what happened, Mark?"

"Two men," Josephson hesitated, "young, just came up behind me on the sidewalk." He paused. "They started making comments about me. Being 'queer,' you know. Then they began hitting me … kicking too."

"Would you recognize them if you saw them again?" Taggart asked. "Anything unusual about them that would help?"

"I don't know. It was dark … but maybe. They were wearing tee shirts, jeans. One thing I did notice … one of them was wearing a Nazi hat."

"A Nazi hat, you mean a hat with a swastika?"

"I don't know if it had a swastika. I call them Nazi hats, because they're the kind you always see the German generals wear in all the old newsreels, like that one in the desert in North Africa, the 'Desert Rat' or something."

"The Desert Fox ... Rommel?"

"That's the one. One of them wore a hat like he always did, with a high peak and a little plastic bill in the front."

"Did you tell that to the police?"

"Yes. Do you think it will help?"

"I don't know. I hope so." Mike reached in his jacket pocket. "Listen, Mark, I feel kind of dumb. I wanted to bring you something, and the thing I always liked best when I was in the hospital was a book. I never stopped to think you might not be able to read.

"Anyway, I brought you a book for when you can move around a little. Have you ever read *To Kill A Mockingbird*?"

"Thanks, Mike. I saw the movie. Didn't read the book. I liked the movie."

"Would you like it if I read some of it to you?" Rhonda said. "I'll be happy to do that."

"I'd like that a lot."

38

Saturday, November 6, 1976 – 9 days to trial.

"Buck," Taggart said, "I'm glad you came. I know you're pissed."

Buck Brown stared at Mike through the smoke of his cigarette and said nothing. They were sitting in a booth at the General Johnston drinking coffee. Mike had been trying to contact Buck ever since the day after Buck stalked out of the football game in the rain. Mike didn't want to go down to the West End to talk to him. Too much temptation for Buck to tell Taggart to go to hell with everyone else looking on.

"Buck, do you remember the first game I ever played for you?"

Buck squinted in an effort to see back across more than ten years.

"I'll refresh your memory. It was down at Wilson on a ninety-five-degree day. All nine of us rode down there jammed into Big Roy's station wagon for an hour and a half with all the gear. No subs. We get there, and what's the first thing we see – a Black guy taking infield for Wilson. Right away there's a big powwow about whether we're even going to play. I threw in my two cents worth that we should to go ahead; and, of course, everyone, including you, told me to shut up and mind my own business."

Mike could tell Buck remembered the game and the argument.

"Point is, Buck, we disagreed about this same issue the first day we met; it didn't keep us from becoming friends then, and I hope it won't keep us from staying friends now."

Was that a slight softening in Buck's countenance or what passed for softening in a visage hardened by almost thirty years working in textile mills and tobacco fields?

"Seems like after all this time, you'd wise up," Buck said. "Hell, I ain't mad at you, Mike. Not really. Guess I'm mad at the situation mostly. Mad at niggers tryin' to shove themselves in where they ain't wanted. You don't see no White man shoving himself into a situation like that. Wasn't much of a game anyway, not with the rain and all ... never been so damn wet." Buck started to laugh.

A sense of relief flooded through Taggart. Ghandi couldn't have changed Buck's mind on this issue. Mike was no Ghandi, nor was he willing to let go of his friendship with Buck Brown. They finished their coffee, paid the bill and walked outside. Mike and Buck shook hands. Buck walked over to an old Harley Davidson motorcycle that he'd been riding since before Mike met him.

"See you're still riding that hawg, Buck."

"Close as I can come to a convertible."

"You know any other boys around here who still ride much?" Mike asked.

"Nah. Not anymore. Most guys my age either outgrowed them or killed themselves by now. My boy, Danny, rides with a bunch of boys from over in Chapel Hill some. Why?"

"Oh, a guy I know got beat up pretty bad the other night, over in Chapel Hill, as a matter of fact. He's a witness in this case I'm working on. You know the one. The guys who did it might be bikers. If you or Danny hear about anybody going around busting queers, would you let me know? I'd like to talk to 'em. They'll never know where I heard it."

"I know the thing you're talkin' about, but ain't heard nothing," Buck said. "If I find out somethin' I can tell you without gittin' Danny or none of his friends in trouble, I'll let you know. How's that?"

"Appreciate it," Taggart replied, adding, "They banged this fellow up pretty bad. Looks to me like they were trying to kill him. Two of them, only one of him. He's not going to be completely right again."

"Hmph. Might could be the guy wasn't completely right to begin with," Buck said. "Well, I'll do what I can."

***

"Are you sorry you ever got yourself into this?" Frank Marello's question surprised Rhonda as she sat on the bench in his cell staring at a chessboard, contemplating her next move. Frank was beating her socks off. She was beginning to regret teaching him to play this stupid game.

"What a strange question. I hope I'm not acting like I'm sorry. I'm tired, and I'm on pins and needles about what's going to happen, but the only thing I'm sorry about is that your family dislikes Mike so much. I think they're so wrong."

"I think they're wrong too. You like Taggart a lot, don't you?"

Rhonda paused so long that Frank added, "I hope you don't think I'm being nosy. It's just that you and I … and Livia, well, we were all friends for a long time before this all happened, and I'd like to see you happy."

"You're not nosy, Frank. You just have too much time on your hands. Not only have you learned how to beat me at chess, now you're becoming a matchmaker."

"I'm sorry." Frank blushed and looked down at the board. "I shouldn't have said anything."

"Frank, look at me. I'm teasing you. It's okay to ask anything you want. Really. As for Taggart and me," Rhonda searched for the right words, "the other day Mike told me he has this friend out in San Diego, Tom Horn, the guy he's partners with."

"Yes, I know. 'Taggart & Horn,' it's on his business card."

"Mike said Horn's one of the few people he's ever known who seems to truly put his friends' interests ahead of his own. He doesn't make a big show of it, just the opposite. He just does it.

"As I was listening to Mike telling me this, I thought, that's exactly the way Taggart does with me. It sounds corny, but I think of him as sort of a 'comrade-in-arms.' Back in law school, we got so we had a kind of telepathy when we were working together. We knew what the other was thinking without being told, what needed to be done and by whom, without even discussing it. It was a powerful feeling, and I'm beginning to see that sixth sense or whatever it is coming back as we work on your case."

Now Rhonda was the one looking down at the chessboard.

"Anyway, that's a long answer to your short question. Taggart and I, we just headed into combat together instead of love, that's all."

"Do you think the two are mutually exclusive?"

"Yes, with Taggart and me, I think they are. Besides, he's practically married. He's head over heels in love with this woman back in San Diego. When Mike went back to San Diego last month, they got engaged."

Frank seemed lost in thought, and Rhonda, lost in thoughts of her own, didn't interrupt him. Finally Frank said, "Your description of your friendship with Taggart reminds me of how I feel … felt about Livia."

The road home from Marlborough wound through Duke Forest. As she drove, Rhonda was still thinking about Frank's comparison of his feelings for Livia with her friendship with Taggart. It made sense. For the first time Rhonda began to understand the facts instead of just parroting them. "Oh, Frank, we've got to get you out of this," she said aloud as she sped through the shower of late autumn leaves cascading onto the highway.

39

Sunday, November 7, 1976 – 8 days to trial.

"Tags, this is Ghost. I have that information you asked for on Marellos."

"Great. Wait just a minute while I get a pen ... By the way, did you hear that guy who was stalking Marcia was found tied up out on Sunrise Highway babbling about someone having cut off his balls?"

"No shit?"

"Yeah. He told the police some guy robbed and kidnapped him and snipped off his manhood, but when they examined him, his balls were still there."

"Sounds like he's a little nuts," Ghost said, then paused. "Maybe he won't bother your friend and her son anymore."

"Hope not. Anyway, if I ever meet the guy who did that, I'd thank him from the bottom of my heart,"

"I'll pass the word. Have you found your pen?"

"All set. Fire away."

"Well, this guy Jim Marello's a car salesman, works for his father, owns part of the business, although it's the old man who calls the shots. Old man's a big Ford dealer. He's a whole lot more interesting than Junior. Nickname's 'Tony' naturally enough, but only people really close to him use it. Not real warm and fuzzy.

"He was a grunt with the First Marines in Korea. Apparently, he damned near froze to death at the Chosin. Hates the cold. Everybody who knows him down here knows about it."

Yes, he is more interesting. "That what happened to his hand?" Mike knew about the Frozen Chosin, fifty below temperatures, the First and Seventh Marines breaking out from an encirclement by a

Red Chinese army some said a million strong, eighty miles of bad road to safety in weather that would have made a walrus weep. Anthony Marello'd spent some time in hell.

"Yeah, frostbite. Wears gloves whenever it's below fifty, even in New Orleans. Tough old bird though. Self-made. Started as a repo man, picking up cars people quit paying for. Some suspect he was in the high-interest short-term loan business on the side." Ghost paused to let that sink in. "Repo men meet a lot of potential customers with a need for that sort of financial service." Collection was no problem. He was a lot rougher back then. Straight enough now. He's bought a lot of respectability in the last twenty years."

"What about Junior?"

"Lots of money. A businessman, likes to play golf, has a boat, belongs to Rotary and Our Lady of Peace Parish. Beats his wife—"

"Hold it right there." Mike nearly dropped the phone. "What do you have on the domestic?"

"Happened twice. October 12, 1973 and December 20, 1973."

"Any investigation?" *The dates are right. The dates are right.*

"Yeah," Ghost said. "Police went out both times. The wife, ... Lauren Marello, it looks like her name is--"

"Are you looking at police reports, Ghost?"

"Yeah, they're right here in front of me."

"Who made the initial complaints to the police, do they say?"

"Just a minute ... yeah, someone named 'Livia Marello,' must be a relative. Doesn't say who she is."

"What did they find when they investigated?"

"Black eye, fat lip, bruises, the basics, nothing broken. He popped her pretty good though, especially the second time. An arrest, no charges the first time, but the wife filed charges the second time, when the son of a bitch gave her a fat lip for Christmas."

"What happened?"

"Says charges were dropped the next day. No explanation beyond a note 'victim withdraws complaint.'"

The old story. How many times as a deputy had Mike been roughed up subduing a drunken husband or boyfriend in response to a complaint by some battered woman, only to have her come into the Sheriff's Office the next day and drop all charges? Stick finally quit accommodating them, refusing to drop charges on request. If hubby was arrested, Stick would file his own complaint and let the women explain to Given Watson why they suddenly were unwilling to testify.

"Ghost, can you get me copies of those investigation reports?"

***

No client ever tells you everything. There's always something undisclosed, sometimes intentionally because they didn't think it important or they're ashamed, sometimes inadvertently because they forgot, sometimes because Taggart hadn't asked.

"Frank, you and Livia had a pretty good relationship, didn't you? I mean, you told each other whatever was going on in your lives, didn't you?" Taggart wanted to make denial of Livia's interference in Jim's marriage, however righteous, as difficult as possible for Frank.

Frank looked puzzled but answered without hesitation. "Sure, as open as I suppose any two people ever are with each other. More than most, in some ways."

"If Livia was thinking of doing something that might hurt or embarrass your family, would she discuss it with you?" Mike studied his client.

"I can't imagine Livia doing anything that would hurt or embarrass the family, but if she did, I think she would discuss it with me first, unless maybe she thought she could protect me from being blamed for the consequences."

"What about Livia's relationship with Jim's wife, Lauren, did she ever discuss that with you?"

"They didn't have much of a relationship. Just what we talked about a few days ago. They met at our wedding and a few times when we visited my folks in the summers--"

"Were you aware Jim beat Lauren up?"

"What? No ... not beat ... .no, gave her a shove or something now and then. He does that to everybody. He's very impatient, I guess you know that by now. But not like physically attack. I don't know anything about that."

"Frank, he was hurting her, leaving marks. Livia knew it. She confronted him during your visit to New Orleans that summer before she was killed. It happened again in October and then again in December, on the twentieth, just four days before she died. Livia called the New Orleans' police both times to report Jim's violence. In December, Lauren apparently locked herself in a room and called Livia, while Jim banged on the door. I've seen the police report. Didn't Livia tell you about that? Didn't she at least seem upset?"

"No. No. I swear I know nothing about this. She never told me anything."

Taggart said nothing, sitting on the cell bunk, leaning against the wall. He knew people who were lying or hiding something sometimes couldn't stand silence and had to fill it up with sound, even the sound of something they didn't want you to know.

Frank remained silent.

"You see the implications these calls, especially the second one, have for your case, don't you? Jimmy sure had a motive to shut Livia up after that."

Frank was up and circling his cell. "It's all supposition," he finally said. "What you want to do is sow the seed of doubt by pointing the finger of suspicion at my brother. I know that, and I appreciate what you're trying to do for me, but I don't want to get off that way."

"What—"

"Mike, Livia's dead. I have no job, no life. Even if I get out of prison, I'll be suspect. The only thing I have is my family, including Jim, like him or not. What you're proposing will drive a wedge so deep into this family that I'll become outcast even from them, on the basis of what … circumstantial evidence of the flimsiest sort. Daddy's going to come down on Jim's side. He always has. Mama's going to stick with Daddy, even though she may disagree with him. Not only will I be destroyed, so will Jim. Most will continue to think I killed Livia, some will think he did. I'll have tainted him without knowing the truth, just to save myself."

Cloud dweller. "Listen, Frank …"

They argued. Mike reviewed in excruciating detail every bad thing he had ever learned of Jim doing to Frank, pointing out what he knew must be just a small part of what really went on. He brought up the bribe note to Susan Hunter. Nothing circumstantial about that – a clear attempt at sabotage. Mike wasn't trying to convict Jim, just protect Frank. They needed a 'reasonable doubt' - let the jurors draw their own conclusions.

"You're very persuasive, Mike," Frank said at the end of an hour, "but I've thought about this a lot, and my mind is made up. I just can't do things your way where Jim is concerned."

40

Monday, November 8, 1976 – 7 days to trial.

San Francisco, West Los Angeles, Greenwich Village.

Mike and Rhonda played the "Best Place To Try This Case" game. Mike's first choice had been Mars. None of their choices had been Marlborough. When Taggart's predecessor made a change of venue motion before the first trial, Hizzoner had denied it. Now the briefs had all been filed in the rematch.

Apart from the lawyers, the courtroom was empty of all but court personnel, everyone waiting for Hizzoner to appear. Rhonda gave her notes a last-minute shuffle. Taggart sized up the playing field. He'd been in this room a hundred times, as a witness, bailiff, occasional spectator, but never as a lawyer. Now it was his workplace, and he assessed the sightlines, the acoustics, the distances voices would have to span. He listened to the chatter of the clerk and court reporter for clues to their temperaments. Little things that never showed up in the official record, but could be the difference between success and failure if unobserved or unappreciated. There were two dark spaces on the wall behind the bench, where portraits of Robert E. Lee and Jefferson Davis had been removed sometime since Taggart graduated eight years earlier. Otherwise, the room was unchanged.

Once Court was called to order, Hizzoner spoke, ""Miss Enright, how is this case different from the identical motion two years ago?"

"Your Honor, we now have polling evidence that did not exist at the time of the first trial. Sixty-seven percent of Johnston County citizens already believe Professor Marello is guilty, forty-three percent think his homosexuality makes his guilt more likely. Those polling results are Exhibit 1 to our moving papers." Rhonda paused and studied the judge, as if trying to discern from his face what he was thinking.

"This is not the only new evidence. The mere fact that this is the *second* time Frank Marello is to be tried on these charges is a new and significant fact. This is a small town, Your Honor, tightly knit. Twelve members of the community having already convicted Frank Marello, it will be virtually impossible to find twelve new jurors who, out of respect, will not be influenced to vote in favor of conviction."

"Ms. Enright, what evidence do you have that the people of Marlborough will be unable to put aside their affection for one another long enough to make up their own minds about the guilt or innocence of the accused?" Hizzoner smiled a tight little smile. "Do you have a poll for that too?"

Sitting at counsel table to the left of the podium where Rhonda stood, Taggart glanced up at her. *How will she handle that?* As expected, Hizzoner was making Given Watson's arguments for him.

"No, Your Honor. All we have is logic and common sense. Who among us can say that, if asked to publicly contradict the action of one of our friends on a matter of life and death - someone with whom we play cards, someone with whom we drink lemonade on a warm afternoon, someone with whom we serve on church committees – Who can say he or she would not at least hesitate before doing something that says to all the world our friend got it wrong? Frank Marello – indeed, any citizen of this country accused of a crime, is entitled to have the matter of his guilt or innocence decided by jurors completely free from such hesitation."

"Well, let's hear what the government has to say about all this," Hizzoner said. "Mr. Watson."

Given Watson stepped to the podium, and Rhonda stepped aside, but did not sit down.

"Your Honor, the accused isn't the only one with a dog in this hunt."

Given the Folksy. Taggart groaned inwardly. Sitting and listening to one's opponent argue, whether twisting the facts or playing it straight, never easy, was doubly difficult when opposing counsel was exploiting an advantage. Watson's use of the vernacular, the 'aw shucks,' good ol' boy lingo of the rural South, was reminding Hizzoner that Watson was a local boy and, conversely, the carpet-bagging defense counsel were not. If the Solicitor was already using this edge with Hizzoner, Mike shuddered to think what Watson would sound like talking to the jury.

On and on he went about the right of the people of North Carolina to a speedy trial, justice delayed being justice denied. Court dockets were crowded everywhere. Why foist Johnston County's problems on another jurisdiction sure to plug the case in at the back end of its trial schedule?

As to the defense's polling evidence, "what kind of snake oil is the defense selling?" It was all "rank hearsay," man on the street stuff, nothing more. The Court was being asked to buy a "pig in a poke." Now Watson was really warmed up. "Let me give the Court just one little example. The defense says forty-three percent of the persons asked believe the fact the accused is a homosexual makes him more likely to be guilty. What this so-called pollster failed to ask is why. The accused's homosexuality is at the heart of his motive for committing this murder. He was engaging in a homosexual affair and wanted out of his marriage. That's not bias, Your Honor, that's logic, that's common sense. This so-called poll proves nothing other than that a clever conjurer of questions can dictate any outcome desired from the git-go." Watson shook his head in a show of disbelief, as if some magic power enabled Hizzoner to see his theatrics.

"Besides, who's to say the attitudes and beliefs of the people of Marlborough are any different from those of every other town in

North Carolina. Where's the evidence of that? This is not the sort of thing the decisions of a court of law should be based on. If Your Honor has any other questions, I will be happy to respond."

"No, I think I understand the government's position, Mr. Watson. Do you have anything you'd like to add, Ms. Enright?"

Watson took a step from behind the podium and Rhonda took his place.

"Your Honor, let there be no misunderstanding. Polling results are admissible in North Carolina courts." Rhonda stressed the word "are" so hard, it might have collapsed under the strain "That was decided once and for all by the *Marigold* case cited in our papers. The company that conducted the survey is a national company with impeccable credentials. Mr. Watson was free to depose the pollster. He could have offered the Court the testimony of a polling expert of his own, if he could find one who would support his position. But he has chosen to do neither. If there's any snake oil being sold here today, it's by the prosecution, not Frank Marello.

"If you listen to the prosecution, you'd think we're in some kind of race. This motion is not for purpose of delay, but to have the trial moved. If delay is involved, it's an unfortunate circumstance, but a small price to pay for an unbiased jury. Whatever delay is involved cannot be laid at the feet of the defense. As the Court may recall, Professor Marello unsuccessfully attempted to have this motion decided two months ago. He's the one in jail. If he's willing to spend a little more time in confinement to increase the chance of receiving a fair trial, the Solicitor hardly has standing to complain. Mr. Watson's still going to go home and eat a big dinner every night. He's not the one in jail--"

"Ms. Enright," Hizzoner said, "you're not down at some comedy club in Durham. Save your jokes for the classroom and stick to the legalities when you're in my court."

"If Your Honor thinks I'm joking, you're mistaken. The fact that Mr. Watson and all the rest of us are free to go home to dinner this evening, whether funny or not, is still relevant. The person imprisoned is the person moving for the change that entails some delay. If he can bear the additional time behind bars for the sake of being tried in an impartial venue, those of us who are free have no basis for complaint.

"The prosecution complains of delay. How much delay is going to occur if this case has to be tried a third time because it is tried this time in a venue incapable of giving Frank Marello a fair trial?"

"Well, Counsel," Hizzoner sat up a little straighter and squared his shoulders, "to the extent your poll indicates some potential for bias may exist, it is the opinion of the Court that any actual prejudice among potential jurors can be filtered out during the jury selection process. Moreover, I've been a judge in this County for almost fifteen years; I practiced law here for another twelve before that, and I have never seen the day when the citizens of Johnston County could not give an accused a fair trial—"

Sounds as if Hizzoner's running for re-election. Taggart turned around to see if there were any reporters present.

"That being the case, Defendant's motion for a change of venue is denied. Does either side have any further motions to present?"

Neither Rhonda nor Mike had expected to win. They'd explained to Frank the necessity of making a record so that, in the event of a conviction at trial, an appellate court would have the chance to find the hostile climate towards Frank had denied him a fair trial.

"Let's hope it never comes to that," Frank said as they huddled momentarily between motions. "What's next?"

Resilience was important in trial practice. Things were never going to go all your way. A bad ruling on the last issue must not dishearten you on the next. In coaching parlance, one had to "bounce back."

"Your Honor," Rhonda bounced back, "the defense moves to exclude from evidence the diary of the victim as inadmissible hearsay."

"I have read the papers you filed on this issue, Ms. Enright," Hizzoner said. "Let's hear what the prosecution has to say about why this diary ought to be admitted."

Given Watson was on his feet. "The relevance is that it contains passages written by the victim shortly before she died that suggest a strong motive for the accused to commit the murder with which he is charged."

"That overstates the content of –," Rhonda said from where she stood beside Watson.

"Counsel, it's not your turn to talk," Hizzoner said. "Proceed, Mr. Watson."

"With respect to hearsay," Watson picked up the thread of his argument, "her mother will authenticate the handwriting of the victim. She will testify her daughter was writing in her diary at her parents' house just three days before her murder."

Watson paused long enough to indicate he was now finished speaking for the time being.

"Your Honor, may I be heard?" Rhonda made sure it was her turn.

"Go ahead, Ms. Enright. Do you have any reason to believe the diary is not that of the victim?"

"Your Honor, the identity of the author is not the issue. The reason why hearsay is excluded, as Mr. Watson so ably pointed out in connection with the preceding motion, is because the speaker is not, and in this instance cannot be in court to be cross-examined about what she said in the diary to test her meaning, to explain ambiguities—"

"Well, she can't very well be in court if she's dead, can she, Ms. Enright?"

"That's exactly right. She can't. And Frank Marello should not be required to defend against some vague, unsubstantiated statement, the prosecution's interpretation of which may be completely unfounded such that the victim herself might well dispute it if she could be here in court to answer questions."

"Your Honor," Watson took his turn at interrupting, "what about the 'state of mind' exception? This diary's a statement of the victim's state of mind. It tells us what she was thinking, and there's every reason to believe what she was thinking was the reason the accused murdered her."

Taggart saw a look of recognition flash across Hizzoner's face at the words "state of mind exception." The "state of mind exception" was evidently something Hizzoner had heard of. It was straight out of law school 101. How many times had Mike seen the use of a law school catch phrase win an argument for the party who came up with it? No matter how badly the proponent might misuse the doctrine, the mere familiar sound of the name of the rule was too often enough to carry the day.

"With all due respect to the Solicitor," Rhonda said, "it's the accused's state of mind that is at issue in this trial, not the victim's. Frank Marello didn't have a crystal ball that enabled-"

"If the late Mizrus Marello was like most wives," Watson exercised the prosecution's apparently exclusive privilege to interrupt and make jokes, "she probably told her husband exactly what she was thinking."

"That illustrates my point," Rhonda said. "If she was here, we could call her to the witness stand and ask her. We'd say, 'Mrs. Marello, did you ever tell your husband such and such?' and if she said 'no,' then it's not very likely her state of mind motivated Professor Marello to kill her, is it?

"Trouble is, we can't call her and cross-examine her, and that's precisely the reason hearsay like this is inadmissible whether it describes her state of mind or talks about the weather."

"There's nothing to prevent you from asking your client if his wife told him what she was thinking," Hizzoner said.

"Sure, we can," Rhonda replied. "But his denial is just what the jury expects to hear. They know he can say anything he wants, because his wife's no longer around to contradict him if what he says is untrue. It is the accused's right to have the jury hear it from the declarant herself or not to have the diary come into evidence at all."

"Be that as it may, Counsel," Hizzoner's tone said he had finished listening. "Mr. Watson is right. State of mind is a well-recognized exception to the hearsay rule. Defense's motion to exclude the diary of Livia Marello is denied."

"Thank you, Your Honor," Rhonda turned back toward Mike and Frank seated at the defense table. Frank was sitting with his hands folded, staring straight ahead. Rhonda wondered what he was thinking.

Taggart, too, was wondering about Frank. *Frank Marello, this poor, tall, awkward, gracious, innocent, condemned, reprieved, simple, complex man sitting on a hard wooden chair in the room where he has already once been sentenced to die, listening to efforts which are the beginning of his last best hope of being saved continue to fall on deaf ears – what's Frank Marello thinking?*

Mike didn't know much about psychiatry and even less about eastern religions, but in a year of infantry combat and more than a hundred trials, he had seen people stripped layer by layer down to places even they didn't know existed, places where they harbored thoughts they didn't even know they had. Psychoanalysis and meditation might be other ways of peeling back all the layers to reach one's essence, or whatever it was called, but being on trial for one's life could sure do the trick.

By the time Rhonda reached counsel table, Howard Julius, the deputy who was riding herd on Frank, had already snapped the cuffs on his wrists for the trip back across the street to the jail. Frank extended both his hands, and Rhonda shook them.

"Nice try," Frank said.

Mike joined them and put his hand on Frank's shoulder. "Hang in there, Frank," he said in a low voice so Howard, who had taken a couple of steps back as an accommodation, could not hear. "Do you know the story of B'rer Rabbit and the tarbaby?"

Frank nodded.

"Well, that diary isn't a wholly unfriendly briar patch. The more Watson thinks we hate it, the harder he's going to try to sell it to the jury. He may discover it's a mixed blessing."

Frank smiled slightly at Taggart's message, lifted his manacled wrists to the level of his chest and made two fists. "Don't worry about me. I understand." He was led away.

"You're unusually quiet," Rhonda said as they walked back to the car.

"Just thinking about Frank. 'Don't worry about me,' he said. Most of my clients don't want me to worry about anything else. Funny, Frank's attitude makes me want to worry about him even more than I already do."

41

Monday, November 8, 1976 – Late Morning

"There's someone sitting on your front steps," Rhonda pointed towards Mike's apartment as they drove up Church Street after the hearing.

Taggart's eyes flicked from the street to his front stoop, then widened in disbelief. "Rhonda," he said, "you're about to meet Eric Gonchar."

The slender figure with slightly Asiatic features stood up and walked toward them. "Hello, Ghost," Rhonda said as she emerged from the car, right hand extended. "Rhonda Enright."

"What are you doing here, Ghost?" Mike unlocked the door and the three of them walked inside.

"Came for the Fall colors."

"Too bad. They peaked about ten days ago. They're fading fast."

"I was busy then," Ghost said. "But in that event, is there anything I can do to help? What's going on in your case?"

"Next thing's jury selection, Ghost. We need to develop a profile of pluses and minuses, questions to ask, things to look for when we're choosing the jury."

"Who are you looking for?"

"People who don't necessarily equate homosexuality with devil worship."

"Pretty tall order."

The three of them talked for a few minutes about the best ways of taking the County's temperature regarding Frank Marello. Brainstorming.

"Stay here if you want, Ghost. There's an extra room." Mike said, "Then you can just wander around the County, engage people about the case without being too obvious. Try to get a fix on their attitudes and backgrounds. It would be nice to have a jury analyst working for us. Maybe that can be you."

"Purpose driven wandering's one of my strengths," Ghost said.

Rhonda laughed.

***

"Hi. I thought perhaps you could use some cheering up. Hizzoner told me he mowed you down in court today."

"Susan," Taggart peered over her shoulder to see if anyone else was in the vicinity as she stood in his doorway. Church Street, Marlborough's busiest, ran past forty feet away. "You can't be here."

"Well, I am here, as you can plainly see." Susan Hunter brushed past him into the living room.

Taggart quickly closed the door and turned to see Susan on the far side of the breakfast bar opening the refrigerator. "I knew you'd have beer," she said, peering at the mostly empty shelves. "Have one." She tossed him a can and opened one for herself. "I think Hizzoner's driven us both to drink today."

She looked around the room. "So. This is the nerve center of the great defense effort. A little Spartan for my taste." Susan eyed Taggart's orange vinyl couch, uncarpeted floor and walls adorned only with a bulletin board to which various scraps of paper were pinned.

"Tell me your version of what happened in court." She sat down.

"Not much to tell. Hizzoner thinks the good people of Johnston County are sufficiently free from prejudice and unburdened by preconceived notions of guilt to enable them to give Frank Marello a fair trial. You know how open-minded the people of the rural South can be."

"Well, where do you think he should have transferred it? The rest of the State's just as 'open-minded.'"

"Any place where Marello hasn't been convicted once already on less evidence than the prosecution will have at its disposal this time around."

"From what I hear, that's only one problem among many."

"Why? What did Hizzoner say about that?"

"Oh, just that the defense made a couple of motions that wasted his time and your friend Rhonda is a smartass to boot, and that he liked you better when you were a deputy sheriff. Nothing that should cause you any concern."

"His feelings don't surprise me," Mike said. "Although I think I felt better when I didn't know for sure."

"If it's any consolation, the old wolverine feels that way about almost everybody. Maybe you should take a break and think about something else for a change," Susan said. "Sit down and tell me about this Marcia woman who's won your heart. How'd you meet her? What made you fall in love?"

Missing Marcia ever more as the weeks before trial went by, Taggart welcomed the opportunity to talk about her and gave Susan long answers to her short questions, including the whole Sullivan saga. When he came to what made him fall in love with her, he smiled. "Like a lot of the same things. She makes me laugh. Why does anybody fall in love? She's courageous."

"Courageous? What kind of courageous?" Susan asked. "Because she's a single mom? Lots of them around. That deal with the crazy doctor?"

"Well, when she was standing there, ready to brain Sullivan with a ball bat if he got away from me, that was no small thing," Mike said.

Susan hadn't said a wortd throughout the entire story. Now she nodded her head as if in homage to Marcia'a sucking up her fear. "She'll do for you," was all she said.

It was after eleven when she stood to leave. "You know, Mike," she was standing by the door, "you're a good guy. Let's always be friends, even after this trial's all over. Stay in touch, I mean. Okay?" She kissed Taggart on the cheek, opened the door and walked out into the night.

***

The morning after his arrival Ghost got a job selling Bibles door to door. At the end of his first four days on the job, he turned in his inventory and resigned. He had almost been bitten by two dogs, sold ten bibles, and had countless conversations about the case with residents across a broad spectrum of Johnston County neighborhoods. Everybody seemed to be aware the trial was about to happen, and many were eager to talk about it.

Evenings he spent in the Marlborough Library, a lovely little building near the north end of downtown, scanning microfilm, focusing and refocusing the blurred images of newsprint on the screen, never able to get it quite right, leaving each night with a headache. *The News of Johnston County – Chapel Hill, Marlborough, Carrboro – Between and Beyond.* What could the local papers tell him about the first trial that might be useful to Mike and Rhonda in the second?

He learned the first jury consisted of eight men and four women; ten Whites and two Blacks, possibly as many as six college degrees, something Mike and Rhonda surely knew already. According to post-trial interviews, the jury had gone home following the first day of deliberations having voted 7-5 for acquittal. After three hours of deliberations the next morning, it had voted 12-0 to convict. Not much about the reason for the shift. Wondering why, Ghost pushed back his chair.

Following the reversal of Marello's conviction by the State Supreme Court three months earlier, an editorial in the News stated:

> Men of good will and intellect may disagree with the Supreme Court's interpretation of the law. Men of good will and intellect may consider the expense of a second trial a waste of hard-earned taxpayer dollars. Men of good will and intellect may find the personal habits of the accused not only illegal, but repugnant. Nevertheless, the law must govern even in distasteful circumstances, if each of us is to remain secure in our constitutional guaranty of freedom.

"I don't think I want any 'men of good will and intellect' on this jury," Taggart said when Ghost showed him a copy of the editorial.

42

Tuesday, November 9, 1976 – 6 days to trial

"Cornelius," Mike and Rhonda stood up as Mike's friend approached their table at the General Johnston, "thanks for coming. Meet a friend of mine, Rhonda Enright."

Taggart watched the two of them shake hands with a mixture of relief and regret - relief Cornelius accepted his invitation to meet, regret at the obvious reserve in his friend's manner. "Cornelius, Rhonda teaches at Duke Law School. I've talked about your situation here in Marlborough with her, and she wants to help."

Cornelius shifted his gaze in Rhonda's direction.

"Cornelius," Rhonda smiled slightly as she said his name, "unless I miss my guess, you not playing on the Marlborough team is just the tip of the iceberg. I mean, when it comes to the complaints of the Black community here in Marlborough. Am I right?"

Cornelius nodded.

"Well, we can talk about all of that in great detail later, but first, let me tell you a bit about myself." Rhonda's civil rights pedigree followed, her forsaking Stanford for a predominantly Black southern college, voter registration in Mississippi, Selma, occasional stints in jails that made Mr. Jack's establishment seem like the Waldorf.

"No question you've been some important places, Miss Enright, the question is, where are you willing to go? Getting school buses to run in Marlborough's Black neighborhoods and the like's not going to make network TV."

Rhonda stirred her coffee, reflecting on what was just said. "Here's the thing, Cornelius," she said, looking up, "I live right next door to Marlborough. Seems like I ought to work at putting my own neighborhood in order before going out to conquer the world. Besides, I have a clinic full of law students not nearly as interested in seeing themselves on TV as they are in seeing themselves in court."

Rhonda's answer coaxed Cornelius' first smile since his arrival.

"But, Cornelius, this won't be easy. If you're going to be the point-man on this effort, expect trouble, not just for you, but for your family, and not just from the White community. There'll be Blacks who resent what you're doing, who think you're just stirring up trouble. So the question's not only where I'm willing to go, but where you're willing to go."

Mike watched his friend straighten, his eyes narrow. "The distance."

43

Friday, November 12, 1976 – 3 days to trial.

The car was sitting with its hood up on Friday when Tremaine Troutman came down the steps from above the empty store on his way to work. Some little white guy in a black windbreaker and pants and a stocking cap pulled down over his ears was leaning over the engine staring at it. As Tremaine reached the bottom of the stairs the man stood up and looked at the sky. Then, evidently hearing Tremaine's footsteps, the man turned towards him. He was young and wore glasses. "Excuse me, do you know anything about car engines?"

Tremaine was in a hurry, because he planned to stop for breakfast before work, but he turned so as to get a better look at the guy with his good eye. The man was wearing a cleric's collar. "Some. What's the trouble?"

"Wish I knew. Has plenty of spark. Turns over, but won't start. It was running fine last night when I parked."

"Carburetor maybe," Tremaine said. "Lemme take a look." He leaned in and unscrewed the wing nut holding the air filter in place atop the carburetor and set the filter on the fender. This uncovered a small hole in which a metal disc was fitted, held there by a tiny node connecting to the rim at each end of its radius. Tremaine poked the disc with his finger and it pivoted up and down.

"What are you doing?" the man asked.

"That's the butterfly valve. Sometimes it get stuck and the engine can't get no air. Then it won't start, but it seems to be working. Git in and try to start it. Lemme listen."

The man got in and Tremaine heard the click of the ignition as he turned the key. The engine turned over immediately, but wouldn't catch.

"Okay." Tremaine held up his hand. "Hmmm. Wait here. Ah got something that might work." He turned and walked back up stairs to his apartment. A minute later he returned holding a spray can.

"Git in and try it again when ah say."

The man got in and opened the choke ever so slightly. Tremaine sprayed whatever was in the can into the hole at the top of the carburetor and said, "Now."

The engine roared to life. Leaving the engine running, the man got out. "Thank you very much. What is that magic stuff?"

"Oh, some kinda high test stuff." Tremaine replaced the air filter. "You maybe had a vapor lock and this stuff just kinda blows it away. Here, you can keep this can case it happens again. But look out, it's almost empty."

"Thank you again. I'm John Kennedy, by the way." The man stuck out his hand.

Tremaine shook it. "Tremaine Troutman."

"Mr. Troutman, can I buy you a cup of coffee, give you a ride somewhere? I was going to stop for a cup myself. How about it?"

"Ah dunno. Gotta be at work by eight. What time is it?"

"It's only six-fifty now. Where do you work? I can give you a ride."

"Workin' at Belmer's Garage over south of downtown on Columbia."

"Perfect. I'm headed that direction myself after coffee. Hop in."

Tremaine hopped in. He put the Bible that was lying on the passenger seat up on the dash.

The cafe on the edge of campus was largely deserted, just a couple of students on the way to early classes getting coffee to go. Tremaine and Kennedy sat down with their coffees in a marred wooden booth. Tremaine noticed that Kennedy bowed his head briefly before taking his first bite of donut. "So, you're a mechanic,"

Kennedy said. "My guardian angel was looking after me this morning."

"Ah'm a bit of everything. You must be a church preacher."

"Yes and no. I'm an ordained minister, but I don't have a church. I work for an outfit called Carolina Prison Ministries. We bring the word of God into the prisons, help the chaplains, try to help the prisoners deal with their burdens. Are you a church-goer, Tremaine? You're certainly a good Samaritan."

"Used to be. My mama raised me up Baptis', but ah ain' been for a long time. You ever work in the prison over in Raleigh?"

"All the time."

Tremaine took a swallow of coffee and set down his cup, looking down as if studying its contents. Without looking up, he asked, "Ever meet a prisoner named Frank Marello?"

"I know about Marello, but I've never met him. I was living here when his wife was murdered and he was convicted. According to the paper, they're going to try him again in a few days. Do you know him?"

"Ah testified in the first trial. Used to do some work for him an' his wife." Tremaine mumbled when he said these words, sighed and looked down. "They was nice people."

"Is something wrong, Tremaine?"

Tremaine hesitated. "You're a real preacher, right?

"I'm not a preacher, because I don't have a church, but I am an ordained minister in the Baptist faith, yes."

Tremaine took a deep breath. "Ah said somethin' that wudn't true in the first trial, and it's weighin' on me."

"What did you say, Tremaine?"

"Ah said that Marello axed me to kill his wife, an' that afterwards he tol' me he did it."

"Wow." Kennedy's voice was soft. "Whatever made you do such a thing, Tremaine?"

"That big Sheriff came around axing me questions about how ah used to work at Marello's an' how ah knew about their apartment an' stuff an' how they had gave me a key to the place when ah was workin' there. It was kinda like he thought ah mighta killed her. Ah got scared. White Sheriff lot rather have a Black murderer than a White one." Troutman was beginning to choke up, swallowing hard.

"Wow," Kennedy said again. "That's a terrible thing you did, Tremaine, but I think you know that, don't you?"

Tremaine nodded. Tears were trickling down his cheeks. "They wants me to testify again."

"What are you going say, Tremaine?"

"Ah dunno. How can ah not? Ah gots one of them papers that says ah hafta be there at the court next Monday. What'm ah gonna do? What can ah do?"

"I suggest that you take it to the Lord, Tremaine. Pray about it. Pray for guidance."

"Will you pray with me, Reverend Kennedy? Help me talk to the Lord?"

"I'd be honored. Give me your hands. Let's bow our heads.

"Lord, I'm here with your servant, Tremaine. He's made a bad mistake, but I know You already know that. He was afraid, Lord. We're all afraid. You know that too. So we've come to ask for Your help. Tremaine wants to do the right thing, but it will take strength he doesn't know he has. He's afraid if he admits his lie to the authorities, they'll punish him, so he's admitting it to You and asking for Your guidance and forgiveness. Please show him the way Lord. Blot out the untrue words from his memory. Help them to fade away and be replaced with the determination to stay right with You and all Your children in the future. We ask this all in the name of Your son, Jesus. Amen."

"Amen," Tremaine echoed. He was still crying. Kennedy offered him a napkin. Tremaine wiped his eyes and blew his nose.

"Thank you, Reverend. Ah thinks ah know what needs be done now. Praise God ah met you this mornin'."

"You're welcome, Tremaine. Praise God my car and I met you."

They both laughed.

44

Saturday, November 13, 1976 – 2 days to trial.

"So, what'd you learn about the customs, conventions and mores of the citizens of Johnston County?" Mike asked Ghost as the two of them sat in Taggart's living room on Saturday morning.

"Pretty good market for Bibles," Ghost said.

Rhonda stood on the kitchen side of the counter separating the kitchen from the living room converting her coffee to dark-colored cream. "In humor there is truth."

Ghost was looking at some notes he'd made. "One thing I found interesting is the way the first jury turned around overnight, seven to five for acquittal when they went home for the night, twelve-zero to convict by noon the next day. Why do you suppose that was?"

"Maybe family pressure," Rhonda said. "Should we request the jury be sequestered?"

They discussed the demographics of the first jury, occupations, married or single, education, family size, race, religious affiliations, information culled from the transcript of the first jury selection and Ghost's microfilm study. Did any of those factors create predispostions? In whose favor?

"It seemed like persons from blue collar backgrounds were more open to the possibility Frank didn't do it than people from more affluent backgrounds," Ghost said. "But sample size is a problem. I mean, all told I probably only discussed it with fifty or sixty people. Hard to draw any conclusions."

Taggart described his conversation about the case with Buck and his pals at the West End. It seemed consistent with what Ghost was hearing.

"On the other hand, that wasn't my experience with Marine Corps' juries," Mike said. "Staff NCOs are the blue collar of the Corps, and they were the hardest horses you could get on a jury – quick to convict, long on sentencing. Officers tended to be much more lenient."

"Yeah," Ghost said, "but the military is kind of a bubble all its own, especially the Corps. Those NCOs are just keeping the bar high within their own organization. They think of themselves as elite; their harshness, or whatever you want to call it, is their way of keeping the organization's standards high, same way in the SEALs. I'm not sure that translates to the wider civilian community."

Through the steam from her coffee, Rhonda studied Ghost. That was a pretty astute observation for someone with ears like that.

Mike and Rhonda argued at length over who was more likely to be sympathetic to homosexuality, Whites or Blacks. "Whites, because as a general rule they're better educated," Rhonda said.

"I might agree with you if this was California, but not North Carolina."

"What's geography got to do with it?"

"My experience in this town is that the educated Whites are the most judgmental, the group most likely to look down its nose at somebody else. Remember that story I told you about what happened to Cornelius Kempton's mother over at Colonial Baptist Church?"

"Well, they're still better than the uneducated ones who've never been outside the County except for a car race," Rhonda said.

"Not if a person's Black. An uneducated Black is no stranger to discrimination," Mike replied.

"You're making a mistake grouping sympathy for sexual preference with race," Rhonda said. "Stop and think. Most people think sexual preference is a matter of choice, and that, unlike being Black, Frank doesn't have to be gay if he doesn't want to. How much sympathy do you think Blacks will have for someone who invites discrimination?"

"Blacks may think that, but so do Whites," Mike said. "That's a constant cutting across both. I still prefer a Black juror, all other things being equal."

So it went for more than two hours. Mike's legal pad was full and the second pot of coffee empty by the time Rhonda and Ghost departed, Ghost in the car Taggart had been using, saying he'd be back in a couple hours. He just wanted to "drive around."

"Oh, Tags," he said on his way out the door, "You know what's interesting? When I talked to that guy, Tremaine Troutman, yesterday. A blind eye can still cry."

45

Monday, November 15, 1976 – Trial Day 1

Jury selection in North Carolina required each side to ask all its questions of a given candidate, and to decide whether to challenge for cause before moving to the next. While being questioned, the candidates sat in the witness stand.

"Johanna Walker," the Clerk droned.

An old lady who looked more like Mammy Yokum from the Lil' Abner cartoon than Taggart would have believed possible for an American woman in the second half of the Twentieth Century stood. She walked slowly to the witness stand. As she sat, she shifted her weight, trying to find a comfortable position for her scrawny flanks on the hard wooden chair.

"Please state your name?" Watson began.

A. Johanna Walker, but my friends call me 'Johnnie' like the whiskey, but not spelled the same.

Taggart smiled. To admit in public that she knew she shared her name with a brand of whiskey, suggested Mrs. Walker might be more open-minded than Mike would have guessed from the look of her.

Mrs. Walker was so short, she could barely be seen over the rail in front of the witness chair. She told Given Watson she was fifty-nine years old, but her face looked seventy-nine, probably from the seven children and fifty-nine years of farm life she proceeded to describe. Her body was wiry and lean, but stooped, her face deeply lined. If she had pulled out a pipe and lit up, Taggart would not have been surprised.

"Mrs. Walker," Mike said when his turn came, "you're aware that Frank Marello has already had one trial on the charges against him, aren't you?"

A. Yes, I am.

Q. Did you read about the first trial in the newspaper?

A. Yes, I did.

Q. Did you hear about it on the radio?

A. Yes, I did.

Q. Did you see and hear reports about it on the television?

Q. Yes, I did.

Q. Now, Mrs. Walker, having in mind everything you heard and read about Professor Marello's first trial, do you think you can give Frank Marello a fair trial?

A. I think he already had a fair trial.

Why couldn't she just say "no?" Was the barb in her last answer sharp enough to hook some of the other candidates? Would they be as candid?

"Your Honor, the defense challenges Mrs. Walker for cause."

Hizzoner granted the challenge. Given Watson stood up to begin his voir dire of the next candidate.

"Someone like that woman could hang a jury," Mike whispered to Frank, who was sitting beside him. "She's too independent to follow anybody else."

"Too bad all she wanted to hang was me," Frank whispered back.

By the end of Day One, twelve candidates had been questioned, all of whom knew the outcome of the first trial and the reason for its reversal. Counting Mrs. Walker, five of the twelve said they were of the opinion Frank was guilty. Hizzoner granted challenges for cause for all five.

Taggart had also challenged the other seven. He argued mere knowledge of the first trial and its outcome was sufficient cause for disqualification, even without an opinion on the issue of guilt. Those seven were still sitting in the jury box. Challenges denied. They would be jurors unless one side or the other used preemptory challenges to exclude them.

Tuesday, November 16, 1976 – Trial Day 2

On the morning of the second day, Watson was questioning a candidate named "Carver Washington," a slightly built Black man about five-eleven, not counting his enormous Afro hairstyle. He wore tiny rimless glasses and a loose fitting shirt with an elaborate, multi-colored pattern. Unlike most Black residents of Johnston County, Washington had grown up in Chicago, attended DePaul University as an undergraduate and UCLA as a graduate student, earning a Masters and Ph.D in history. Although now an assistant professor of Black History at the University in Chapel Hill, he'd been a member of the Black Panthers and had known Lucinda Edwards, the militant Black professor from UCLA.

Watson's next question said he was thinking along the same lines as Taggart when it came to which jurors might be soft on homosexuality.

Q: Dr. Washington, you are a member of a race that has been a victim of discrimination throughout the history of this country. If the evidence shows the accused is a homosexual, do you think you would be more sympathetic towards him than you would otherwise be, because he, too, is a member of a group against whom discrimination has historically been practiced?

A: I'd say it's about time someone other than Blacks felt the brunt of this country's prejudices for a change.

Q: So you would not feel any particular sympathy for the accused because you think prejudice against homosexuals might somehow lessen discrimination against Blacks?

A: Mr. Solicitor, I have no illusions that's going to happen. The white man's got enough hatred to go around.

Taggart could see no basis for a challenge for cause in any of that and passed on Carver Washington for the time being.

By three o'clock on the second day, fourteen candidates had successfully run the gauntlet of challenges for cause, enough for twelve jurors and two alternates. It was time for preemptory challenges, the ones requiring no justification. Each side had six. If a challenge was exercised, the challenged candidate was gone, no questions asked.

The prosecution went first, challenging a high school English teacher from Chapel Hill named Carol Lindsey. Taggart had known she wouldn't survive. Although she had lived in the County for eight years, she had grown up in New York and gone to college in the Northeast. By Marlborough standards, she smelled like a raving liberal.

The candidate called to replace her was a Black man who ran a country store outside the rural community of Dare. His name was James Landers, and he was sixty years old. Mike had been in his store several times when he was a deputy and knew Mr. Landers was a leader in the Black community. *Does Landers remember me?*

"Mr. Landers," Given Watson began, "are you married?"

A. Yes, Sir.

Q: Any children?

A: Yes, Sir. Six, all grown.

Q: How long have you lived in the County?

A: All my life. Born jest outside Mebane. Reckon I'll die there.

Q: Are you a high school graduate?

A: No, Sir. I don't have no school, but I can read 'n write an' do my sums.

Q: How did you come to read and write if you've never been to school?

A: Kinda like Mr. Lincoln did, I jest figured it out, and my kids helped me some when they commenced to school.

Q: You a church going man, Mr. Landers?

A: Yes, Sir. Mt. Zion Holy Baptis'.

Q: You've heard questions these last two days about the first trial in this case, haven't you?

A: Yes, Sir.

Q: Were you aware of the first trial when it was taking place?

A: I heard it was going on, but I didn't pay no mind.

Q: Do you happen to know the outcome of the first trial at the time it happened?

A: I have to answer "No." If I knew, I've forgot. Seems like the first I've heard how it came out is here the last couple a days.

Taggart could tell Watson was fishing for a reason to challenge Landers, but not having much luck. With five Blacks already seated in the Box, including Dr. Carver Washington, there would be a significant number of Black jurors unless Watson used all his preemptories against them. Even that might not work if the luck of the draw replaced them with other Blacks. If the prosecution challenged a popular Black like Mr. Landers, it might antagonize other Blacks who wound up on the jury. *Things were so much simpler before integration.*

Finally, the questioning of Landers ended. The prosecution declined to challenge him for cause, so did the defense. Now it was Taggart's turn to exercise his first preemptory.

"The defense challenges Tyson Catchings."

A tall, weathered man of about forty dressed in faded denim work clothes stood up and made his way out of the jury box. Tyson was a tobacco farmer with whom Mike had played ball a couple of seasons. He liked Tyson and thought Tyson liked him, but to the best of Mike's recollection, Tyson's level of tolerance for anyone different from himself was latex thin. Any temptation on Tyson's part to do an old teammate a favor would be heavily outweighed by his antipathy for queers, college guys and foreigners. Frank Marello qualified on two counts, maybe three, inasmuch as his name ended in a vowel.

Catchings was replaced by a twenty-two year old white woman named Kelsey McTavish, who sold tickets at the theater in Chapel Hill. Hizzoner displayed what all the deputies had long referred to as his "gum radar." He couldn't see a person chewing gum, but somehow knew when anyone was doing it in his court.

"Spit out your gum, Miss McTavish," Hizzoner ordered.

"There's no wastebasket. Where do you want me to put it?"

"Hold it in your hand if you have to. Just spit it out."

The court clerk held a wastebasket out towards the witness stand and McTavish spit out her gum. "Gum gone, Judge," she said.

She told Watson she didn't remember hearing about the first trial when it was happening and that her hobby was listening to music. Taggart had no trouble believing either answer. Ordinarily he might have exercised one of his preemptories on her on the suspicion that she would be too easily influenced by other, older jurors. But, after the first day of trial he had seen her being picked up outside the Court House by a Black man approximately her own age, a pairing that still took courage and a measure of independence in Marlborough.

The prosecution challenged a white male nurse at the University Hospital, and he was replaced by a white housewife who belonged to the Marlborough Historical Society and Daughters of the American Revolution. In honor of Marian Anderson and Eleanor Roosevelt, Taggart burned his next preemptory on her.

She was replaced by an engineer of Chinese ancestry who worked at one of the new businesses beginning to move into the Research Triangle industrial park of which Chapel Hill was part and Marlborough was not.

Finally, Given Watson announced, "Your Honor, the State is pleased with the jury as presently constituted," leaving it up to Mike and Rhonda to decide whether to bump Carver Washington off the jury. If the government liked Washington well enough to keep him, that made Mike think he had better challenge him.

On the other hand, Washington had only said he wouldn't mind if homosexuals took some of the heat off Blacks; he had not said he believed discrimination was right or that he personally was prejudiced against homosexuals. Washington was an independent thinker, but Taggart didn't think he would lead any other Blacks on the jury the way James Landers might.

Rhonda slid Mike a note that said only "WASHINGTON!!" So it was clear what she thought he should do. Ancient trial wisdom decreed the best one could hope for when picking a jury was to keep off the worst jurors, not insure you were getting the best. It was like making a Christmas list. It was a lot more realistic to hope you wouldn't receive a piece of coal in your stocking than to expect a Ferrari.

Mike didn't think Carver Washington would have any qualms about letting the citizens of Johnston County know they screwed up the first time around. Would he be able to say that of whoever replaced Washington if he decided to challenge? Mike stood up. "The defense is happy with the jury as presently constituted and waives further challenges.

"The jury is empaneled," said Hizzoner. "Will the Clerk please administer the Jurors' oath?"

The jurors stood. Linda Tillman, the Clerk, read the oath. As he watched, Mike felt like he had just ordered a meal in a foreign country. The names of his choices meant nothing to him, and even after he saw what he'd selected, he had only the vaguest idea what it was.

46

Wednesday, November 17, 1976 – Trial Day 3

Taggart remembered the Gillette Friday Night Fight telecasts when he was in high school, how the fighters danced down the aisle and into the ring shadow-boxing in shiny robes, towels draped over their heads. Were they still experiencing apprehensions, or had their preparations overtaken their fears, leaving them eager to use the skills and strategies they had worked so hard to hone?

"How you feeling?" Ghost asked, as Mike slid into the front passenger seat, while Rhonda climbed in back.

"Mediocre to piss poor. Just want to get started."

The theater in Marlborough had been closed since before Taggart first moved there, another "Whites Only' business gone down in the flames of integration. Apart from the high school gym and the sanctuary at Colonial Baptist, the courtroom was the largest room in town. Long wooden benches, each designed for twenty people, this morning held twenty-two or twenty-three. Others stood two deep around the walls. It was like Easter Sunday at Colonial Baptist.

Stick and a couple of the deputies were in the front row reserved for town officials, along with Mayor Lund, his wife, Edna, Cathy's old nemesis, and Reverend Claiborne. Beside them sat Susan Hunter, impassive as a Buddha, and a couple of other members of the Town Council. Farther back, Cornelius, taking some vacation in order to watch, sat with his wife, Josie. Buck Brown, half a dozen of Rhonda's Duke law students, Jim and Anthony Marello, of course, a couple of reporters who had unsuccessfully tried to interview Taggart about the case during the last two months, and dozens of others. Rhonda looked around and saw not a single one of Frank's former colleagues from UNC.

"Close as you'll ever come to being a rock star," Mike muttered to Rhonda as the crowd parted to let them pass through the swinging gate separating the entertainers from the audience.

"Here for the hanging," she said, and rolled her eyes.

Within a minute or two, Tubby Mayes arrived from the jail with Frank Marello. Frank, dressed in a dark blue suit, white shirt and blue tie, had seemed open and relaxed during jury selection, but today his face was clouded, as if he was trying to think himself somewhere else. As usual, he said little while in the courtroom.

The defense table was on the far left side of the room, the side away from the jury box. Frank sat on the far end, closest to the wall, Rhonda in the middle, where it was easiest to confer with either Mike or Frank, and Taggart had the inside chair closest to the witness stand, directly in front of the bench. He would be doing most of the talking. After parking the car, Ghost took his post among the spectators standing in back, the team's eyes and ears in the audience, the sensor, there to detect which of their strategies were taking flight and which going "*Clunk.*"

The two counsel tables were separated by a space of approximately ten feet containing the podium and its microphone. Hizzoner's bench, a throne, sat centered at the front of the room. To its right, close to the jury box, was the witness stand.

"Keep your eyes and ears open, Frank," Mike reminded, as he handed his client a legal pad on which to make notes. Don't hesitate to mention anything that seems unusual."

Mike gave Frank what he hoped was a reassuring grin. "Here we go," he said, sticking out his hand. Frank shook it but did not grin back.

"Are the parties ready to proceed?" Hizzoner began.

Given Watson strode to the podium, turned it to face the jury box set down his notes, and looked up at the jurors. "The purpose of what I am about to tell you is to let you know what the evidence in this case will show." There followed an unremarkable description of the discovery of Livia's body, the cause of death and a promise to prove Frank had strangled her. "Why did he murder her?" Watson asked. "For a reason as old as the story of David and Bathsheba, but with a twist—"

"Objection." Mike was on his feet. "Objection, argument."

Opening statement was supposed to be a simple, direct, non-argumentative recitation of the facts the speaker expected to prove. Watson could save his Bible stories for final argument.

At the sound of Taggart's objection, Given Watson turned in a show of surprise, no doubt feigned, hoping the jury would think him shocked at the rudeness of Mike's interruption. Hizzoner, too, turned his head toward the sound of Mike's voice. "Counsel will approach the bench," he said.

"One lawyer doesn't ordinarily interrupt another's opening or closing remarks in this Court, Counsel." Hizzoner's voice was low enough so the jury could not hear. "It's not polite."

"Objections aren't against the rules, Your Honor," Mike said, "but turning opening statement into a Bible parable is."

"Don't tell me what the rules are in my own courtroom. Your objection, Sir, is denied."

Taggart was turning to go back his seat, then paused as Hizzoner continued, "But Mr. Watson, be careful. I will not have this case reversed a second time because of improper remarks of counsel. Do I make myself clear?"

"Yes, Sir."

Lose a battle, win a war. Hizzoner's admonition to Watson was worth the price of twenty overruled objections.

Watson resumed. "The evidence will show the accused had a motive to kill his wife as old as the Old Testament itself - the proverbial 'other woman.' However, in this case, the affections of the accused were not for another woman, but for a man".

Frank's night spent with Josephson, the insurance, the midnight argument, the shopping trip with "Mark," so contrary to his wife's wishes, all were trotted out for the jury. "You will hear and read entries from the diary of his victim as she agonizes over the problem and how to deal with his deviance in a way that will not injure the accused's precious self-esteem. Livia, pregnant with the accused's child, despairing over his homosexual orientation." Watson drew the words out, "ho • mo • sex • u • al o • ree • en • taa • shun" and followed with a pause, letting the jurors imagine the fears Livia Marello must have harbored over the prospect of motherhood in a marriage to a homosexual man.

Watson reviewed the telltale signs the killer was left-handed, just like Frank Marello. He pointed out that Livia was still in her pajamas and the absence of any signs of forced entry, robbery or rape, all circumstances diminishing any chance her assailant was a stranger.

Finally, Watson placed a portrait of Livia on a tripod before the jury. "In the next few days you will come to know Livia Marello, the person she was, her cares and concerns ..." Watson paused, as he picked up an 8 x 10 glossy of Livia's corpse on the kitchen floor, her head and arms lolling at unnatural angles. Moving from the podium down close to the front of the jury box, he held up the photo, "and what the accused did to her."

Immobile, silent, a totem pole, Watson stood in front of the jury holding up the picture of the dead Livia for several seconds. Then he sat down without another word. Taggart's turn had come.

Mike was not a podium person. With Hizzoner's permission, he stepped in front of counsel table, into the well of the courtroom, being careful not to approach the jurors too closely. He was still the relatively unknown lawyer from California, whose proximity might make them uncomfortable. An unknown lawyer talking to them about a taboo subject. Homosexuality was obviously the centerpiece of Watson's case, and Taggart knew better than to be defensive.

"Your Honor," Mike began with a nod of respect towards Hizzoner, "Counsel," a nod towards Watson, "Ladies and Gentlemen of the jury, Frank Marello loved and respected his wife. He did not murder her.

"He loved her so much that he was honest with her about everything, no matter how painful. How many of us can say the same? So complete was his honesty and respect that, as he came to understand he was sexually attracted to other men, he discussed it with Livia. Homosexulity was not just his problem, but their problem, and they faced it together, with as much understanding and caring as two people who love each other could command.

"Frank and Livia Marello did not *fight* over this issue; they did not *argue* over it. There will be no evidence of any kind, not a diary entry, not a next door neighbor's testimony, not a shred of evidence in any way suggesting Frank Marello's emerging homosexuality was ever the subject of a quarrel between him and his wife." Taggart shook his head as he spoke, as if to confirm the absence of any such proof. "Indeed, on the night he told Livia about what had happened between him and Mark Josephson, Frank and Livia made love.

"That is not to say they did not cry about it. You will hear the testimony of Dr. Suzanne Lefler, a professor of psychiatry at Duke University Medical School, the counselor to whom Frank and Livia turned with their problem. Dr. Lefler will explain the nature of homosexuality and how little choice any of us have in the matter of sexual orientation.

"Frank and Livia Marello's lives took a turn neither of them foresaw. Together, they peered into the unknown with both sadness and apprehension about what this unexpected development might mean for them.

"Frank Marello will take the stand and tell you he had no affairs, only a single experience, an episode, a red flag that so troubled him, he could neither sleep nor eat for days until he shared what had happened with his wife. No sneaking around behind his wife's back. No leaving her to learn what had happened from rumors accidentally overheard, gossip among friends who thought she wasn't listening – the meanest, most cruel way to learn something about someone you love.

"You have heard Livia Marello's diary is filled with agony and despair. Not so. Judge for yourselves whether these are the words of a woman locked in a loveless marriage."

Taggart picked up the diary off the evidence table and began to read.

"Sunday, December 16, 1974, just nine days before she died."

> Sunday morning. Lazy time – no place to go. No place either of us had to be. I woke up in Frank's arms. He was still asleep, but not for long. We made love real long and slow. He is so gentle and tender and pleasing to me. It was delicious. We are making progress.

The words sounded like the purring of a cat, and Mike paused to let the jurors soak up the sound of Livia's contentment.

"Ladies and gentlemen, Frank Marello had a problem which he bravely and honestly confronted. He loved his wife. He is not a murderer."

Taggart paused again. After a second or so he walked over and slowly drank a swallow of water. This was the point where he needed to be able to say, "Well, if Frank Marello didn't kill his wife, who did?" Then follow it up by pointing the finger at a more obvious culprit – Jim Marello, in Taggart's mind. But the evidence to support such an assertion was too thin. Trying to make a scapegoat of your brother to save one's own hide was risky business, especially on the basis of no more than the fact that Jim, indisputably in New Orleans at the time of the murder, and Livia disliked each other. Better to wait.

Taggart explained Frank's behavior in the wake of the night spent with Josephson, the Marello's decision to buy insurance from Mark, the shopping trip - details, details, exculpatory details, but no alternative suspect.

"Ladies and gentlemen," Mike said, taking a step closer, "during jury selection you each promised me you will keep an open mind and not decide this case until you have heard both sides of the story. This was a terrible crime, but no more terrible than it will be to convict an innocent man of its commission. Terrible crimes are not always solved. Frank Marello loved and respected and honored his wife and did not kill her. I am sure, when you have heard all the evidence, you will agree the law needs to look elsewhere than at Frank Marello in its search for who did this awful thing. Thank you."

47

Thursday, November 17 1976 –Trial Day 3 - Afternoon

Open and close strong, sandwich weaker witnesses in between – classic trial advocacy wisdom. The prosecution's first withess was Stick Hatcher. Given Watson and Taggart had read the same books.

Q: Sheriff Hatcher, please describe your involvement in the investigation of Livia Marello's death.

Stick launched into a description of how he happened to be in the Chapel Hill substation wishing his troops "Merry Christmas" on Christmas Eve, when the call from Claudia Wilmer came in reporting her discovery of Livia's body, of arriving at the Marello apartment and of how it was immediately clear Livia hadn't died of natural causes. He authenticated a photo of the corpse laying on the kitchen floor and close-ups of bruises on Livia's neck, four on either side in back, one on either side in front.

Q: Did you notice any difference in the bruises on one side as compared to the bruises on the other?

A: Yes, Sir.

Q: What differences did you observe?

Stick held up Exhibit 3 so both Watson and the jury could see. Hizzoner gave Taggart permission to approach the witness so he could get a closer look at what Stick was about to explain.

A: The four bruises on the right side of her neck (Stick pointed to them with his pencil and paused to let the jurors focus on what he was showing them) are brighter or deeper, whatever you might call it ... more severe. They are more purple, darker purple than the ones on the left side of the spine.

Q: Do you know the reason for the difference?

A: No, Sir. I know what I think, but you'll have to ask a doctor about that.

"Objection. Move to strike everything after 'No, Sir'."

It was a great answer. By refusing to testify about something outside his expertise, Stick made whatever he did say more credible. But he had no business directing Watson, and, indirectly, the jury to later testimony from the coroner, thereby bestowing additional credibility on that witness.

Besides, Mike wanted to break up Stick's testimony, which he feared might be mesmerizing the jurors. The objection wouldn't bestow more emphasis on the testimony than Stick had already created, and Mike wanted to remind the jurors, "Hey, we're still here."

"Sustained, the jury will disregard everything in the last answer after the words, "No, Sir."

The jurors looked baffled by the entire exchange.

Q: Did you observe any signs of a struggle?

A: No, Sir. The place was neat as a pin.

Q: Any sign of forced entry?

A: No, Sir.

Watson then guided Stick through Frank's appearance on the scene, of warning him of his right to remain silent and to consult a lawyer, followed by their conversation while sitting in Stick's car.

Q: Did the accused seem upset by what had happened?

It was a leading question. "Upset" was a conclusory word, an indirect request for an opinion - at least two bases for objection. But Taggart knew he would have to swallow lots of objections without making them or risk being perceived as trying to hide evidence from the jury. This was one of those.

A: He was very quiet. A couple of times I heard him ask "Who would do such a thing?" an' "This can't be happening." Otherwise, he was calm enough. He was able to understand and answer all my questions. He an' I went out to my car to talk. Mostly he just sat there in the front seat and kind of rested his forehead in his hand.

Q: Any tears?

A: None that I saw.

Q: You say you asked the accused some questions?

A: Yes, Sir.

Q: So, the accused was an immediate suspect?

Another leading question, but again, Taggart didn't object. If Hizzoner wouldn't let Stick answer, the jurors would answer it in their own minds. Maybe Stick's answer would be better than theirs.

A: At that point no one and just about everyone was a suspect … we didn't have no one else.

Q: Please describe what you asked the accused and what he said in reply.

A: I asked if he knew about any enemies his wife mighta had, and he said he didn't. Once the victim's body was removed, I asked him to go back in and see if anything was missing. Turned out, nothing seemed to have been stolen.

Q: What else did you ask him?

A: I asked him if he and his wife had been gettin' along, and he said they'd been gettin' along alright. I asked him what he'd been doing that morning, and he said he'd been Christmas shopping.

Q: Did he say with whom?

A: No, he didn't mention bein' with anybody.

Q: He said they had been 'gettin' along alright?'"

A: Yes, Sir. That's what he said. Said they'd been gettin' along fine and had just learned they were going to have a baby.

Q: Just your typical happy young couple on Christ—

"Objection, argumentative."

"I withdraw the question," Watson said before Hizzoner had a chance to rule.

Q: 'Gettin' along fine,' eh. Did he say anything about any trouble between 'em over him sleeping with Mark Josephson?

"Objection, leading question."

"Overruled."

Taggart had to flex his face to hide a grimace. Watson's last question was perhaps the single most leading question in the history of jurisprudence. *Hizzoner's becoming more interested in the prosecution's theory than keeping the playing field level.*

A. Not a word.

"Humphf. No further questions."

Hizzoner recessed for lunch.

"Sheriff Hatcher," Mike began when court reconvened, "when Professor Marello told you he'd been shopping that morning, did you ask him whether he had been with anyone?

A: I don't recall that I did.

Q: Professor Marello did not say he had been alone, did he?

A: No, Sir. He did not say one way or the other.

Q: How long after he arrived at the apartment was it that you asked him where he was that morning?

A: Within fifteen minutes.

Q: So, less than a quarter hour after the shock of discovering his wife was dead, murdered on the floor of their kitchen, it's your testimony Professor Marello didn't answer a question you didn't ask?

A: If he was the one who put her there, he'd had a lot longer than fifteen minutes to get used to the idea.

Q: Well, Sheriff, if Professor Marello "put her there" as you put it, don't you think he'd have an alibi ready to go and most assuredly would have mentioned having been with someone while shopping?

"Objection, calls for spec—"

"Not if the person he was with was his boyfriend," Stick said before Watson could finish speaking.

Watson left his objection hanging in the air.

Taggart hated the answer and wished he could withdraw his question. He eyed his old boss, a veteran of more trials than Mike.

Stick sat like the coiled rattlesnake on that first Marine battle flag – "Don't Tread On Me." Mike changed directions.

Q: Mrs. Wilmer, the next door neighbor was the person who reported finding Livia Marello's body?

A. Yes.

Q. She told you that when she went over to visit Mrs. Marello, she found the back door of the Marello apartment standing open?

A. Yes.

Q. Standing open as if someone had left in a hurry?

A. Or wanted to make it look like that. We asked all the neighbors we could find if they saw anybody comin' out of the Marello apartment that morning, and nobody had.

Q: But they did tell you about a black motorcycle that was parked in the parking lot that morning?

A: Yes.

Q: A black motorcycle with a long front fork?

A: Yes.

Q: Three different neighbors mentioned seeing that motorcycle that morning, didn't they?

A: Yes.

Q: You checked and no one in the complex rode such a motorcycle, did they?

A: No. No one did.

Q: At the time you first observed Livia Marello's body, she was wearing a nightgown?

A: Yes.

Q: And a bathrobe?

A: Yes.

Q: And some slippers?

A: Yes.

Q: So, she was still in her nightclothes?

A: Yes.

Q: At the time of her murder, Mrs. Marello hadn't gotten dressed yet after getting out of bed?

A: Probably not. I don't know what she wore to bed.

Someone in the gallery giggled at the thought Livia might have been sleeping naked. Hizzoner jerked his head around toward the direction of the sound in disapproval, but said nothing.

Q: She wasn't dressed to receive visitors, was she?

A: No.

Q: She wasn't wearing any make-up?

A: No, she didn't appear to be.

Q: On the kitchen table there were two tea cups?

A: Yes, as I recall.

Q: And each of those cups had an unused teabag in it?

A: Yes, Sir. That's right.

Q: On the stove there was a tea kettle with a hole in the bottom and its plastic parts melted, wasn't there?

A: Yes, Sir.

Q: Mrs. Wilmer told you that when she came in and found the body, she also found the stove on and the tea kettle melted through and glowing and she turned it off, didn't she?

A: Yes, Sir.

Mike picked up Defense Exhibit B from the evidence table, a scorched tea kettle with a large hole in its bottom and all the plastic fittings melted and showed it to Stick, who identified it as the tea kettle from the Marello apartment.

Q: Evidently Livia Marello had a guest and she was fixing tea?

A: Or she and her husband were going to have a cup, but he killed her instead.

Q: I thought you might say that, Sheriff, but in addition to those teacups, didn't you find a new bathrobe with the tags still on it in a box on the kitchen table?

"Objection, this is all irrelevant. It also exceeds the scope of the direct examination."

"Counsel will approach the bench."

Once congregated on the side of Hizzoner's throne away from the jury and witness stand, he asked, "Mr. Taggart, what's the point of all this?"

"Your Honor, the defense obviously contends someone other than Professor Marello entered the apartment that morning and killed Mrs. Marello. Two cups with unused teabags and a tea kettle boiled dry certainly support the inference she might have been killed while waiting for the water to boil, and the assailant fled in haste after committing the murder without turning off the tea kettle or closing the door. The answers to these questions couldn't be much more relevant."

"Objection overruled. But don't be long in tying this all together, Mr. Taggart, or I'll disallow the entire line of questions."

Once back at the defense table, Mike repeated his question.

Q: In addition to the teacups on the kitchen table, you found a box containing a new bathrobe with the tags still on it?

A: Yes, Sir.

Q: It was a man's bathrobe?

A: Yes, Sir.

Q: I hand you Defense Exhibit C. Is this the bathrobe and box you found on the Marello kitchen table that afternoon?

Mike handed Stick a box containing a dark green bathrobe.

A: Yes, Sir.

Q: There were a number of tags still attached to the bathrobe when you found it, weren't there?

A: Yes, Sir.

Q: But the price tag was no longer on the robe?

A: Yes, Sir. It had been cut off.

Q: The price tag was lying on the table beside a pair of scissors?

A: Yes, Sir.

Q: The size of the bathrobe is "Extra Long?"

A: Yes, Sir.

Q: You also found Christmas wrapping paper, some tape and a bow on the table?

A: Yes, Sir.

Q: You also found a little card with some handwriting on it?

A: Yes, Sir.

Q: I hand you Defense Exhibit D. Is that the card you found on the Marello kitchen table beside the box with the bathrobe?

Stick examined the card. "Yes, Sir, it is."

Q: Please read to the jury what the card, Exhibit D, says.

A: "To Frank, With Love, From Livia."

Q: "To Frank, With Love, From Livia." Does the presence of this card lying beside a box containing a brand new extra long bathrobe with the price tag cut off and Christmas wrapping and scissors nearby suggest to you that Livia Marello had started to wrap her Christmas present to her husband shortly before she was killed?

"Objection, calls for speculation."

"Sustained."

Taggart didn't care if the jurors heard the answer so long as they heard his question. He walked over to a large blackboard on wheels standing against the far wall and wheeled it into the well of the court, positioning it at an angle that allowed Stick and the jury to see it at the same time. Watson rose and moved over to where he could see it too.

"Let's look at the possible explanations for the presence of the two teacups and the melted teakettle. One explanation would be that she was making herself two separate cups of tea?

A: Yes, Sir.

Taggart printed: "1. 2 separate cups of tea for self;" on the blackboard.

Q: A second explanation might be that Mrs. Marello was making tea for herself and her husband?

A: Yes, Sir.

Taggart printed: "2. 1 cup for self; 1 for husband."

Q: Finally, she could have been making tea for herself and a visitor?

A: Yes, Sir.

Taggart printed: "3. 1 cup for self; 1 for visitor."

Q: Can you think of any other explanations, Sheriff?

A: No, just those three.

Q: As for explanation number one, it doesn't seem likely that Mrs. Marello would make herself two separate cups of tea, does it?

"Objection, calls for speculation."

Taggart crossed his mental fingers.

"Overruled."

Whew.

"She probably wasn't making tea for herself in two different cups," Stick agreed.

Taggart erased the explanation number one from the blackboard.

Q: The fact that she appeared to be have been wrapping her husband's Christmas present when she started to make tea makes it less likely that second cup was for her husband, doesn't it? Wouldn't that spoil the surprise?

A: I have no idea whether she intended to surprise him.

Despite Stick's equivocation, Mike erased the second alternative.

Q: So, in light of the presence of the two cups and the partially wrapped gift to her husband, don't you agree explanation number three, that Livia was making tea for herself and a guest, is the most likely, Sheriff?

A: No, I don't agree. The woman was still in her nightgown, wasn't wearin' any makeup. It doesn't seem at all likely to me she was entertainin' any visitors. I think it was her husband she was makin' the tea for, and she didn't give a damn whether she surprised him or not after some of the surprises he'd given her lately.

Q: It's your opinion that Mrs. Marello wouldn't be entertaining in her nightclothes?

A: That's right.

Q: It's not entirely proper for a woman to be parading around in front of strangers in her pajamas?

A: My point exactly.

Q: If Livia Marello was going to go around in her nightgown and robe in front of someone other than her husband, she'd have to know that someone awfully well, wouldn't she?

A: Awfully well, that's right.

Q: Maybe another woman friend, or neighbor she sees all the time?

A: Maybe.

Q: Or maybe another family member?

A: Maybe.

Q: If it was a friend or neighbor or another family member, that would explain why there was no sign of forced entry, wouldn't it?

A: It could.

"No further questions."

Redirect examination was for patching holes punched in a witness's testimony by your opponent's cross-examination. Given Watson didn't have much to patch, but he did establish that as part of his investigation Stick had determined that all the members of Livia's family were either in Greensboro or New Orleans at the time she was killed. Then he wrote "2. 1 cup for her; 1 cup for her husband" back on the board and erased explanation number 3.

Hizzoner recessed trial for the day

As Mike began to stuff what he would need for the night's labors into his briefcase, he noticed Jim and Anthony Marello talking to Frank across the wooden rail dividing the courtroom out of the corner of his eye. Rhonda stood at Frank's side listening. Waiting to escort Frank back to jail, Howard Julius stood just out of earshot. Jim was jabbing his index finger at Frank's chest, and Frank was nodding his head as if agreeing.

Curious, Mike interrupted his packing to investigate. As he joined the group, Jim and Anthony walked away.

"What was that all about?"

"Mike, we need to talk," Frank said. "Come over to see me after you get your things together." He gestured at the papers strewn across the table.

Howard led Frank away, and Ghost joined Mike and Rhonda at the table. "I think the Marello family is unhappy with those last few questions about who Livia was having tea with."

"Move to the head of the class," Rhonda said. "Mike, you know what Frank thinks about that tactic, and believe me, his view is mild compared to Jim's."

"I don't give a rat's ass what Jim thinks. What do you think?"

"I think we're raising a specter that'll come back to haunt us, if we can't come up with some pretty convincing evidence tying Jim to the murder."

It was almost dark and had begun to mist when the three of them, laden with briefcases, walked out of the courthouse.

"Rhonda, I'm going over to see Frank" Mike said. "Want to come along?"

"I don't think so. I'm going back to the apartment to work on jury instructions. I've seen enough blood spilled for one day. Why don't you run me up to the apartment, Ghost, and then come back for Mike?"

Ghost and Rhonda walked around the corner to the car, and Mike started for the jail. As he stepped into the street, Jim and

Anthony Marello pulled up to the opposite curb in their large black rental car.

Jim rolled down the window. "Get in."

Mike climbed in the back seat and slid over to the passenger side, pulling his briefcase in behind him.

"What the hell are you trying to do with this 'family member tea drinking' bullshit, Taggart?" Jim stared at him in the rearview mirror.

Jimmy's nothing, if not direct. "You know very well what I'm doing."

"That's not what this case is about." Jim turned and glared directly at Mike as he spoke. "Frank says he told you he didn't want you defending him like that. That's not why we hired you."

"You hired me to get your brother off. Making those jurors believe someone else killed her is the only way to do that. We're sure not going to do it by trying to persuade the jury Frank's not homosexual."

"No, we sure aren't. Not after that opening statement."

"Not after those diary entries. Not after Frank has confirmed everything they say and then some," Mike said. "If you have any better ideas, I'd like to hear 'em."

"'Family member killed her.' Bah. What good's finger pointing, if you've got no facts to back it up? You're just going to make Frank look stupid and selfish."

"I'll tell you what I've got," Mike said. "Two complaints to the police against you for spousal abuse, both filed by Livia, and witnesses who will say there was a confrontation between you and Livia five months before she died about the way you were abusing your family. I have a your admission you tried to bribe the Judge, and a strong suspicion you hired those two thugs who beat Josephson senseless."

At Taggart's mention of the attempted bribe and beating, Anthony, who'd been turned looking at Mike from the passenger seat, shifted his gaze to Jim. "What's this about a bribe?"

Jim gave a wave of dismissal. "Another pipe dream." Then to Taggart, "Witnesses, what witnesses have you got to any confrontation between Livia and me? As for your police reports, they'll never stand up, those complaints were dropped. There was never any conviction."

Taggart could feel the momentum of the conversation beginning to turn in his direction. "I don't care if you were convicted, *Jimmy*. Livia calling the police on you gets me where I want to go. Shows your motive to shut her up. As for witnesses," Taggart reached into the inside pocket of his suitcoat, "here's a subpoena for each of you." Taggart dropped two folded pieces of paper in the front seat between the two men. Opening the car door, he said, "Jim, you've fucked Frank over your whole life. Now he has someone in his corner who might just fuck you over if it will help Frank,. So tape your ankles, 'cause this game's just getting started."

On the way to the apartment Rhonda asked Ghost, "How do things look from the back of the bus?"

"If this was a prize fight," Ghost said, "I'd say we're behind on points, but so far no knock downs. I don't think we'll win if all we do is prove homosexuals aren't natural born killers."

Rhonda laughed in spite of Ghost's negative assessment. She had noticed it happened a lot, Ghost making her laugh. "What kind of a name is 'Gonchar' anyway? You don't look like a 'Gonchar.'"

"Gonchar's Russian. According to family history, Grandpa Gonchar came over in the '20s about one step ahead of the Gulag. I think he jettisoned a couple of syllables when he came through Ellis Island."

"Where'd you grow up?" Rhonda asked.

"New York City. My dad was a translator at the United Nations. He actually met my mom at the San Francisco Conference, where the U.N. began. She had something to do with the Nationalist Chinese delegation. I'm one of the first manifestations of post-war international good-will. What about you?"

"Cody, Wyoming. Both my folks were lawyers. They started the first title company in Wyoming."

"Hmm," Ghost said. "You're the second person from Wyoming I've met recently."

48

Thursday, November 18, 1976 – Trial Day 4

Given Watson had decided this would be "Science Thursday." His first witness of the morning was the coroner, Dr. Winifred Bordick, a squat, buxom woman with a thin head, pointy nose, almost invisible lips and a brow with furrows permanently plowed. She squinted as she talked.

"Bordick looks like she got someone else's head," Ghost noted in his little spiral pad.

Dr. Bordick testified she was a private practitioner specializing in internal medicine, not pathology. There wasn't enough work to keep a full time coroner busy, so various members of the Johnston County Medical Society volunteered to take one year turns as coroner for a little extra money. If Livia Marello had been murdered eight days later, the examination and autopsy would have been some other doctor's problem.

Dr. Bordick told the jury she first examined Livia Marello's body at the crime scene at approximately 2:00 p.m. on the twenty-fourth and had performed an autopsy at the morgue about two hours later. Merry Christmas.

The Solicitor had Dr. Bordick describe her examination and autopsy detailing the procedures she performed and what she observed, and then asked the Doctor whether, based on her examination, she had an opinion about the cause of Livia Marello's death.

A: In my opinion, she died from a combination of cerebral hemorrhage caused by strangulation resulting from the closure and ultimately the crushing of her carotid artery, the large artery carrying blood to the brain, and, secondarily, from the severance of the spinal cord due to a broken and displaced vertebrae at the C-3 point in her cervical spine.

Q: Can you explain that in layman's terms, Doctor?

A: Simply stated, whoever killed this woman strangled her and broke her neck. Either event was enough to kill her, but both appear to have been the result of the same force, and, in my opinion, she was strangled before her neck broke.

Perhaps because she had been only a part-time coroner in a county where the homicide business was real slow, Dr. Bordick hadn't formed the detached demeanor Taggart was used to seeing among full-time pathologists in Southern California. There the abundance of daily atrocities was such that even the most idealistic young emergency room doctor or pathologist soon developed the insensitivity of a gunnery sergeant. Bordick's frequent contemptuous glances at Frank made it clear he had already been found "Guilty" in the court of Bordick.

Q: Are you able to estimate the time Mizrus Marello died?

A: Yes, within a range of approximately four hours.

Q: What is your estimate of the time of her death?

A: I estimate she died sometime between 6:00 and 10:00 a.m. on December 24, 1973.

Q: Can you be any more specific than that?

A: No, I cannot.

Q: Why not?

Bordick launched into a long and detailed explanation of Livor Mortis and Rigor Mortis, phenomena having to do with the behavior of bodily fluids once a person's heart is no longer pumping them around the body and gravity takes over. Out of the corner of his eye, Ghost saw a movement in the front row of the jury box. McTavish, the ticket-taker, had turned her head away from the witness and was twisting a hankie in her hands as if she was strangling it as Bordick continued to describe a body shutting down.

Oblivious of the dismay she was creating among some in her audience, Bordick went on. "Comparing the extent to which these processes have progressed against the known rates at which they occur, I was able to narrow the time of death to between 6:00 and 10:00 a.m."

It had been an oversimplified description. But Taggart was sure Watson could elicit a more thorough explanation if required. Would that help his client? Probably just the opposite. If Mike couldn't score any points for his own side, the least he could do was avoid scoring points for the opposition. Once more he stifled an objection.

Watson moved on to the damage to Livia's breathing apparatus, carotid artery and cervical spine with gruesome thoroughness. He left out nothing that might horrify the jury into voting for convicion, if for no other reason than being sure to punish someone for such a brutal act. Frank just happened to be handy. Eventually he arrived at the bruises on Livia's neck.

Q: Dr. Bordick, Are you in agreement with Sheriff Hatcher that these dark marks on the victim's neck are bruises?

Leading question. Another unmade objection.

A: Yes.

Q: Did you notice any difference in the bruises on the left side of Mizrus Marello's neck compared to those on the right side?

A: Yes.

Q: What difference did you notice?

A: The bruises on what would be the right side of Mrs. Marello's neck were more severe than those on the left side.

Q: What do you mean "more severe?"

A: Bruises are an accumulation of blood under the skin that come from blood vessels and capillaries, which have been broken by some force. The greater the force, the greater the breakage; the greater the breakage, the greater the leakage. In simplest terms, more blood leaked out on the right side than on the left, and this is what creates the deeper purple color and somewhat greater coverage on the right side. In other words, more force appears to have been applied to the right side of Mrs. Marello's neck than to the left.

Q: Greater force such as would be applied by a left-handed person grabbing Mizrus Marello's throat with more force from his strong hand than with his weaker hand?

"Objection. Leading. Calls for speculation."

"Sustained," Hizzoner surprised Taggart by agreeing with him. "Mr. Watson, you'll have to lay more of a foundation if you want an answer to that question."

Watson shrugged.

Q: Dr. Bordick, can you determine from the pattern of the bruises in what manner the force was applied to Mrs. Marello's throat?

A: Yes.

Holding up the two photos of Livia's throat in one hand and using her pencil as a pointer, she explained, "The location of two bruises on the front of the victim's throat and eight points of most intense bruising on back of her neck is consistent with the pattern that would be created by someone standing in front of the victim and choking her, like this."

Dr. Bordick stood up, putting the photographs down as she did so. She turned to Given Watson, who had not retreated to the podium since handing her the photographs, and took his throat in her hands, thumbs on either side of his windpipe, fingers clawlike on the back of his neck .

How many times have they rehearsed that? Taggart couldn't resist blurting out, "Let me try!"

This earned Mike the first good laugh of the trial. Watson quickly attempted to dampen the mirth by raising his voice as Dr. Bordick released his neck and sat back down.

Q: According to your observation, Doctor, which hand do the bruises in these photos indicate exerted the greatest pressure?

A: The assailant's left hand.

Q: Dr. Bordick, you testified that Mizrus Marello was pregnant. Could you determine how far advanced the pregnancy was at the time of her death?

A: Yes, from my examination of the fetus, she was approximately ten weeks pregnant.

"Thank you, Dr. Bordick. No further questions ... Oh, one further question. In the course of your examination, did you find any indication Mizrus Marello had been sexually assaulted?"

A: No. There was no evidence of any sexual activity.

"No further questions."

The cause of Livia's death was now firmly established and had never really been an issue in the first place. No point in going over that again. But Bordick's estimate of time of death threw way too big a loop, one that couldn't help but lasso Frank unless challenged. Tedious, but unwise to ignore.

"Dr. Bordick," Mike said, "your estimate of the time of death is based on your knowledge of the rates of livor mortis and rigor mortis, is that right?

A: Yes, obviously.

The Doctor's tone suggested she didn't see any difference between Livia Marello's murderer and Taggart, and would very much like to perform her strangulation demonstration on him.

Q: The rate at which livor mortis occurs can vary depending on a number of factors, is that correct?

A: Somewhat.

Q: For example, it is likely to occur more rapidly in a small person?

A: Yes.

Q: You measured and weighed Livia Marello, didn't you?

A: Yes.

Q: She was 5′ 1″ and 105 pounds?

A: Yes.

Q: She was a small person?

A: It depends.

Try to be as elusive as you can, Doc.. Mike bowed and shook his head in frustration.

Q: Among adult middle class American women of Northern European ancestry born and raised in the middle third of the twentieth century, Livia Marello was of below average size. Is that correct?

A: Yes.

Q: And when you said a moment ago that the rate of livor mortis could vary depending on body size, you were speaking in terms of adults, weren't you?

A: Yes.

Taggart paused for a second in the hope the jury would appreciate that Dr. Bordick was playing games with him and wasting everyone's time, including theirs.

Q: Now, Doctor, let's turn to rigor mortis. Rigor Mortis is the stiffening of the muscles which you described in response to the Solicitor's questions?

A: Yes.

Q: I wrote down your answer in which you said it takes "approximately twelve hours for rigor mortis to be complete." Taggart held up a sheet of yellow paper as if he was reading. But the rate of rigor mortis isn't the same for everybody, is it?

A: Not exactly.

Q: Twelve hours is just an average across the broad range of the population?

A: In a manner of speaking, yes.

Q: The length of time it takes rigor mortis to be complete actually varies from person to person depending on a variety of factors, including body size?

A: Yes.

Q: We've already established that Livia Marello was a small person?

A: Relatively small, yes.

Q: So, rigor mortis might be expected to occur faster than the average rate in her case?

A: Somewhat.

Q: Do you know how much?

A: No.

Q: You have no facts or figures to tell you how much the rate of rigor mortis for Livia Marello would be accelerated by the fact that she was so tiny?

Winifred Bordick hesitated, as if maybe she didn't like the characterization of Livia Marello as "tiny" and was considering whether it was worth getting into another battle of semantics. After a couple of seconds, she answered "No."

Q: You just know the rate was faster because of Mrs. Marello's size?

A: Probably.

Q: So, rigor mortis did not necessarily have to have begun at six a.m. in order to reach the point to which it had progressed by the time you observed her?

A: Possibly not.

Q: A moment ago you said "probably." Isn't it probable that in a person as small as Livia Marello rigor mortis would have advanced to the point at which you observed it, even if it started somewhat later than six a.m.?

A: I will say that "possibly" it could have, I will not say "probably."

In the back of the courtroom Ghost was laughing to himself. Taggart should go into dentistry. Wisdom teeth would be easier to extract than a concession from this witness.

Q: Doctor, you also made a second observation for the purpose of determining the time of Mrs. Marello's death, didn't you?

A: No, I don't think so. To what are you referring?

Q: I am referring to the fact that, according to your autopsy report, when you arrived at the Marello apartment, you took the temperature of Mrs. Marello's liver, didn't you?

A: Yes, but—

Q: The rate at which the liver cools is one of the ways of determining time of death, isn't it?

A: I did not use it for that purpose.

Q: Nevertheless, you are aware it is a method that is used to determine time of death?

A: I am aware it is sometimes used for that purpose, although I regard it as unreliable – too many variables.

Q: The reason for using the temperature of the liver is because it is the organ deepest inside the body, the most insulated from variations of external temperatures?

A: Among those who use the temperature test, yes.

Q: The "variables" you mentioned, those are things like room temperature, body temperature at time of death, things like that?

A: Yes.

Q: You knew liver temperature test was susceptible to these variables before you took the temperature of Livia Marello's liver, didn't you?

A: Yes.

Q: But you took it anyway?

A: ... Yes.

Q: It was the first thing you did after visually examining the body according to your report. Am I reading that correctly? (Taggart held up his copy of the autopsy report.)

A: I think that's correct.

Q: By your own estimate, Livia Marello had been dead at least four hours at the time you took the temperature of her liver?

A: Approximately.

Q: And at the time you took it, the temperature of her liver was eighty-five degrees?

A: Yes.

Taggart walked over to the blackboard and picked up a piece of chalk.

Q: When external temperatures are within a range of sixty-five to seventy-two degrees, you expect a rate of liver cooling to be approximately three degrees per hour, correct?

A: Under laboratory conditions that would be the expectation, but you hardly had—

Q: So, assuming that before her death Livia's temperature was a normal 98.6 degrees, her liver had cooled thirteen and one-half degrees?

Mike wrote "13.5 degrees" on the blackboard.

A: Yes ... but—

Q: So, if I divide that—

"Objection, Counsel is interrupting the witness."

Hizzoner sat silently for a moment, considering the sequence of questions and answers he had just heard. "Overruled," he said at last. "Those are questions that can be answered with a 'yes' or 'no.' The time to develop whatever limitations may exist is redirect examination, Mr. Watson."

Q: So, if you divide the number of degrees Mrs. Marello's liver had cooled at the time you took its temperature by three, the three degree per hour rate of cooling ...

Taggart made the division sign to the right of the "13.5 degrees/3" on the board.

... you get four and a half hours. Is my math right, Doctor?

A: Yes.

Taggart wrote “13.5 degrees/3 = 4.5 hours” on the board to complete the equation.

Q: Then, if we count back four and a half hours from the time you took that temperature, we come to approximately nine forty-five a.m.?

A: Yes, if she died in a laboratory and not in an apartment in and out of which all sorts of people had been coming and going since the murder was discovered, if not before.”

Taggart wrote “9:45 a.m.” on the board and drew a circle around it.

Q: Dr. Bordick, when you arrived at the Marello apartment on the afternoon of the 24th, how many people were in the apartment?

A: Let me see, there were two persons with the ambulance, two persons from the Sheriff’s office, a news photographer and a reporter … and me … and Mr. Marello, eight not counting the victim.

Q: So at least eight people had come into the apartment since the time of Mrs. Marello’s death?

A: Yes.

Q: Did the doors to the Marello apartment open to the outside?

A: To the outside … what do you mean?

Q: As opposed to opening to an inside corridor?

A: Oh, yes … yes, they opened to the outside.

Q: What was the weather like at the time you arrived at the apartment, generally speaking?

A: It was clear and cold, very brisk as I recall. I was wearing my winter coat, and I don’t do that very often.

Q: What effect would these “comings and goings,” as you put it, of eight people in that small apartment have on the room temperature?

A: It would lower the room temperature.

Q: Now I want you to assume that there will be evidence in this case that the back door to the apartment, the one between the kitchen and the outside, was left open for an hour or more prior to approximately one-thirty p.m., that, too, would tend to lower the room temperature, wouldn't it?

A: Presumably, yes.

Q: And if the room temperature was lowered, that would accelerate, speed up, the rate of cooling of the liver, isn't that right?

A: I don't know that.

Q. Dr. Bordick, are you telling this jury a liver would cool just as slowly in a fifty-degree room as in a seventy degree room?

Off to the right behind Taggart he heard a rustling sound from the direction of the jury box, as if some of the jurors were turning in their chairs so as to better hear the battle over liver temperatures.

A. No. Room temperature could affect the rate of cooling. But you're making up numbers now.

Q. Yes, to illustrate the general principle that room temperature is a factor, a principle, I take it, with which you *now* agree?

A. In principle, yes.

Q. And if it took even less than four and a half hours because of the door being left open and all these 'comings and goings,' that would place the time of death even closer to the time of your examination, wouldn't it?

A: That is sheer speculation. You're focusing on a single variable. You don't know what the room temperature was to start with. You don't know the impact of the amount of clothing the victim was wearing. Mrs. Marello was wearing a warm flannel full length nightgown, a heavy man's style terry cloth robe and fleece lined slippers. That would make a difference. You don't know what her temperature was before she died. She was pregnant. Often pregnant women's temperatures are higher than normal. All these things could make a difference.

Mike paused long enough to make sure Dr. Bordick had finished her answer.

Q: And if it took even less than four and a half hours because of all these 'comings and goings' you've described, that would place the time of death even closer to the time of your examination, wouldn't it?

Dr. Bordick gave Given Watson a look that said, "Say something. Get me out of this," and then, briefly, at Hizzoner. Watson put his hands on the table in front of him as if to push himself to his feet, but evidently thought better of it and relaxed them without standing. Hizzoner, not hearing an answer, said, "The witness will answer the question."

"Yes," Winifred Bordick almost whispered, as if by speaking in a voice difficult to hear she could somehow make what she said less true.

"I'm not sure the jury could hear your answer, Dr. Bordick," Mike said, cupping his hand to his ear. 'Was your answer 'yes?'"

"Yes," she replied in a normal tone. "My answer was 'yes'."

Q: Doctor, let's turn to the subject of the bruises on Mrs. Marello's neck. You have concluded the greater severity of the bruises on the right side of the neck is attributable to the assailant being left-handed?

A: Yes.

Q: You did not observe the attack yourself, did you?

A: Of course not.

Q: You've never heard from anyone else that the assailant was left-handed?

A: Not as far as I can recall.

Q: So, you don't know the assailant was left-handed, do you?

A: No, I don't actually know, I suppose.

Q: It's just an assumption on your part?

A: That's right, a very good assumption.

Q: Well, let's see about that. Can you think of any other explanations for why the bruises would be more severe on the right side of the neck?

A: No, I cannot.

Q: Let me help you. Do you think that when she started to be choked, Livia Marello tried to struggle?

A: I don't know, she might have … probably … but maybe not. I didn't find any skin or blood under her nails.

Q: It would be human nature to struggle against being strangled, wouldn't it?

A: Obviously.

Q: Okay, assume for the purposes of discussion that she struggled by placing both of her hands on the right arm of her attacker, attempting to wrest it off of her throat. That could have reduced the pressure exerted by the right hand, couldn't it?

A: … Yes.

Q: Thereby resulting in the bruises from the attacker's left hand being more severe?

A: Yes.

Q: Even though the attacker was right-handed?

A: Yes.

"No further questions."

Science Thursday continued with the prosecution's fingerprint expert, an agent from the State Bureau of Investigation in Raleigh named George Cavanaugh. He testified he had dusted the entire apartment for fingerprints and found only those of Frank and Livia Marello, no one else, with the exception of a single print on the outside of the glass in the back door belonging to Tremaine Troutman, a handyman who had painted the door two weeks earlier.

On cross Taggart was able to establish that anyone wearing gloves would have left no prints.

Q: So, your search for fingerprints in the Marello's apartment does not eliminate the possibility that someone other than the Marellos were there that day?

A: No, it does not.

49

Thursday, November 18, 1976 – Trial Day 4 – Late Afternoon

Thursday ended with one of those witnesses who testifies for no more than half an hour, but has potential to impact the outcome of trial all out of proportion to the length of her appearance. Claudia Wilmer, the elderly woman who lived in the apartment next door, described discovering Livia Marello lying on the Marello's kitchen floor. She repeated her testimony from the first trial about hearing loud talking coming from the Marello apartment about three a.m. on the morning of December 24th. Mrs. Wilmer's bedroom shared a common wall with the Marello bedroom.

During pretrial motions, Rhonda had tried to have Wilmer's testimony excluded on the ground that what she had heard was irrelevant and too ambiguous to be capable of supporting an inference of anything. Hizzoner disagreed.

Watson asked, "How long had you lived next door to the Marellos as of December 24th, 1973?"

A: Ever since they moved in a year and a half earlier.

Q: Had you ever heard any loud talking coming from the Marello apartment on any other occasion?

A: Oh, no. They were such nice, quiet neighbors. Mrs. Marello was such a pleasant, friendly young woman … a shame what happened.

Q: Could you understand what was being discussed in this conversation you heard?

A: No. I was trying to sleep, not eavesdrop. The only word I could make out was "money." I heard that word used at least twice.

Q: How long did this conversation last?

A: No more than a couple of minutes, at least the sounds I heard.

Q: You were familiar with both Frank and Livia Marello's voices?

A: Yes. Mrs. Marello and I, we'd talk whenever we saw each other. Sometimes we'd have tea. I knew Mr. Marello's voice too.

Q: Whose voice did you hear on the occasion you've been describing?

A: At one time or another, I heard both. But more Mr. Marello than his wife ... poor thing.

"Thank you, Miss Wilmer. No further questions."

As evidence of an "argument," Wilmer's testimony barely got its chin over the bar, but Taggart knew Watson would make the two-minute conversation, only one word of which was discernable, and that heard through a wall, sound like a fist fight on final argument. He needed to give the jury a bit of perspective.

Q. Good morning, Miss Wilmer. I'm Michael Taggart, and I represent Frank Marello in this trial. Do you think it's important for anyone accused of a crime to get a fair trial?

A. Of course, I do.

Q: You've talked to Sheriff Hatcher a couple of times about what you heard on the night of December 24th, 1973?

A: It was early morning actually, but yes, I've talked to Sheriff Hatcher two times.

Q: And you've also talked to Mr. Watson here, haven't you?

A: Yes.

Q: How many times have you talked to Mr. Watson about what you heard?

A: Counting times on the telephone?

Q: Yes, all conversations.

A: At least a half a dozen. Three times in person. He would call before he would come to see me.

Q: And you always agreed to talk to him?

Miss Wilmer froze.

A: … Yes.

Q: I called and asked to talk to you about what you heard, didn't I?

A: Yes.

Q: You refused to talk to me about it, didn't you?

A: I had nothing to say to any lawyer for Mr. Marello.

Q: Did Mr. Watson tell you not to talk to me?

A: Mr. Watson said it was up to me.

Q: Now, you told Mr. Watson the conversation you heard "only lasted a couple of minutes." By that do you mean approximately two minutes?

A: Approximately, yes.

Q: And the only word you could actually discern was the word "money?"

A: Yes.

Q: All the rest of what you heard was just sound so muffled that you could not make out any of the words?

A: Yes.

Q: Ms. Wilmer, I want you to take a look at the clock on the wall above the entrance to the courtroom … now wait with me until the second hand reaches the twelve. Okay, there it goes – let's see how long two minutes is, starting now.

A silence, seeming like ten minutes instead of two, ensued.

"There," Mike said as the second hand finally climbed up the left side of the clock face and swept past the twelve after the passage of one hundred twenty seconds. "That was about the length of time you heard these "sounds" coming from the Marello's apartment. Is that right?"

A: Certainly no more than that. Maybe a little less.

Q: During that entire time the only word you heard was the word "money?"

A: Yes.

Q: That left a lot of time for other things to be said, didn't it?

A: Yes.

Q: But you have no idea what?

A: That's correct.

Q: You never heard the word "homosexual?"

A: No.

Q: You never heard the word "Josephson?"

A: No.

Taggart took a chance. "What you heard was too faint and muffled to tell whether either of the Marellos were angry?

A: All I know is the sound woke me up and that's the only time I ever heard any sound coming from their apartment.

Q: But you were unable to discern the emotions of the Marellos?

A: No, I just assumed—

Q: They could have been happy and celebrating something, like one of them getting a raise. That might have led to the mention of "money."

A: At three a.m.? Anything's possible, I suppose.

Taggart thought he'd gone about as far as he could safely go in his effort to erode any possible inference that what Wilmer had heard was an "argument." If he antagonized Miss Wilmer by pushing too hard, she might suddenly remember something really harmful, or think she did. He had seen it happen. So he left the subject and turned to Wilmer's testimony that Livia, was a "nice, friendly person." Eventually she conceded that Frank, too, was nice and friendly. It had been a grudging concession made only after being reminded how Frank had rescued her cat from a tree, chased a bat out of her apartment and always carried her trash can out to the curb and back on collection day.

As Mike paused to review his checklist of things to ask Wilmer, he considered probing further, trying to get her to admit the Frank Marello she knew would never have murdered his wife. In the midst of this contemplation, Rhonda stuck a note under his nose. It read, "Shut up and sit down."

"No further questions."

Watson had no redirect, and Hizzoner recessed court for the day.

For Taggart, stopping to relax or even eat at the end of the day was deadly, especially a day of trial – after listening so closely to every word, for every nuance, trying to say exactly the right thing to convince but not antagonize, keeping ten thousand facts big and small at the forefront of his thinking and instantly understand how they related to whatever he was hearing from the witness, the judge, the prosecution. If he relaxed for even half an hour at the end of such a day, inertia would take over. His body at rest would tend to stay at rest. Having both eaten and relaxed, Mike was in his classic couch slouch, staring at a place no one else could see, when Rhonda began to prod.

"C'mon, Mike," Rhonda said, "We need to go over the stuff on Mrs. Lindholm one more time. You know she's going to be Watson's next witness."

Rhonda the goad.

Margaret Lindholm was Livia's mother. She had been cooperative with Avery Carleton, Frank's first lawyer, but that was before she discovered and read Livia's diary. Mike had asked to speak to her, so had Rhonda. Mrs. Lindholm refused. They had considered having Ghost try to sell her a Bible, but decided against it. If it ever came out that they had surreptitiously interviewed the victim's mother against her wishes under the guise of trying to sell her a copy of the Good Book, they would be "viewed with disfavor" as Ghost had put it.

Mrs. Lindholm would authenticate Livia's diary, but what else would she have to say? Cross-examining a murder victim's parent required delicacy. Fear of how wrong it could go was enough to overcome Taggart's post-dinner paralysis and get him back in harness for the evening. Back and forth, back and forth, Mike and Rhonda played the "What if she says …" game. Playing out different scenarios, making notes, oblivious to the passage of time.

"God, it's way past eleven." Rhonda reached for her purse. "I have to get out of here. Where's Ghost? I loaned him my car."

"Who knows where or when, if Ghost's involved. Take my car. I'll walk out with you. I want to get some stuff out of it."

They walked down the steps from the porch to Taggart's car. Out on Church Street a lone car cruised slowly past. Otherwise, the street was empty. Although no longer raining, everything was still wet and dripping from the earlier showers, and there were no stars. Mike watched Rhonda drive away. He stood leaning against the building staring at the reflection of the street light in the puddles on the road.

What are Marcia and Matt doing? Taggart was homesick as a kid at camp.

50

Friday, November 19, 1976 – Trial Day 5.

Margaret Lindholm wasn't hard to recognize. She was the attractive middle-aged woman dressed for a funeral seated in the front row of the gallery immediately behind the prosecution table. Despite the way she was dressed, she did not look severe as she settled onto the wooden witness chair without any of the stiffness or discomfort often displayed by persons unused to such surroundings.

"Mizrus Lindholm," Watson began, "what was your relationship to the victim in this case, Livia Marello?"

A: She is ... was, my eldest daughter.

Q: And I presume you're acquainted with the accused?

A: Yes, he is my former son-in-law.

Q: I hand you a photograph marked Prosecution Exhibit 4, do you recognize it?

A: Yes. (Mrs. Lindholm sat staring at the picture.) It's a portrait of Livia.

Q: When was this portrait taken?

A: I persuaded Livia to have it taken in the Fall of 1973, in late October. I had intended to give it to Frank for Christmas that year.

Q: Does this portrait accurately depict the way your daughter looked at the time of her death?

A: Yes ... to the extent anything like that can capture the vibrance and vitality of a living person, I suppose.

Margaret Lindholm bit her upper lip at the end of her answer while Watson moved the admission of the portrait into evidence.

What Livia looked like before she died was irrelevant, but it was an objection Taggart would never make. As he had come to know some things about Livia Marello earlier in the case, even he had been curious to see what the woman lying dead on the floor in the earlier photos really looked like when she was alive. No doubt the jurors were experiencing the same curiosity. For Mike to deny them that opportunity would be a sin they were unlikely to forgive.

Q: When did you last see your daughter alive?

A: On Sunday, December 23, the day before she died. The school where Livia taught had started Christmas vacation, and she came over to Greensboro on that Friday night and stayed with us, her dad and me.

Q: What was the purpose of her visit?

A: She drove over so we could go Christmas shopping together … Livia and me and her sister, Ellie, my other daughter … she stayed for church the next day, and Sunday dinner and then drove home.

Q: Did Frank Marello come with her?

A: No.

Q: Mizrus Lindholm, I hand you a book marked Prosecution Exhibit 5, do you recognize it?

A: Yes, Livia's diary.

Q: How can you tell this diary belonged to your daughter?

A: Well, her name is on the first page in the space that follows the words, "This is the Diary of…" (Margaret Lindholm held the diary up open to the first page so the jury could see.) And, of course, I recognize my daughter's handwriting throughout.

Q: When did you first see this diary, Mizrus Lindholm?

"Objection, irrelevant."

"Overruled," Hizzoner said, annoyed.

"When did you first see this diary, Mizrus Lindholm?"

A: On that Saturday night Livia stayed with us … the Saturday before she died, … before she was murdered, December 22nd. I came into her bedroom, she was staying in her old room, and I came in to say "Goodnight," and she was writing in it. Ever since Livia was a little girl, she had always been faithful about recording things in her diary,

Margaret Lindholm was breathing life back into her daughter, compelling the jurors to like the little girl who still went Christmas shopping with her mom and loved to write in her diary, and making them want to punish someone for her death. Mike pushed back his chair to stand, the impulse to object strong within him. Rhonda reached out her right hand, touching his arm. He relaxed and settled back in his seat.

Q: After Livia was murdered, did you give the diary to the investigators?

Mrs. Lindholm swiveled slightly in her chair so that she was facing the jury, not Watson, and in that minimal movement seemed to wrap her arms around its members, gathering them to her, fourteen children about to be told a bedtime story.

A: "May you outlive your children, ..." That's a curse I read somewhere a long time ago, but I never stopped to think about what a terrible thing it was until it happened to me ... Her voice began to crack for the first time. When Livia died, some of me died too. I couldn't force myself to go into her old room where I watched her play so happily growing up, where I helped her get ready for her first day of school and, years later, her first date.

I didn't go into Livia's room again until about six months ago. Finally, I walked in one day and just wandered around, touching things, opening drawers here and there, and in her nightstand was her diary. She must have forgotten to pack it when she went home that Sunday, and since she was coming back just two days later for Christmas day, she didn't call to have me send it to her.

Taggart studied the jurors. McTavish, the ticket-taker, was crying. James Landers was staring at his lap. The impassive faces of the rest gave no clue.

"Go on Mizruz Lindholm," Given Watson said.

A: Even after I discovered the diary, it must have been two months before I let anybody know. It took me that long to finish reading, because—"

"Objection, irrelevant, non-responsive." Taggart said. *Why the hell did I let her go on like this?*

"Overruled. Mr. Taggart..." Hizzoner began, but evidently thought better of whatever he was about to say. "never mind. Proceed Mr. Watson."

"Mizrus Lindholm, you were saying?"

A: It ... it took me a long time to read, because I kept crying, and I would have to stop. I think you will see the ink is smudged on some of the pages ... well, those smudges are from my tears.

She was crying as she finished her answer.

"Mrs. Lindholm, would you like to have a moment to compose yourself?" Hizzoner asked.

If she evoked sympathy in as hardened a courtroom veteran as Hizzoner, Taggart was nearly in despair over what effect she must be having on the jury.

"No, thank you, Judge." Margaret patted her eyes with a folded handkerchief and squared her shoulders. "I'm sorry to have to be this way. I'm alright now."

Once the diary was admitted, Watson asked, "Mizrus Lindholm, before we get into what the diary says, please compare the handwriting to what purports to be your daughter's signature on Prosecution's Exhibit 6, the application for life insurance. Does that signature appear to be your daughter's handwriting?

A: No. It looks like Frank's.

Q: You're sure?

A: I'm sure it's not Livia's.

Q: Now, will you please turn to the diary entry for Saturday, January 5, 1973?"

Margaret Lindholm leafed through the pages until she came to the requested date.

Q: Will you please read the last two sentences of the second paragraph beginning with "[w]e so seldom?"

A: "January 5 … we so seldom go on to real passion. If we go there, it's only because I'm driving…"

She read in a voice that began clear and strong, but which became progressively more husky.

Watson selected only those passages directly alluding to Livia Marello's concerns about her husband's sexuality, omitting her even greater number of acknowledgments of Frank's tender and caring behavior.

"Mrs. Lindholm," Hizzoner said, "please try to keep your voice up just a little louder, so the jury can be sure to hear what you're reading."

Mrs. Lindholm stopped, took a deep breath and continued.

"…February 5 … first time this year … Frank is so hesitant … April 1 … thinking of talking to a marriage counselor … what's not going on between Frank and me—"

Taggart was out of his chair. "Your Honor, may we approach the bench?"

Hizzoner hesitated. Finally, he said "Approach."

"Mr. Taggart," Hizzoner said when everyone was assembled, "this had better not be a repetition of something that the Court has already addressed. I will not have you interrupting the flow of the prosecution's case on matters that have already been decided. Now, what is it?"

"Your Honor, I move that the State be required to have the witness read the entirety of the passage for each entry, particularly October 8th, which I am sure he is coming to. There is no way the accused can receive a fair trial if the prosecution is allowed to pick and choose what parts of these entries, particularly that one, the jury is allowed to first hear—"

"Counsel can have the witness read whatever he wants on cross," Watson said.

"Don't interrupt me, Mr. Watson." Mike snapped. "I don't interrupt you—"

"You will direct all your comments to me, Mr. Taggart," Hizzoner said, "not opposing counsel. Now, are you quite finished?"

"No, Your Honor, I'm just warming up. To force any passages that give context to what this witness is reading, which may be favorable to the accused, to come into evidence only at a point in time widely separated from those portions the State wants to emphasize distorts what the victim actually wrote. It is not a fair and accurate presentation of what the entries say."

"Counsel," both Hizzoner's voice and jowls were trembling, "you are in contempt. That motion was fully argued and denied as part of the pretrial motions. Your re-making of motions already disposed of distracts the jury and interrupts the flow of the prosecution's evidence, and I won't have it. You are fined one hundred dollars and, if it happens again, it will be twice that. Do I make myself clear?"

Taggart glared at Hizzoner, saying nothing. There had been no such pretrial motion.

"Do I make myself clear, Sir?"

"Yes, ... Sir."

"Very well. Pay the clerk at the end of the day. Now, let's get on with it."

Watson, wanting no distractions from Margaret Lindholm's recitation of her daughter's diary, waited until Mike and Rhonda had resumed their seats before asking her to continue.

A: "... April 16 ... went to the marriage counselor ... when it comes to sex, he never heated up ... She asked if I had ever wondered if Frank is homosexual ... August 15 ... doubts about Frank's sexuality worsening ... He sees more and more of this man Mark Josephson ... I think he's homosexual ...

Q: Directing your attention to the entry for Tuesday, October 8, 1973, Mizrus Lindholm, will you read the first paragraph of that passage to the ladies and gentlemen of the jury?

A: "If clarity was what I wanted, I have my wish, and now I'm sorry I ever wanted it. Last night Frank told me he is a homosexual, that he has strong feelings for Mark Josephson, and he has slept with Mark. Despite all my earlier concerns, it was like having a bomb explode inside my heart to hear that it's true. I feel like someone hit me in the stomach with a baseball bat."

"Thank you, Mizrus Lindholm." Watson said. "I know this was extremely difficult for you. I have no further questions."

He turned and looked at Taggart. "Your witness."

Mike almost leaped from his seat, the words of his first question on their way as he rose.

"Mrs. Lindholm, I'd like to tie up a few loose ends here. At the first trial of this case, you testified on Frank Marello's behalf, didn't you?"

A: Yes.

Taggart picked up some pages from the transcript of the first trial.

Q: At the time you testified that you had known Frank Marello almost four years?

A: Yes.

Q: And it was your opinion he had a kind and gentle and non-violent character and would not be capable of acting with force or violence towards your daughter?

A: Yes.

Q: Frank Marello had been a guest in your home on many occasions during those four years?

A: Yes.

Q: During the course of those visits, you had the opportunity to observe whether he preferred coffee or tea?

A: Yes.

Q: Frank always drank coffee, didn't he?

A: Yes.

Q: Never tea.

A: Not that I recall.

Taggart walked to the evidence table beside the Clerk and picked up a small card and handed it to Mrs. Lindholm. "Mrs. Lindholm, I hand you Exhibit D, the card found on the Marello's kitchen table at the time your daughter's body was discovered. Do you recognize the handwriting on the card?"

A: Yes, it's Livia's handwriting.

Q: Please read what the card says.

A: 'To Frank, with love, from Livia.'

Q: By the way, did Livia mention to you that she was giving Frank a new bathrobe for Christmas?

A: Yes. I was with her when she bought it.

Mrs. Lindholm sighed. Inwardly, so did Mike.

Q: Now, I want to go back over all those passages that the Solicitor just asked you about. Will you please turn back to the diary entry of January 5 and read that to the jury?

Margaret Lindholm hesitated for a moment and then turned to a page near the front of the book lying in her lap.

A: Saturday, January 5, 1973

End of the holidays. Classes are back in session for Frank. I'm glad we didn't go anywhere for Christmas. Nice just to be together - no demands of either his classes or mine for a couple of weeks.

Frank must feel the same way, but I sometimes wonder how much beyond "niceness" his feelings go. He's so gentle and kind, he's impossible not to love. But I wonder what "love" means to him. Here we are in this relationship filled with tenderness, and we seldom go on to real passion. If we go there, it's only when I'm driving.

Maybe Frank has spent too many years alone with his books. It's as if "love" is some idealized concept existing in his brain like the page of some book. He says lovely things to me; he does nice things for me; but he doesn't do nice things to me. Sometimes a girl wants to be literally swept off her feet, and I don't think he understands this.

Q: Now February 15, please.

Friday, February 15, 1973. Yesterday Frank gave me a wonderful old volume of John Donne's love poems for Valentine's Day, and we took a walk through campus in the late afternoon after the crowd from the basketball game was gone. It was lovely.

We made love last night. The first time this year. I never thought I'd be counting!

Mrs. Lindholm had beeh holding the diary up with both hands, but as she finished reading this entry, her hands sank to her lap and she bowed her head. After no more than a second or two, she raised her head, and with a look of resignation, took a deep breath.

Q: April 1.

A. Monday, April 1, 1973

April Fool's Day! Spring has certainly come to Chapel Hill, and that's no foolin'. The azaleas are rioting! What a satisfactory flower.

I'm thinking of talking to a marriage counselor about what's going on or, more correctly, not going on, between Frank and me. Maybe it's me. Sometimes I ask myself am I a wanton person? I listen to other women complain about being pressed for sex by their husbands, and I wonder if I'm just asking for trouble. But when everything else about the relationship is so filled with warmth and tenderness, our failure to find the ultimate expression of those feelings seems a lot different to me than the kind of sex those women are talking about.

Q: April 16.

A. Tuesday, April 16, 1973. I went to the marriage counselor yesterday during the noon hour. I felt like some kind of traitor to

Frank to be telling her about our problem (or is it my problem?). There I was, paying this woman fifty of our oh so scarce dollars, just to tell her our most intimate secrets. Livia, darlin', are you going crazy?

I think the jury's still out on that one. Actually, Dr. Lefler is very nice and says I'm not a sex maniac. At first she said that couples just naturally "cool down" after a while, but after we talked some more, I think we agreed that the trouble isn't Frank cooling down. When it comes to sex, he really never heated up very much. Dr. Lefler says the fact Frank pays so much attention to me otherwise suggests the problem is something else. She agrees it's probably just a lack of confidence, but one thing she said is something I never thought of before. She asked if I had ever wondered whether Frank is homosexual.

Homosexual! I don't think I even know what the word really means, not really. I just have this mental picture of real effeminate men mincing around and holding hands with each other, and then I don't even know what. I mean, I kind of do, but not really. I want to just say, "No, no, that's not the problem," and leave it at that, but if that is the problem, how does that help Frank, or me, for that matter? Dr. Lefler says if he's homosexual, it will become increasingly clear, although she can't necessarily say how.

For the time being I guess I'm just going to try to give Frank as much encouragement and reason for confidence as I can without attempting to force things. I just hope I don't make this all a bigger problem than it is by paying too much attention to it.

Q: August 15.

A. Thursday, August 15, 1973. My doubts about Frank's sexuality are worsening. We haven't made love in two months. How can someone so kind and caring not want to have sex? God knows no man ever had a more willing partner! That sounds funny when I read it back to myself, but it's not. He sees more and more of this man Mark Josephson. I think he's "gay" or whatever it's called these days. I just can't believe that Frank would sneak around or lie to me, but something's certainly wrong.

Q: Mrs. Lindholm, in addition to asking you to read only parts of certain entries, Mr. Watson also left out some other entries which expressed your daughter's and her husband's feelings for each other?

A: Ye … yes.

Q: For example, will you turn to the entry for Sunday, May 6, 1973, and read that to the jury?

Margaret Lindholm thumbed through the pages to the May 4 entry.

My birthday! A lovely day. Chapel Hill was never more radiant – blue skies and sunshine all day. Frank made breakfast, and when I came to the table, beside my plate was a poem, one he wrote. It made me cry, I was so happy. I have read it over and over today.

Q: There is a poem pasted in the diary following this entry, isn't there?

A: Yes.

Q: Will you please read the poem?

A: Livia,

My door unopened
Stood for years,
Curtained heavily,
Dark within,
To the contents
Offering no clue.
Ideas, feelings, thoughts,
Seeds without sunlight,
Dormant, imprisoned,
Masked,

Secured by a lock
For which
I came to believe
There was no key.
Until one day
I discovered
I was not alone
In the room.
You
Had joined me.
Instead of saying,
"You could…"
You whispered,
"You are…"
Expecting nothing,
You gave me everything,
Caring only
For the way things are,
Instead of for what
They might become.
You made me believe
In your belief in me,
And in so doing
Unlocked the door.

Love, Frank

Q: What words did your daughter write immediately following that poem?

A: Just reading those words fills me with love.

After a pause, Mike said, Thank you, Mrs. Lindholm.

Rhonda turned and looked at Frank sitting next to her at counsel table. That was lovely, Frank.

"Poem," Ghost jotted in his notes, "many jurors staring at Marello, McTavish still crying." He thought for a moment, then added, "If Marello wrote this to Livia, what did he write to Josephson?"

Q: Mrs. Lindholm, will you please turn to the entry for October 8, 1973, and read that one it its entirety?

A. If clarity was what I wanted, I have my wish, and now I'm sorry I ever wanted it. Last night Frank told me he is a homosexual, that he has strong feelings for Mark Josephson and he has slept with Mark. Despite all my earlier concerns, it was like having a bomb explode inside my heart to hear it's true. I feel like someone has hit me in the stomach with a baseball bat.

Frank was so distraught when he told me. He's having all kinds of problems with what he has done. He says he still loves me, but that it's more of a 'friendship love.'

Although the problem has become clear, the solution seems murkier than ever. I asked Frank if this means he wants to leave me, and he said 'no.' Apparently this attraction to Mark is not the first time Frank has had a sexual experience with another man, but the others were years apart and a long time ago. He doesn't know why this happens and says he feels like a 'traitor' to me, and he wants to stay with me and love me and live with me, but he has these other feelings he doesn't want to have, and he doesn't know what to do about them.

We talked for hours. Sometimes Frank was crying; sometimes I was crying; sometimes we both were crying. It was as if we were the last two people on Earth and all the identities that define us for others were stripped away and we were lying there with nothing but our feelings. I came to see it's like Frank has a disease, and one of the symptoms is that he doesn't know who he is, or if he does know, he doesn't want to be that person. In the midst of it all, we made love, and it was very comforting for me and, I think, for Frank, despite all the confusion. Thinking about it now, it seems ironic that the source of our comfort and discomfort is in some ways the same thing separated only by a razor's edge.

Taggart paused to let Livia Marello's words of anguish and the Marello's continued love for each other even in the wake of his infidelity, sink in.

Q: Mrs. Lindholm, have you read your daughter's diary from cover to cover?

A: Yes.

Q: From front to back, there is not a single reference anywhere suggesting your daughter was considering leaving her husband, not one, is there?

A: No.

Q: Nor, and this is important, is there a single word or reference that suggests Frank Marello wanted to leave your daughter?

A: No.

Q: In fact, your daughter says she asked him that direct question, "Does this mean you want to leave me," and he replied that he did not?

A: Yes.

At this point Mike wanted to ask whether Livia ever told her mother that either she or Frank was considering giving up on the marriage. He did not know the answer. In that case, conventional wisdom said, don't ask the question. Better no answer than a bad answer.

On the other hand, the diary was filled with expressions of the couple's determination to overcome the problem and stay together. If Livia had ever told her mother such a thing, it seemed unlikely she would have testified on Frank's behalf in the first trial. Watson had not attempted to elicit any such testimony. *Is this a trap he had set, hoping Taggart would ambush himself by venturing into unexplored territory?* Maybe he could inch his way up to the dividing line between the explored and unexplored and get a feel for what might be waiting for him on the other side.

Q: Your daughter used to tell you about the boys she went out with?

A: Yes.

Q: She told you about the places she went and the things she did on her dates?

A: Yes.

Q: So, you and your daughter shared an open and candid relationship with each other?

A: Yes, we did.

Here goes.

Q: Yet, at no time did your daughter ever suggest to you in any way that either she or her husband were thinking of giving up on their marriage?

A: No, she didn't.

Whew.

Q: To the contrary, her diary indicates that following Frank's disclosure of what had happened, they faced the situation together, doesn't it?

A: Yes.

Q: And that they were determined to try to overcome the problem?

A: Yes.

Q: And make their marriage last?

A: Yes.

Q: Even on the very night he told her about his homosexuality, in the immediate wake of his telling her, Livia and Frank made love?

A: Yes.

Q: Your daughter thought she and her husband were making progress with the problem?

A: I don't know what she thought.

Q: Mrs. Lindholm, please turn to the entry of December 16, 1973.

Taggart did not want this entry read with tears or meekness. He wanted it read with strength and resolve, with emphasis in all the places it belonged. So, he read it aloud himself ever so slowly and deliberately.

Q: The entry for December 16, 1973 reads,

Sunday morning. Lazy time – No place to go. No place either of us had to be. I woke up this morning in Frank's arms. He was still asleep, but not for long. We made love real long and slow. He is so gentle and tender and pleasing to me. It was delicious. We are making progress.

Did I read that entry correctly, Mrs. Lindholm?

A: Yes.

Another pause. Taggart glanced at his notes and took a swallow of water.

Q: Please turn to the diary entry for October 12, 1973.

Margaret Lindholm stole a quick glance towards the prosecution table.

Q: Have you found that entry, Mrs. Lindholm?

A: Yes. I have it.

Q: On October 12, your daughter wrote,

Terrible night. Lauren called, weeping. She and Jim had an argument. I could hear him yelling at her. Lauren was hysterical. She said she had locked him out of the bedroom so she could call. He picked up a phone somewhere else in the house and said awful things to me, called me a 'nosy slut' and told me to 'butt out of their marriage or he'd butt me out.' I said nothing.

Lauren said he hit her. She thinks her jaw might be broken. I told her to call the police. Lauren kepts asking 'what about the family? But what about 'The family' anyway? Nobody seems to be doing anything to stop Jim. 'The Family' deserves all the embarrassment it gets. I have half a mind to call the police myself.

Q: Did I read that correctly, Mrs. Lindholm?

A: Yes.

"No further questions."

"Mizrus Lindholm," Given Watson began, "defense counsel asked you about the testimony you gave at the first trial of this case. Do you recall his questions?

A: Yes.

Q: Is your opinion of your former son-in-law's character at present the same as it was at the time of the first trial?

A: No, it most definitely is not.

Q: Why not?

A: At the time of the first trial, it was also my opinion Frank Marello would have been incapable of being unfaithful to my daughter with another woman, let alone a man. Livia's diary certainly showed me how wrong I'd been in my assessment of him on that score, and that my overall opinion of him was ... tragically mistaken.

"No further questions."

51

Friday, November 19, 1976 – Trial Day 5 – Afternoon

"The Prosecution calls Mark Josephson." Margaret Lindholm was just stepping down from the witness stand when Watson spoke. As she reached the double doors at the back of the courtroom, they opened, and Mark Josephson came through in a wheel chair pushed by Deputy Meachum. Margaret's upper lip curled in disgust as Mark was wheeled past, but she said nothing.

Rhonda had turned in her chair watching Margaret depart, wondering how the woman ever found the strength to live and re-live this awful time. Josephson's sudden appearance, the unexpected tableau of him and Margaret Lindholm facing each other, made Rhonda gasp. Anguish versus anguish. It was one thing to hear about the intensity of trial in a Trial Advocacy class in law school and quite another to be in the cauldron as it boiled.

"Lindholm wants to spit on Josephson," Ghost, who was sitting no more than five feet from the unloving pair, noted.

Mark was dressed in slacks and a sport shirt. His left arm was in a sling and casted, only the tips of his fingers peeked out. Most of the swelling in his lips appeared to have subsided in the two weeks since Mike and Rhonda's visit, and the stitches had been removed, but his left eye still looked like a ripe plum. Unable to take the witness stand, which was slightly elevated, Josephson sat beside it in his wheelchair. He looked shriveled, a deflated human ball without resilience.

Mike looked at Frank. *What's he thinking?* A lot had happened since that shopping trip three years ago. "Keep a poker face when Mark is called," Mike had cautioned during a prep session, but now he saw a slight wince flicker across Frank's countenance as Josephson raised his hand and stated his name and address.

Q: You are acquainted with the accused, Frank Marello, is that right?

A: Yes.

Q: How long have you known each other?

A: We first met in mid-1972, in August, I think.

Q: How did you meet?

A: In a bookstore. We were standing at the counter. We were both buying the same book, and we started talking.

Q: What kind of bookstore?

What does Watson think? Some adult porn place? C'mon. Some show of solicitude, however feigned, was usual towards a witness whose injuries were as serious and undeserved as Mark Josephson's. But this was not business as usual judging from the way Watson ripped through his questions with the abruptness of a Prussian colonel.

"Watson not soft on queers," Ghost noted.

A: It was the Tarheel bookstore ... the book was *The Best And The Brightest* ... about President Johnson's advisors during the Viet Nam War.

Did Josephson see the implication of Watson's question? His voice, weak and slightly halting, sounded like he was having trouble breathing, but his words were firm.

Q: The two of you became good friends?

A: We became friends.

Q: The accused was married when you and he became friends?

Watson was aggressively leading his own witness, but Taggart didn't care. Whatever help Josephson had to offer the prosecution would be more effective coming from the witness, not the examiner. *If Watson sees it another way, break a leg.*

A: Yes, he was married.

Q: When did you learn that?

A: I don't remember. Probably that first day. We went and had a cup of coffee.

Q: So you *knew* the accused was married throughout your so-called friendship?

A: I think so.

Mike whispered to Frank, "Pay attention to the way Watson is questioning. You'll get the same third degree."

Q: You had known for a long time the accused was married?

A: For at least a year, yes.

Q: By October 1973 the two of you had become very good friends?

A: Yes.

Q: The two of you went out together socially?

A: Yes, from time to time.

Q: You went to movies together?

A: We did once ... something Livia didn't want to see.

Q: You mentioned the name "Livia," are you referring to the accused's wife?

A: Yes.

Q. The wife he is accused of killing?

A. Yes.

Q: You were not on a first name basis with her, were you?

A: What do you mean?

Q: You only met Livia Marello two times, is that right?

A: Yes.

Q: Once just to shake hands?

A: Yes.

Q: And the other time when she begged you to stay away from her husband?

A: I wouldn't put it that way, but yes, when she asked me not to see Frank.

Q: In October, 1973, you and the accused became homosexual lovers, didn't you?

A: On one occ—"

"Your Honor," Watson said, "may the witness be instructed to answer the question with a simple 'yes' or 'no?'"

"Your question is ambiguous, Counsel. I think the witness was going to clarify your question in the course of his answer. You may proceed with your answer, Mr. Josephson."

A: On one occasion Frank and I did become involved, yes.

Q: "Became involved?" You and the accused had homosexual sex, didn't you?

A: Yes.

Q: You spent the whole night together?

A: Yes.

Q: This occurred in October 1973?

A: In late September.

Q: Just three months before Livia Marello was murdered?

A: Approximately.

Q: And it was after you and the accused had sex together that Livia Marello begged you to leave her husband alone?

A: She asked me not to see Frank any more, yes. It was after that one time.

Q: You told her that you would stop seeing her husband?

A: Yes.

Q: But you did not stop seeing him?

A: ... Not entirely. I stopped initiating contact.

Q: So, it was the accused who continued to call and ask to see you?

A: Not exactly. He called once or twice, but it was on business.

Q: Ah, yes. Business. Let's talk about business. You're in the insurance business, aren't you?

A: Yes.

Q: You sell life insurance.

A: Yes.

Q: You sold a policy of life insurance to the accused on his wife's life?

A: Yes.

Q: The face amount of the policy was $25,000?

A: Yes.

Q: The accused bought this policy from you on December 13, 1973?

A: I believe that's the date he submitted the application.

Q: Just eleven days before the newly insured Livia Marello was murdered?

A: Yes.

Q: Did you have any dealings with Mrs. Marello in connection with the purchase of this insurance?

A: She signed the application along with Frank.

Q: Did you see her sign the application?

A: No, Frank brought it in signed.

Q: You're not familiar with Livia Marello's handwriting?

A: No.

Q: So, you don't know whether that really was her writing on the application?

A: No, I guess I don't.

Q: You don't know whether Livia Marello even knew her husband had purchased insurance on her life, do you?

A: Well, I didn't see her sign the forms.

Q: When the accused visited you to buy the insurance, the two of you made a date to go Christmas shopping?

A: A 'date?' No, not a date in the sense that your question implies. Frank came into the office to pick up the policies, and we chatted for a moment. It turned out neither of us had finished our shopping, and we thought it would be more fun to go together than alone.

Q: So you made plans to go Christmas shopping together?

A: Yes.

Q: This shopping trip was not for "business purposes," was it?

A: No.

Q: It was for social purposes?

A: Yes.

Q: The two of you made a plan to go out socially?

A: Yes.

Q: On what day did you make these social plans?

A: I think it was December 18, the day he picked up the policy.

Q: So, on the eighteenth of December you and Frank made a plan to go Christmas shopping six days later?

A: Yes.

Q: You made this spur of the moment plan to go Christmas shopping together six days in advance of the actual day you intended to go?

A: Yes.

Q: That's pretty careful planning, don't you agree?

A: I guess.

Q: You and the accused are together in your office planning a shopping trip and you select a day six days into the future on which to do it. Was that because he needed to have an alibi that morning?

A: No

Taggart turned in the jury's direction. *Jesus, are any of them still awake? Watson's beating the shopping trip to death.*

Q: You had six days in which to do your shopping, seven if you include the eighteenth itself. Don't you think you were cutting it a little close by waiting until the day before the holiday?

A: Maybe, but it was the only day both of us could do it.

Q: So, there were some earlier times during that six day period when you could have done it, but the accused couldn't?

A: As I recall, yes.

Q: And there were some earlier times during the six day period when the accused could do it, but you could not?

A: Yes.

Q: The twenty-fourth was the only time the two of you could go shopping together?

A: Yes.

Q: Either of you could have done the shopping at some other time, but the twenty-fourth was the only time you could do it together?

A: Yes.

Seated in the back row, Ghost wrote, "Shopping. ZZZZZZZZZZZZ!" in his notebook.

Q: So, the important thing about the trip on the morning of the twenty-fourth was the two of you being together, not the shopping?

A: The important thing was to make the drudgery of shopping more fun by getting it done together.

Q: By shopping together?

A: Yes.

Q: Livia Marello was a school teacher, wasn't she?

A: I believe so.

Q: School was out the week before Christmas?

A: Maybe … I really don't know.

Q: Typically, school gets out for holiday vacation a few days before Christmas, doesn't it, Mr. Josephson?

A: I suppose so.

Q: So, if his wife wasn't teaching school, the accused could have gone shopping with her?

A: Unless perhaps he was shopping for her gift or she for his, I guess.

Q: So, the accused asked to go shopping with you instead of his wife?

A: I don't know that. Maybe he went shopping with both of us at one time or another, but, yes, he did ask me if I wanted to go shopping, and it turned out the twenty-fourth was the only day we could both go.

Q: Was that because his wife would be dead on the morning of the twenty-fourth and couldn't go?

A: I have no reason to believe that.

Q: Who drove on this *shopping trip*?

A: I did.

Q: What time did you pick up the accused?

A: Approxiimately 9:15.

Q: When you picked the accused up on the 24th, did you enter his apartment?

A: No.

Q: What'd you do, just pull up to the curb and honk?

A: No, Frank was waiting outside when I arrived?

There was a murmur in the gallery. "Oooo, bad fact." Ghost noted.

Q: There has been testimony that even at two o'clock on the afternoon of the twenty-fourth, it was cold enough for a winter coat. It must have been even colder at nine-fifteen in the morning. Are you sure he was waiting outside when you arrived?

A: It was cool, but he had a coat.

Q: So, you never went inside the Accused's apartment?

A: No.

Q: You had no opportunity to see what was lying on the kitchen floor.?

Even though he would have asked the same question, if he'd been Watson, Taggart hated hearing it. "Objection, there's no evidence anything was lying on the kitchen floor at nine-fifteen."

"Sustained. The jury will disregard Mr. Watson's last remark."

Taggart wished Judge Hunter could see the smirk on Watson's face. "No further questions." The Solicitor relinquished his examination with a sneer.

As Taggart hoped, Hizzoner recessed court for the weekend without embarking on Josephson's cross-examination. Maybe the passage of a couple days would dim the bad facts in the jurors' minds.

***

"Any thoughts? Ideas?" Mike said after they were seated. "Impressions? Anyone?" No one said anything until after they ordered. They were having Friday's dinner at the Holiday Inn in West Durham, a click up the dining scale from the General Johnston.

"That was a nice poem Frank wrote," Ghost said, "but if I was Watson, I'd argue he gave it to the wrong person,"

"But he didn't give it to Josephson, did he?" Mike said. "He gave it to Livia. He and Josephson may have fooled around one time, but his heart was with Livia. I think we're okay on that. Couldn't ignore it, since it's in the diary. You can bet the jurors will read it."

"Frank signing Livia's name to the insurance application and choosing to wait outside for Josephson' are such bad facts," Rhonda mused aloud. "They feed on each other."

"Yeah, but we knew they were coming," Taggart said. "Besides, it's like my partner Horn, says, 'If it weren't for bad facts, nobody'd need lawyers.'"

"What about Mrs. Lindholm?" Ghost asked.

"She was good for Watson," Mike said. "I'm just glad to have her off the stand early. She'd have been my last witness, if I were him. The more time between her departure and the beginning of deliberations, the better."

"I think homosexuality's been talked about so much in this case, it might be losing some of its stigma," Ghost said.

Rhonda pursed her lips, considering. "What makes you think so?"

"When the subject first came up during jury selection, people back where I was sitting were rolling their eyes and shaking their heads, but I didn't see any of that today, even during Josephson's questioning, where you might expect it. It's as if it's become so familiar now, it's not a big deal any more. Like a new car that no longer seems new after being driven a couple of months."

Taggart hoped Ghost was right, but didn't think so. Homosexuality had been an "abomination" in biblical times, and now, twenty centuries later, people were still smearing queers, just ask Mark Josephson. Homophobia had a lot of staying power.

52

Friday, November 19, 1976 – Evening, Trial Day 5

Ghost dropped them off at the apartment and drove off in Mike's car for parts unknown. Rhonda headed for home less than a minute later. Lugging his briefcase, Mike started up the steps. As he stopped to unlock the door, someone said, "Mike." Buck Brown stepped out of the shadows at the end of the porch.

"Whoa, Buck, you startled me."

"Sorry, I wanted to wait until the others left."

"C'mon in. What's up? Want a beer?"

"Probably not much, but my son, Danny, was down at the West End after work this afternoon, an' the news on TV showed that boy coming out of the courthouse in the wheelchair. Guess he testified, right?"

Buck had been at the trial only on the morning of opening statements.

"Josephson, yeah," Mike replied. " He started this afternoon." *Easy, Mike, don't get excited yet.*

"Anyway," Buck continued, "Danny's standing there with a bunch of other boys when they show this fella being wheeled out. Lee Roy Thigpen's there too, an' he says he met that guy once an' how he's a real fairy or some such. Danny didn't say nuthin', an' Lee Roy didn't say no more, but you gotta believe there's only one way Lee Roy ever met this guy, an' it wasn't because Lee Roy was buyin' insurance. He was either beatin' him up or stealin' his car."

Taggart was astonished. Breaks like this didn't happen in Southern California. Asking someone in San Diego to keep their eyes and ears open was like throwing a pebble in the ocean. In Marlborough the ocean was a puddle.

"Who is this guy, Thigpen?" Mike asked. "Do I know him?"

"Probably not," Buck replied. "Lee Roy's no ballplayer. He's a repo man when he works at all. I think he steals more cars than he repos. Lives over east of Dare on the Lebanon road. Got a trailer out there."

"Does he ride a motorcycle?"

"Yeah, come to think of it, he does. Big ol' Harley with a long fork and high bars ... damnedest contraption."

"Buck, any idea how I can get a look at this guy if I need to?"

"Last few months he's been playin' pool down at the West End 'bout every night."

"Describe him."

"Lee Roy ain't no movie star. He's in his late twenties, about five-eleven or six feet, got a gut on him, but pretty solid. Don't shave more than once or twice a week. Dark hair ... always smokin'. Wears an old Harley-Davidson cap all the time. Don't ask me what color his eyes are. Lee Roy an' I don't know each other that well."

"A Nazi hat," Mark Josephson'd said. "Okay, no eye color. No problem. Buck, you've given me plenty. Thanks. Thank Danny for me. Tell him I'm buyin' next time I see him ... By the way, since when did that television down at West End start to work?"

"Lester got himself a new one for home an' brought his ol' one down to the bar. Ain't noticed it's increased his business none.

"One other thing," Buck said, "don't tell nobody where this information come from. I'd hate for Danny to get cross-ways of Lee Roy. He's more'n half mean."

***

Saturday night, the night after Buck passed along what Danny Brown had heard, Ghost, driving a big Harley with Georgia plates coasted to a stop in front of the West End Tavern, put down the kickstand and went inside. His Levis were faded almost white, but covered with smudges of dirt and grease, his denim jacket only marginally less faded and dirty. He was wearing an old Atlanta

Braves baseball cap with a Marine Corps' Eagle, Globe and Anchor lapel pin stuck to its side.

He stepped up to the bar, nodded to a couple of men standing there, ordered a Black Label, and looked up at the television.

"You new around here?" Lester asked. "Don't think I've seen you in here before."

"Just here for a few days," Ghost replied. "With the crew putting in the irrigation at that golf course they're building over north of Durham. We're out of Valdosta, Georgia. Stayin' at the Rebel Yell, an' the guy there said this was a good place to shoot pool."

"What happened to yer ears?" Bobby Mack, a West End regular, who was standing next to the newcomer asked. He was grinning.

"Viet Nam," the small man said, putting down his beer. "Long story."

"No shit!" Bobby Mack was no longer grinning. "Here, let me buy you that beer. My name's Bobby Mack." He stuck out his hand.

"Eric Ragan." Ghost lied, shaking hands. "Thanks." He lifted the can and tipped it slightly in Bobby Mack's direction.

Ragan had a hell of a grip for a little man. "So you play pool?" Bobby Mack asked. "Any good?"

Ragan shook his head. "Nope. Just play to relax. How 'bout you?"

"I ain't played in years. But Lee Roy over there does." He pointed to a thickset man wearing jeans, a black tee shirt and a Harley-Davidson hat. "Hey, Lee Roy, come here for a minute."

Two hours later, when Lee Roy Thigpen kicked his bike to life and drove away from the West End, he was fifty dollars richer. He was also pretty drunk, too drunk and too happy to pay any attention to the single headlight, a pinpoint in his mirrors.

***

Good, there he is. Taggart got out of his car and walked across the street to the front of the Colonial Baptist Church. Eleven o'clock services were just letting out.

"Sheriff, sorry to interrupt your Sunday, but I need your help on something."

Stick Hatcher looked in Mike's direction, said something to his wife, who headed off towards where a group of women were standing in the sun talking.

Stick waited as Taggart came up to him. "I ain't sure I'm in the favor-doin' business. You and I ain' on the same side no more."

"We are on this one, Sheriff. I think I can tell you who mugged Mark Josephson over in Chapel Hill a couple of weeks ago. But there may be more to it than that. That assault might be related to the Marello murder."

Stick rubbed his chin. "I'm listenin'."

Mike opened a large brown envelope he was holding and withdrew two pictures. "Take a look at these. Recognize this guy?"

One photo showed a man, a cue in his hands, bent over a pool table lining up a shot. The other showed the same man coming out of the door of a mobile home with a cinder block front step. Both showed the man's face clearly.

"Sure, I recognize him. That's Lee Roy Thigpen. What about him?"

"Lee Roy's one of the guys who beat up Josephson," Mike replied. "I showed these photos to Josephson this morning, just asked if he knew the guy. He identified Lee Roy immediately."

"G'damn," Stick gazed at the photos. "Where'd you get these pictures?"

Two hours later Taggart was sitting with Mark Josephson in the empty office at the Sheriff's Department when Stick and Tubby Mayes walked in with Lee Roy Thigpen. Despite having been read his rights and knowing the reason for his arrest, at the sight of

Josephson, Lee Roy's usually insolent expression melted with momentary alarm before re-freezing.

"You know this fella, Lee Roy?" Stick asked.

"Ne'er saw him before in my life."

"Well, he says he knows you. He and Mr. Taggart here come in with these two pretty pictures of you and sayin' you're the guy who gave Mr. Josephson that black eye he's sportin' and a whole lot of other trouble to boot." Stick dropped the photographs on the table in front of Lee Roy. I also got a bunch of witnesses who'll say they heard you braggin' you knew Mr. Josephson when you seen him on television the other night down at the West End. Guy you played pool with last night says you mentioned him too.

"Those are admissions, Lee Roy, and together with your victim's eye witness identification, I'd say you're going to be out fixin' the roads of the sovereign state of North Carolina for the next ten years or so."

Convicts in North Carolina still worked on road gangs. The thought of a career detour into road repair put Lee Roy in a somber mood. Stick sat silent for thirty seconds or so to let him contemplate his future.

At the end of the time, Stick went on. "Of course, the thing I'm wondering about is why ya'll did it an' who the other boy was you did it with. Can't believe you had anything personal against Mr. Josephson here, or that you rode all the way over to Chapel Hill just to beat someone up, when you coulda found someone right here in Marlborough.

"That makes me think somebody put you up to it, maybe even paid you to do the job. Shame for him to get off while you're doin' time on the road. On the other hand, if you were to cooperate an' tell me who was in on this with you and whose idea it was, I might be willin' to put in a good word when your trial comes up. I ain't makin' any promises, but it'd be better to have me talking for you than against you. Understand?"

Lee Roy understood. "Guy said his name was Joe Cooper. Only seen him twice, once before an' once after. Me and Tyler Cosby done it.

So much for the right against self-incrimination. Taggart was constantly amazed by how Stick knew what buttons to push.

"Cooper, he called up and said he'd heard I might be willing to beat up a queer for five thousand dollars. Said he wanted this guy Josephson 'gone,' and it had to look like someone was just out huntin' queers. I told him if he wanted it done right, so it'd look the way he wanted it, he oughta have two people, an' that I'd find someone. An another thousand for the second guy."

Mike strained to keep a poker face. He glanced at Josephson. *How's he handling hearing the plan for his own murder?*

"Cooper said 'okay' an' we set it up, half in advance and half when the job was done. I met him at the rest stop out on the Interstate, an' he give me the first half of the money. I met him again out there afterwards, but the prick wouldn't pay me the rest, on accounta the queer lived."

Red-necked asshole. Mike leaned over and whispered something to Stick.

"Lee Roy, you left-handed?" Stick asked.

"Yeah. What of it?"

"Well, Lee Roy," Stick said, "I'm glad you're smart enough to be civic-minded and willin' to help law enforcement any way you can. Now I want ya'll to take a look at these pictures an' tell me if any of them's this Joe Cooper."

Stick handed Lee Roy a stack of thirty mugshots, and Lee Roy began to leaf through them, tossing his rejects back across the table at Stick like he was dealing cards.

"That's him," Lee Roy said, holding up one of the photographs.

He handed Stick a mugshot of Jim Marello taken by the New Orleans Police Department on December 20, 1973.

Four days earlier, on the Wednesday immediately following his confrontation with Jim and Anthony about his having raised the specter of some family member in the Marello apartment when Livia was killed, Taggart had gone to see Frank.

"I thought I told you I didn't want Jim implicated," Frank said as soon as Mr. Jack departed, not even waiting for an exchange of hellos.

"Frank, I'm not implicating Jim in anything. You have to understand that. To the extent he's implicated in Livia's murder, he's implicated himself."

"That's a bunch of sophist nonsense. You're the one who once told me that in trials there is no truth, only versions. Well, this is my trial and my version, and my version isn't going to contain any suggestion my brother murdered my wife. If you won't go along with that, then I'm going to get another lawyer."

"What if he did?"

"Wha … what if who did what?"

"What if Jim did murder Livia? You tell me you didn't. I believe you. The fact remains, she was definitely murdered. If you didn't do it, who did? Somebody with a motive other than robbery or sex. Who can you think of who fits that description? You've seen the diary entries. You tell me you loved Livia. How do you feel about her killer?"

Taggart looked down in the middle of his speech and saw he was wagging his index finger at Frank, something Mike hated when people did that to him. He put his hand in his pocket.

"You know Livia reported Jim to the police twice, that he called her a 'nosey slut,' that just four days before she was murdered Jim was actually in jail in New Orleans because of a complaint Livia had filed. Jim Marello, big time businessman, honorable Rotarian, in jail for wife-beating all because of his goddamned sister-in-law. Who do you think killed her?"

Frank had been standing, leaning with his hands wrapped around the bars of the cell door, looking down at the floor. "I don't know. I don't know. I don't know."

"This isn't about loyalty, Frank. This is about justice. Maybe you're willing to die despite your innocence to protect your brother, but are you willing to let Livia's killer go unpunished?"

Frank straightened up. "No, I'm not. I just don't believe Jim's the one. I mean, I talked to him in New Orleans that afternoon. Every minute of his time that day was accounted for. Maybe he did have a motive; maybe he even threatened her; but there's not a shred of evidence he did anything about it. I don't want to be acquitted at my brother's expense."

Taggart drummed his fingers on the bench where he was sitting. *Is Frank's resolve cracking? Hard to tell.* "Fair enough," he finally said. "No more attempts to implicate Jim unless I come up with something more than I have so far that points to him. Is that what you're saying?"

Taggart stood staring at Frank. Loyalty versus justice. *Life's full of tough choices.* Frank stared back.

Finally, Frank exhaled and put his palms together, fingertips up, almost as if he was praying, except the tension in his arms and shoulders was pressing his hands together like a vice. "Okay, let's see what happens."

That had been last Wednesday night. It had been raining. Now it was late Sunday afternoon. The sun was shining, and the weather wasn't the only thing that had changed. In the interim Taggart had broken his promise about Jim. He had cross-examined Margaret Lindholm about Livia's October 12 diary entry describing Lauren Marello's call. Frank was angrier than he had been four days earlier.

Taggart needed to patch things up with Frank. He hoped Lee Roy's recent account of current events would be the needle and thread to do the job.

"Listen, Frank, I know you're more pissed off than ever, and you should be, but let me tell you what's happened." He described the events of the last forty-eight hours.

"What's Jim have to say about these charges this Thigpen guy is making?" Frank asked.

"He doesn't know yet. Thigpen may have let himself be stampeded into confessing he beat up Mark. He's probably not even sure that's illegal. But he's not admitting he murdered anybody, no matter who put him up to it."

"So, you still don't have any evidence Jim is responsible for Livia's death?"

"I think we've taken a giant step in that direction. Now we not only know Jim had a motive, but also the willingness to hire someone to kill another person."

"What I can't figure out," Frank said, "is what Jim thought could possibly be gained by killing Mark."

"My guess is, when he hired Lee Roy, he was still hoping you'd deny the homosexuality when you testify," Mike replied. "With Josephson gone, he was hoping it couldn't be proved."

"Yes, but there was still the diary."

"When he hired Thigpen, Jim didn't know what it said.

"Anyway, if Jim would hire someone to kill Josephson, presumably to protect you or the family or whatever, then there's reason to believe he'd hire someone, Lee Roy Thigpen, to kill Livia to protect himself. Lee Roy rides a big old chopper like the one that was seen outside your apartment the morning Livia was murdered ... and he's left-handed."

Frank was pacing, wall to wall, three strides to a lap. He kept rubbing his hand across his forehead, saying nothing. Mike let him digest what he'd just heard.

"If Thigpen denies killing Livia, what makes you think Jim will admit it?"

"Maybe we can make Jim think Thigpen's confessed. At least that's the plan."

"You mean trick him?"

"Yeah, 'trick him.' I don't think we'd ever get him to confess. That only happens on TV. But at least we may get enough to support an argument that, as between the two of you, Jim's the more likely candidate to have murdered her – pile on a little more reasonable doubt."

"I don't kno—"

"My God, Frank, Josephson, someone you care about, 's in a wheelchair. He may never see out of that eye again. Even that wasn't enough for Jim. He wanted Mark dead, just like Livia's dead."

Frank stopped pacing and stood with his back to Taggart, his forehead pressed against the cell bars. He was staring through the window on the far wall overlooking the town square. He turned. "You're right … you're right."

53

Monday, November 22, 1976 – Trial Day 6.

Stay in the moment. Do this right. Don't get ahead of yourself. The trap was set, but first they had to finish Mark Josephson's examination. With luck this would be the last day of trial. Taggart wanted to go home.

Tubby Mayes rolled Mark through the packed courtroom and into place beside the witness stand.

"Mr. Josephson, do you understand you're still under oath?" Hizzoner asked.

"Yes, Sir."

It was easy to look good cross-examining friendly witnesses. Mike's only concern was that Mark might come across as so eager to help Frank, his bias would destroy his credibility. They had talked about it, and Josephson seemed to understand.

Mark explained to the jurors that he and Frank never planned to have sex. It was just "something that happened." They were friends who became lovers once, no more. Frank had expressed immediate remorse. Frank had been the first to insist they stop seeing each other, well before Livia made her request.

Q: Mr. Josephson, according to your understanding, why did Frank Marello come to see you again after both he and his wife had said that shouldn't happen?

A: It was really because Livia got pregnant. They decided she needed insurance, something neither of them knew anything about, if they were going to be parents.

Q: Why just a policy for Livia, none for Frank?

A: Frank already had a policy his parents had given him.

Q: Was December 24th really the only day the two of you could find to go shopping together?

A: Yes. The quarter at the University had just ended. Frank had a bundle of final exams he had to grade and turn in by the 21st. I was having a party on the twenty-third. When we looked at our calendars, the twenty-fourth really was the only available day.

Q: Was Frank invited to your party?

A: No, but it seemed like the rest of the world was. Making all the arrangements was driving me crazy.

Q: When Livia Marello asked you not to see her husband anymore, what did she say?

A: She said in view of what had happened, she would appreciate it if I didn't call or try to see Frank. She and Frank were going see if they could make a go of things, and she thought this would be best.

Q: Describe her manner of asking. Did she sound desperate?

A: No, not at all. She was very nice. I could see she was firm in her resolve, but she wasn't "begging."

Q: What was your response?

A: I told her Frank had already made the same request, and it was not and never had been my intent, nor Frank's, for any of this to happen. I certainly wasn't going to do anything she thought would threaten their marriage.

Q: Having had this conversation with Mrs. Marello, did you make any attempt to clear this shopping trip with her?

A: No.

Q: There was a note found on the Marello's refrigerator in Mrs. Marello's handwriting, that said you called for Frank on the 23rd. Did you place such a call?

A: Yes.

Q: You spoke with Mrs. Marello on that occasion?

A: Yes.

Q: What did she say?

A: Nothing other than she would give Frank the message.

Q: She didn't remind you of her earlier conversation with you?

A: No.

Q: Now, Mr. Josephson, you told Mr. Watson Frank was waiting for you when you picked him up on the 24th, how was it decided you would drive?

A: Frank said Livia might need their car. They only had.one.

Q: Did Frank say why he was waiting outside?

A: Yes. He said Livia liked to sleep late when she wasn't teaching, and he didn't want to risk waking her up.

Q: Describe Frank's demeanor that morning.

A: He was chipper. On the way over to Durham I asked him how things were going, with him and Livia, I mean. He said they were getting better, that he was talking more about his feelings, and that was helping, and she was being a terrific support for him.

Q: Why go over to Durham instead of shopping in Chapel Hill?

A: I'd ordered a book to give my mother from a bookstore in Durham and needed to pick it up.

Q: So going to Durham was your idea, not Frank's?

A: That's right.

Q: When did you return to the Marello's apartment?

A: It was about one-thirty. I remember looking at my watch, because I had an appointment at two, and had to go home first.

Q: What took so long?

A: Frank was trying to find something for Livia, and nothing seemed quite right. Of course, a lot of the selection was depleted because we were shopping so late, so it took a long time. We went to a lot of stores.

Q: Did he ultimately buy something for his wife?

A: Yes. He eventually found a sweater for her and a decoration, a Christmas angel.

Q: When you dropped Frank off, did you go inside?

A: No. I didn't get out of the car.

Q: Did you notice anything unusual when you dropped Frank off?

A: Yes. I dropped him off in the parking lot behind their place, and saw the back door was standing open. Frank did too, because he said maybe Livia had gone to the laundry room and had her hands too full to close the door. Also, there was a police car in the parking lot.

Q: Did he say anything else?

A: No. We just shook hands and wished each other 'Merry Christmas.'

Q: Mr. Josephson, after shaking hands and exchanging Christmas wishes and driving away that afternoon, have you ever spoken to Frank Marello again?

A: No.

Q: Have you ever written to each other?

A: No.

Q: In view of your past friendship, why have you neither written nor spoken to each other?

A: I knew Frank still intended to try to live a straight life. If he wanted to see me, he would get in touch.

Q: And he never did?

A: And he never did.

"Thank you, Mr. Josephson. No further questions."

Given Watson was on his feet.

Q: Mr. Josephson, you've been inside the Marello's apartment, haven't you?

A: Yes.

Q: It's a two-story apartment, isn't it?

A: Yes.

Q: The bedroom's upstairs on the second floor, isn't it?

A: I believe so.

Q: So there wouldn't have been much risk of awakening someone sleeping upstairs in the bedroom, would there?

The question called for speculation, but the point was already made. Why underscore it with an objection? Taggart kept his seat.

A: Depends on how lightly someone sleeps, but probably less than if the bedroom was downstairs.

Q: You weren't planning on making a big hulabaloo, if you came inside, were you?

A: No.

Watson went on too long. He revisited aspects of Josephson's earlier testimony, trying to create inconsistancies where there weren't any and, above all else, remind the jury this was Frank Marello's homosexual lover they were listening to. He wrapped up with Josephson by handing him phone books for Chapel Hill and Durham and having Mark count the number of life insurance agencies listed, a total of thirty-eight within the fifteen-mile radius. Having received his answer, he scooped up the two books and plopped them on the defense table in front of Taggart as he walked back to the prosecution table. "No further questions." After studying a pad full of crossed-out notes, he finally he looked up. "Your Honor, the State rests."

In the back of the room Ghost noted, "No Troutman."

"Is the defense ready to present?" Hizzoner inquired at the conclusion of the mid-morning recess.

Time to play poker. "Yes, Your Honor."

"Very well. Mr. Taggart, call your first witness."

"The defense calls James Marello."

Jim stood up. He knew he would be the first to be called. Rhonda had spent the previous afternoon with him discussing the character testimony they wanted him to think he was being called to give. It had been an unpleasant afternoon.

"Do you swear to tell the truth, the whole truth and nothing but the truth in these proceedings, so help you God?"

"I do."

"Please state your full name and address."

"James Calfee Marello. 22 Rue de Marseilles, New Orleans, Louisiana."

"Please be seated."

"Mr. Marello," Taggart began, "are you related to Frank Marello?"

A: Yes. I'm his brother.

Q: Are you his older brother or younger.

A: I'm his older brother, four years older.

Q: How would you describe your relationship with your brother?

A: Well, I wouldn't say we're terribly close as brothers go. We don't share a lot of the same interests. However, we did share a room until I was fourteen and Frank was ten, and we do share the same immediate family, which is pretty close.

Q: So, you've had ample opportunity to observe your brother?

A: Yes, ample.

Q: Since becoming adults, how has your relationship with your brother progressed?

A: We would often see each other on holidays and vacations and such. Although Frank and I didn't have a lot in common, our parents, particularly our Mama, made sure the family stayed close. There has always been a lot of visiting back and forth.

Q: Have you been here for this entire trial?

A: Oh yes.

Q: What about the first trial?

A: Yes, that too.

Q: Did you ever see how your brother behaved in times of stress?

A: Absolutely.

A simple "Yes" would have sufficed. *Jimmy's beginning to feel comfortable.*

Quickly, Taggart established that Jim had observed Frank's behavior in all types of agitation, frustration, embarrassment, anger, when threatened, when denied.

Q: Have you had a chance to observe him in these circumstances I've described since he became an adult?

A: Yes.

Q: Given this lifetime of opportunities to observe your brother, have you formed an opinion about his character when it comes to the use of force and violence?

A: Yes.

Q: What is your opinion in that regard?

Jim Marello turned his head slightly towards the jury just as Rhonda had suggested in yesterday's session.

A: My brother truly wouldn't hurt a fly. Anybody who's shared a room with a brother or sister, knows fights are inevitable, and Frank and I were no different, except for one thing, Frank wouldn't fight.

Q: He wouldn't fight?

A: No, he'd just go off somewhere and read and let things blow over. No matter how much guff I gave him, and I gave him quite a lot from time to time, he'd never hit me. It just isn't in him.

Jim's confidence pump, never in need of much priming, had been topped off. *Time to change the subject.*

Q: Mr. Marello, how would you describe your relationship with your late sister-in-law?

A: With Livia?

Q: Yes, Sir.

A: We had some disagreements.

Jim shifted in his chair.

Q: Disagreements about what?

A: About her interfering with my relationship with my wife.

Q: By "interfering," are you referring to the incident described in Livia Marello's October 12, 1975, diary entry regarding your wife's call to her?

A: That diary entry makes a mountain out of a molehill. My wife was upset. We were having an argument. Nothing happened. I never hit her.

Q: Livia Marello reported you to the New Orleans Police Department as a consequence of that incident, didn't she?

"Objection. This witness is not on trial."

"Sustained."

Sustained! If that objection stuck, Taggart couldn't question Jim about his quarrel with Livia, and the defense might as well fold its tent. "Your Honor, may we approach the bench?"

"You may."

The lawyers congregated along with the court reporter on the far side of the Judge's bench, away from the jury and witness stand.

"Your Honor, the diary entry for October 12 read by Mrs. Lindholm, shows this witness was antagonistic towards his sister-in-law. I should be allowed to expand on this antagonism in order to show someone other than Frank Marello had a motive to kill his wife."

"Mr. Watson, I think I know your position, but go ahead and say it for the record," Hizzoner said.

"Your Honor, this is nonsense. The undisputed evidence is that this witness was in New Orleans at the time of the crime. The Defense is just trying to distract the jury. We are already in our sixth day of trial. It's time to move on."

Weak response.

"No, Mr. Watson. I disagree," Hizzoner said. "Let's see what the witness has to say about all this. But, Mr. Taggart, if this goes where you seem to think it will, I may terminate your examination on self-incrimination grounds. You understand "

"Yes, Sir."

The cast members resumed their places.

"Ladies and Gentlemen," Hizzoner said, "I am overruling myself. Mr. Taggart's last question will be allowed."

Q: Mr. Marello, did your sister-in-law report you to the New Orleans Police as the result of your wife's October 12th call?

Jim hesitated. Mike figured he was weighing whether this was a good guess based on the diary or did Taggart have something else?

A: Yes, she did. She overreacted. The police came out to our house, but nothing happened. I was not charged. My wife explained the whole thing was a misunderstanding.

Mike withdrew a sheet of paper from a file on the table in front of him, making sure Jim had enough time to start wondering what was written on it.

Q: You say "nothing happened." You were arrested, weren't you?

A: Arrested, but not charged.

Q: October 12, 1973 was the first time Livia Marello reported your abuse of your wife to the police, but she reported you a second time, didn't she?

At this, Jim leaned forward in his chair. His eyes narrowed.

A: Yes.

Q: December 20, 1974?

A: Yes.

Q: Four days before she was murdered?

Jim turned his face away from Taggart and the jury. When he turned back, his lips were a thin line across his face, and his words were hissed through clenched teeth.

A: Yes.

Q: Her second complaint to the police was also for wife beating?

A: Spousal abuse.

Q: You were arrested?

A: Yes.

Q: On that second occasion, you were charged with assault and battery?

A: Yes.

Q: A felony.

A: Yes, but the charges were dropped the next day.

Q: You were actually put in jail?

A: Yes.

Q: How did you like being in jail?

A: How would you like it?

"The witness will answer the question."

A: I didn't like it much.

In the back of the courtroom, Ghost noted, "Jurors wide awake."

Q: Returning to the first instance in which Livia Marello reported you to the police, you actually spoke to her by telephone on the occasion of your wife's call to her, didn't you?

A: Maybe. I don't remember.

Q: In fact, you called her a "nosy slut," didn't you?

A: I don't know. I might have. I was mad.

Q: You told her to "butt out or you'd butt her out," didn't you?

A: Something like that.

Q: But she didn't "butt out" did she?

A: No.

Q: Her second report brought much more serious consequences, didn't she?

A. Like I said, the charges were dropped.

Q: Along with your father, you are the owner of a Ford dealership in New Orleans, aren't you?

A: What's that got to do with anything?

Taggart repeated his question as if he hadn't heard Jim's response.

"The witness will answer the question."

Good. Hizzoner's on board.

A. Yes.

Q: As a matter of fact, it's the biggest Ford dealership in the Southeast, isn't it?

A: What do you mean by biggest?

Q: I mean your dealership sells more cars than any other dealer in Ford's Southeast Region.

A: Yes.

Q: That's been true for the last five years in a row?

A: Yes.

Q: This dealership has made you a wealthy man?

Jim took a deep breath, letting pride temporarily replace anger.

A: We're comfortable.

Q: The source of that comfort is the income you receive from that dealership, isn't it?

A: Primarily, yes.

Taggart picked up a multi-paged document from the table and began to leaf through it. Jim studied Mike as Mike studied the paper.

Q: This dealership you own, it's based on a dealership contract you have with Ford?

A: Yes.

Q: One of the provisions of your contract with Ford is that, if the dealer is convicted of a felony, Ford can terminate his dealership, isn't that right?

A: How should I know? That contract's forty pages long.

Q. But you have read it, haven't you?

A. Yes.

Q. Would it refresh your memory if I showed the provision to you, Section III, Paragraph H.1.?

Taggart began to step out from behind counsel table.

A. Don't bother. I'm sure it's in there.

Q: Ford doesn't want any wife beaters for dealers?

"Objection, argumentative."

"Sustained. The jury will disregard the last question."

Q: So, when Livia Marello began reporting you to the police for beating your wife, she was jeopardizing your livelihood, wasn't she?

A: I told you, the charges were dismissed.

Q: Had the charges not been dismissed, a conviction of felonious spousal abuse would have jeopardized your relationship with Ford Motor Company, isn't that right?

A: I don't know. It never happened.

Q: But you agree Ford had the right to terminate your dealership in the event one of the owners, you for example, was convicted of a felony?

A. Yes.

Q: Mr. Marello, are you acquainted with a man named "Lee Roy Thigpen?"

Jim turned and looked at the Judge and then looked back at Taggart.

A: I don't believe so.

Rhonda rose and walked out of court.

Q: You recall Mark Josephson, the witness who testified last Friday and again this morning from his wheelchair?

A: Of course.

Rhonda re-entered the courtroom through the double doors followed by Stick Hatcher and Lee Roy Thigpen. Thigpen was wearing handcuffs. Rhonda resumed her seat between Mike and Frank. Stick and his prisoner took seats in the front row of the gallery that Tubby Mayes cleared for them.

Q: Mr. Marello, isn't it true that just last month, you hired two men to kill Mark Josephson, one of whom was Lee Roy Thigpen?

"Objection. This witness is not on trial."

"Counsel approach the bench."

"Your Honor," Taggart said, "before we move on, I would like to make an offer of proof."

"I assume it has to do with your last question."

"Yes, Sir. We have just established this witness had a motive to kill Livia Marello, and with a few more questions, I can prove he had not only the motive, but the willingness to kill people and, in fact, had hired a person who fits the description of the possible killer, a left-handed motorcycle rider, to commit another murder, that of Mark Josephson.

"Just exactly how are you prepared to prove this witness had anything to do with that assault, Counsel?"

"One of Josephson's assailants is sitting in court with Sheriff Hatcher right now, Your Honor. He has confessed and has independently picked Jim Marello's photograph out of a lineup as the person who paid him to commit the assault—"

"Wait a minute." Given Watson said. "Why wasn't I notified of this?" He turned and searched the courtroom looking for Stick Hatcher as he spoke.

Hizzoner held up his hand for silence. "It doesn't make any difference, Mr. Watson. What else have you got, Mr. Taggart?

"Your Honor will recall Sheriff Hatcher testified witnesses reported that on the morning Livia Marello was murdered, a large black Harley-Davidson motorcycle, one of those with the long front fork and the high arching handle bars, was seen parked outside the Marello apartment at about ten o'clock a.m. One of the Josephson assailants owns and rides such a motorcycle.

"In addition, Dr. Bordick testified that Livia Marello's murderer was left-handed. That same assailant, Lee Roy Thigpen, is left-handed. These are not coincidences, Your Honor. Taken together, these facts support the inference that, not only did Jim Marello have the motive to kill Livia Marello, he's both capable of and willing to hire someone to do it on his behalf."

"No, no, no! It does no such thing." Given Watson was practically dancing with impatience. "How many left-handed motorcyclists are there in the world? There's nothing unique about that. That narrows the field to what, perhaps ten thousand persons in the state of North Carolina? In terms of a signature common to both crimes, it's worthless. This is nothing more than a transparent attempt to create a red herring, a false clue to mislead the jury."

"Your Honor," Mike said, "the State is glossing over—

"Mr. Taggart," Hizzoner was holding up his hand for silence again.

Taggart stopped talking.

"That's better. Now, I am inclined to agree. This is more than a matter of ten thousand left-handed motorcyclists, Mr. Watson. I think I need to advise the witness regarding his rights before you ask your next question, Counsel. Then let's hear what Mr. Marello has to say about all this.

Judge Hunter turned in the direction of the witness stand as Taggart and Watson resumed their seats "Mr. Marello, before you answer the question Mr. Taggart is about to ask, you should be advised you have a right against self-incrimination; you have the right to remain silent, and anything you choose to say may be used against you. You also have a right to confer with an attorney of your own choosing before deciding whether to answer any further questions. Do you understand these rights?"

"Yes, Sir."

"You may proceed, Mr. Taggart."

Q: Mr. Marello, isn't it true that just last month, you hired two men, one of whom was Lee Roy Thigpen, to kill Mark Josephson?

A: No.

Taggart turned and motioned to Stick. Stick and Lee Roy stood up.

Q: Mr. Marello, you see the man standing next to Sheriff Hatcher?

A: Yes, I see him.

Q: I represent to you that this man is named "Lee Roy Thigpen." You hired this man to kill Mark Josephson, didn't you?

A: No, I did not.

What's a little perjury compared with attempted murder?

Q: Once more Mr. Marello, you met Mr. Thigpen, the gentlemen on the Sheriff's Hatcher's left, out at a rest stop on I-85 just west of Marlborough on October 29th of this year and paid him a three thousand-dollar first installment on the price you'd agreed to pay in exchange for Mr. Thigpen and another man killing Mark Josephson?

A: Absolutely not.

Q: Mr. Marello, isn't it also true that, following your release from jail after Livia Marello's second complaint against you for beating your wife, you hired someone to kill your brother's wife?

"Again..." Hizzoner repeated Marello's constitutional rights. "You understand your rights?"

"Yes, Sir."

"Do you wish to remain silent?"

"No, Sir. I do not." Jim Marello turned and looked at the jury, this time without any prior coaching by Rhonda. "I had nothing to do with killing Livia Marello. I deny having anything to do with her death from the bottom of my soul."

Taggart announced that he had no further questions. Given Watson, pleading surprise, asked the Court for some time to consider his cross-examination of the witness. Hizzoner recessed the trial until after lunch. No sooner had the jury left the courtroom than Stick walked through the swinging gates into the front of the courtroom and placed Jim Marello under arrest for assault with intent to kill and attempted murder.

Mike, Rhonda and Ghost sat around the mostly empty courtroom during the recess, which went on until after three-thirty because Watson asked for more time after lunch. Dead time.

"Did you expect Jim would deny hiring Thigpen when Lee Roy's standing right in front of him in handcuffs?" Ghost asked.

"No. I thought he'd take the Fifth and refuse to answer. That would have been almost as good as an admission for our purposes."

"So, what's Plan B?"

"Call Lee Roy. He's waived all his rights. So long as he says Jim hired him to kill Josephson, he rides a big black motorcycle and he's left-handed, Jimmy can shit in his hat."

"Lee Roy won't admit having anything to do with Livia's murder," Rhonda said.

"Doesn't matter much. He rides a motorcycle like the one seen in the vicinity of the crime, he's left handed like Livia's killer, and he admits attempting another murder on Jimmy's behalf. That ought to be enough to raise a reasonable doubt about whether Frank killed her, despite Lee Roy's denials ... or Jim's for that matter, don't you think?"

"You know, it's ironic. If Jim had paid Lee Roy the second installment, he might not be charged with attempted murder," Rhonda said. "By stiffing Lee Roy because Mark survived, he's as much as said he intended Mark be killed."

"Suppose Mr. Jack will put Jim in the cell next to Frank's," Ghost said.

Mike laughed. "There goes the neighborhood."

"Mike, you need to ask Mr. Jack to keep Jim downstairs," Rhonda said. "Otherwise, it's going to interfere with our conferences with Frank. It'll be better coming from you."

Taggart agreed. Given Watson was still closeted up in his office plotting his next move, so Mike walked over to see Mr. Jack. On the way back, he noticed Anthony Marello sitting all alone in his car. He looked so forlorn, Mike was tempted to go over and say something to him, but what could he say? *Nothing he wants to hear from me.*

Once Watson was finally ready, Frank and Jim brought back from the jail, the jury ushered in from the jury room, Hizzoner back on the bench and all the court personnel reassembled, Watson asked Jim only four questions.

Q: Mr. Marello, where were you on the day of Livia Marello's murder?

A: I was in New Orleans all day.

Q: Did you hire Lee Roy Thigpen or anybody else to kill Mark Josephson?

A: No

Q: Did you hire Lee Roy Thigpen or anybody else to kill Livia Marello?

A: No.

Q: Did you have anything whatsoever to do with either crime?

A: No, I did not.

Hizzoner recessed court for the day.

That night Mike and Rhonda were sitting around decompressing, discussing the next day's schedule, including Lee Roy's expected testimony. Ghost, by far the best cook in the Gang of Three, was making pizza. The phone rang. Mike answered.

"Mike, this is Sheriff Hatcher. I have some bad news for you."

"What's that?"

"Your client's brother couldn't have hired Lee Roy to kill Mrs. Marello.

"Why not?"

"Lee Roy was in jail the day she was killed. In fact, he was a guest of the County the entire month of December 1973, doin' sixty days for assault."

"Maybe Frank did kill her," Ghost mused, when he heard the news.

Rhonda put down her beer. "What are you talking about?"

"Well," Ghost stopped sprinkling mushrooms on the pizza shell, "despite all the signs pointing right at Jim, despite you and Mike urging Frank to at least consider the possibility Jim killed her, up until two days ago, Frank wouldn't hear of it. Maybe it was brotherly loyalty, but maybe he knows for a fact Jim's innocent. That'd explain such dogged opposition in the face of all logic."

Taggart scratched his head and made a face, considering. "Can't let myself think like that, Ghost," he finally said. "Wouldn't do anything different at this point anyway, even if I could think what that might be. All such thoughts do is infect what we're already doing with doubt. If the jury senses Frank's own lawyers aren't all in on his behalf, we'll lose for sure."

"I understand what you're saying," Ghost replied, " but if Frank didn't kill her, who did? Troutman?"

54

Tuesday, November 23, 1976 – Trial day 7

As soon as Court convened Tuesday morning, Watson moved to exclude any testimony or argument suggesting that Jim hired Thigpen to kill Livia or anyone else, including Mark Josephson. Taggart argued that even though Jim couldn't have hired Thigpen to kill Livia, because Lee Roy was in jail at the time, evidence that he paid to have Mark killed showed a predisposition on Jim's part to hire a murder and was therefore relevant.

"The Defense is painting with too broad a brush," Watson responded. "Livia Marello was killed three years ago. The events are too remote in time from each other to support the inference the Defense seeks.

Hizzoner sat and considered. Then, speaking slowly to insure the reporter got every word, "I am in agreement with the prosecution. The probative link between hiring someone to kill victim A and the likelihood of having hired someone else to kill Victim B three years earlier is too weak. Evidence of an attempt to hire a murder is provocative; it is emotional. A jury is likely to want to punish Jim Marello for attempting to kill Josephson by blaming him for killing Mrs. Marello three years earlier, thereby exonerating the accused on the basis of evidence of low probative value. The prejudice outweighs the probity. The motion is granted. I will instruct the jury that all possibility of Lee Roy Thigpen having killed Livia Marello has been eliminated and is not to be considered.

With that, the answer to "if Frank didn't do it, who did?" went glimmering. Knowing Hizzoner was probably right did not ease Taggart's disappointment. He was glad the next witness was Rhonda's. It would give him time to regroup.

Rhonda was beyond ready. Her first trial witness ever. For several days Taggart and Ghost had been teasing her about her uber preparation.

"Maybe we should break a bottle of champagne over her bow to celebrate the launch of the Good Ship Rhonda on the sea of trial practice," Ghost said.

"Like one of those rituals signifying the onset of puberty," Mike suggested.

"Maybe we could devise some kind of pin commemorating the occasion and have a pinning ceremony," Ghost said. "When I was pinned in the SEALs, I thought they'd punctured one of my lungs."

"We could shave her head like they do when a person crosses the equator for the first time," Mike said.

Rhonda looked up from the notes she was studying, eyebrows arched, chin held high. She cupped her right hand to her ear. "Hark, methinks I hear the bleatings of a low species." She went back to work.

Now Rhonda stood at counsel table in one of her zones where only she and her objective resided. Taggart watched her flip through her notes without apparent purpose, lost in thought. Seldom had so much brainpower been devoted to the presentation of a single witness.

Dr. Suzanne Lefler was petite, stylishly dressed, with shimmery blond hair that Ghost noted as "metallic, a color not found in nature." Without even speaking, she projected a cheerful energy that seemed more genuine than her hair color. Her smile revealed a small gap between her two front teeth, an engaging imperfection.

Q: Dr. Lefler, for whom do you work?

A: I am a professor of psychiatry at Duke University Medical School, and I have my own private practice in Chapel Hill.

Q: Will you please describe your educational background for the jury?

"Your Honor," Watson was standing, "The State will stipulate that Dr. Lefler is a qualified psychiatrist. There's no need to take up the jury's valuable time with a recitation of credentials not in dispute."

Under the guise of being cooperative, Watson was trying to prevent the defense from impressing the jury with the witness's sterling credentials. Old trial trick. Rhonda was having none of it.

"Your Honor, I appreciate Mr. Watson's offer, but Dr. Lefler has some remarkable professional achievements that are especially relevant to the issues in this case, and the jurors should know who it is they're hearing as they listen to what she has to say. May I touch on the high points and make an exhibit of her full resume' for the jury's review during deliberations."

"That will be acceptable, Miss Enright."

Q: Dr. Lefler, please describe your education and experience as it relates to the psychiatric aspects of homosexuality and marriage.

A: I received my medical degree from the University of Chicago. I did my residency in psychiatric medicine at Johns Hopkins University Hospital. I have been a visiting professor at the University of Vienna School of Medicine in the field of human sexuality, and I have a grant from the National Institute of Health for the study of dimorphic changes in the brain associated with homosexuality. I am also a certified marriage and family counselor.

How did Livia Marello find this woman? Rhonda had told Taggart Lefler had all the academic firepower they needed. *Understatement.*

Q: Are you acquainted with the victim in this case, Livia Marello?

A: Yes. In April 1973, Livia Marello came to see me about her misgivings having to do with her husband's sexuality, and after a couple of sessions I began to counsel them both.

Q: Before we get into your advice to the Marellos, will you explain what causes homosexuality?

A: I will explain what I think causes homosexuality. Based on my studies, I believe actual dimorphic changes take place in the brain that are responsible for a person's sexual orientation.

Q: What do you mean "dimorphic changes?"

A: I mean actual biological differences between the brain of a heterosexual and the brain of a homosexual. Usually "dimorphism" refers to well-established and emerging information about how male and female brains differ. However, we can also apply the term to stable biological differences between homosexuals and heterosexuals."

Dr. Lefler was facing the jury, talking to them in a conversational tone as if they were all sitting around a dinner table. "In other words," she continued, "if you look at the part of the brain that controls sexual response, the brain of a heterosexual person would actually appear different from that of a homosexual person upon close medical examination. In fact, a male homosexual's brain resembles that of a female according to this hypothesis."

"I didn't think human sexual response had anything to do with the brain," Ghost had said when Rhonda told him and Mike what Dr. Lefler would say.

"It doesn't with men," Rhonda had replied.

Q: What do you mean by 'changes?'

A: It is likely that from the beginning of existence the homosexual brain is different from the heterosexual brain, although there may be a strong additional "push" or influence caused by endocrine differences.

Q: What causes these differences?

A: It is either genetics or very early events, and by "very early," I mean events taking place in earliest childhood, perhaps while the person is still in the fetal stage, and are biological in origin. An example would be an influenza attack resulting in an extremely high fever that somehow affects the development of the brain before the baby is even born ... while it is still in the mother's womb.

"Objection, relevance. We're not here to decide why the accused is a homosexual."

"Overruled. Homosexuality has been talked about so much in this trial, the jury is entitled to know something about it by way of background."

Hizzoner's getting interested. Taggart's greater concern was the jury. *Are they getting it?*

Q: What's your basis for this opinion, Dr. Lefler?

A: In 1968, I began a study of seven hundred fifty persons. Each was interviewed according to a set of predetermined criteria for the purpose of determining whether these persons had experienced any sexual ambivalence.

Q: Sexual ambivalence?

A: Doubts regarding their sexual orientation or preference.

Q: What did you learn?

Lefler proceeded to describe culling out ninety persons who had experienced significant sexual ambivalence from the larger field. The efforts of those ninety to resolve their ambivalence had been monitored. Eighteen had achieved resolution, seventeen in favor of homosexuality.

Q: What did you conclude from that outcome, Dr. Lefler?

A. In those seventeen cases, the level of ambivalence was extremely high. Just from a statistical standpoint, this indicates a very strong biological force at work dictating the outcome. If it was merely a matter of choosing one orientation or the other, homosexual or heterosexual, based on randomly distributed factors, for example the environment in which a person has been raised, a greater number of persons would have certainly resolved their ambivalence in favor of heterosexuality.

Q: What does this mean in terms of Frank Marello?

A: Dr. Marello repeatedly returned to sexual encounters with males over a long period of time and lacked sexual interest in his wife, whom he seemed to love very deeply in every other respect. This indicates that, if one were to examine his brain, it would be found to contain biological characteristics common to homosexual persons.

Q: So, in your opinion, Professor Marello is a homosexual.

A: Yes, I believe he is.

Q: Is there anything he can do about it? Can he change?

A: No. This isn't the movies. People can't change their brains. That brings up an interesting point however, which tends to validate the conclusions we are reaching in our studies.

Q: What's that?

A: Throughout history right up to present day, homosexuals are treated badly, like sideshow freaks, at least by a significant segment of heterosexual society and even, in some instances by law and government; certainly by religion. They are blackmailed, fired from their jobs, denied admission into the military, imprisoned, refused ordination, routinely beaten and scorned ... Why would anybody subject themselves to that kind of treatment voluntarily, if there wasn't some compelling force overriding their freedom of choice and dictating that they be as they are – homosexual?

Q: So, Frank Marello would be heterosexual if he could?

A: In my opinion, yes. Frank Marello can suppress his homosexual instincts and feelings for a time, but sooner or later these forces assert themselves. The human sex drive, both homo- and hetero-, is right up there with the need to eat and breathe.

Q: Just one more question, Dr. Lefler. Is there any scientific evidence homosexuals have any inclination towards violence against members of the opposite sex?

A: There is no such evidence. None whatsoever. To the contrary, it has been my observation that homosexual men get along very well with women. Indeed, to the extent homosexual males' behavior and brains resemble those of women, they are less violent than the "normal" man. The fact that they aren't interested in women sexually is also a great factor for harmony, as is the fact that heterosexual men are interested in women sexually is often the source of enormous friction and violence between heterosexual men and women.

"Thank you, Dr. Lefler. No further questions."

Out of the corner of his eye, Taggart caught one or two or the women jurors nodding their agreement with Lefler.

Rhonda sat down. Mike slid a note over to her. "Nice job!"

"Dr. Lefler," Given Watson said, "you've never actually seen these biological differences that you were telling the jury about, have you?

A: Seen them? No, I haven't seen them.

Q: In other words, you haven't actually looked at the brains of known homosexuals under a microscope and seen something different from what you would see if you looked at the same part of a heterosexual brain?

A: No.

Q: If a knowledgeable person was to look at the brain tissue of a homosexual, could one visually detect differences from the brain of a heterosexual?

A: I won't kid you, Mr. Watson, the scientific evidence in this regard is in its early stage. However, some studies using high resolution x-ray techniques suggest some subtle differences in the size of brain structure that may relate to the regulation of hormones.

Q: So this is all just speculation in which you've engaged based on how homosexuals behave?

A: No, it's not speculation. It is a scientific deduction. Based on what I do know, I can deduce other things I believe to be true.

Q: You "believe" these deductions to be true, but you don't know them to be true, do you? You haven't experienced the things you are deducing with any of your own senses, have you?

A: I'm not sure what you mean.

Q: Well, you've already told us that you haven't seen the differences. Have you heard them?

A: No.

Q: Have you smelled them?

A: No.

Q: Have you tasted them?

A: No.

Q: Have you felt them?

A: No.

Q: All of the evidence on which you are relying is circumstantial evidence, isn't it?

Dr. Lefler smiled.

"I see that you're smiling, Dr. Lefler," Watson said. "The jurors and I aren't scientists and doctors like you, so I'm sure my questions seem funny to you, but all I'm trying to do is give the jury a clear picture of—"

"Objection. Move to strike. That's a speech, not a question," Rhonda said.

"Sustained. The jury will disregard Mr. Watson's explanation that the rest of us aren't doctors."

Suddenly Taggart was no longer so sure whose side Hizzoner was on. *Probably nobody's, like he ought to be. Just having a little fun.*

Q: All you have is circumstantial evidence, isn't that right, Dr. Lefler?

A: I smiled, Mr. Watson, because I knew you'd ask me that question, and I'll answer it the same way I did the last time a lawyer asked it of me. Imagine you are looking out the window on a winter day and you see the branches of a tree moving. You do not see, hear, feel, taste, or smell the force that is moving the branches, but because the branches are moving, you know it is a windy day. Just as you deduce it is windy from observing the moving branches, I deduce there is a biological force at work in the brains of homosexual people making them the way they are. Does that answer your question?

Watson changed the subject, attacking the foundation of Lefler's study. During an excruciating few minutes, the jury learned that of the seven hundred fifty persons interviewed and tested, Dr. Lefler herself had conducted only three percent. The rest had been performed by post-doctoral research assistants using questions Lefler developed. However, she had performed all the follow-up interviews with the ninety persons who'd admitted experiencing sexual ambivalence and personally monitored their process of resolution.

"Ten minutes spent on the road to nowhere," Ghost noted.

Q: All this while working as a full-time professor at Duke Medical School and maintaining a private practice?

A: Yes.

Q: Are you married, Dr. Lefler?

A: Yes.

Q: Do you have children?

A: Yes, two, Twelve and Fourteen.

Q: So, in addition to being a full-time professor and having a private practice, you are also a full-time wife and the mother of two teenagers?

A: Yes, I'm a busy girl.

Q: That must not leave you much time for this seven hundred-fifty person study with all its follow-up and monitoring?

A: Let's just say I don't watch a lot of television.

Why is Watson continuing to cross swords with Lefler like this? Taggart met Rhonda's eye as she turned so that the jury couldn't see her reaction to the last couple of exchanges. The last thing they wanted was for the jury to think Frank's lawyers were smirking or arrogant. There had been precious little to smirk about.

Q: Dr. Lefler, I understand you counseled both Livia and Frank Marello?

A: That's right.

Q: And it is your opinion that Frank Marello is a homosexual?

A: Yes.

Q: And there's nothing he can do about it?

A: There are lots of things he can do about it. Whether they are successful is another matter. I don't mean to be flip with you, Mr. Watson, but Dr. Marello is what he is, but he can try to suppress his homosexual feelings and instincts.

Q: You believe that sooner or later those homosexual feelings or instincts will assert themselves?

A: Usually they do.

Q: Livia Marello wanted to preserve the marriage, didn't she?

A: Yes. They both did.

Q: I thought you just told me that Frank Marello is a homosexual?

A: I did.

Q: In other words, his sexual preference was for other men, rather than his wife?

A: Among other things, that's what it means.

Q: You're not suggesting that a homosexual man with these irrepressible feelings and instincts wanted to stay married to a woman, are you?

A: I'm not suggesting anything. I'm simply saying that in my talks with Frank Marello, he told me he wanted to try to make his marriage work, and I believe he truly did. There are lots of reasons besides sex to stay married. Children are one – the Marellos were going to have a baby. Economics are another.

In this case, I would say "love" was a big reason. Frank Marello seemed to me to adore his wife and to be profoundly sorry he'd hurt her. One of the biggest things he needed to deal with going forward was to accept that no matter how perfectly he wanted to love Livia, he was human, and humans are never perfect. If they were, they'd be God. One of the great things about Livia Marello was that she already understood that.

"Thank you, Dr. Lefler. No further questions." Watson sat down with a nonchalance Rhonda was sure was feigned, hoping the jurors would think the witness's last answer was exactly what he had been looking for.

"I have no further questions of this witness, Your Honor," she said.

"The defense calls John Waldrip."

"G'damn," Stick whispered to Mayor Lund, who was taking a break from the rigors of his mayoral and pharmacy duties to watch a little of the trial, 'I'd forgotten Mr. Jack's got a real name."

Stick wasn't the only surprised person in the courtroom. Mr. Jack walked in looking like a seventy-five year old cub scout ready to stand inspection. It was the first time Taggart had ever seen Mr. Jack without a hat on and without chewing tobacco. His sparse white hair was parted and slicked down. He was clean shaven and wearing a semi-white shirt and a tie with a picture of some men hunting ducks on it, tied at the throat with a knot as big as Taggart's fist.

"Please state your name," the Clerk said after Mr. Jack took the oath.

"John Waldrip ... but you should call me 'Mr. Jack.'"

"Have a seat, Mr. Jack," Hizzoner said.

Q: Mr. Jack, where do you work?

A: Hell, Depity, you know where I work.

Laughter flickered across the courtroom.

Q: It's not for me, Mr. Jack, it's for the jury.

A: Oh ... yeah ... I work at the jail. I'm the superintendent of the jail.

Q: Do you know Frank Marello?

A: Sure do ... saved my life.

Out of the corner of his eye Mike could see Given Watson put his hands on the edge of the counsel table in front of him as if he was about to push himself to his feet to object.

It was one of the anomalies of the law of evidence. While a witness could give his opinion of the accused's character or reputation in response to questions from the party seeking the character endorsement, the law left it to the opposing party to get into specific examples if it chose. Taggart had explained this to Mr. Jack, but it was a finer distinction than Mr. Jack was capable of making.

Watson rose half out of his seat and then sank back down, knowing he would probably just give greater emphasis to the objectionable testimony by objecting.

Q: How do you know Professor Marello?

A: He's been a guest over at my place of business for the last two and a half months. He was also there for five months back in the first part of '74.

Q: How often have you had the opportunity to see and talk to Frank Marello during the time he was in jail?

A: Lotta the time he was the only prisoner. Been alone since the wife died back in '71. Nobody to talk to most of the time after that. Sometimes the Prof an' I'd play checkers at night. I'd jest set up the board right outside his cell. I brought him all his meals an' mail. We'd talk about stuff. The Prof's pretty smart.

Mike remembered Mr. Jack's "fudgepacker" remark the first day he visited Frank. There had been no more friendly checker games once Mr. Jack heard Frank was gay, at least not until he returned from the hospital after his heart attack. Upon his return, Mr. Jack would hear no ill of "the Prof.'"

"Hell, Mr. Jack," Howard Julius, the youngest and largest of the deputies, had said on Mr. Jack's first day back at work, "maybe that homo just thought you were cute."

Mr. Jack had jumped up and tried to hit Howard with a chair.

Q: During the time you have known Frank Marello, have you formed an opinion about his character for violence?

A: Yep.

Q: What is your opinion?

A: Hell, the Prof's about the most non-violent person I've ever known or heared anything about. Why, he wouldn't even lemme sweep the spider webs out of his cell. Said the spiders needed a place to live too. He's gentle as a flower.

Taggart paused to let the jury appreciate Mr. Jack's poetic side.

Q: Based on your opinion of Professor Marello's character, do you think he would be capable of committing murder?

A: Shitfire, Depity, what've I been tellin' ya? It's just the opposite. The Prof saved my life, gave me CPR when I had my heart attack an' called the ambulance when he coulda just walked on outa the jail an' left town. I know folks say he's a homo, an' I don't know what to think about that, but he's no killer. He's a saver!"

Taggart glanced at Watson to see if Mr. Jack had finally goaded him to the point of objecting, but the Solicitor appeared lost in study of what Mike suspected was a blank legal pad, as if to say by his inattention how unworthy he thought Mr. Jack's testimony.

"No further questions."

All Watson wanted to say to Mr. Jack was "good-bye." "No questions."

55

Tuesday, November 23, 1976 – Trial Day 7 - Evening

"Hi. I saw your light on and thought you might need some company." Susan Hunter stood in Mike's doorway. He was glad to see her in spite of himself, whatever the hour, whatever conclusions an onlooker, had there been any, might draw.

"Aren't you going to invite me in?" Susan barged past him into the apartment.

"Sure. Make yourself at home. What brings you out at eleven o'clock on a school night?"

"How's the trial going?" Susan said over her shoulder as she opened and closed cupboard doors. "You certainly don't have much in the way of snacks for entertaining."

"You ought to know how it's going. You've seen as much of it as I have. How do you think it's going?"

"I think your client needs to have a big day for himself tomorrow. He is testifying tomorrow, isn't he?"

Susan came back into the living room and set down a bowl full of dry Cheerios between them on the couch.

"Frank'll do alright," Mike said. "He's used to teaching. Tomorrow's lesson is a big one."

"Too bad about Thigpen being in jail on the day of the murder," Susan said. "I thought you were on to something there. What about the other guy who helped beat up Josephson? What was his name, Cosby? Nice boys, those two."

"He had a good alibi too," Mike said. "We checked him out." Mike yawned and rubbed his face.

Susan didn't miss the gesture. "You're falling asleep. You want to go to bed?"

Mike looked at her.

"I don't mean with me. You need sleep more than you need to please some sex-starved old lady."

Taggart exhaled a breath he didn't know he'd been holding.

"Mind if I ask you a personal question before I leave?"

"Go ahead."

Bang! Bang! Bang! Someone was knocking hard on the door.

Mike jumped at the noise. Susan gasped.

"Jesus, who do you suppose that is?"

"Probably nobody I want to see." Susan headed out of the room. "Don't answer until I get out of sight."

Susan disappeared, taking her coat and purse. Mike went to the door and looked out. Standing there, still wearing his skycap uniform with his collar turned up against the cold was Cornelius Kempton.

"Cornelius, what are you doing here? C'mon ..." Taggart hesitated. *Don't trap Susan in the bedroom.*

"C'mon in, Cornelius," Susan said, emerging from hiding.

"Missus Hunter," Cornelius nodded before taking a step inside and looking around to make sure Hizzoner or someone else unexpected wasn't lurking in the shadows.

"Where've you been the last couple of days?" Susan said. "I missed you at the trial."

"Ran out of vacation. Had to go back to work. That's where I just came from. Mike, I need to talk to you about something ... something about the trial." Cornelius glanced at Susan.

"Go ahead and talk, Cornelius," Mike said. *What can he have to say about the trial so urgent it requires a visit at this hour?* Taggart nodded towards Susan. "It's okay."

"Well, Josie says you're kinda pointing the finger at this Jim Marello, suggesting he was the one who really did the murder ..."

Wishful thinking at this point. Mike said nothing, waiting.

"... but I don't think you've got the right guy."

56

Wednesday, November 24, 1976 – Trial Day 8 - Morning

"Morning, Frank," Mike sat down at counsel table. "Ready to go?"

Frank nodded. "Don't think I can be any more ready. I didn't get much sleep last night. Hope that's a good sign."

Bet you got more than me and Rhonda. Mike chose not to put his thought into words - not a confidence builder.

Moving his chair closer to Frank's, Mike lowered his voice. "We're going to change the order of the questions a little from what we rehearsed. There's nothing you haven't heard before, so just answer the questions as they're asked. Remember . . . from the heart."

Frank shook his head, but said nothing.

"Court will come to order. Mr. Taggart, you may resume the defense presentation."

"The defense calls Frank Marello."

Frank stood up, walked to the witness stand, took the oath, stated his name and sat down. He peered at Mike through his thick glasses.

Q: Professor Marello, did you kill your wife?"

A: No. I did not kill Livia. I loved her.

Taggart paused, to let the jury absorb Frank's denial.

Q: Okay. Now, let's go back to the beginning. How old are you?

Step by step Mike walked Frank through the emptiness of a friendless childhood filled with disparagement and lack of understanding, of being outshone by an older brother in all things most people, particularly his father, seemed to value. Saying only enough to serve as a directional marker for the story Frank was telling, Mike stayed out of the way of his client's words, letting Frank paint the picture.

"Then one day in a discussion class I was leading, things changed. I was just a Graduate Assistant, only a few years older than the undergraduates in my classes. Those who cared enough to say anything in class usually were trying to prove whatever I said was wrong. Things changed the day a pretty sorority girl began firing back at my critics in class. Livia."

Frank described bumping into Livia on campus several months later, their discovery of shared interests in books, music and, eventually, each other. "She was the first person who ever told me I made them laugh," he said, staring into space as he talked, as if seeing in his mind the scenes he was painting for the jury. "She was the first person who ever even tried to make me laugh.

"Our monthly meetings to discuss books over coffee, or tea in Livia's case, became weekly and more about each other, me mostly, than books. The time we spent together each week soon became the most important time of my life. Our afternoon chats became dinners; dinners became breakfasts - weekends. By the time Livia said she thought we should get married, I would have followed her to the moon."

Courtrooms are seldom noisy. Rarely does more than one person speak at a time. Yet Taggart noticed as Frank spoke the room became even more still. When Frank finished his last answer, Mike waited to allow the command Frank had achieved to permeate the occupants of the jury box. He wished he did not have to ask the next question.

Q: Professor Marello, why did you allow yourself to become involved with Mark Josephson?

A: I've asked myself that question a thousand times. When I married Livia, I didn't consider myself homosexual. I didn't think of myself as anything, just lonely. When Livia and I got married, I didn't think I'd be lonely anymore. But then that night happened with Mark. After talking it through at great lengths with Livia and

Dr. Lefler, after thinking about the feelings and emotions I experienced, that's what I've concluded, that … I am … homosexual.

Frank stammered and struggled to swallow, took a deep breath and went on.

… Livia was the only one who understood what it meant for me, for us. When I told her what I'd done, she believed in me enough to know I hadn't done it to hurt her. She said she wanted to try to work things out, but if I had to go, she would understand. She didn't try to rush me. She just said she wanted me to be able to find peace. I loved my wife. I did not kill her."

Enough about homosexuality. They'd had to address it. Watson certainly would. But of all the issues before the jurors, Taggart was sure this was the one for which they were least willing to feel sympathy, least capable of understanding. Giving the matter any more attention would sound defensive without without gaining any ground. They needed to move on, but Frank needed to remain on the witness stand until the arrangements required by what they'd learned from Cornelius last night could be made. Otherwise, Hizzoner might close presentation of evidence, and Frank's best chance for exoneration could be lost forever. Mike looked around hoping to see Ghost in the courtroom, but he wasn't there. He asked for a recess.

"Listen," he said as Frank stood stretching, rotating his shoulders, trying to relieve some of the tension, "you're doing great. But, you're not going to be the last witness after all. We changed the order of questions around to set this up a little. That's the reason for the change."

Frank looked puzzled and started to speak. "Who –"

"Frank," Mike put his hand on his client's shoulder, "Just stay focused on your testimony. Trust me on this one, okay?"

"No point in stopping now," Frank replied as Hizzoner re-entered the courtroom signaling the end of the recess.

Frank testified about his and Livia's surprise and happiness at the news of her pregnancy, the decision to buy insurance and why they chose to buy from Mark Josephson. Next came the question Taggart would rather have walked through fire than ask, but if he didn't Watson would. Frank's answers would sound better volunteered in response to friendly direct examination than extracted by a hostile cross.

Q: Professor Marello, I hand you Prosecution's Exhibit 6 and direct your attention to the signature of Livia Marello. Do you recognize the handwriting?

A: Yes. It's mine.

Q: How did you happen to sign your wife's name to this application?

A: She told me to. We'd decided to buy the insurance, and when I was filling out the app, Livia was busy and told me to go ahead and sign her name.

A shudder rippled through Taggart. How often did spouses sign each other's names out of sheer convenience? He and Cathy certainly had. An innocent convenience or an incriminating circumstance – same fact, different spin.

Q: Now, Professor Marello, I want to talk a bit about the morning of December 24, 1973, the day Livia was killed. Taggart changed subjects, leading Frank through an account of his Christmas Eve morning as he waited for Josephson to pick him up. Waking up around seven, showering, shaving, dressing, breakfasting on toast and coffee, clearing and wiping the table, washing the dishes, all the mundate little details.

Q: When you left that morning to go shopping, what was the condition of that table top?

A: Clean and bare. Empty.

Q: How about the stove? Did you use the teapot?

A: No. I never drink tea. All the burners were off when I left.

Q: What time did Mark Josephson arrive?

A: Around nine-fifteen.

Q: Did Livia get up with you?

A: No. She liked to sleep late, and vacation was the only time she could do it because of teaching.

Q: So, she was still asleep when Mark arrived?

A: Yes.

Q: Why did you wait outside for Mark to arrive?

A: Same reason. Livia was asleep. She was a light sleeper, and our doorbell sounded like Big Ben. I wanted her to get all the rest she could, especially now that she was pregnant.

Q: Had you and Livia argued sometime during the night?

A: No, not really. Livia had awakened in the middle of the night, and when she came back to bed, she was feeling sad because we didn't have a Christmas tree or any lights, and she woke me up to tell me about it.

Q: Why no tree or lights?

A: We had agreed ... to save money. We'd just learned we were going to have a baby, and we didn't have much money anyway. We figured we'd save Christmas decorations until next year when the baby could see them too.

Q: Were you angry when she awakened you?

A: Maybe a little put out, I guess. Not angry. I just said something like, "you mean you woke me up for that?" She started crying. Then I could see how much it really meant to her, and I was holding her, and I told her we'd work something out in the morning, and we both went back to sleep. I have to believe that's the conversation Mrs. Wilmer testified about.

Q: What time was it when you and Mr. Josephson returned from shopping?

A: About one-thirty, maybe a couple of minutes before.

Q: Which door did you use when you came back from shopping?

A: Mark drove into the parking lot behind the apartment when he dropped me off. I asked him to, so I could sneak in the back door with the presents. But the back door was already open.

Q: Did you think it was unusual that the back door was open?

A: No, not too unusual. I thought Livia might be carrying a basket of clothes to the laundry room and not had a free hand to close it.

Q: Describe what happened when you went in the apartment.

A: Well, I peeked in the back door to see if Livia was around, but there was Sheriff Hatcher standing with his back to me. At first, he blocked my view into the kitchen, but as he turned around, I saw there was a body lying under a blanket on the floor … Livia -

Q: What happened next?

A: The Sheriff told me Livia had been killed and asked me to come outside to talk to him. Once I'd recovered myself, we sat in his car and talked.

Q: Describe that conversation.

A: I was in shock. I don't remember much about it. Sheriff Hatcher didn't say anything for quite a while. I think I asked the first question, something like "what happened." He said Livia appeared to have been strangled. He wanted me to say where I'd been.

Q: Did you tell Sheriff Hatcher you had been shopping with Mark Josephson?

A: I don't remember. If Sheriff Hatcher says I didn't, then I probably didn't. But only because he didn't ask. I wasn't trying to hide that I was with Mark. I never dreamed I'd be a suspect.

Taggart turned and glanced around the courtroom again. Still no Ghost. He turned back towards Frank Marello.

"No further questions."

Taggart's choice of a place to conclude his examination appeared to catch Given Watson by surprise, but he quickly recovered. He began his cross-examination by asking Frank about his other episodes of homosexual behavior. Then he asked:

Q: Now Professor Marello, you claim you loved your wife?

A: Yes.

Q: You claim you felt great tenderness for her?

A: Yes.

Q: That you regarded her understanding and caring for you as a blessing?

A: Yes.

Q: Livia Marello was the first person to treat you like a good and special person?

A: Yes.

Q: And you repaid this loving and generous spirit to whom you'd been married for just a year and a half by having sex with a man?

A: It had nothing to do with repayment.

Q: You must have felt pretty strongly about Mark in order to violate this wonderful trust you and your wife shared?

Watson pronounced the word "Mark" with mock tenderness.

A: I didn't approach what I did as a violation of trust at the time I did it, although afterwards I came to see that is exactly what it was.

Q: So, you didn't have any strong feelings for Mark?

A: No, I didn't say that. I did have strong feelings for Mark.

Q: But despite these strong feelings, you decided that you weren't going to see Mark again?

A: That's right.

Q: You told your wife you weren't going to see Mark again?

A: Yes.

Q: And then within a three-month period you proceeded to see Mark at least three more times?

A: Yes, well the first two -

Q: You've answered the question, Professor. So you lied to your wife about not seeing Mark again, didn't you?

A: No.

Q: Wait a minute, Professor, one minute you're filled with remorse and telling your wife you're not going to see your homosexual lover anymore, and the next minute you're going Christmas shopping with him. Isn't that a lie?

On a ten-point scale of objectionability, Watson's question was a 9.95, but Taggart thought Frank could handle it and said nothing.

A: I didn't lie to her.

Q: Did you tell her you were going shopping with Josephson?

A: Actually, Mark told her the day before when he called. That was what the note on the refrigerator was about.

Taggart looked away from the jury in case his face betrayed how much he would have preferred Frank to have been the one who told Livia of his plans with Josephson. *Will Watson pursue this or let it lie?*

Pursue.

Q: So, you didn't tell her?

A: No, I didn't tell her, although I intended to.

Q: You had made these plans several days earlier?

A: Yes.

Q: Yet on the eve of the shopping trip you still hadn't told your wife you were going shopping with Mark despite the passage of several days?

A: Yes. More than three months had passed. Mark had been a friend a long time before he and I became involved that one time. Both Livia and I knew I couldn't just stay in the apartment all my life, hiding from all homosexual men. There would be others, if not Mark. They really weren't the issue. I was. I had to find out what was normal for me, and on that would depend what happened to our marriage. Livia and I agreed I had to find out for myself, how I really felt. A Christmas shopping trip seemed like a pretty safe experiment.

Q: An "experiment" you didn't bother to tell your wife you were about to perform?

A: I was in the midst of grading papers. Livia was over in Greensboro with her mom part of the time. I didn't do it.

Taggart's impassive face was at war with his churning stomach. For the first time since taking the stand, Frank's answers to the last two questions sounded defensive, as if he had something to feel guilty about. "Yes's" or "No's," were all Watson's inflammatory questions deserved. Save the explantions for friendly questions from Taggart. They had practiced this. But talking about it was one thing, doing it another.

Q: Now I heard you tell the jury in response to a question your lawyer asked you that you are a homosexual. Did I hear that right?

A: Yes.

Q: So, you've decided the answer to the question of whether you could "function" without having homosexual relationships is "no," is that right?

A: No, I can function without them. I prefer not to.

Q: Having sex with men is what's normal for you?

A: Having sex with men is what feels right for me for reasons over which I have no control.

How humiliating. It was like undressing in public – only worse. Expressionless, Taggart's earlier aggravation morphed to sadness and pain.

Q: So, you decided you would prefer to have sex with men?

A: It's the conclusion I have come to since all this has happened. It was still a question at the time.

Q: And you bought a $25,000 insurance policy on your wife's life?

A: Yes.

Q: You bought the policy from Mark, the man with whom you'd had your most recent homosexual affair?

A: From the man with whom I'd recently had a single sexual encounter.

Q: The man who is your alibi for the morning your wife was murdered?

A: The person with whom I went shopping that morning.

Q: Then you killed your wife in order to collect the insurance and be free to pursue your sexual preference with Mark or one of the other men you knew would be out there?

A: No. Absolutely not.

"No further questions."

Marello's testimony hadn't been perfect, but Taggart thought any attempt to patch it up would only focus the jurors' attention on the weak parts. He had Frank repeat once more that he loved Livia and did not kill her. Then, having spoken more than two hours in his own defense, Frank Marello left the stand. As he rose, Rhonda thought she heard a faint sigh throughout the courtroom, as if the conclusion of Marello's testimony finally allowed the listeners, jurors and audience alike, to relax.

57

Wednesday, November 24, 1976 – Trial Day 8 - Afternoon

By the time Ghost showed up with Cornelius and a young Black woman dressed in some kind of yellow and black uniform, the noon recess was nearly over. Taggart and Rhonda were already sitting at counsel table with Frank . They stepped back to the rail separating the trial area from the gallery to confer with Ghost, while his two companions took seats near the rear of the courtroom.

"Her name's Angela Cummings," Ghost said, referring to the woman sitting with Cornelius, "and she's on board."

"She remembers it the way Cornelius remembers it?"

"Yeah, one hundred percent."

"I talked to Anthony," Rhonda said. "He knows he's going to be called after all."

Anthony had not been on the original witness list. Taggart thought calling one's father as a character witness was a waste of time. Of course, a father was going to praise his son. Such testimony added nothing and only highlighted the shortage of character witnesses outside the family.

"Anthony's not too pissed about the way we used Jim?" Mike asked.

"He's angry, but he's doing it for Frank, not you."

"Good. Then we're set to go. Any last thoughts?"

Ghost and Rhonda both shook their heads.

"Keep your fingers crossed." Mike turned back towards counsel table.

"Court will come to order. Mr. Taggart, call your next witness."

"The defense calls Anthony Marello."

Big Tony Marello hoisted his bulk up off a bench in the gallery, took the stand and was sworn.

Q: Mr. Marello, you are Frank Marello's father?

A: Yes.

Q: You and your wife, Frank's mother, live in New Orleans?

A: Yes.

Q: I have seen you and Frank's brother, Jim, in court almost daily. Why hasn't your wife been here?

A: Mary Sulah has a bad heart. The doctors told her to stay away. I bring her up to date every night.

Q: You've been in the air between New Orleans and Raleigh/Durham a whole lot these last two years?

A: A whole lot.

Q: Just out of curiousity, how long does that flight take?

A. Direct flight, three and a half hours; more than five if you have to go through Tampa.

Q: Mr. Marello, along with your son, Jim, you are the owner of a Ford dealership in New Orleans?

A: Yes.

Q: Who is the majority owner?

A: I am.

Q: By what name are you known in the advertising for your dealership?

A: The King of Cars.

Q: Did you consider Livia Marello a friend of yours, someone with whom you were on good terms?

A: A friend? She was my daughter-in-law. Yeah. We were on good terms. I liked her.

Q: How well were the two of you acquainted?

A: How well did I know her, is that what you're asking?

Q: Yes.

A: We met several times. She and Frank came to visit once before they were married and a couple of times after they got married, I think for a week each time, and they stayed at our house.

Mary Sulah and I went up to their wedding in Greensboro, where we met her family. I would say we were pretty well acquainted.

Q: When Frank and Livia visited you before they were married, were they already engaged?

A: Yes.

Q: So, you knew Livia was about to become your daughter-in-law?

A: Yeah.

Q: In view of that fact, did you make any special effort to get to know her?

A: I don't know whether it was me or her that made the effort. But, for example, if I was going somewhere, like on an errand, she'd hop in the car and say she'd go along to keep me company. So, there were several times she and I were together, just the two of us, talking. She did the same thing after they were married too.

"Objection, Your Honor. Move to strike. What's this have to do with the issues in this case? Irrelevent."

Please just rule without making me explain. Mike did not want to have to spell out his objective in front of Anthony.

"Overruled. I presume you're going to tie this all together at some point, Counsel?"

"Yes Sir."

Q: Did Livia have anything to fear from you?

A: Fear? No, not at all. She wasn't a fearful person anyway. She had spunk.

Q: Mr. Marello, I don't want to embarrass you, but I couldn't help noticing when you held up your right hand to take the oath, you are missing parts of two fingers. Will you show the jury what I'm referring to?

Anthony hesitated for a couple of seconds and then held up his right hand.

"May the record reflect that the witness is missing the top two joints on his little and ring fingers on his right hand?"

"So ordered."

Q: Mr. Marello, how did that happen?

A: I was in the Marine Corps during the Korean War. It was in the winter at a place called the Chosin Reservoir. I froze my hands, and those two fingers had to be amputated.

Q: Does it interfere with your ability to grip things?

A: A little. I can still hang on to things, but I'm not as strong in my right hand as my left.

Q: As a result of having been frozen, your hands and fingers are abnormally sensitive to the cold, aren't they?

A: Yeah, they are.

Q: You wear gloves whenever the weather turns a little cold.

A: Yeah.

"Objection, leading."

"Overruled."

Hizzoner's getting it. "Mr. Marello, you're a tea drinker, aren't you?"

Anthony, like a giant rock, sat silent.

"The witness will answer the question," Hizzoner said.

A: Yeah, I drink tea.

Q: You seldom, if ever, drink coffee?

A: ... That's right.

Q: Mr. Marello, you were in Chapel Hill on the day Livia Marello was murdered, weren't you?

A: No. I spent the entire day hunting on my farm outside New Orleans. I didn't find out what happened until I went into the dealership in the late afternoon and Jimmy told me.

Taggart turned towards the gallery and gestured for Cornelius to stand.

Q: Do you see that man standing in the gallery?

A: Yeah.

Q: His name is Cornelius Kempton, Sir. Mr. Kempton works at the Raleigh/Durham airport, and he will testify he saw you at the airport on the morning of December 24, 1973, at about ten o'clock in the morning. Now, is it still your testimony that you were not in Chapel Hill on the day Livia Marello was murdered?

"Just a minute, Counsel," Hizzoner said. "I think the witness needs to be warned of his rights. Mr. Marello, I hereby advise you that you have a right against self-incrimination. You have a right to remain silent, to not answer any more questions. You have a right to consult with an attorney before you decide whether you want to make any further statement. I further advise you that any statement you make may be used against you in a court of law. Do you understand what I am telling you?"

"I understand."

"Do you want to speak to a lawyer before you make any further statements?"

"Yes."

Although he'd expected it, Anthony's "yes" rocked Taggart. He looked over his shoulder to see how Frank was taking the bad surprise.

Frank Marello's eyes were closed. He wanted to put his head down on the table. "Jim, yes; Daddy, no. Why can't I just die instead? he thought. "Why can't I, the son of whom you thought so little, just sink from sight? Do you hate me so much just because I can't be like Jim?"

Mike could see Frank had begun to weep. He motioned to Rhonda, who had been studying Anthony, and she turned and put her arms around Frank, talking low and slow, the way Mike had seen Marcia talk to Matt when he was hurting.

Hizzoner's clerk was whispering in the Judge's ear, describing the scene at defense table.

Tubby Mayes, who was on duty as bailiff and Frank's keeper, rose at the first sign of disruption, but stopped and stood, stroking his chin, watching. What did one do to make someone stop crying?

"Counsel, do you want a recess?"

"Yes, Sir," Taggart replied. *I need to throw up.* "In light of Mr. Marello's exercise of the privilege, I have no further questions."

Anthony's assertion of his right to remain silent foreclosed any cross-examination. So, Mike called Cornelius to the stand after the recess.

Q: Mr. Kempton, where do you work?

A: I'm a skycap at Raleigh Durham Airport.

Q: Were you working on the morning of December 24, 1973?

A. Yes sir.

Q: Did you normally work the morning shift?

A: No. I usually worked at night, but I was pulling a double shift because of the holiday and other guys wanting to take vacation. I just did it for that one day.

Q: You were in the courtroom during the testimony of the previous witness, Anthony Marello. Had you ever seen him before today?

A: Yes.

Q: When did you first see him?

A: The first time I remember seeing him was on the morning of December 24, 1973, at approximately ten o'clock.

Q: Was there anything in particular about him that caused you to remember him?

A: Yes. For one thing, he's big and he was wearing camouflage hunting clothes in the airport on Christmas Eve.

Q: How can you be so sure it was the morning of Christmas Eve 1973?

A: Because I know it was daylight when I first saw him, and that was the only time I ever worked in the daylight until more than a year later.

Q: Was that the only time you saw him before today?

A: No, I have often seen him going in and out of the airport since.

"No further questions."

Given Watson walked to the podium.

Q: This day you say you first saw Anthony Marello, December 24, 1973, that was almost three years ago?

A: Yes.

Q: Airports are pretty busy places during the Christmas holidays?

A: Yes.

Q: Lots of people coming and going?

A: Not so many on Christmas Eve, but still busy, yes.

Q: You say you're a "skycap?"

A: Yes.

Q: That means you're one of the guys that carry people's suitcases for them when they arrive at the airport for their flights?

A: Yes, most of the time, but sometimes when they are arriving home from their flights and need help with the luggage to their cars.

Q: You didn't help Mr. Marello on that Christmas Eve morning, did you?

A: I don't believe he had any luggage.

Q: So, it's your testimony that you just noticed him among the crowd of holiday travelers?

A: Yes.

Q: You knew about this case when it was first tried back in 1974?

A: Yes.

Q: But you didn't come forward at that time with your alleged sighting of Mr. Marello?

A: No.

Q: Mr. Taggart was your high school baseball coach for three years, wasn't he?

A: He was an assistant coach my last two years.

Q: In fact, he was assigned as your special coach to help you with the catching position?

A: Yes.

Q: He helped you in other ways as well?

A: Yes.

Q: In fact, he helped you obtain a scholarship to the University of Michigan?

A: Yes.

Q: University of Michigan just happens to be where Mr. Taggart went to college, isn't it?

A: I believe so.

Q: So, Mr. Taggart got you in to his alma mater?

A: Mr. Taggart gave me a good recommendation. I got myself in.

Q: How many times have you visited with Mr. Taggart since he came back to town from California for this case?

A: Four or five times.

Q: What have you done during those visits?

A: Sat around his place, went fishing, shot baskets, had dinner.

Q: So you and he are good pals?

A: I would say that he and I are good friends.

Q: You didn't bring this story about seeing Mr. Marello to anyone's attention during the first trial, but now that your friend Mr. Taggart's in town, you suddenly remember seeing Anthony Marello on the day of the murder?

A: I didn't know the man I saw had anything to do with the case back in '74. I didn't even know his name was Anthony Marello.

Q: So your answer is "Yes?"

A: Yes.

Q: It was Mr. Taggart who told you who Mr. Marello was?

A: Yes.

Q: When did you first tell Mr. Taggart that you had seen Anthony Marello on the day of the murder?

A: Last night.

Q: Last night, right after Jim Marello was eliminated as a suspect?

A: I don't know anything about that.

"No further questions."

"Redirect, Mr. Taggart?"

"Yes, Sir."

Q: Mr. Kempton, what prompted you to tell me about your having seen Anthony Marello on the day of the murder?

A: I watched the trial last week, and my wife was here this week when Jim Marello testified. From what she told me, it sounded like you were trying to point the finger of suspicion at him. After I thought about it, I thought maybe you were barking up the wrong tree.

Q: Mr. Kempton, is there anything about our friendship that would cause you to lie under oath?

A: No, nothing.

"No further questions."

"For its next witness, the Defense calls Angela Cummings."

Ghost stood up, went to the door of the courtroom, stuck his head out and said something. The young woman wearing the black and yellow uniform who had earlier accompanied Ghost and Cornelius entered and came forward to be sworn.

"Miss. Cummings," Taggart began after she gave her name and address, "by whom are you employed?"

A: Hertz Rent-A-Car company.

Q: What's your job with Hertz?

A: I'm a rental counter agent at Raleigh Durham Airport.

Q: How long have you worked there?

A: A little over three years. I started in September 1973.

Q: Where were you on the morning of December 24, 1973?

A: I was working at the Hertz counter at the airport. Junior person works the holidays.

Q: Are you acquainted with Anthony Marello?

A: I know who he is.

Q: Did you see Mr. Marello at the Raleigh Durham Airport on the morning of December 24, 1973?

A: Yes, I did.

Q: How do you happen to remember seeing him that long ago?

A: Mr. Marello came to the counter and rented a car from me. He didn't have a reservation. So, it was a little unusual. He's so big, and he was wearing those funny military clothes, and he joked about how he should be home playing Santa Claus instead of flyin' all over creation.

Q: What time of day did you see him?

A: It was some time around ten o'clock in the morning.

Q: Did you ever see him again after that?

A: Oh, yes. Mr. Marello has rented cars a lot of times when I've been at the counter. Sometimes I wait on him; sometimes I just see him while I'm waiting on someone else. Like I said, he's hard to miss because he's so big.

"No further questions."

"Miss Cummings," Given Watson said, "how old are you?"

A: Twenty-one.

Q: You say you live out in Boxelder?

A: Yes, Sir.

Q: You any relation to Mossy Cummings?

A: Mossy's my daddy.

Q: So, you're kin to Cornelius Kempton, who just told the same story you're telling?

A: Cornelius is my cousin.

That's a revolting development. Taggart wished he'd known that. He would have asked the question himself.

Q: Cornelius help you get your job at the airport?

A: He'd heard there was an opening at Hertz and suggested I apply.

Q: Christmas is a pretty busy season in the car rental business at the airport?

A: Yes, Sir, one of the busiest.

Q: Long lines?

A: Yes.

Q: Lots of people in a hurry?

A: Yes.

Q: More things to do than there is time to do them?

A: Yes.

Q: Now, Miss Cummings, when someone rents a car from Hertz, they have to sign a contract, don't they?

A: Yes.

Q: A person renting a car has to sign this contract in a couple of places and initial it in a couple more?

A: Yes.

Q: Hertz keeps the original of this rental contract?

A: That's right.

Q: Otherwise, the Company wouldn't have any record of who had its cars?

A: Yes, Sir.

Q: Of course, you don't have a copy of any rental contract showing Anthony Marello rented a car from Hertz at the airport on December 24, 1973, do you?

A: No.

"No further questions."

"Miss Cummings," Mike said, "are you testifying because Cornelius Kempton is your cousin?

A: No, Sir.

Q: Or because Cornelius helped you get your job?

A: No, Sir.

Q: Would either of those facts cause you to lie under oath?

A: No, Sir. Definitely not.

Q: Did you look for a copy of Anthony Marello's rental contract for December 24, 1973?

A: No, Sir.

Q: Why not?

A: Because I know it's not there anymore. Old contracts are only kept for one year and then destroyed. That's part of my job to do that. I do it every month.

"Thank you, Miss Cummings. No further questions."

Mike leaned over to Rhonda. "Anything else we need?"

Rhonda scrutinized their list of evidence to be presented, which was covered with cross-outs and check marks. "Looks like that's it."

"Your Honor, the Defense rests."

The presentation of evidence by both sides drew to a close.

Hizzoner excused the jury, but instructed counsel to remain.

"Counsel," he said once the jury had filed out, "as you heard me tell the jury, being as how tomorrow is Thanksgiving, we will recess until nine o'clock Friday morning, at which time you should be prepared to argue I will then instruct the jury and deliberations will begin. Have a good Thanksgiving."

Ghost dropped Mike off at the apartment. Rhonda was going home to start Thanksgiving dinner. Ghost had offered to help. Taggart said he'd rather stay at his place and work on the final argument. After Ghost and Rhonda drove off, Mike changed clothes and went for a walk.

It was already dark, and the air was cold. He had no particular destination in mind, but recognized where his feet were taking him. He had forced himself not to go there until now.

A short mile back toward downtown, then just over a mile up Oak Grove Road, two rows of trees arched over a long lane like an arcade. Beyond the trees, an open lawn stretched for another fifty yards, at the end of which a giant house loomed in the moonlight. Devon Hill.

Mike walked up the path people had been walking up since 1815, when the place was built by William Perkins of Devon, England, to reign over a five-thousand-acre plantation and all its minions. Continuing past the south end of the house, a three-story pile of red bricks topped by a five-chimney roof, the lane forked, turning to the left and running across the back of the mansion, while to the right it ended after a few yards in more rolling lawn.

There on the right, during the years 1965 to 1968, Taggart and Cathy had lived in a tiny cinderblock house, now vanished, they called the "slave quarters." On these lawns he had first seen Feodot run as a puppy, her body smaller than her ears over which she often tripped. Across the same lawn on warm summer nights had come the sound of their landlord, Gifford Perkins, the eighty-year old last of the line, carousing drunk with his wife, Pauline, thirty years younger, hollering that he'd give her a "good screwing" when he caught her, and Pauline, equally drunk, yelling back that maybe she wouldn't let him catch her this time.

He and Cathy would lie listening to the revelry beneath the ancient ceiling fan humming their only defense against the Carolina heat and humidity, sooner or later forgetting Gifford and Pauline and catching each other.

"Glad you're quicker than ol' Giff," Cathy would whisper as they lay panting together afterwards.

"Glad you're so willing to be caught," Mike murmured in reply.

It was the last place they had been happy.

Thinking the place would make him too sad, Taggart had stayed away. To his surprise, it had the opposite effect. Of course, things had changed; happiness had been lost, but at least it was possible. Things would change again, were changing. It was hard to see, to think beyond the fortunes of the trial, but now as the end drew near, he sensed the glimmer of the future, Marcia and Matt. *Cathy's already found her future. My turn. Funny thing, they aren't that different.*

His feet followed the road around the big house without stopping and headed for home.

58

Thursday, November 25, 1976 - Thanksgiving

Thanksgiving morning. At ten, Ghost picked up Taggart for the trip to Rhonda's for an early Thanksgiving dinner. There would be work to do that night.

"I notice you didn't make it home last night," Mike gave Ghost a look as he slid into the car.

"By the time the last pie was in the oven, it was too late."

"I wish you'd call. You know how I worry."

Rhonda lived in a small red brick house nestled well back from the street among some sycamore trees. The yard was covered with unraked leaves. Ghost parked at the curb. The sky was bright blue and there was a breeze that wanted to become a wind. Leafless branches rattled. Mike felt like gravity had slightly relaxed its hold on him, better than he had felt in weeks. *Nothing like a viable alternative suspect.*

He opened the front door and was instantly struck by a sixty-pound ball of flying boy. "Happy Thanksgiving, Coach," Matt said, leaning back with his legs wrapped around Taggart's waist. "Are you winning your case? Mom's here too."

"Wow! Matty, great surprise. When did you get here?"

"Last night. I slept on the plane. Mom didn't."

"Where's your mom? Did she just drop you off and go home?"

"I'm in the kitchen." Marcia's voice. "Come in here. I'm up to my elbows in dressing."

"What's going on," Mike entered the kitchen and inhaled, "an aroma festival? I smell a little league mom. Fee, Fi, Fo, Fum."

"I smell a big, bad wolf," Marcia said. Dressed in a pink apron, Rhonda's team colors, over a blue, green and white plaid flannel shirt and jeans, she was standing at the kitchen table. Her face was flushed from the warmth of cooking, and a wisp of her hair dangled over her right eye. She hadn't been lying about the dressing. Mike grabbed her around the waist from behind and kissed her neck. "How are you, Love? I'm glad you're here."

"Get whatever you want to drink from the frig," Rhonda said. "Dinner won't be ready for another hour."

After dinner and the dishes, Mike and Marcia took a walk. Matt was watching the football game with Ghost, who was teaching him to walk on his hands.

"Matt and I are staying here tonight, Mike. You need to finish this without any more distractions. Besides, Matt needs to catch up on sleep, and so does his mom."

"Wish you weren't, but you're right. You coming to the closing arguments tomorrow?"

"Are you kidding? If I don't go, Matt will go without me. He brought his whole lawyer get-up, including the glasses I got him for Halloween."

They walked a little farther holding hands.

"How does your last Thanksgiving as a single man feel? You're not sorry, are you?"

Mike stopped walking, turned towards Marcia and took both her hands in his. "Marsh, I'm the most un-sorriest guy you will ever meet."

59

Friday, November 26, 1976. - Trial Day 9

Not even Billy Graham, a North Carolinian at the height of his fame, could have filled the courtroom more completely than Given Watson and Mike Taggart did on Friday, November 26, 1976. Stick Hatcher and every deputy not actually out on patrol were sitting in the front row along with Susan Hunter, Mayor Lund and Edna and Rev. Claiborne and his wife. Cornelius and Josie were half way back sitting next to Mark Josephson, who had been wheeled in. Betty Lou Combs, the waitress from Lund's drug store, was there along with a couple dozen people Taggart didn't recognize. In the back row sat Buck, Big Roy, Lester, Alvin Wade and Bobby Mack wearing what looked like the same coats and ties they'd worn to Mike's graduation eight years earlier.

In the second row on the aisle, where Jim and Anthony Marello formerly sat, were Matt and Marcia, sitting next to Ghost.

"Mr. Watson, you may proceed."

Mike settled into his chair. He steeled himself to listen to his opponent twist and spin the facts, an ordeal that always made him squirm with impatience.

Watson stepped to the podium.

"Ladies and Gentlemen of the jury, it's been a long trial. On behalf of the State of North Carolina, I thank you for your attention.

"Now, the defense has tried to make this case a whole lot more complicated than it really is. Why, the accused has offered up just about his entire family as sacrificial lambs in his attempt to wriggle out of his guilt. First his brother, then his father. It's a good thing for his mama she stayed home in New Orleans, or the accused would have found a way to point the finger at her too."

So, Frank's attempt to sacrifice his family is going to be Watson's keynote. Taggart had expected him to trot out Frank's homosexuality for openers. *It's coming.*

"Strip away all the California-style drama from the accused's case; analyze it with a critical eye, and you cannot help but recognize that no one in the Marello family except the accused had either the motive or the opportunity to kill Livia Marello. Strip away all the drama, and you cannot fail to recognize the following hard facts.

Watson launched into a review of why neither Jim nor Anthony could be the killer, of how "this fella Kempton" was too beholden to Taggart to be believed.

Why doesn't Watson just call Cornelius "boy" and get it over with? Taggart hoped the jurors saw Watson's use of "fella" instead of Cornelius' name for what it was.

According to Watson, Livia's complaints to the police about Jim's abusive behavior couldn't be a motive, because all charges had been dropped. There was no evidence Ford ever heard a word about them.

"Even if Ford Motor Company doesn't want felons for dealers, Anthony, not Jim, is the 'King of Cars.' Do you suppose the folks up at Ford are going to sacrifice their biggest dealer in the Southeast because of some charges against a minority owner? How likely is that?

"If push ever came to shove, wouldn't it have been a whole lot easier for Anthony just to ease Jim out of his minority ownership than to get on a plane the day before Christmas and fly across the country, crack a few jokes at the rent-a-car counter, then drive over to Chapel Hill and murder his own daughter-in-law, a woman he liked and admired?"

Watson picked up a dictionary and opened it to a place he had marked.

"I'd like to read to you the definition of the term 'red herring.' 'Red herring' – 'something intended to divert attention from the real problem or matter at hand; a misleading clue.'

"All this stuff about Jim Marello and Lee Roy Thigpen, all this stuff about Anthony Marello and Defense Counsel's two pals from the airport, are exactly that – red herrings. Maybe that's the way things are done out in California. That's where they make movies, isn't it? Thank God this isn't California. Thank God this is North Carolina, where we rely on evidence, not red herrings, not false clues.

Rhonda slid a note over to Taggart as Watson stopped for a drink of water. "The longer he talks about Jim and Anthony instead of Frank, the better for us."

Taggart agreed. So far he was squirming less than expected.

Watson, too, sensed that he had spent enough time on Anthony and Jim. He shifted gears.

"On the other hand, when we're talkin' motive, we're talkin' Frank Marello. In the year and a half since Frank Marello married Livia Lindholm 'until death do us part,' he'd decided he was homosexual. At the age of thirty-two, it was foreseeable he would spend the next forty years married to a woman he didn't even want to sleep with."

In the gallery, Matt turned to Marcia and whispered, "Mom, what's a … "

Marcia put her finger to her lips. "Shhh."

"Frank Marello needed to free himself from the baggage his wife and soon his child would become. So on the morning of December 24, 1973, he killed Livia Marello. Sometime that morning between six and ten o'clock, after a quarrel so loud it was heard by the neighbors, he strangled her, choked her to death, broke her neck. Suddenly all the complications of his life disappeared and he was free … free to pursue the homosexual life he himself has told you he prefers."

As he listened, Taggart stared across the courtroom at the jurors. *How are they responding to all this?* At least none of them were nodding their heads in agreement.

Watson turned to the two teacups, the tea kettle boiled dry and the bathrobe in the midst of being wrapped "Folks, remember Dr. Bordick? Remember she told you Livia Marello was murdered sometime between six and ten a.m. Miss Wilmer didn't discover the murder until twelve-thirty. At a minimum, the accused had two and a half hours, more likely four and a half, to set out those teacups, set out that nice new bathrobe and the Christmas wrappings, and to boil that teakettle dry. If ever there were three clues easier for a murderer like Frank Marello to manufacture, to invent to deflect suspicion from himself, I'd like you to tell me what they are.

Watson stepped from behind the podium and bent towards counsel table, as if to get a drink, but immediately straightened. "Another thing, how many people choose to wait for their ride outside on a morning so cold they need a winter coat? What's the Accused's excuse for that – he didn't want to risk that notorious noisemaker, Mark Josephson, waking Livia up as she slept in an upstairs bedroom? That dog won't hunt. What he didn't want to happen was for Josephson to see what he'd left on the kitchen floor.

"What kind of an alibi is it to say 'I was out shopping with my homosexual partner who just sold me the insurance policy I'm going to collect on my dead wife's life? Ladies and gentlemen, the accused went shopping with the very fellow who helped him figure out he didn't want to be married any more and who helped put him in a position to enrich himself by means of his wife's death. What a coincidence! If that's not a compass pointing directly at Frank Marello as Livia's killer, I don't know what is.

"Here's a couple who can't even afford a Christmas tree, and the accused's out buying life insurance for a twenty-five year-old woman in the bloom of health, so if she happens to fall over dead, he'll be provided for. And, what do you know, a few days later, she does fall over dead. What a coincidence!

"Here's another so-called 'coincidence'– the Accused signed his wife's name to the policy application, just like he would if he didn't want her to know what he was doing. Defense counsel's probably going to argue Livia Marello knew about that insurance policy, but to that, I say, 'So what?' That doesn't change a thing. Whether she knew about it or not doesn't lessen its force as a motive for her husband, the beneficiary of that policy, to kill her.

"We have only the Accused's 'word' that Livia knew about the insurance – the Accused, Frank Marello, the same guy who told Sheriff Hatcher on the day of the murder that he and his wife were getting along 'just fine.' I guess he just forgot about all those troubles Livia recorded in her diary. As my daddy would have said, Frank Marello's 'word' ain't worth spit.

"Not only is the Accused asking you to believe Livia agreed to the purchase of the insurance, but that she agreed he should purchase the insurance from 'Mark,' the man with whom her husband had committed adultery just three months earlier. A man whom the accused says he promised his wife he would stay away from. It's not as if there weren't a few other insurance salesmen in town.

"Ladies and gentlemen, the Accused had a homosexual affair with Mark Josephson. His wife found out about it, and so he promised to stop seeing 'Mark.' Just to be sure he would, Livia Marello made a point of meeting Josephson and begging him to stop seeing her husband. But did they stop seeing each other? No.

"Instead, the Accused bought life insurance from 'Mark' despite the existence of dozens of other life insurance companies in Chapel Hill and Durham. He and 'Mark' went Christmas shopping together, a fact he never did get around to telling Livia despite the fact the trip had been planned for several days.

"If the Accused had nothing to hide, if he didn't think Livia would object, why didn't he just say, 'Oh, by the way, Mark and I are going Christmas shopping on Christmas Eve.' Simplest thing in the world … unless he knew she would object, unless he knew it's the thing Livia wants least in the world to happen. Then maybe you don't say anything. Then, because the thing Livia wants least in the world to happen is the thing you want most in the world to happen, you kill her.

"Frank Marello lied to his wife. He lied to Sheriff Hatcher. He's lying to you. The time has come for you, as the voice of the citizens of North Carolina, to tell him one true thing. It's time for you to tell Frank Marello that murder will not be tolerated in our community, and those who commit murder will be punished with all the severity the law can command. Ladies and gentlemen, the time has come to do your job. Thank you."

Given Watson collected his notes from the podium and sat down.

Rhonda gave Taggart a "thumbs up" as he rose from his chair. He walked slowly around counsel table to the blackboard on wheels standing against the wall, dragged it out to about twelve feet directly in front of the jury, picked up a piece of chalk and in large letters slowly wrote the words, "REASONABLE DOUBT."

He stepped just to one side of the board so as not to block the jurors' view and turned to face them, standing closer than at the time of his opening statement, more familiar now after eight long hard days spent together, no longer a stranger.

"Your Honor, Counsel, Ladies and Gentlemen of the jury." Mike nodded to each in turn.

"There was a brutal game played by Russian peasants back in the last century in which the peasants would capture one bird, say a starling, from among a flock. They would paint the captured bird and release it. The rest of the flock would no longer recognize the painted bird as one of their own, nor would they understand the difference had been created by a force over which the bird had no control. To the peasants' amusement, the other birds would peck the painted bird to death."

Taggart spoke slowly, letting the injustice of the painted bird's fate seep in.

"The prosecution is inviting you to be like those Russian peasants, to seize on the fact of Frank's difference, his homosexuality, and because of that difference, to convict him of murder and, in effect, peck him to death.

"Remember Dr. Lefler's testimony. Suzanne Lefler is a scientist and psychiatrist. She is a professional listener and observer. She, more than any other third person, had the opportunity to see inside the Marello's marriage all the way to its essence, to its core. It is her professional opinion that, despite being homosexual, Frank loved Livia just as deeply and intensely as any of us love our spouses, love our families. The Frank Marello Dr. Lefler knew loved Livia for all the reasons we love others that have nothing to do with sex. He loved her because of her abundant kindness, her compassion, her humor, her intelligence, her beauty – he loved her in countless ways, for countless reasons. Frank Marello did not murder his wife. He loved her.

"The prosecution's trying to twist that love into a bad thing. Out of consideration for Livia, Frank waited outside for Mark despite the cold rather than risk awakening her. Mr. Watson says that's because he didn't want Mark to see what had happened, but, if Frank was really planning to kill Livia that morning, why didn't he offer to drive, instead of letting Mark pick him up? What if Mark had come early? What if Mark had come to the back door while Frank waited in front? If, as the prosecution would have you believe, Frank Marello planned this whole thing, why didn't he volunteer to drive and eliminate all risk of Mark stumbling on what had happened? Ask yourselves, have you ever been awakened by the sound of a doorbell? Maybe the chances were slight, and it was a small thing, waiting outside. But Frank Marello cared enough to do it. Like the song says, 'Little things mean a lot.' Frank Marello loved his wife. He did not kill her.

"'If he loved his wife so much' you may ask, 'why did he chose to hurt her so by doing as he did with Mark Josephson?' Fair question. Once again, we turn to Dr. Lefler. As she explained, being homosexual is *not* a matter of choice. Frank himself asked Mr. Watson, 'Who would choose such a life?' Homosexuality is a function of brain chemistry, what scientists call 'dimorphic changes.' Putting scientific terms to one side, the bottom line is, God makes people different, both inside and out. Some people are born smarter than others; some are born better athletes; some are born homosexual.

"You may profoundly disapprove of homosexual practices. That is certainly your choice to make. But the fact remains, homosexuality is the cross Frank Marello has been given to bear. God painted Frank Marello every bit as much as those peasants painted that poor bird. The point is, Frank never intended to hurt Livia. He acted in response to a chemical force within him he could neither understand, nor successfully control.

"He was immediately remorseful, repentant, filled with anguish. Don't take my word for it. Take Livia's." Taggart picked up the diary from the evidence table, "On October 8, 1973, she wrote:

> ...Frank was distraught when he told me. He's having all kinds of problems with what he has done. He says he still loves me, but that it's more a "friendship love."
>
> ... I asked Frank if this means that he wants to leave me, and he said no ... He doesn't know why this happens, and he feels like a traitor to me and he wants to stay with me and love me and live with me, but he

> has these other feelings he doesn't want to have, and he doesn't know what to do about them.
>
> We talked for hours. Sometimes Frank was crying; sometimes I was crying - sometimes we both were. It was as if we were the last two people on Earth, and all the identities that define us for others were stripped away, and we were lying there with nothing but our feelings. I came to see that it's like Frank has a disease, and one of the symptoms is that he doesn't know who he is, or, if he does know, he doesn't want to be that person.

"But it's one thing to be remorseful, and it's another thing to do something about it. Frank *did* something about it. He joined Livia in her consultations with Dr. Lefler. He sought to understand why he is the way he is. From Dr. Lefler, Frank learned, just as you have *learned*, that homosexuality is not something people choose; that he cannot be blamed for *having* homosexual feelings. But, if he and Livia were to preserve their marriage, he was going to have to make up his mind not to *act* on such feelings.

"And that is what Frank made up his mind to do – to *not act* on those feelings. Tough job - Dr. Lefler says so - but not impossible, not if you're married to a person like Livia Marello, someone who understood and accepted his imperfections and gave Frank countless reasons to love her every day of their lives."

Taggart walked over to the defense table, checked his notes and walked back in front of the jury.

"It's time for another question. 'Well, if he was determined not to act on those feelings, why did he buy the insurance from Josephson? Why did he go shopping with Josephson?'

"Immediately following his night with Josephson, Frank resolved never to see him again and told him so. That was Livia's first impulse as well, and, as you know, she asked Josephson to stay away, but life is complicated, and you cannot hide from it.

"Livia became pregnant. Frank and Livia decided they needed insurance. Frank already had a policy his parents gave him, but really knew nothing about insurance. Neither did Livia. How much did they need? What type? What's the best company? How much should they expect to pay? Who should they ask? Whom did they know who knew about insurance? Mark Josephson.

"Frank and Livia asked each other, should we ask Mark in light of what happened? The question itself made them realize they could not hide from life. If Frank could not meet and do business with Mark, interact with him as a friend, without becoming romantically entangled, then he and Livia might as well have given up on the marriage right then. As Frank told you from the witness stand, seeing Mark Josephson again was a kind of 'experiment.' He couldn't hide from all men; he couldn't hide from all homosexual men. He needed to know he could be married and live a happy life in the community without acting on his homosexual feelings. If he could do that with Mark, he could do it with anybody.

"And he did. There was no homosexual affair, no ongoing romance. It was a one-night indiscretion, nothing more. In their subsequent interactions Frank and Mark Josephson went back to being just friends, nothing more.

"The prosecution points to Livia's diary as if it is some great revelation in support of its case. I tell you it is just the opposite. Why does the prosecution need the diary? To tell you Frank Marello is a homosexual? Nonsense. Frank admits it.

"That diary does not advance the prosecution's case one inch. But it is *the most eloquent witness* Frank Marello could possibly have in his own defense. You can search Livia Marello's diary from cover to cover, put it under a literary microscope, and you will not find a single passage, not a single word, not one, to suggest Frank wanted to leave Livia.

"Do you think the Livia Marello you have come to know in this trial would have failed to detect any lack of resolve by Frank to preserve their marriage? Livia Marello was on full alert, and what she saw was just the opposite. The Frank she saw was doing everything he could to strengthen their marriage. The Frank Marello she saw is the person about whom she wrote this passage on December 16, just eight days before she died."

Taggart picked up a large piece of stiff white pasteboard off the defense table and set it on the courtroom easel to display Livia's December 16 diary entry greatly magnified. He read it aloud slowly.

December 16, 1973

> Sunday morning. Lazy time – No place to go. No place either of us had to be. I woke up this morning in Frank's arms. He was still asleep, but not for long. We made love real long and slow. He is so gentle and tender and pleasing to me. It was delicious. We ARE making progress!

"Ladies and gentlemen, Livia Marello is sending you a message. She is telling you Frank did not want to end their marriage, did not want to leave her. She is telling you Frank Marello has told you the truth."

Taggart walked over and stood behind Frank. He put his right hand on Frank's right shoulder, looking at the jury.

"Remember, in order to convict Frank Marello, you must believe he is guilty *beyond all reasonable doubt*. Can any of you believe *beyond all reasonable doubt* that the kind and gentle person the evidence reveals Frank Marello to be, the person who, in Mr. Jack's words, is 'as gentle as a flower' could have committed *any* murder, let alone that of the one person he loved most in the world?

"Without considering another fact beyond the kind of person Frank Marello is and the depth and breadth of his love and respect for his wife, *reasonable doubt* exists."

Mike returned to the blackboard and underlined the words "REASONABLE DOUBT," paused, and stood staring, as if contemplating their meaning.

Then he turned, half smiled, and asked, "Well, if Frank didn't kill Livia, who did?"

Taggart paused, hoping the jurors were answering his question for themselves as he was about to - letting them have the chance.

"Anthony Marello.

"The prosecution contends this crime was carefully planned, that Frank Marello made all these careful preparations to commit murder and then methodically carried them out. I tell you that the murder did *not* happen that way. This murder has all the earmarks of a crime of passion, beginning with the way it was done.

"If someone is planning to kill another person, strangling is not the method one selects. Too many things can go wrong, especially if you are a person, like Frank, with no experience of any kind with physical violence or combat. What if the victim slips out of your grasp? What if the victim suddenly kicks her assailant right in the groin? What if the victim manages to scream?

"No, if someone is *planning* a murder, they adopt another method. Too many things can go wrong with strangling.

"The way Livia Marello was strangled required her killer to look her right in the eye as he was squeezing the life out of her. That hardly seems like the Frank Marello whom you've come to know through Livia Marello's diary and there on the witness stand, the man who saved the life of his own jailer … the man who's 'gentle as a flower.'

"No," Taggart raised his hands in front of him as if he was holding someone by the throat and squeezing, appearing to strain every muscle in his body with the effort, "the man who strangled Livia Marello wasn't seeing his victim, he was seeing only the object of his own rage and frustration.

"He was seeing only an 'obstacle' standing in the way of his desire, an 'obstacle' who refused to do what he desperately wanted her to do, an 'obstacle' who was threatening the killer's own comfort and safety and that of his family as he viewed it. That killer was Anthony Marello.

"Anthony Marello claims he was hunting in Louisiana on the day Livia was killed, but two people, Cornelius Kempton and Angela Cummings, saw him at the Raleigh/Durham airport that morning around ten o'clock. Mr. Kempton and Miss Cummings both *know* it was Anthony Marello they saw that morning, because they have seen him many times since. Anthony's a big boy, hard to miss.

"Remember, Anthony Marello is the patriarch of the Marello family, the captain of the ship, the 'King of Cars,' a self-made man. Anthony was the king, and there was trouble in his kingdom. Just four days earlier, Livia Marello had Anthony's eldest son, Jim, his firstborn, his crown prince, his heir apparent, thrown in jail for beating his wife ... and it wasn't the first time it had happened. The first time, things were all smoothed over, but the second time Jim Marello actually had his fingerprints taken, his mugshot snapped, had actually gone to jail, heard the sound of a steel door clanking shut behind him. The second time, charges were actually filed. What would happen the third time? If Jim was convicted of a felony, the Marellos could lose their Ford dealership.

"Quite apart from any potential troubles with Ford, Livia was embarrassing them. Livia Marello was parading the Marello family's dirty laundry in public for everyone could see. There it was in black and white in the newspaper, 'James Marello, prominent car dealer, arrested for wife beating.' Livia Marello was shaming the Marello family in front of their friends and neighbors and business associates in the New Orleans community. The desire to avoid embarrassment is a powerful thing. Anthony Marello is a proud man. Something had to be done.

"I'm not suggesting Anthony came to Chapel Hill planning to kill Livia. A man of his wealth and power – if he wanted someone killed, he could find someone to do it for him, no questions asked. Killing Livia Marello wasn't something Anthony planned to do.

"Anthony Marello came to Chapel Hill to talk some sense into his daughter-in-law, to make her see she was embarrassing the family, that she was endangering its financial welfare. Jim had been arrested and charged on the night of the twentieth. It had taken all day the twenty-first to get him out of jail and the charges dropped. Perhaps Anthony did intend to go hunting when he got out of bed and left the house that Christmas Eve morning, but he'd been brooding about the situation for three days.

"Instead of heading for the bayou, Anthony Marello catches the six-thirty flight to Raleigh/Durham. Three and a half hours. Intending to do nothing other than talk to Livia, he makes no effort to avoid being seen when he arrives, he jokes with Angela Cummings at the car rental counter, he is seen by Cornelius Kempton. Both Angela and Cornelius remember him. The rest isn't hard to figure out.

"Anthony rents a car and drives over to Chapel Hill, parks in the lot behind the apartment, walks up and knocks on the door.

"Livia, still in her robe and slippers and in the midst of wrapping presents, peeks through the curtain, sees it's her father-in-law and opens the door." As he spoke, Taggart pushed an imaginary curtain aside then opened an imaginary door.

"'Anthony, what are you doing here? Come on in.'" Taggart softened his voice as he became Livia.

Then, shifting personae, he turned a half turn to face Livia, voice deepened. "'Phew, it's cold out.' Anthony claps his gloved hands together as he steps inside. 'Let me just stand here and warm up.'"

"'Frank's gone shopping. I'm just wrapping his present and making a cup of tea. Want one?'"

"'Yeah, that would be good. Listen, you're the one I really want to talk to.'"

"'Me? What about? Is it about Jim?'"

"'Yeah. Livia, don't ever do that again. Don't go to the police. Don't cause trouble.'

"Livia sets Anthony's cup with the teabag in it down next to hers. 'Anthony, you've already got trouble. Don't you think having a son who beats up his wife and kids is trouble?'"

"'Maybe so, but it's trouble we'll take care of inside the family. We don't need any outsiders. You need to understand that. How's it going to help Lauren or the kids if suddenly the money's all gone? That don't help anybody.'"

"The tea kettle is whistling, and Livia's about to take it off the stove as Anthony speaks, but she drops her potholder and whirls around.

"'Nonsense, Anthony. No, bullshit, just plain bullshit! Jim bullied and beat up Frank for twenty years and the family never did a damn thing to stop it. Why should I believe it's going to be any different for Lauren and the boys? Fat lot of good money does them, if all it's used for is to pay their hospital bills.'"

"'Yeah, but—'"

"'Yeah, but,' nothing, Anthony. Jim can't talk to someone, not someone he thinks he's tougher than, without punching them, pinching, poking them in the chest. I've seen it myself. It goes on all the time, and nobody does anything. When I tried to talk to him on the phone, he called me a 'slut' and threatened me."

Ghost, the jury watcher, noted, "Jurors engaged but would prefer better looking actor." He looked up from his notebook as Taggart, in the role of Livia, continued.

"'I've seen what it did to Frank, and I see what it's doing to Lauren. The poor woman walks on pins and needles, afraid of her own shadow. Same with the boys. If you don't see that, you're either blind or you don't give a damn. Well, I give a damn, and every time I hear of it happening, I will call the police, I'll call the FBI, I'll call your priest, I'll call anybody I can think of who might be able to stop that bully you call a son.'

"Anthony had had enough. Who the hell does she think she's talking to?

"'You listen to me, bitch—'

"'Bitch ... Bitch' is it now? Welcome to the Jim club, Anthony. Now I see where he gets it.'

"'Shut up—'

"'I won't shut-up. Maybe all the other women in the Marello family shut up when you and Jim start throwing around the 'bitch' word, the 'slut' word, but I won't. What're you going to do? Hit me? That solves everything for you and Jim, doesn't it?'"

"The tea kettle is shrieking; Livia is shrieking. Anthony, pissed out of his mind, 'You'll shut up.' Grabs her ..."

It had been at this point last night that Ghost, the theater arts major, began yelling at Mike, "Punch it up! PUNCH IT UP! If you're going to do this, do it right. You need to *be* these people. You need to *be* Livia. You need to feel all her rage and frustration. You have to *be* Anthony. You have to *be* the 'King of Cars.' You have to *kill* Livia. You have to *feel* it, if you're going to make the jury feel it. Punch it up."

Taggart punched it up.

Murder was being committed. Mike's face was red with strain, his teeth clenched and his lips drawn down in a cold hard line. His hands extended in front of him, squeezing, choking, shaking the writhing, clawing, gasping, gagging Livia they held.

"… But this isn't Mary Sulah, this isn't Lauren, this is Livia. Livia kicks – hard; Livia scratches if she can just reach him, struggling to scream, but Anthony's not letting go. He's squeezing, for the moment more afraid of what might happen if he lets go than if he doesn't. Anthony's big; Livia small. It only takes a moment."

Suddenly, Taggart's shoulders sagged and his arms relaxed.

"Livia Marello slid from his fingers and fell to the floor. Anthony stared down at her body, realizing that, in the midst of his uncomprehending rage, he has killed her."

Seconds passed in the suddenly silent courtroom.

"It wasn't planned," Mike said at last. "Anthony never even got his gloves off. Tea was never poured, and suddenly Livia Marello was dead. Anthony had killed her."

"Panic. Anthony bolts out the back door leaving it open in his haste. Flees. It's not quite eleven o'clock in the morning. Dr. Bordick says Livia was dead by ten, but, like she said, that's laboratory conditions. This is no laboratory; this is the Marello kitchen where the door stood open for hours on a day so cold that Dr. Bordick herself wore her winter coat, accelerating, speeding up the body's loss of heat. Livia was a tiny person, her body cooled fast.

"Livia's killer wasn't left-handed. The difference in the bruises was caused by the missing fingers on Anthony's right hand…" Mike held up his right hand with the ring and pinkie fingers curled under. "The absence of fingerprints by the gloves Anthony wears whenever it's cold.

"Ladies and gentlemen, neither Frank Marello nor I take any joy in telling you that his father killed Livia, but kill her he did. The Marello family has been trying to tear itself apart for thirty years, and on December 24, 1973, it finally succeeded.

"If you don't believe me, believe Anthony. He sat right there in front of you and heard me all but accuse him of killing Livia Marello. It would have been the easiest thing in the world for him to deny. But did he deny? When given the chance to look each of you in the eye and say, 'Ladies and gentlemen of the jury, I did not kill Livia Marello,' what did he do? He refused to answer. He refused to answer and asked to talk to a lawyer. He took the Fifth! Anthony Marello *ducked* the easiest question in the world for an innocent man to answer.

"You folks have been given a big job, bigger than most juries. You not only have to decide the guilt or innocence of Frank Marello, but in so doing, you need to decide whether you can stand up to the slings and arrows of all the people out there who would condemn Frank merely for being different … different, but no more guilty of murder than a painted bird.

"The days when such discrimination was the norm are coming to an end, but the braking process has been slow and painful. You are in a position to set an example of which everyone in this community should be proud. Thus far you have been attentive and punctual, and, on behalf of Frank Marello, I thank you. But now the hard work begins.

"When you have reviewed all the evidence, I am sure you will agree Frank Marello did not kill his wife. Anthony Marello did. It's up to you to say so, to announce to the world that in Marlborough, North Carolina, in Chapel Hill, in Johnston County, we do not convict a person on the basis of an unrelated fact over which he has no control.

"Thank you."

Given Watson stood up and began to clap.

"I'm clapping, ladies and gentlemen, because that's what folks do when they see a great actor. But remember, that's all you just saw and heard – a great act. California - Mr. Taggart sure practices law in the right place."

Watson went on, pointing out that everything Taggart had said was speculation, a good story, but argument, not evidence, Taggart had concocted the entire fairy tale on the basis of a disputed identification made three years after the supposed sighting. The defense was asking the jury to believe this based on the testimony of two people who owed Mr. Taggart and each other big favors.

"'May you outlive your children...'" Watson said, invoking Margaret Lindholm's curse, "Ladies and Gentlemen, you cannot bring Margaret Lindholm's daughter back to her, but you can let her live the rest of her life knowing the man who killed her daughter does not go unpunished."

It was eleven-thirty. Final argument had taken two and a half hours. In the thirty minutes that remained of the morning, Hizzoner instructed the jury about the various rules they were to follow during deliberations. Then they disappeared into the jury room, where one of the deputies brought them lunch.

60

Friday, November 26, 1976 – Trial Day 9 - Afternoon

The waiting was always the worst part. There was nothing more to do. Had what they'd done been enough? Did those twelve jurors see things as clearly as Mike and Rhonda?

"Do you think the jury will take long?" Marcia asked once Mike and Rhonda joined her and Matt in front of the courthouse. "I'd like to wait it out with you, but I'm wondering about Matt."

"No way to know," Rhonda said. "Several hours at a minimum. They're going to want to go over all the evidence at least once, and there's bound to be a lot of discussion."

"I think they'll finish by five," Mike said. "Jurors like to get home early on Friday, and don't like to come back on Monday. Still, it'll be a while. At least come join us for lunch."

They walked over to Lund's, where Betty Lou Combs had returned to duty and was practically running between tables trying to get her orders out. The café was crowded with court watchers, but Susan Hunter had a table and motioned for them to join her. Ghost excused himself, saying he'd just thought of something he needed to do.

"Susan, I'd like you to meet my fiancé, Marcia Banning, and her son, Matt."

Susan stood up and shook hands with Marcia and Matt. "Mike and I are old friends. I've heard a lot about you both."

"So, Susan," Mike said once they'd ordered, "what do you think that jury's going to do? Susan's Judge Hunter's wife," he explained to Marcia. "She's seen more trials than Rhonda and me put together."

"I think it's closer than I wish it was," Susan said, "although given a chance I might have convicted you of the murder after that re-enactment. Jury's going to have to believe Anthony did it. The mere fact Frank Marello's a good guy won't be enough. Too many good guys kill people."

Later, when most of the crowd had left and they were lingering over coffee, Susan said, "Did I ever tell you that when Hizzoner was practicing here, before he became a judge, one day he was going to the toilet in the men's room up on the second floor of the courthouse while he was waiting for a jury to decide one of his cases. As he stood there, he heard voices coming from the floor below, and it dawned on him the bathroom was right above the jury room. So Hizzoner got down on his knees and put his ear down to the open commode, and he could hear just about every word being said. After that, Hizzoner waited out jury deliberations in all his cases in that toilet stall. I'd take a chair and wait outside the door and rap on it if somebody was coming."

Mike and Rhonda looked at each other.

"But as soon as he became a judge, he had the floor fixed," Susan added. "Just in case you two were thinking what I think you were thinking."

It was a great story, but Taggart was beyond laughter. His mind was beginning to adjust to the idea that there was no further effort for which it must steel itself, and his two week adrenaline rush was subsiding. He felt light-headed, almost groggy.

"Matt and I are going back to Rhonda's," Marcia said twenty minutes later, "where there's a TV and somewhere he can run around. He can only stand being a lawyer for half a day. Call if you can and let me know how things are going."

Susan and Rhonda continued to chat about how they thought the trial had gone while Mike stirred his coffee without drinking any and nibbled his half-eaten sandwich. Two or three people came up to tell him they thought he'd done a good job, but most left them alone.

On the way back to the courthouse Rhonda stopped, put her hand on Mike's wrist and turned to face him. "Mike, there's something I want to say before we get back with lots of other people around and before the jury gets back too."

"What's that?"

"Just that, no matter how this turns out, I'm glad I asked you to come out here and do this with me. That's all."

"Thanks," Mike said. "I'm glad you did too."

There were no other matters on the court calendar for the day, so Hizzoner was letting them wait in the courtroom. Reporters from the Raleigh, Durham and Chapel Hill papers were all there and a couple of television crews as well, but Rhonda screened them from Taggart, and other court watchers and kibitzers drifted away from his silence.

Frank was sitting at counsel table doodling on a legal pad. "When I was a kid, about eleven or twelve," he said, "I had a dog named 'Shady' because she had an uncanny ability to find shade even in the most barren surroundings. She was my best friend during those years.

"One day she went into terrible convulsions. The vet told me and my folks someone had poisoned her, and she would have to be put to sleep. We left her at the vet's, and I cried all the way home.

"Three days later, the vet called and said he'd kept Shady sedated while administering an antidote, and she seemed to be recovered. We could come and pick her up. You can imagine how I felt. I could have run all the way to the vet's office. We couldn't get there fast enough. I was out the door and into that office before Daddy even turned off the car. That night Shady was curled up at the end of my bed where I never thought she would sleep again.

"A couple days later Shady went into convulsions once more, and this time she didn't recover. It was much harder the second time." Frank sat staring at the ballpoint pen he was twiddling between his fingers.

Wonder if Jimmy poisoned that dog. "Well, they say lightning doesn't strike the same place twice," Mike didn't think his words did much good. *How could they?*

Frank went back to doodling. Rhonda was talking to some of her students who'd come over to Marlborough to watch the morning's arguments. Mike wandered out of the courtroom and into the Sheriff's office.

"If you want to hide, you can use that empty office." Stick pointed in the direction of the room where they'd confronted Lee Roy Thigpen five days earlier. *Or was it ten years ago?* Taggart closed the door behind him and sat down by the window looking out on Church Street.

When he had lived there during law school, Mike, fresh from the Midwest, had thought Marlborough a peculiar place. Now, watching the people of the town walking along the sidewalk on their way to whatever brought them out, unaware of being watched, he wondered whether Marlborough was so peculiar after all. People were people wherever they were. Loves and hatreds, virtues and vices – were the stories Marlborough had to tell any different than those of hundreds of other small towns? Large towns? Cities? At heart, they all consisted of people just trying to get from one end of their lives to the other as best they could, making choices, risking consequences, hoping all went well.

Generous, selfish, noble, base, wise, foolish, choices creating outcomes, both foreseen and unforeseen, sometimes beautiful, sometimes tragic, sometimes both. How was Frank's story going to turn out? How was his own?

What about Livia Marello? Had she ever been to Marlborough? In terms of time and place, Chapel Hill and the University were fifty years and a thousand miles away from the town where her husband's fate was being decided. Mike imagined he could see her walking down Church Street, poking around the shops, squinting in the late autumn sunshine. He felt a tremendous sense of loss for this woman he had never met, but thought he knew.

That's right, Livia Marello. I know you. I know your ways, your wisdoms and your fears. I've read your diary, you see, not just read it, but visualized the things you describe. I know you, Livia Marello, and I'm sorry you died.

Rhonda stuck her head in the door. "What are you doing in here?"

Mike shrugged. "Meditating. Wondering what it all means."

"Well, Swami, when you get it all figured out, let me know. Meanwhile, the jury's gone to supper, but the Judge is bringing them back afterwards. He sent a note out with the bailiff. I'm going up to the apartment. Ghost stashed some leftovers from yesterday in the refrigerator. Want to come?"

"No thanks."

"Want me to bring you anything?"

"No … thanks."

Like the dream that begins to retreat from memory as soon as the dreamer awakens, Taggart's ghosts had vanished with Rhonda's appearance. After she left, the walls were just walls again. He continued to stare out the window.

Opportunity lost is never to be regained." The words from a saying Horn had framed on the wall of his office came into Mike's head. Would Marlborough, blind to so many wrongs throughout its years, find a way to admit to itself it had wronged Frank Marello two and a half years ago and make it right? Opportunity regained came along so rarely.

After a while he walked into the outer office. A young man was sitting at the dispatch desk where Mike had sat on hundreds of nights during law school. The current occupant was studying a ten-pound law book while the white noise from two shortwave radios sitting on the table behind his chair droned, punctuated now and then with a screech of static followed by some deputy reporting that he was going to be out of his car for something.

"Hi, I'm Mike Taggart. I used to have this job."

"Chris Carver. I know. The other deputies have all told me stories. I think it was more interesting back then, with all the civil rights stuff and moonshiners."

"Interesting times aren't necessarily the best of times," Mike said. "Where do you go to school?"

"Duke. I'm a second year at the law school. But I live out here in Marlborough. My wife teaches school at Evanston Park."

The more things change, the more they remain the same. It was as if Mike was seeing himself through a telescope pointed back through time. He and Carver sat swapping yarns about working for Stick, the antics of various professors they'd both endured and stories about what practice had been like since Mike graduated.

Eventually Rhonda stepped in to announce her return and again later to say Hizzoner had sent out another note saying he was going to keep the jury deliberating until ten o'clock and would bring them back on Saturday morning at nine if they failed to reach a verdict this evening. Whether by coincidence or because the threat of having to come back on Saturday clarified its thinking, Rhonda was back a third time about twenty minutes later to say the jury was coming in. A note to the Judge said they had reached a verdict.

Mike sighed. His stomach turned over. He slid off the desktop on which he had been sitting opposite Carver, slipped on his suit coat, straightened his tie and hurried into the courtroom. Given Watson came down from his office upstairs and followed Mike in. Behind them others scurried to take their places in the gallery. There was none of the chatter that usually preceded Hizzoner's appearance. Everyone sat in solemn silence, a congregation waiting for church to begin.

After the longest two minutes in recorded history Hizzoner emerged from chambers and took the bench.

"Bring in the jury," he ordered Tubby Mayes, who was again the bailiff.

Like elders about to serve communion, the jurors filed in and took their seats. Solemn. No one stirred.

"Ladies and gentlemen, have you elected a foreperson?" Hizzoner said.

"Yes, Sir. I am the foreman," the tall tobacco farmer, Otis Burwell, stood as he spoke.

"Have you reached a verdict, Mr. Foreman?"

"We have, Your Honor."

"Please hand it to the bailiff."

Otis Burwell handed an eight and a half by eleven sheet of paper folded once across the middle to Tubby Mayes, who in turn handed it to the clerk, who stepped behind the bench and read the verdict to Hizzoner in a whisper.

Hizzoner nodded, and the clerk handed the verdict back to Tubby, who handed it back to Burwell.

"The accused and counsel will please rise."

The fingertips of Rhonda's right hand were clutching the hem of Taggart's coat as they stood shoulder to shoulder; with her left hand she held the edge of Frank's jacket in equal desperation. "C'mon," she muttered, "get on with it."

When the bailiff had announced to those waiting that the jury was coming back with a verdict, Frank Marello felt his heart rate start to climb. The curtain of numbness he'd draped over himself as armor against the awful things that had happened and the promise of further awfulness to come fell away. "My God," he said to himself, "please let this nightmare finally end."

Burwell unfolded the paper and read: "It is the verdict of this jury, duly sworn, by unanimous vote in secret session, that the accused, Franklin Allan Marello, is not guilty."

A murmur that nobody standing at the defense table heard rippled through the courtroom. Hizzoner gaveled it into submission and verified that the verdict was indeed the will of the entire jury. That done, he complimented the job counsel had done and thanked the jurors for their service, releasing them in time for the late news.

Then Hizzoner turned to face the defense table, where Mike, Rhonda and Frank were still standing. "It is my pleasure to order that the accused be immediately released from custody," he said, thereby signaling his agreement with the verdict. "This Court stands adjourned."

With the adjournment the tide of their victory began to wash over the trio. Quiet jubilation composed in equal parts of joy and relief from the excruciating tension inherent in the question, "What if we lose? What if we lose?"

Given Watson was the first to offer congratulations, followed by countless others, including Stick, deputies, jurors, townspeople, reporters. In the midst of the hubbub Mike freed himself and called Marcia with the news.

"Congratulations, Mike," Marcia said. "Wish I could have been there. Are you coming back here tonight or staying at the apartment?"

"I think it's time you and Matt and I all have breakfast together, don't you?" Mike replied.

"Absolutely."

Twenty minutes after the verdict was announced there were still twenty people clustered around the defense table when Tubby came in and said they would have to leave because he wanted to lock up the courtroom.

Frank and Ghost waited while Mike and Rhonda gathered their briefcases for the last time and the rest of the crowd slipped away.

As Mike was about to close his briefcase Frank handed him the piece of yellow paper folded in the middle on which he had been doodling when Taggart fled the courtroom early that afternoon. Mike unfolded the paper and there was a poem Frank had written entitled "Trial." Slowly Mike read the words Frank had written, then looked up with a smile. "Thanks, Frank. I'll hang this on my office wall.

Side by side Mike, Rhonda and Frank walked down the corridor towards the outside entrance trailed by Ghost, the last to leave except for Tubby, who was holding the door for them. As they passed the outer office of the Sheriff's Department, Mike glanced in and saw Chris Carver still poring over some law book to the accompaniment of the radios.

The white globes of the lights on either side of the small plaza in front of the building cast a dim light, too feeble to completely obscure the stars that sparkled overhead in the crisp November air. Taggart looked down Church Street, which was deserted. Off to their right Buck Brown's sleek Black Chevrolet Impala with the spinner hubcaps pulled out and honked at them before heading back towards the West End with a carload of good ol' boys who would never be anything else and never wished to be.

Right behind them Cornelius and Josie Kempton pulled to a stop.

"Nice work, Counsellor," Cornelius called before turning in the opposite direction from that taken by Buck.

Taggart nodded his thanks. *Nice work Marlborough. You've turned a blind old eye on many sins, but you're still young enough to weep.*

The street was again empty.

"Frank, why don't you come up to the apartment and bunk there for the night … or for as long as it takes to sort out what comes next. We've got the place until the end of the month," Mike said. "You don't have anywhere else to go, do you?"

"Sure … yeah, I mean, thank you. It just began to dawn on me that I don't have anywhere to go. Mr. Jack says I can come on back up there, but you know …

"I don't even have any money, at least not with me. After all your dire predictions, I didn't let myself plan on an acquittal. I guess I just assumed I'd go with Daddy and Jim if that happened."

That was a subject no one wanted to talk about.

"Good," Mike said.

When they reached the car, Ghost opened the trunk, withdrew a cooler and took out a bottle of champagne. "Knew we'd need this," he said, "but I forgot to buy cups."

"Open that baby," Mike said. "I don' need no stinkin' cup."

Ghost popped the cork and offered the first swig to Frank, who deferred to Rhonda. "Ladies first." After five circuits around the group, the bottle was empty. They'd drunk in silence, too drained for further celebration.

"Ghost," Frank said as they prepared to climb in the car, "do you mind if I drive? It's something I've really missed."

Ghost smiled, tossed Frank the keys and climbed in back with Taggart. Rhonda rode shotgun.

"Do you mind if we drive around a bit before we go back to the apartment?" Frank said as they drove out of the parking lot. "Or are you both too tired? You're the ones who've been doing all the work."

Rhonda looked over her shoulder into the backseat where Taggart was sprawled. Mike shook his head indicating he didn't care.

"You're the pilot, Frank," she said. "The tank's full. We can drive all night as far as I'm concerned."

They drove out onto I-85 and headed west. Frank lit a cigarette, but immediately crushed it out. "Now I have to quit this habit."

For more than fifteen minutes no one said anything. Finally, Frank asked, "What's next for the three of you?"

"I was just going to ask you the same question," Rhonda said, glancing again over her shoulder at the still silent Taggart and the usually silent Ghost, to see if they had fallen asleep.

"You first," Frank said.

"Just keep teaching, maybe handle an appeal now and then if something really interesting comes along. I think I'm going to see what I can do about getting Cornelius Kempton onto the Marlborough baseball team. I'll sic some of my students on the town and see what we can do."

"You next, Ghost," Frank said, glancing in the rearview mirror.

"I'm going to stay in town for a while, see if something really interesting comes along."

Rhonda smiled.

"How about you, Frank?" Rhonda asked, "You must be feeling as if you've been reborn, but as an adult ... kind of like the old saying about wishing you could relive something knowing what you know now."

In the backseat, Taggart winced at all the melancholy memories the idea of reliving Frank's life might kindle, but he said nothing, and Frank didn't stumble over the notion.

"I suppose I'll stay around long enough to see whether there's anything I can do for Daddy and Jim – " he began.

"You're shitting me," Ghost straightened in his seat. "After everything they've done?"

Frank shrugged. "I know. But Ghost, things that make other people mad mostly make me sad. Probably they won't even want me around. Sooner or later, I'm going to do just what we're doing now. When I was a little boy, I used to go to sleep at night thinking, fantasizing about traveling all over the country in a big van equipped like a house so you could live in it. That was before these campers on pickups you see all over now. I want to get one of those and just move around. One of the worst things about being in jail is watching other people move from place to place and knowing you can't. I used to stand in my cell watching the cars go up and down Church Street and wonder if I'd ever be able to do that again."

Taggart, too, had often dreamed of losing himself on the world's highways. *Before Marcia and Matt, I would have been tempted to go with you, Frank.*

Then he caught himself. Frank's gay. What would travelling together mean?

Mike shook his head in disgust. *Why does it have to mean anything?* He'd just dedicated three months of his life to convincing twelve other people Frank's homosexuality shouldn't mean anything, and here he was flinching at the thought of what might be the trip of a lifetime with someone he liked and respected - a friend – because he's gay. It was one thing to pledge oneself not to be prejudiced, even to act without prejudice, but quite another to purge the sentiment from one's brain. *So much for enlightenment.*

"What about you, Mike?" Frank said. "What's next for you?"

Brooding at his unheroic thoughts, Taggart pretended to be asleep and didn't answer.

Saturday morning. Mike, Marcia, Matt and Rhonda were eating breakfast. Ghost had stayed at the apartment to keep Frank company. Beneath the table, Marcia's left hand rested on Mike's knee.

"Coach," Matt said, "what's 'homosexual' mean?"

Made in the USA
San Bernardino, CA
21 April 2018